THE MIDAS TOUCH—FUN AND GAMES (BOOK I)

A SCIENCE FICTION NOVEL

SERGEY ILYN

BLACK DRAGON ARTS

1st Edition
ISBN: 978-1-7346176-1-0

WARNING: The book contains strong language, intense violence that may not be
suitable for children and require parental guidance.

ACKNOWLEDGMENTS

I'm eternally grateful to my wife, Valentina, who inspired and helped me write The Midas Touch trilogy. She was as important to this book getting done as I was—from reading early drafts and spending countless hours on development editing.

Character illustrations by David Enriquez (https://www.den-riquez.com)

Development Editor: Valentina Ilyn

Editors:
- Eanna Roberts (https://www.penmanshipediting.com),
- Amanda Sumner (https://www.engagededitor.com)

UPDATES AND OTHER BOOKS IN TRILOGY

For updates, official art, previews and bonus material related to the Midas Touch universe and its characters visit author's website Sergey Ilyn Worlds (https://sergeyilyn.com) and the trilogy Facebook page (https://www.facebook.com/javatina)

The Midas Touch—Snares of Power (Book 2 of the trilogy) is planned for release in Q3–Q4 2020.
    https://sergeyilyn.com/product/snares-of-power

The Midas Touch—The Crack of Doom (Book 3 of the trilogy) is planned for release in Q1–Q2 2021.
    https://sergeyilyn.com/product/crack-of-doom

To my love and wife, Valentina
— always together till the last breath

"Meantime we shall express our darker purpose."

WILLIAM SHAKESPEARE

CONTENTS

ONE

22 YEARS AGO

Thunder and lightning rolled across the west, cracking the world in half and unleashing the fury of gods. Two jet fighters flying in tight formation approached rapidly from the east. Both aircraft stood out against the background of the vanishing sun. The jets streaked across the sky with a deafening roar, flying into the storm.

F-15 Eagle fighters had launched on an intercept mission over the Great Basin Desert in central Nevada. David Stroud, a young air force captain with the callsign Stinger, piloted the lead aircraft. In the rear seat sat Chris Kline, his Weapon Systems Officer. Neither man spoke, focused on doing their jobs.

The voice of the mission controller crackled over David's radio. "Stinger One, climb and maintain flight level two-zero... Bogey is bearing one-five-zero at one niner miles."

The flight leader and his wingman changed their heading slightly, now flying into the eye of the storm while ominous dark clouds billowed in from the west and sprawled across the sky. Lightning cut crazy zigzags out of the raging, tenebrous covering hanging over the desert and the mountain ridges.

A target-locking tone prompted David to contact the air base. "Control, bull's-eye at zero-zero-eight for twenty, and I... Ahh, lost it... It didn't look like a bird. Two, try to stay away from seventeen thousand."

"Copy that," the "Two," David's wingman, responded.

The mission controller cut in, "Stinger flight, the target at your three o'clock—do you have a tally?"

"No joy..."

Locking tone the second time—David turned his head left and right, trying to get a visual on the target amid the flashes of lightning. "I've picked it up again. It's seventeen-seven... seven miles... no, three miles off my nose... No airspeed indicated."

The mission controller spoke up. "Stinger flight, that's not what we see on our radar. State your intentions."

"I'm gonna... Climb up slightly here and slow down to get a better look... Two, try to follow if you can."

The flight leader climbed higher as a lightning bolt illuminated his wingman's jet. David could see it breaking left and accelerating. The wingman warned, "Approaching position... I'm gonna descend to sixteen five."

"Two, start coming back toward the—"

Another locking tone coincided with a powerful and prolonged lightning strike illuminating the clouds in front of and below David's jet. "Holy shit! We've got somebody else out here with it."

His Two didn't react. A couple of seconds later, David heard his voice. It sounded like someone or something was strangling him. "Stinger... Stinger! Break—"

Then silence. Desperate, David tried to understand what had just happened. He rolled his aircraft left and right, looking underneath the fighter on either side, keeping his head on a swivel, trying to see behind him—to no avail. His wingman's plane was gone. There was nothing visible in the splashes of lightning, and nothing on David's radar. Two had vanished into thin air as if he'd evaporated.

Suddenly, total silence fell, and all lights were extinguished as the jet's main and backup power went out. The emergency power system kicked in, but controls remained slushy. The aircraft lost altitude fast. A cold chill ran through David's body. *Mountain ridges below. No way to find a strip here. The wingman's gone. We're next!* "Chris, bailout! Bailout!"

David pulled the ejection handle, and both seats rocketed up, one after another, into the gloom.

David fell into turbulent darkness, heavy rain battering him from every direction. His flight suit got soaked through in seconds. The large, cold droplets hit his neck and the exposed portion of his face like ice pellets.

He was terrified as a lightning bolt struck not too far from him, lighting up his parachute. For a second, he thought the electric discharge had struck the chute itself. Strong upward air currents pulled him up, only to yank him earthward again seconds later in the downdraft.

Heaving, airsick from the up-and-down cycles, David tried to guess how close he might be to hitting the ground. But the rain, the darkness, and the chaotic air currents completely disoriented him. David's only wish was to end this torture. He was tired of fighting the storm.

To make things worse, the strong wind drove the parachute onto a mountain range—David noticed it in frequent lightning strikes around him. He attempted to change the direction of the descent using the control lines, but the wind was too strong. The treacherous air currents carried him over a stand-alone cliff, and when he thought the worst had passed, he hit an upthrust rock. A sharp pain pierced the whole right side of his body like a hundred knives.

I'd probably be dead if I didn't have a helmet. Relief flashed through him.

The chute canopy collapsed, and David started sliding down the rock's face—certain death waited for him at the bottom of the canyon. Luckily, the parachute lines got tangled in the rocks somewhere above. The canopy, soaked with water, slipped under its weight and hung near him. He was helplessly stuck on the near-vertical wall of the abyss.

With David on one side and the heavy canopy on the other, the balance was fragile. As the lines repeatedly fouled on projecting rocks, both slipped in convulsive movements farther and farther down along the steep face of the cliff, falling a few dozen feet at a time, before jerking to a stop.

David poked around with his hands and feet, trying to find something to hang onto, something that could stop him from falling and dying at the bottom of the abyss. In the flashes of lightning, he noticed not far from him a rock formation reminiscent of the letter Y. David scrabbled toward the wet cavity, desperate for a firm grip. Unexpectedly, the crag under his hands disappeared, and he tumbled twenty feet, hitting a flat, rocky surface. The parachute and its lines fell on him. With what was left of his strength, he crawled inside an opening in front of him and blacked out.

When David regained consciousness, the cave was almost pitch black—but there was a barely perceptible glimmer of light coming from somewhere inside. He unhooked from the parachute harness and removed his helmet. Every movement caused pain.

As his eyes adjusted to the faint light, he realized that the opening to the cave had disappeared. Somehow, it had been replaced by a wall covered with strange symbols, vanishing into the dimness. The vastness of the space surrounding David gradually registered in his mind.

He tried to get to his feet, but groaned in pain and fell to the floor. He refused to give up, however. Enduring the breathless pain pulsing through him, he finally found enough strength to stand. Dragging his right foot, he slowly hobbled toward the light.

As he moved, space narrowed. The passage turned in a wide curve and opened into a large, dimly lit chamber. A strange device in the shape of an upright torus stood in the middle.

Rather tall, nine or ten feet high, it rested vertically with its lower part sunk below the chamber's rocky floor. The artifact's soft, pale-blue glow was the only source of light in the room, and the device flickered at irregular intervals. As David watched, several bluish sparks fell to the floor from above. The sound of electric arcs and discharges added to the impression that something had gone wrong here.

David approached the torus and started circling it. Every step required deliberate effort. Finally, he stopped behind it, leaning with his hand against the artifact. He closed his eyes and tried to relax.

On the other side of the chamber, a woman appeared. She wore strange clothing—something like a tight-fitting jumpsuit with a high collar, solid hiking boots, and a couple of small devices attached to her belt, all a metallic light-blue color. At first glance, the several small implants on her face could have been mistaken for exotic jewelry matching the tattoos on her neck and upper chest, which was visible in the cleavage of her suit. Despite her unusual outfit and look, she might have passed for a charming modern woman.

Her soft but distinct voice made David open his eyes. "You are not allowed to be here."

David flinched and stared at the woman. All he could say was, "Who are you?"

"My name is Nox. Please tell me why you are here."

A whiff of mystical power radiated from her, and David instinctively felt he owed her an explanation. But as soon as he opened his mouth to tell his strange tale, he realized he had no idea where to start. *From the moment we scrambled? Or before that? Should I mention that I had to eject from my fighter?*

Nox Ell

The truth was that David could give no reason as to why and how he had gotten here. He was following orders. But more importantly, he was in such great pain, and so weak, that the prospect of talking to her and explaining things terrified him. "I don't know. It just happened…" he gasped.

Nox took her time to examine David from head to toe. "You are a pilot. United States Air Force. What is your name?"

"David... David Stroud."

"I apologize, David, for what happened to you. And I am willing to help. All you need to do is to tell me what you want. Your wish..."

That confused him even more. It seemed surreal—he didn't know what he wanted, at least at the moment. Or, perhaps, he wasn't sure what he could ask this strange-looking beauty. Could he say that he would like to be in his quarters at Nellis Air Force Base in Nevada, near Las Vegas? Or wish to end the nightmare that had started as a UFO intercept mission?

When did it start? An hour ago, or was it yesterday?

He looked around, trying to get some clues about what he wanted. Finally, he uttered, "To get outta here? That'd be nice, ma'am."

Nox scrutinized David for a few more seconds, then held out her hand. "Come."

Spellbound, David made a step under the donut's arch toward Nox. At that point, he lost any sense of reality as a strange lightness in his body and an inexplicable sensation of joy, power, and excitement overcame him. He went blind for a second—and realized that he was no longer in the cave.

A breath of fresh air brought David back to reality. *That woman, Nox —a ghost? An illusion? But I didn't hallucinate—my instant teleportation from the cave was real. As soon as I passed through the torus... An alien technology?* Confused thoughts swamped his head. *Darn it! What should I say in my report?*

He stood on a mountain plateau near the edge of the cliff. His eyes, accustomed to the darkness of the cave, couldn't at first appreciate the austere beauty of the place. But as they adjusted, a remarkable view opened up in front of him. Mountain ridges were separated from the plateau by the canyon. The rugged terrain, sparse vegetation and patches of snow on some mountain tops made an indelible impression on him. The storm had passed. With the warm and welcoming weather, harsh nature didn't appear as frightening. Unfortunately, the place was deserted—no roads, no dwellings, no people, no help.

As the shock from last night's events dissipated and David plunged into more immediate realities of life, he realized the gravity of his situation. He was weak and in bad shape. His flight suit was torn in multiple places, and parts of it were soaked with blood from wounds that were still bleeding.

David touched the right side of his chest and moaned in pain. *Several ribs broken and God knows what else inside, he decided. Idiot... I should have at least asked her to take me closer to civilization.*

The lower part of his body didn't look any better. David examined his right leg, which had taken the heaviest hit. *Is it broken? Crap...* Exhausted, he dropped to the ground.

After a few moments, having regained some strength, David recalled that inside the kneeboard still strapped around his thigh, there was a detailed map of Nevada. By circling the map with the approximate landing area and looking at the net of major highways, he could choose the best strategy to get closer to a populated place.

David studied the map for a while until blank sheets in the kneeboard caught his eye. *I better write down everything that I saw while it's fresh in my memory. Not sure, though, if it's a good idea to talk about aliens... Still...*

He moved closer to the edge of the cliff and meticulously documented the landmarks, precisely as they looked from his position. On a separate page, David drew a stand-alone cliff, described its location, and added the Y-shaped rock inclusion he'd touched before ending up in the cave. On other pages, David sketched the artifact, its place inside the cave, and Nox in front of the torus. She didn't come out convincingly—cursing his artistic talents, he added to the female figure an outstretched hand. Somehow, it made the drawing more persuasive. Satisfied with his effort, David rose from the ground and hobbled away from the edge of the cliff toward the tree line visible in the distance.

Later, when the Nellis AFB investigators tried to estimate the length of the route he covered trying to get out to the highway, they came up with twenty to thirty miles, an impossible undertaking for the injuries he must have sustained. Still, David did it somehow, and a truck driver found him unconscious by the side of Route 50.

When an Emergency Air Ambulance Service helicopter delivered an unconscious David Stroud to the Millennial Hills Hospital close to downtown Las Vegas, a medical team was already standing by, prepared for multiple urgent surgical procedures.

The surgeon's assistant began by cutting off David's flight suit. The right side of David's body looked a total mess.

The surgeon picked up David's dog tags and gave them to the circulating nurse. "Inform the air force their pilot is in critical condition. I suggest they contact his family as soon as possible."

To say the surgery went well was like saying, "Thank God David didn't die on the operating table," so severe were his wounds. Five broken ribs, a collapsed right lung, a ruptured liver, and a fractured fibula topped the list. The worst of all was the prolonged bleeding he'd suffered. As a result, the surgeon had to perform a liver resection to remove the necrotic tissue and source of the bleeding.

Surrounded by monitors and support equipment, stuffed with painkillers, antibiotics, and who knew what else, David lay in the intensive care unit, awake but groggy after the four-hour surgery. A nurse scurried around him checking equipment and IV bags.

A shy knock came from the door, and a young woman poked her head through. "I'm Sarah... Sarah Stroud, his wife. The doctor said I could see David."

"Please come in. He's very weak—don't tire him." The nurse looked at Sarah disapprovingly. "I'll give you some privacy, ma'am."

The nurse left the room, and Sarah, timid and frightened, came in. With a big baby-belly typical of late pregnancy, she waddled. She looked at her husband, and tears rolled down her cheeks. "Oh, David... You're alive, and that's all that matters," she whispered. Maybe because of her helplessness and desperation, it seemed to her that whispering might help him, might make his suffering and pain less severe. "I love you so much! The wounds will heal..."

She wanted to touch his hair, caress him, her most cherished being in this world, but she moved her hand away, afraid of causing him pain. Instead, she took David's hand in hers and gently pressed it to her belly. "That's our baby, David."

David opened his eyes and tried to smile—it didn't come out convincingly. Then, barely audible, he said, "You came... Sit..."

Sarah sniffed loudly, wiped her face, pulled a chair closer to the bed, and sat down.

"You should rest... Our baby..." David's voice trailed off.

Her eyes filled with tears again. "He's due in two days. I want us to be together when I give birth. Everything will be fine, you'll see."

David tried to say something else, but couldn't. His fingers moved slightly as if inviting Sarah to come closer. She got up from her chair, bent over David, and kissed his forehead.

David's lips and chin moved slightly—Sarah brought her ear closer to his mouth. He kept talking for a minute and then, exhausted, stopped and closed his eyes.

Sarah straightened up. "Please don't worry. Rest. I'll do it now. I'll be back."

I have to do what David asked me... I have to do it... That simple, repetitive thought throbbing in her head was like a lifeline to save her from the delirium Sarah had been sinking into since the moment she saw her husband.

She stumbled into a member of the hospital staff, who showed her to the storage for patients' belongings—a drab room full of cabinets, with a stainless-steel table in the middle. The medical assistant opened one of the lockers, pulled out a plastic bag tagged "Stroud, David," and plunked it on the table. "Please don't remove anything," he said. "If you or your husband need something, let us know. We'll get it for you."

Sarah unzipped the bag and looked inside. There was what remained of his flight suit, soaked in now-hardened blood, a flashlight, a folding knife, and a few odds and ends from his USAF survival kit. She made sure the hospital's attendant left her alone and pulled out the kneeboard.

Not much to see there—a laminated list with some operating procedures, a folded map covered in blood, and several pages filled with pencil sketches. Trembling with chills, Sarah ripped out the last four with David's notes and put them under her blouse. Just then, the tramping of people dashing through the corridor outside the storage room distracted her. She froze.

As Sarah stood there motionless, filled with premonitions, the door opened, and the surgeon rushed in. "Ms. Stroud, I was told I could find you here. I'm very sorry to tell you this, but your husband has passed away."

Sarah had to catch hold of the table to keep from falling. Her knuckles turned white, and that was the last thing she saw before hitting the floor in a dead faint.

Recent events had left their mark upon Sarah. Doctors pointed to her bout of severe stress due to her husband's death as the main reason for a long and exhausting labor and delivery. Her contractions were irregular, and when they occurred, the pain was excruciating. A knot inside would seem to tighten and twist, getting worse and worse until it would finally peak and drop off. Soon after that, the whole cycle would repeat again and again and again. Sarah shook, unable to let go of the midwife's hand.

"Don't be afraid, my dear. Everything will be fine."

Sarah didn't feel any fear. Deep sorrow and a feeling of blatant injustice obscured everything—her pain, an uncertain future, and whether she would ever learn this mothering thing. With red eyes full of tears, she lay silently staring at the ceiling of the maternity ward. Yet, when Sarah's child decided to finally see the light of day, and the midwife took her hand and placed it on the baby, the sense of a miracle occurring overwhelmed Sarah and helped her regain her usual optimism. With the newborn resting on her chest while they both received routine care, she smiled for the first time since she'd heard about David's death.

The baby lay quiet but eagerly responded to the nurse's touches as she examined him and checked his breathing. "He's alert and energetic. Congratulations, you have a wonderful, healthy son!"

Sarah gently touched his face and said, "Welcome to this world, Elias David Stroud. We'll make it together, and your father will always be with us... always!"

"Ms. Stroud," announced a nurse, "Eli is due for his heel stick. Dr. Phyns will do the screening."

"Screening? Is something wrong with my son?"

The door opened, and a tall man with a sunburnt and stern face entered the room. "My name is Kond, Dr. Kond Phyns. Nothing wrong with your son, Ms. Stroud. Screening is one of the things that happens a few days after every baby is born. You can decline it on religious grounds, but I don't recommend it. Testing helps make children healthier."

"Definitely, Doctor Phyns. Please proceed," said Sarah.

"I'll prick Eli's heel to collect a small sample of his blood... Can you please hold him? He'll feel more comfortable if you do."

The doctor skillfully landed a small sample of Eli's blood on the porous part of the screening card. "Done. You see, quick and simple." Kond smiled. "You have a handsome son. And brave—he didn't cry at all, not a tear, not a sound."

"When will I know the results?" asked Sarah.

"We'll send the screening card to the state laboratory for a full analysis. It may take several days."

"So long? I'll worry. Anything sooner?"

The doctor rested his chin in his palm. "I can tell you results for the most important blood components, but the portable analyzer I have is still experimental. I can't put its results on the card. Do you understand?"

"I do. How long does it take?"

"Seconds. I can do it right here."

Kond Phyns pulled a small device from his pocket and rubbed its pointed end over the blood smudge on the card. He stared at his gadget until his face brightened—the doctor turned to Sarah. "You have a healthy son, Ms. Stroud. Everything looks splendid!"

"Thank you, doctor. Then there's nothing to worry about?"

"Absolutely nothing. I'm sure your son will have a great future."

A man in an air force service dress uniform approached the registration desk. "I'd like to see Sarah Stroud. My name is Chris Kline."

"Are you a relative?"

"No. Her husband died several days ago. I am... I was his weapons officer and a good friend."

The woman behind the counter measured Chris with her eyes. Evidently, a uniformed air force officer inspired in the strict and vigilant receptionist enough confidence to pick up the phone and confer with her superiors. "There's a gentleman here who wants to see Ms. Stroud. Chris Kline... Yes."

As she put down the phone, her face softened. "Please sit down. The nurse will be with you soon."

Sarah lay sleeping in the postpartum room when a maternity nurse knocked at the door. "Sorry to bother you, ma'am."

Sarah blinked the sleep out of her eyes. "Please, come in. I'm taking a nap."

"There's an air force officer named Chris Kline here. Says he was a friend of your husband. He wants to see you."

Sarah, still woozy from waking up, slowly took in what the nurse was saying.

"Ma'am, if you don't want to—"

"No, no... Please invite him in. If you don't mind, can you please bring me my bag?"

"Yes, ma'am. I'll be back in a minute." The nurse opened the door. "Mr. Kline, please come in."

Chris entered the room. "Ms. Stroud, I'm Chris. I used to fly with David. I'm very sorry for your loss... And... I wish all the happiness in the world to you and your son, Ms. Stroud. God bless."

Chris seemed, to Sarah, much older than David. Also, he was heavier and taller, and there was something touching in his figure, in how this man stood hesitantly in the middle of the room, shifting from foot to foot. A warm feeling of gratitude spread over her. "Please sit—call me Sarah. If I recall correctly, we've never met before. I work at Palomar Observatory in San Diego... I'm glad to see you. You were together that night, right?"

"Always behind him in the cockpit. It's a two-seater."

"Can you tell me what happened?"

"Very little. We experienced a flameout—total systems failure. We ejected, and that was the last time I saw him. I guess I was luckier than... than David." Chris stumbled over his words. This seemingly strong air force officer looked like a small boy grieving over the first loss in his life. "They found me quickly... but... there was no trace of David."

Sarah looked at him, not taking her eyes off his face, holding her breath and heeding his every word and every gesture, every move of his head. No matter how sad his story was, she wanted to hear more.

Chris thought for a second and then went on with his tale. "Even if he had a hard landing, we still should have been able to spot his parachute or locator beacon... but nothing! He showed up three days later near Route 50."

The nurse entered the room right then and put Sarah's bag on the nightstand. "Do you want to see your son?" she asked.

Sarah turned to Chris. He sighed with relief. "I'd love to see him!"

Sarah looked at the nurse and smiled. "Yes, please." She waited until the nurse closed the door behind her and continued, "There's something David asked me to do."

Sarah opened her bag, pulled out an envelope, and handed it to Chris.

"You talked to David?" he asked.

"He only wanted me to give you this. He died a few minutes later."

"Anything he wanted me to do with this?" Chris waved the envelope.

"No..." For a split second, Sarah hesitated. "As far as I understood it, that's something David wanted to be kept safe. 'Nobody should see this,' that's what he told me." She turned an inquisitive look on Chris. "Anything else you can tell me about what happened?"

He withdrew his gaze from Sarah. "Honestly... The air force investigation is ongoing. They may have developed some information that I'm not privy to." Chris paused for a moment and added reluctantly, "But if David asked you..." He pointed to the envelope. "You know... we were scrambled to intercept an unidentified target, but things went awry. The wingman's jet vanished. We lost control over our plane and ejected." Chris paused again. "I guess David knew or saw something... I promise I'll respect his wish, and—"

The door opened, and the nurse appeared, pulling behind her a hospital bassinet containing Eli. She wheeled it up closer to the bed and moved out.

Sarah looked at Chris. "Can you give him to me?"

"Ms. Stro—Sarah... I can't... I'm—"

"Do you have kids?"

"A daughter, Ashley."

"How old is she?"

"She's three."

"Then you know how to handle babies." Sarah held out her hands.

Chris put the envelope in his pocket, carefully took Eli from the bassinet, and handed him to Sarah. "I guess I do. You know, I'm so glad I came to see you and your son. He looks like David, doesn't he?"

Sarah smiled. "I thought so too."

TWO
ELI

The home in Las Vegas that Sarah had inherited from her parents usually stayed empty. With her job at NASA's astrophysics division, she often traveled around the country and abroad, which made constant use of her home impractical. At one point, she wanted to sell it and move to Washington, DC, the location of NASA headquarters. However, with her life on the road, while Eli was growing up, Sarah decided to postpone any decision in this regard. She hoped that her son might find a job and stay in Las Vegas upon graduating from Croffts University—he was in his final year of studying mathematics, specializing in computer science.

Indeed, Eli was a frequent guest in the house during academic breaks. He often stayed in Las Vegas instead of traveling and spending time with his friends at popular vacation destinations. So the fact that Eli lay on a couch with empty bottles of beer on the floor nearby and another one, half empty, in his hand while playing computer games wasn't unusual. With one minor exception—it was still spring term, and Eli was supposed to be at the university campus in Kendan, New York, gnawing at the fruits and secrets of science in search of hidden truths unknown to those unimpaired by knowledge.

The adult version of Eli looked like his father—his delicate corporeal attributes were fully compensated by remarkable agility so necessary in feats demanding suppleness of limb and quickness of eye. Eli's open face exhibited honesty and sincerity, qualities that made most people comfortable around him.

Elias (Eli) Stroud

Lubricated a little by his beloved Hobba Yobba from the local Shaggy Hudie brewery, he sat in front of a big TV set in the family room and enjoyed himself, shooting lazily at the enemies supplied in abundance by the FPS game. Laser pistol in hand, he was picking targets at random and putting virtual slugs in them one after another without using the gunsights, getting a bull's-eye every shot—something Eli expected and accomplished without effort. Alas, that didn't give him any satisfaction. He was bored.

It was during one of these rapid-fire strings that Sarah opened the front door, pulling a bag behind her, with a duffel over her shoulder. Alarmed by the loud gunshots coming from loudspeakers, she rushed to the family room and saw her son. "Eli? What are you doing here?"

The unexpected appearance of his mother had no effect on her son. After several more lucky shots, still playing and without turning to look at her, he finally acknowledged his mother's presence with a cheerful, "Hi, Mom!"

"Aren't you supposed to be in Kendan? At school?"

"Ah…" Another delayed response—"I, uh, dropped out."

"You what!?"

"Mom, please, don't tread on my psyche."

"I'm not treading on anything! You need to be someone and have a purpose in life. You need to *learn* in order to do that. You can do anything you want if you work hard."

"Right… That's why there are so many people who can fly." Eli put more slugs into bad guys. "And please don't start talking about my father. I've heard enough. I've learned enough. Learning's boring. Why can't you understand that?"

"Elias, your father was a hero! He gave his life protecting this country. Show some respect for that, at least."

After putting the game on pause, Eli calmly got up and approached his mother, giving her hand a quick squeeze. "I'm sorry, Mom. That's not what I meant. It's just that… well, I don't know him. I wish I knew more about Dad."

"I know. Sometimes I forget that you're not a kid anymore." Sarah wiped a tear off her cheek, went to the closet, and pulled out an old suitcase. "Speaking of your father… This is what I got when he died. I don't think you've seen it before."

Sarah opened the suitcase. Inside, there were personal items and some old military stuff. She pulled out a tattered flight suit with the embroidered tapes U.S. AIR FORCE on one side and STROUD on the other. "I cleaned it. It was soaked in blood. I think the legs and torso were cut apart in the hospital before surgery. Your Dad was in it when he was found."

Eli looked into the suitcase and then at his watch. "Oh, shit! I have to run. My job starts soon," he said regretfully but kept looking over things in the suitcase.

"You have a job?"

"Yeah… casino."

"Moving up in the world?" snorted Sarah.

"Ha! It's computers… I keep my eyes open."

As Eli was touching his father's belongings, Sarah gave her son a sidelong glance. His boredom had disappeared, and his eyes glowed with delight.

She realized that something had suddenly changed in him. *He didn't know his father—only my stories and my tears. Could these simple things help Eli understand at last that he's his father's son? Will they let him connect to David? Why didn't I show them to Eli before?*

David's kneeboard caught Eli's attention. "Cool. Can I take this with me?"

Sarah nodded. "It's all yours. Go, don't be late."

Eli grabbed his backpack, threw the kneeboard into it, and disappeared behind the door. Already running down the street, he shouted, "Love you, Mom!"

Eli walked down a back-street alley, a place of dumpsters, odd smells, and crime. Graffiti on the walls and casino silhouettes behind concrete structures with service entrances, utility ducts, and electrical boxes unmistakably screamed Las Vegas—and not the best part of it. He thumbed through the kneeboard without concerning himself about what was happening around him. Too bad, because someone followed Eli in a car, an old clunker whose miserable condition would have been remarkable in itself if it weren't for the driver who deserved even more attention—at least for the discerning observer.

Abaddon (Ab)

The man behind the wheel was called Abaddon, often abbreviated by friends and enemies to "Ab." In his forties, with long dark hair and the grayish-brown skin that on Earth can only be found among indigenous people of Australia, he already presented himself as quite an exciting and vibrant individual. But the most intriguing part of his appearance was his eyes. They were the same color as his skin, with one of them squinted as if to increase the penetrating power of the other. A frequent devilish smile revealed snow-white teeth. The shadow of stubble and a tiny English-style mustache complemented Ab's image.

Still studying his father's kneeboard, Eli also ignored a group of three young men hanging around on the other side of the street. However, they spotted him and moved in, cutting across his path.

This didn't go unnoticed by Ab, who got out of the car and sauntered closer, trying not to show his interest in the brewing street drama. He got there just in time as the tallest and most menacing-looking guy, likely the gang's leader, blocked Eli's way. "Look who's here!"

Another tough-looking hoodlum took a position at Eli's right. "A welch?"

Moving to Eli's left, the third and the youngest didn't fall behind either. "A mooch?"

"I'm not a mooch."

"What d'ya call someone who imposes on other people's generosity?" asked the leader.

"I told you, I need more time."

"You kiddin' me, bro?" smirked the tough-looking guy on the right, punching Eli in the stomach.

Eli folded in half but stayed on his feet.

"Huh," snorted the gang leader. He hit Eli in the chin. "Need a lesson?"

Eli fell on his back, and the kneeboard flew out of his hands. Ab caught it and whacked down the boy who had punched Eli in the stomach.

Either surprised by the unexpected help or scared by Ab's disturbing smile, the other two backed off. "Hey, dude! Chill out. We want what's ours," protested the leader.

"Get lost!" barked Ab.

The gangbangers immediately retreated, cursing and threatening from afar with their fists as Ab helped Eli stand up. "That what they wanted?" Ab gave him the kneeboard.

"No, that's mine. Rather, it was my father's."

"He's a pilot?"

"Was... Killed in action. Many years ago."

"Interesting... I was a pilot myself. You know what?" Ab nodded at the hooligans. "Your friends are still there, and you have a scratch on your brow. Let's go to my car."

"I'm fine," Eli assured him and pulled his phone from the back pocket of his jeans. The device was bent, with a crack across its screen. He tried to turn it on, but the phone was dead. "I must have fallen on it." Eli heaved a sigh and had to grab Ab's hand so as not to lose his balance. "Ahh, dammit, my head's spinning."

"Don't argue—my car is close." Ab's devilish smile was long gone by now. All courtesy, he walked Eli to his junker. Eli trudged next to his savior with downcast eyes, feeling sad and despondent.

"That nasty cut on your forehead…" worried Ab once they were inside the car. "Very deep. We need to disinfect and dress it." He rummaged in the glove compartment and took out a first aid kit. "This might be a bit painful. Relax, it'll only hurt a little." Ab popped open the box and withdrew a few articles before deftly treating the cut with ointment and sticking a bandage over the wound. His movements were quick, sure, and economical. "Okay, good as new. You can go now."

"Thanks," Eli said uncertainly.

"Don't mention it. Always glad to help the son of a hero." Ab peered at Eli. "You know what? I'd better drive you home."

"Is this what you want from life, Eli?" nagged Sarah, examining his bruises and frowning at the bandage.

Eli wasn't sure what he wanted from life, but he definitely didn't want to continue this conversation. *What has this got to do with what I want from life?* he wondered. No words could describe his state of mind after what had happened two hours before. Was he frustrated? Annoyed? Fearful? Piqued? Resentful? A bit of everything, perhaps. He knew he hadn't been prepared for what had happened. At all, either physically or mentally, but most importantly, mentally. Standing in front of those three juvenile troublemakers, Eli hadn't reacted in any rational or spontaneous way—he just stood there like a damn punching bag. Why? He had no explanation.

"Yep… It looks that way, doesn't it?" An apologetic but vague answer to his mother's rhetoric seemed to Eli the best way to end the conversation. Anyway, he didn't feel that sorting out his feelings could help him now.

Sarah had opened her mouth to continue her fault-finding mission when someone knocked. "I'll get it." She went to the entrance door. "Who's there?"

"FBI, Special Agent John Smith. Can I talk to you?"

"Seriously? John Smith?" she muttered. Turning back toward her son, she called, "There's an FBI agent here! What else have you done?" She opened the door and said in a resigned tone, "Please come in, Agent Smith. I imagine you're here to talk to Eli, my son."

Smith flashed his badge upon entering the family room. "Nice to meet you, Eli."

Sarah turned pale. The man was of Asian descent, in his thirties, wearing jeans and a checked shirt. He didn't look like any FBI agent she'd ever seen on TV or the movies. She shifted her eyes to Eli and then back to the visitor.

"Ma'am, please don't worry," Smith said smoothly. "We know that a man who calls himself 'Ab' or 'Abaddon' was in contact with Eli." Agent Smith showed them both Ab's photo. "Do you recognize him?"

Sarah shook her head. "Never seen him before."

Eli looked at the picture. "Yeah, I met him today. He's a former pilot. Right?"

"No, that's a cover to collect information on air force installations in Nevada. Anything you can tell me about him?"

"Well, he had an interesting car, a real rust-bucket. He helped me when I fell, and he gave me a lift home. He thought I was a pilot. You know... He's a pilot... I'm a pilot..."

"Are you?" Smith said, lifting an eyebrow.

"No, he saw..." Eli looked around for the kneeboard.

"... my husband's air force cap. Eli loves it," piped up Sarah. From the pile of David's things still on the table near the couch, she took an old cap with the name, unit, and rank embroidered on its front.

Eli was puzzled by his mother's sudden butting in but decided not to contradict her.

"Can I talk to your husband?"

"He was killed in the line of duty many years ago."

"Ma'am, I'm sorry to hear that. That's a great loss for you and our country." Smith reached into his pocket. "Here's my business card. Ma'am, if you or Eli see this man again, please call. It's a matter of national security."

"We will," said Sarah, walking the FBI agent to the door.

"Thank you for your time, ma'am." Eli heard Agent Smith exiting the house and then the sound of the closing door.

Sarah returned and began to pack things back into the suitcase.

"Dad's cap?" Eli demanded. "He saw the pilot book in my hands!"

"Your father didn't want strangers to know about the kneeboard."

"Whatever." Eli approached the table and took the kneeboard. "Hey, Mom, I saw some drawings in that book. Are they a treasure map or something?"

"I don't know. We didn't have time to talk." Sarah sobbed. "He passed away so quickly. But he mentioned that... He didn't want his superiors to see the notes."

Eli hugged her quickly, then asked, "Did you try to do any research?"

"I did. I even tried to use the database at work. At NASA, we have 3D projections of the Earth's surface maps. These mountains in Nevada are all the same, though. There are so many of them, so alike. If your father drew this after he crashed, I think he did it for himself... Maybe to go back to the place where it all happened."

That night, Eli couldn't sleep. He kept tossing and turning in his bed until he got an idea. He took his laptop and started searching the internet.

First, Eli tried *Nevada geography of military installations*. Nothing interesting. He pondered his next step and decided to try *Nevada geography tours*. Nothing interesting either.

Eli was about to give up when, on the ninth page of search results, a link to a page titled *Nevada Safari to Explore US Military Past* caught his attention. He clicked the link.

The web page opened with a showy picture of a man in front of a small aircraft with the following caption underneath:

PIPER PA-20/22 PACER AIRCRAFT

Unique air tours - contact Rurik Cavell at info@rurikcavell.tour, a former jet fighter pilot and Ponolah (NV) based licensed tour operator, with an intimate knowledge of Nevadan geography and history. From $699.95.

Paragraphs below yielded more details.

For the adventurous at heart, a trip from all major destinations in Nevada to the abandoned military installations in a Piper airplane will provide the thrill of a lifetime. The narrated aerial tour is a unique opportunity to experience the majesty of Nevada and its history with a full-day, all-inclusive tour by air. Enjoy a round-trip scenic flight and touch-downs at the forgotten airstrips. Only with Nevada Safari.

Your trip can be customized to include flyovers with sweeping views of many natural landmarks. Hear informative narration from your expert pilot while you soak in views of Nevada's fantastic landscape.

The page had a map of Nevada showing arrows originating from a small town of Ponolah to various locations.

Eli opened his email and, with a "Eureka!" face, started typing. He finished with a loud bang on the keyboard to send his message to Nevada Safari.

Rurik Cavell, a fifty-three-year-old former navy pilot, widower, and alcoholic, sat on a plush blue sofa in the lobby bar at the Yellow Mountain Casino. With a puffy face under a mat of salt-and-pepper hair, a baggy and dingy outfit, and a glass of brownish liquid in front of him, he looked like a man who had seen enough of life and its shitstorms.

His career in the navy had taken a sharp turn during the 2003 invasion of Iraq when he received a general discharge after disappearing from his aircraft carrier with no plausible explanation. Nobody could find him for five days on the ship cruising in the open sea. On the sixth day, he was found sleeping on his bunk with no one having seen him getting into his stateroom.

Ruke—that's what most people called him—claimed he was abducted by aliens. The crew and his commanders concluded—based in part on previous drinking problems—that he had been hiding and binge-drinking in the carrier's anchor well. According to Ruke's testimony, aliens who were planning to create an outpost on Earth had interrogated him, which led to a severe psychological trauma he tried to alleviate with alcohol.

Though at times direct and blunt, Ruke was a soft, easygoing, and kind person. He was still full of optimism, with a rather philosophical approach when facing the quirks of life. When drinking, Ruke was usually calm, short-spoken, often claiming that his heritage went back to Rurik, the legendary ninth-century Norseman chieftain who founded the Rurik Dynasty, which ruled Kievan Rus and later the Tsardom of Russia until the 17th century.

Rurik Cavell didn't exactly look like he did in the picture posted on his website. But given the few people in the bar and the fact that Ruke was wearing an aviator jacket, Eli couldn't miss him. "Mr. Cavell? Good afternoon."

"It's nice to meet you... Umm..."

"I'm Eli. Eli Stroud."

"Right."

"Mr. Cavell—"

"Call me Ruke. I'm a Norseman. A man from the North!"

"Okay. Thank you, Ruke."

Ruke took a long chug from his glass and looked around with a renewed interest in life. "So... what's up?"

"As I said in my email, I'd like to learn more about my state, its glorious past, and—"

"Glorious past? Cut the crap, son. What do you want?"

Eli, uncomfortable and not knowing how to explain what he wanted, hesitated. "You do custom tours, right?"

"And?"

"I need to find a place. I thought that using a plane would be the best way to do it under the circumstances."

"What circumstances?"

Eli took his father's drawings from his pocket and showed them to Ruke. "You see this skyline and other landmarks? That's the view from a place I need to find."

"What's so special about the place?"

"My father crashed somewhere near there. He was an air force pilot."

A nod of respect broke through Ruke's forthright attitude. "Can you narrow down the area? Nevada is big."

"I think it's near Ponolah. Probably twenty to forty miles northeast."

"What was your father's name? By the way, I'm a former navy pilot myself."

"David Stroud. Did you know him?"

Ruke squared his shoulders. "I'll help you. Let's go!"

"You mean… Now?"

"Why not? I know the place. My plane is here—fuel's on you."

Sarah was right when she told her son that all mountains in Nevada were the same. Well—maybe for geologists, zoologists, and wildlife biologists that's not true, but if you're a layperson and want to find a few mountains stuck together in a particular config-uration, your quest will most likely fail.

Nevada is the most mountainous state in the Union. Depres-sions, flats, dry lakes, pans, and sinks are scattered between ribbons of mountain ranges. That's Nevada—dry, hot, and windy, especially in the summer, with a lot of contrasting lunar land-scapes, few human ventures, and only a few picturesque settings and trails that could entice visitors hungry for the wonders of Mother Earth. With the exception of some natural attractions and parks, as soon as you move away from larger cities, Nevada becomes monotonous and dull. There's nothing for the human eye to stop on, to rejoice in, or to marvel at.

As Ruke admitted later, his confidence that he knew the place David depicted in his sketches didn't materialize in a quick result. By the second day, Ruke and Eli were ironing several areas, trying to stay as close to the ground as possible with both of them glued to the windows of Ruke's Piper Pacer, comparing the view from the cockpit to David's sketches.

No matter what, Eli wanted to find the place. He became concerned about Ruke losing interest and giving up. However, Eli soon discovered that his newfound partner, albeit for unknown reasons, had developed the same obsession with the quest and stubbornly continued their search.

Repeatedly making sharp turns, changing altitude, and going back to view the landscape from different angles turned out to be a daunting task. What eventually helped was David's note pointing to a line of woods, one of the few useful landmarks. Flying time and time again over the edge of a small forest, Ruke finally pointed to the rock on a mountain plateau a mile ahead. "That's it!"

He banked hard right and began a rapid descent... and abruptly the cockpit became quiet. After two days, the annoying, constant sound of Piper's engine was gone. All Ruke and Eli could hear was the wind from the aircraft's wings, wing braces, and landing gear.

"What happened?" asked Eli.

"We're going down—that's what happened," snarled Ruke.

Struggling with the controls, he dropped the airplane's nose, trying to maintain a flying airspeed and avoid a stall—but alas, the ground was getting closer and closer. The Piper shook as its landing gear brushed against a group of boulders, but by sheer luck, Ruke avoided a collision. Fortunately, the plateau was broad enough to land the plane safely.

While Ruke was inspecting his Piper for any damage after its hard landing, Eli walked to the edge of the plateau. He checked his father's notes and compared them to the panorama in front of him. There was no mistake—the skyline looked exactly as it did on the sketch. This was the place.

To his left and right were rocky outcrops and stand-alone boulders. Eli examined two more pages marked LEFT and RIGHT with some details, mostly rocks, near the edge of the plateau itself. Something was wrong. It occurred to him that the position where the drawings were made was different than his, but by using those two pages, he could identify the exact spot where his father stood on that fateful day. His heart pounded in excitement—he knew that he was on the right track. Eli started moving left, comparing what he saw to the sketches every ten or fifteen steps. Then he stopped abruptly.

This is it! This is where he was... Eli kneeled and stroked the grass with his hands. *What now? I don't believe my dad spent all that time sketching the place to show where he was. There's something special about this spot.*

Eli looked around. These few square yards of grass and rocks where he stood seemed no different from the rest of the plateau. He approached the edge of the cliff and looked down the canyon—nothing unusual there, either. *Mom should know more. She was rather secretive about the kneeboard. Oh, crap, I didn't even tell her where I was going. She must be mad as hell!*

He took out his new phone to call Sarah. No luck in such a remote place, with the nearest cell tower many miles away. "Ruke!" shouted Eli. "How's the plane?"

"I still need to check something."

"I need to get back to town and call my mom."

"You can use my satellite phone. It's in the cockpit."

To Eli's surprise, his mother took the call from the unknown number. "Sarah Stroud," he heard in the bulky box of Ruke's phone.

Eli covered his other ear with his hand to isolate the noise from the wind. "Mom? Hi, Mom! It's me. Can you hear me?"

"Eli! That's not your phone. Where are you?"

Eli hesitated. "Uh... in Ponolah. Well, sort of..."

"What? What did you do now?"

"Nothing, just researching."

Eli wanted to tell Sarah that he'd found the place of the crash, but Sarah didn't give him a chance. "Did you go to see Chris?"

Being on the other side of the line, Eli couldn't see Sarah's face when she asked this question, because if he'd gotten a glimpse of it, the conversation would have taken a different turn. Eli would have had no doubt that Sarah had said much more than she intended. But without seeing her, Eli simply asked, "Chris? Who's Chris?"

Sarah went silent for a second or two. Finally, she uttered,

"Chris Kline, your father's crew member... I thought I'd told you about him."

"Do you know his address?" asked Eli. He caught a flicker of motion in the corner of his eye and turned his head to look at Ruke, who was pointing toward something behind Eli.

Eli turned around. A small flying object, like something he'd only seen in sci-fi films, slowly and silently rose from the canyon and landed softly, not far from Ruke's airplane. A moment later, a young woman in a tight, light-blue jumpsuit emerged from the craft.

Still holding the phone tight to his ear, Eli didn't listen to Sarah anymore—the events developing right before his eyes were too strange to keep talking. Ruke rushed to his plane's cockpit. From the pile of rubbish on the floor, he pulled out a Kalashnikov and shouted, "She's one of them!"

"Them?"

Ruke pointed the gun at the woman. "Stay where you are!"

"Are you listening? I don't know his address. Who's with you?" Eli realized that Sarah was still on the phone.

"Fucking aliens!" Ruke shook his weapon, not daring to do anything else.

Eli covered the phone's mic with his hand. "You mean she's an alien? C'mon..."

"Eli! Eli! What's going on?" demanded Sarah.

"Mom, sorry... Got to go. Not a good time to talk." Eli ended the call.

"Abducted me when I was with the navy. See? They didn't believe me! I can prove it now!" Ruke yelled, advancing toward the woman.

"Whoa, man! Chill out!" Eli stepped back, away from Ruke's gun. "She seems to me to be rather Earthy... No tentacles or anything." He turned to the woman. "Who are you?"

"My name is Nox. Don't worry, Eli, he cannot harm me."

"You know me?"

"I knew your father."

"My father must have been *en vogue* in these godforsaken places." Eli tilted his head slightly and examined Nox from head to toes. "How old are you?"

Nox smiled. "I thought it wasn't polite on Earth to ask a woman her age."

Ruke bellowed, "You candy bitch, shut up!"

Paying no attention to Ruke, Nox, now sad, continued, "I truly regret what happened to your father. The storm damaged our systems that night. I faced a dilemma—"

"On the ground, or I'll kill you!" raved Ruke.

"Gentlemen, please be reasonable. The best thing you can do now is to leave and forget this place exists. Others may not be as forgiving as I."

As if her words were prophetic, another alien spacecraft at least ten times bigger than Nox's flyer emerged from the canyon and hovered above the plateau, accompanied by a light rumbling sound. It had a predatory look, with two wings protruding and curving forward as if trying to catch a victim in its claws.

"They've already traced you!" announced Nox, looking agitated.

"Traced?" Eli raised his eyebrows in disbelief.

"Yes." Nox shook her head at the spaceship. "That's Abaddon's ship. He either followed you or bugged you. He had no clue about this place. See? You're here—he's here."

The spaceship's hatch opened, and out stepped the man Eli knew as Ab, with two more individuals in military-style uniforms. With a theatrical gesture, Ab declared, "Let the party begin!" and broke into a smile. "Aren't we all happy to be at this wonderful place?"

Ruke looked confused. He kept shifting his Kalashnikov from Nox to Ab and back again. "It's them!" he exclaimed, but this time he sounded less convincing.

"Serious weapon you have. Are you ready to use it?" Ab made a hand signal to one of his guards. "Drach!"

Drach walked leisurely to Ruke and knocked him down with one blow of his huge fist. "The man from the North. Nice to meet you again."

Ab approached the unconscious Ruke lying on the ground. "A couple of clowns short of a circus, this one. And Eli, must I say thank you. Couldn't have done better myself." Ab poked Ruke with his foot. "You and your friend can go. For now." Ab turned to Nox. "You, my darling, are coming with us. Drach, Lobo, escort the prisoner inside the ship. Make sure she cannot escape... Oh, and dispose of that." Ab pointed to Nox's craft. "I don't want any traces of it on this planet."

THREE

ASH

Eli and Ruke sat inside the Piper's cockpit. "Can you fly?" Eli asked anxiously, looking at Ruke, who was still shaky after the blow to his head.

"Ohhhh... and they didn't believe me."

"They? Who?"

"The discharge review board. They claimed I was hiding and drinking for five days."

"Were you?"

"No, that was him!"

"The guy who hit you?"

"No, the other one... Their boss. You know him?"

"Ab?"

"Whoever..." Ruke touched his head. "Oww... Fucking aliens. He interrogated me and my cellmate for days. Mind you—he's a very bad guy."

"So, you're telling me *aliens* are living on Earth?"

"Dude, you've just met four. Who else did you think they might be? Creatures from the Black Lagoon?"

"They looked like humans..."

"Humans—but not from Earth! Did you see their ship? And their weapons?"

"I'm thinking," pondered Eli. "If there are aliens, then this place is like a magnet, a honeypot that attracts them. There must be something special about it. I think it's no accident my father asked Mom to be careful with his notes."

"You didn't tell me about that."

"I'm telling you now. Hey, do you know a Chris Kline?"

"Ponolah's Chris Kline?"

Eli nodded.

"I sure do—Ponolah is a small place. Chris died last year. His daughter, Ashley, is still there. Why?"

"My mom told me over the phone that Chris was my father's crew member. He should have known something about my dad. His daughter may also know something."

"I'll show ya where she lives..." Ruke mumbled. He continued after a long pause, "I don't like it. I don't like this at all. Be careful and let me know if you need help. Now let's go."

Ab's ship approached Pat'zan, the only inhabited planet in the Mulgruus star system and the central planet of the Elder Keep Alliance. Mulgruus was an old, dying sun, a red, cool, high-mass dwarf—an unexpected occurrence in this universe. In a way, the star was a whim of nature. But Pat'zan was even more unusual.

What was called a planet was, in reality, one of the two large moons orbiting near Pat'zan Prime, a gas giant with one hemisphere constantly facing Mulgruus. As was true for most gas giants, Pat'zan Prime radiated more heat than it was receiving from its sun. Strong winds in the giant's dense atmosphere helped distribute energy evenly and create habitable conditions on both moons.

Like many other planets in this part of the Milky Way, Pat'zan had been colonized by the humans abandoning Earth in search of new worlds. The migration had started more than a hundred thousand years ago and continued until about 20,000 BC. That's when the Grand Cleanup took place, and a few enthusiasts, willing to stay, founded the cradles of modern civilization on Earth.

The purpose of the Cleanup was to leave Earth in a pristine condition and provide Earth's biosphere a chance to renew the natural cycles of all its ecosystems. It was a complicated process that involved removing all human-made deposits and additions to the planet, from microscopic particles of chemicals not occurring naturally to the removal of all major alterations to Earth and the solar system. It used everything from nanomachines to world-sized engines to accomplish this project.

The few people remaining on Earth knew that they would have to set out on a grueling life, relying only on their skills and knowledge to survive. In reality, it was much worse than that. It meant that it would be tens of thousands of years before they could reach a technological level comparable to the one their ancestors had possessed when leaving Earth.

It's worth mentioning that the hundred-thousand-year exodus wasn't a continuous process—it took place in three waves. But each ended in a way similar to what had happened after the last mass departure. Pat'zan's inhabitants, who called themselves Pazons, were members of the Third Wave and were among the least advanced of Earthlings spread around the galaxy.

At first glance, Pat'zan, about the size of Earth, didn't look appealing to the settlers. Rocky areas alternated with oceans and flats covered with purple plants, illuminated by the dim light coming from both Mulgruus and Pat'zan Prime. The moon seemed to be a dark, dreary place—an etude in dark violet, with streaks of blue and purple.

The strange succession of nights and grim days, with complex transitions between the two, appeared chaotic and unfriendly. Many of the first colonists who came to Pat'zan didn't care for it and didn't stay long. However, among those who stayed, the mood changed quickly. What once gave the impression of being unwelcoming and depressing became full of harmony and beauty.

Some said it was the ideal environment and climate on Pat'zan that changed their minds. Year-long mild, stable temperatures, no extreme meteorological disturbances, friendly flora and fauna, and no disease-inducing microorganisms made life easy. Others found comfort in worshiping Tyanis, the God of Night and Gloam, and justified their desire to stay on the moon by proclaiming that everything around them was the result of the will and wishes of their newly minted god.

The belief was eagerly adopted by the planet's ruling party, the Elder Keep, and not without using the divine providence to strengthen their power. With time, the Congregation of Tyanis, the institutionalized form of the Elder Keep religion, became a formidable political and social force.

With or without Tyanis at the center of the Elder Keep political movement, Pazons found little to complain about. In fact, they thrived. With time, they adapted perfectly to the darkness of the place, building mega-cities defined by illuminated veins of busy roads with Gothic-like gleaming towers overshadowing the less affluent districts and slums.

After the successful colonization of the moon came the consolidation of power and expansion. Either by means of conquest or peaceful associations formed for mutual benefit, the Elder Keep grew into a strong alliance of planets and races occupying a vast area around Pat'zan.

The Pazons were a conservative race. Throughout hundreds of centuries, they remained mostly immune to things like arts, fashion, or architecture in which other sentient beings would find pleasure and joy, enriching their lives beyond purely physical existence. On Pat'zan, the useful functionality of things, along with a set of rigid religious tenets, ruled the lives of its inhabitants. That's why visual signs of changes were a scarce commodity, with one notable exception. Science and technological developments, fed by the need for expansion, flourished.

With time, the church and the military became the two fundamental pillars of Elder Keep society. Both were built on strong hierarchy and bureaucracy, both were aggressive and unscrupulous, both strongly believed that the end justified any means, and both served the same goals, using their own strategies and tactics. The military guaranteed security and expansion, whereas the church brought values and gave comfort and salvation to the people's souls. The Congregation of Tyanis still provided the ideological foundation of almost all facets of life in the Alliance, and it tacitly enjoyed an aura of superiority.

Undoubtedly, the two backbones of the Elder Keep sometimes became involved in power struggles to gain more influence. Such fights, though, were considered family matters that didn't concern outsiders and were never shared with them. Also, the church always won, even when the military seemingly had the upper hand. After all, the Alliance's name for its armed forces was the Knights of Tyanis, a clear sign of the level of religious indoctrination among military personnel.

With this in mind, it should come as no surprise that Xiir Zanrod, the Lord Guarantor of the Congregation, was intimately involved in many operations conducted by the Knights of Tyanis' Security Chancellery. Some of the most important undertakings that required the use of the Elder Keep security apparatus were inspired and initiated by Xiir.

His huge office was dark, as Gothic windows with intricate tracery patterns didn't provide much light. But that was how Xiir liked it. He sat motionless behind his desk, staring at the barely perceptible ghostly shadows on the stone floor left by the dim rays of Pat'zan Prime passing through the glazing bars of office windows. An enormous statue of an ancient warrior in a cape and hood, leaning on a sword, stood behind Xiir Zanrod.

The Lord Guarantor looked as if he had come from a late seventeenth-century portrait of a nobleman on Earth, distinguished by a long, craggy face framed by curly gray hair falling to the shoulders. His long black silk coat, with ruffled sleeves and a small cravat, accentuated his strong personality. In his seventies, he was a man of advanced age on Pat'zan. That hadn't resulted in any deterioration of his mental abilities. On the contrary, years seemed only to further sharpen his wit, acumen, and political sagacity.

Xiir Zanrod

There were few people who could enjoy the Lord Guarantor's graces. The smarter someone was, the more difficult it became to break the moat of suspicion and distrust separating Xiir Zanrod from the rest of the world. Ab was an exception. He was smart, but that didn't stop Xiir from having a weakness for his protégé. Nobody knew why, but the fact that he treated Abaddon, the Aspirant Inquisitor of the Congregation of Tyanis and its rising star, with apparent kindness was well-known. Ab's reputation as the church's favorite didn't provide him with many friends. On the other hand, Xiir's support and patronage had launched Ab's remarkable career at the Security Chancellery, where he now served as the chief of special operations.

Ab knew whom he had to visit first after booking Nox and taking her down to the high-security prison in the Chancellery's basement, and he didn't need to go through the Congregation's Protocol Doyen to see Xiir Zanrod. The Lord's doors were always open to Ab. All he had to do was knock.

"My Lord Guarantor," said Ab, entering the Lord's office and bowing. "I want to thank you for your wisdom and guidance and congratulate you with the capture of Nox, the Guardian of the Game."

"You always know how to make my day." Xiir rose and came up to Ab. "But don't be too shy about your doings for the glory of our God and the Alliance. You've done a good job, Aspirant Inquisitor Abaddon." Xiir sucked in his lips while thinking. "What's next?"

"Nox is not a regular flesh-and-blood individual. I have something special in mind to make her useful. Meanwhile, I'll return to Earth to take advantage of the momentum."

"Prosperous providence, Abaddon. But remember, many important players, including our allies, may become angry if they learn about our efforts to seize the Game. Asphalis, your boss at the Chancellery, should know that."

"Thank you for reminding me, my Lord. I will not fail."

Let us not offend the inhabitants of Ponolah by saying that the small town was a miserable hole. Once an important place for mining ventures, the settlement lost its role as one of the richest silver strikes in Nevada history with the end of gold and silver mining production, and it gradually transformed into a stopover and rest spot for travelers on a lonely highway. With a population of fewer than three thousand people, the town relied on the nearby government facilities as its main source of employment. That was where Ashley, the only child of Chris Kline, lived with no expectations or prospects to change her life and fulfill at least some dreams any unpretentious twenty-five-year-old woman might have.

Though Chris had survived the crash that killed David Stroud without a scratch, he'd run out of luck when he was diagnosed with multiple sclerosis. But that wasn't the end of his problems chasing the family. Five years after the incident, when Chris had already resigned from the air force, Jenifer, his wife and Ash's mother, died from cancer. At the time, Ash was eight years old, and after that, her life became a living hell.

Chris and Ash remained in the old house in Ponolah they'd inherited from Jenifer. Chris' debilitating disease consumed him gradually but steadily. The medical bills mounted, and despite his health problems, Chris had to work, but he could find only low-paying jobs. His feeble attempts at fatherhood, no matter how laudable they were, produced the opposite effect, with Ash having to help her father more and more.

Despite the many challenges, Chris' daughter grew up optimistic and confident in life. Somehow, after crying at night in her room, she could find the strength to do all her daily chores and be nice and supportive of her father. Ash got good grades at school, perhaps because of her sharp and inquisitive mind. Among her fellow students, she acquired a reputation of a kind, unassuming, and honest person—a typical girl next door.

Ash's dream was to continue her education and become a scientist and researcher. But because of her aging and ailing father, she decided to stay in Ponolah after graduating from high school. Thanks to Chris' remaining connections at the US Air Force, Ash found a civilian job at Ponolah Test Range.

Ruke, as promised, drove Eli to Ash's house. The nondescript construction with rickety walls wouldn't stand out against

Nevadan rural town dwellings. Nevertheless, the house looked clean and tidy.

As Eli approached, its door opened, and Ash emerged with two bags ready to dump into the trash can for the next day's collection. There was nothing fake about Ash—jeans, a simple T-shirt, not too baggy and not too tight, neat but not over-styled blond hair, only traces of makeup. She looked like a non-superficial but subtle beauty.

"Ashley? Ashley Kline?" called Eli from the street, waving his hand.

Ash glanced at Eli and remained silent. She knew who he was— moreover, she had just finished speaking to Sarah Stroud over the phone. Eli's mother had warned her that he might show up and begged her not to give him David's notes.

It never occurred to Ash to question Sarah's motivation for the phone call. After all, Eli was her son, and Sarah was talking about her husband's notes. So even if her explanations, which Ash had never asked for, were confusing and erratic, the request didn't bother her. She had never seen Eli before in person and wasn't in the habit of meddling in other people's lives.

Eli caught her glance and continued, "I'm looking for Ashley Kline, the daughter of Chris Kline. My father was in the air force with Chris."

"How can I help you?" Ash brushed Eli off with an impersonal and bureaucratic cliché, evidently believing it would be the best way to get rid of him.

"I'm Eli Stroud. My father's plane crashed in this area years ago. I'm trying to research what happened. I wasn't even born when he died."

"I'm sorry, Eli. I don't know anything about it." Ash turned and moved to the house.

"Wait! Do you know someone who can help me?"

Ash gave Eli an icy stare. "My dad died last year. Your best bet is to inquire at the air force base where your father served."

Ash Kline

Eli wanted to add something, but it was too late. She had already disappeared back inside. He sat on the curb in front of the house and covered his face with his hands. *Damn her! Why bum me out like that?* He was tired and didn't know what to do next.

Ash showed up again a moment later, this time on the driveway, to get into a truck. As she swung out into the street, she stopped and opened the window, calling to Eli, "Anyway, why is it so important to you?"

This time, Eli could sense some empathy in her voice. "Because I suck at life!" burst out of his mouth. She wouldn't understand, he decided, and added, "This is the first time I've felt I'm doin' something worth doin'!"

"Better late than never," Ash commented sarcastically, hitting the gas.

Eli sat there and watched Ash driving away. *Bitch!* He put his hand into his pocket, reaching for the phone, and suddenly felt a piece of heavy paper under his fingers. *That's the business card the Fed left. He should know more regarding what's going on.*

A glimpse of hope dawned on Eli's face. He quickly tapped in the number. "Agent Smith?"

"Who's calling, please?"

"Eli Stroud. Mr. Smith, you... Whoever you are... We need to talk."

Early the following afternoon, Eli sat in the bar of an old hotel, sipping a beer. The place was cozy, with a curious mixture of Old West and Victorian decor. He was waiting for John Smith. Eli had already imbibed a hefty dose of Gulden Ark, full-bodied Trappist ale, and was taking pleasure in the peace and tranquility around him.

The barman came up to Eli and asked, "Another beer, sir?"

"Yes, please." The strong ale helped him stop thinking about recent events and put him in a pleasant state of mind.

He leaned back into a deep, plush armchair and watched the bartender carrying over a new bottle of ale, placing it on a small table in front of him and opening it with an elegant move of his hand. Copper-colored liquid moved smoothly out the bottle and into a branded chalice.

"Enjoy your beer, sir."

Eli raised the goblet, holding it up to the light from the dim sconces on the wall. *Not a bad place, this Ponolah, if they have Ark...*

He lowered the beer and touched the creamy head to his lips, savoring the moment. Far from the first time in his life, Eli was alone with himself, but he was at peace for once. *What's different now?* he pondered, and couldn't find the answer. But it felt good.

Maybe it was because Eli was no longer floating free, disconnected from half of his heritage. From the moment he'd touched his father's kneeboard, he'd gained purpose and stopped drifting through life, cutting corners and trying to find the path of least resistance. He had now to make decisions and search for answers. And he'd already done something—he'd found the place where his father had crashed. *Is it that simple?*

"Hello, Eli." John Smith's deep voice interrupted Eli's soul-searching.

"Ah, Mr. 007! What's your real name?" Eli bared his teeth in a predatory smile.

"I told you—John Smith. You asked to meet me. You have something new on Ab?"

"I have—" began Eli and stopped. "C'mon, man, Russian spies don't fly on spaceships... cause Ab does. Really, who are you?"

"That's classified. Anything else?"

Eli felt a flash of anger. "Do you take me for an idiot, 'Mr. Smith'?"

"That's not what I meant. You have to admit—I did agree to come and see you on short notice, even when you didn't want to explain why."

"Oh, I'll tell you why. How about Ab kidnappin' a hot babe who looked like she belonged in a fuckin' beauty contest but who appeared out of nowhere in a flying fuckin' saucer in the middle of nowhere?"

"I see..." The so-called FBI agent fell silent, digesting what he'd heard, then stated in a low voice, "Okay. First, stop shouting about flying saucers. Second, can I join you?"

"Be my guest." Eli pointed to an empty chair on the other side of the table. "Want a beer?"

"No, thanks." John looked into Eli's eyes. "You're correct. I'm not an FBI agent. My name is Nayo, but people usually call me by my first name, Yow. I'm a private eye hired to investigate this Ab character. This person intends to steal a piece of technology that would be highly dangerous in the wrong hands. Its important component is here on Earth."

"But *you're* not from Earth, are you?"

"No, I'm not," Yow replied flatly.

"So, you're the good guy... How do I know you are not lyin'?"

"Just trust me."

Eli looked at Yow. *An honest face, so the dude is probably telling the truth. But the guy lied already when he said he was a suit. Well, that's okay, what else could the man tell me?*

"I will... for now." Eli was curt. "Go on."

"The 'babe' you described... She's special. An android, I think, but I'm not sure. Her name is Nox. She guards the artifact on Earth. If she's been kidnapped, then Ab is close to his goal. Not without your help."

"I never helped him."

"Perhaps not directly. But remember how Ab found you? By the way, how did you end up in that 'nowhere'?"

"I was researching my father's death. I have his notes. They led me to the place, but there's nothing there. Only mountains."

"Ah, your father. Makes sense. Let me guess. Nox tried to stop you, and Ab showed up?"

"Nox was certain he tracked me somehow."

"It does seem that way. What exactly happened?"

"They took her and flew away."

Yow breathed a sigh of relief. "So Ab doesn't know where the device is. That's good. And he wants to use Nox to learn more about it."

"What? You mean he's gonna torture her?" Eli asked, instantly concerned.

"He may try to, but that's not what we should focus on right now."

"What do you suggest?"

"First, let me check to see if you're bugged." From his coat pocket, Yow produced a small device with blinking lights on one end, placing it on the table in front of Eli.

"What's this?"

"A scanner. It can detect most known bugs in the galaxy. It'll take a minute or two."

Eli and Yow sat silently, watching the scanner. *Is this some kind of joke?* Eli wondered. *Or is the guy a nut? Probably not—he seems to be trying.*

The device emitted a squeak, and the lights turned off. "Nothing," announced Yow sullenly.

"But that's good news, right?"

"Honestly, I'd prefer we had found a bug. At least we'd know what to do. But now I have to assume that Ab followed you directly. Anyway, don't worry, he's not going to touch you. Probably, he'll keep watching... for now."

Blood rushed to Eli's head. "If Ab followed me, he may know the other people I contacted. Ruke, the pilot... I bet the man doesn't care about Ruke. But Ash, she's the daughter of my dad's crewman. I think she knows more than she says about what happened to our dads."

"When did you see her?"

"Yesterday."

"Where?"

"At her home."

Yow shook his head. "I know who Ashley is. You need to warn her immediately. I'll try to contact my client and join you later at her house."

Eli's excitement about the last several days of his life evaporated. "What am I supposed to tell her?"

Yow's face expressed disappointment. "Do you still want to find out what happened to your father or not?"

"Of course I do."

"Then figure it out. You're a big boy." Yow was mocking Eli, who turned red with embarrassment and anger. "Now run, before Ab kidnaps Ash."

When Eli showed up for the second time at her place and knocked at the door, Ash Kline was standing in the kitchen, hunched over the sink, washing dishes by hand. There was no dishwasher in the house. She was hot, and every time she began a new scrub-and-rinse cycle, she tried to use her upper arm to remove a stubborn strand of hair that kept falling across her forehead.

The knock at the door was welcome at first since Ash got a break from her chore. But when Eli's face appeared in the peephole, she didn't know what to do. Sarah's phone call was still fresh in her memory. Irked, Ash opened the door and growled, "You again?"

"We need to talk!"

Ash raised her hands as water dribbled from her latex gloves. "I'm a little busy right now, okay? Besides, there's nothing to talk about."

"Can I come in? It's important."

Ash rolled her eyes and stepped aside.

Eli entered, mulling over what to tell her. While he stood hesitantly shifting from foot to foot in front of her, Ash was pondering her next and final move to get rid of him once and for all. The silent face-off ended when Ash blurted out, "I'm trying to be polite here, but I'm not going to give you the map!"

Map? Several pages were torn from the book—does she have the second part of my father's notes?

Trying to hide his surprise and injecting as much confidence as he could into his tone, Eli said, "Listen, things have changed. I need to find that place."

"Why do you need it? What do you want?"

It was Eli's turn to get frustrated. *This is my father, for God's sake!*

You birdbrain... Is it so difficult to understand? He threw himself on a couch and put his hands behind his head. "To have sex with you. Wouldn't mind, would you?" sneered Eli.

"What!?" She tore off her gloves, hurled them into the kitchen sink, and pointed to the door. "I'm done with you. Get out!"

"Sorry, sorry! I didn't mean it. It's just—"

"Who the hell is that?" squealed Ash, pointing at something behind Eli.

Eli jumped to his feet and looked back. *Dammit! You've got to be kidding me!*

The door was still open, so Ab came right in and bowed gallantly. "I hope I'm not interrupting?"

"Are you with him?" Ash demanded, jerking a thumb at Eli.

Eli grabbed Ash's hand and yanked her away from Ab. "Run!"

"No, no, my darling," Ab assured her soothingly. "I'm with myself. I find your boyfriend annoying and useless. I trust you guys have fun?"

"Run! He'll kill you!" Eli yelled.

Ab snapped his fingers and pointed at Eli. "You, boy, shut up." He turned to Ash. "But you know, he's right. Can't argue with that. Unless you give me that map."

Ash shook off Eli's grip. "Both of you leave me alone!"

"My dear, please hurry." Ab became icy cold. "Or I'll have to kill you, as your boyfriend suggested."

"He's not my boyfriend. Don't you... Don't you ever say that again!"

Ab took a step forward and pulled out a strange-looking handgun from his waistband. "This is a powerful weapon, missy, and I'm losing my patience," he announced, pointing the gun at her.

"Give him the fucking map!" Eli shouted. "Or we'll die because of your stubbornness!"

Ash raised her hands. "Okay, okay, no problem... I'll get it for you." She moved around the couch and then opened her eyes wide in horror, looking past Ab. She slowly stretched out her hand, fixing her eyes, and pointed somewhere behind Ab. "Eli... What's that?" she whispered.

Later on, Eli and Ash laughed every time they recalled the moment that changed the course of events and saved their lives. Ab's split-second distraction was enough for Ash to reach for a semi-automatic shotgun hidden between the couch's wooden back-board and cushions, pull it out, and fire. She missed, destroying part of the foyer wall, but Ab lost his momentum. She pulled the trigger twice more while reaching for a huge handgun hidden in the same place and tossing it to Eli.

Ab fired back at Ash. The sibilant ray of light that burst out of his weapon left an inch-wide hole clear through the wall of the living room, letting in the sunlight, as Ash dodged the shot by plopping onto the floor. Leaving no chance for Ab to shoot again, Eli lunged at him, giving Ash time to recover. Ab shot at Eli, and he dropped on the floor like a bowling pin, writhing in pain.

Smoke, shattered glass, and flying debris filled the house as Ash kept shooting, giving Ab no chance to aim. The chaotic firing continued for only a few more seconds, but the only result was more damage to the house. Finally, Ab decided discretion was the better part of valor, preferring to escape rather than face Ash's determination to push back.

As Ash rushed to Eli to check on his wound, the front door swung open, and Yow Nayo rushed into the house. Ash shot on sight but, thank heavens, missed.

"Don't shoot!" yelled Eli. "He's on our side!"

Yow showed his empty hands. "Whoa, lady! Slow down. Know your enemies and know your friends."

Ash lowered her shotgun, but not her guard. "I don't know you. Stay where you are!"

"Take it easy—*he* knows me." Yow hurried to Eli and examined his injured leg. "You're lucky, merely burned flesh. No bleeding because of it... When we get to my ship, I'll take care of it."

"Who *are* you?" insisted Ash.

"His name is Yow. He's an alien," blurted Eli.

"Alien? You mean like Chinese?"

Eli rolled his eyes. "No, more like an extraterrestrial."

"What? He looks Asian…"

"Yow, where are you from?" Eli demanded, wincing as he flexed his leg. "You never told me."

Rising, Yow said, "Korango, a space station roughly a hundred light-years from Earth." He dusted himself off. "Guys, we can talk later. Right now, we need to find something before Ab finds it. Eli, I couldn't contact my client. We're on our own. Where's the place you mentioned earlier?"

"We need Ruke Cavell. He knows the mountains where it's hidden. The missing piece should be on the map." Eli pointed at Ash. "She has it."

"Miss, may we?"

Ash was already across the room, opening a closet whose door had been riddled with buckshot. She pulled out a shoebox and handed it to Eli, who was still sitting on the floor. He flipped it open, and inside were several pages with sketches in what he recognized as father's meticulous hand. Eli picked them up. "These are my father's drawings," he breathed.

Nobody paid attention as what was left of the front door opened, and Sarah Stroud entered. "Yes," she sighed. "David asked me to give them to Chris, to make it more difficult to find the place."

"Mom, what are you doing here?" Eli demanded.

"I was worried and couldn't sleep. Once I told you about Chris, I knew you'd find Ash." Sarah walked to Eli and helped him get to his feet. She looked around at the devastation. "What happened here?"

"What *happened*? Mom, you lied to me!"

Sarah narrowed her eyes at Yow. "And it seems I'm not the only one."

Yow took the initiative. "My apologies, ma'am. I'm Yow Nayo. I'm human, but not from Earth—you'd say I'm 'extraterrestrial.' I'm investigating Ab, a criminal who's after a piece of dangerous technology left on this planet. He believes that your son and this lady"—Yow nodded at Ash—"know its whereabouts."

"Is he trying to kill my son?"

"Whatever it takes, Ms. Stroud," Yow admitted. "This technology is worth a great deal to many. Now, I'm sorry, we don't have time to talk. Eli, find your friend Ruke. Ash, we need your car. I'll take care of the rest."

"So… aliens. It's all true! Can I go with you?" pleaded Ash.

"You're welcome if you ask me. Don't forget your gun and plenty of ammo if you join us. Okay, people, let's move."

Ash opened a kitchen drawer and started packing ammunition for her shotgun. Meanwhile, Eli picked up Ash's handgun from the floor. He looked at the markings on its barrel. *Hmm, not bad… .50 caliber.* "Ash, can I keep the gun for now?"

"I didn't see you shooting. Can you handle it?"

"You have no idea."

"Okay, then." Ash nodded. "I owe you my life, so the gun is yours. Don't forget the ammo." She threw two magazines and two boxes of rounds to Eli, who caught them awkwardly. "Here's the holster."

FOUR

THE GAMER

Yow's shuttle was small but fast and convenient for his line of work, which required mobility and low maintenance with no need for considerable firepower. But with all the wannabe guardians of the alien technology along for the ride, space was at a premium inside the ship. Eli and Ruke had to stand behind Yow, bending over him and holding onto bars on the bulkhead. Sarah and Ash huddled on narrow benches in a small cargo area, strapping themselves in as best they could.

When Yow took off, the stars still shone in the sky, and the day had sent ahead only a feeble vanguard of light, just enough to see the horizon to the east of Ponolah. He piloted the ship at low altitude among the labyrinth of mountain ranges and valleys, following Ruke's instructions. Still, it took some time to find the area that Eli and Ruke had located two days before. By the time they came to the plateau, the sun had risen high enough to show the total splendor of the blue desert sky.

"Damn sun!" Ruke blocked his eyes with his palm.

"Be glad you can see it," Yow muttered. "I grew up in a tin can.

For me, it's a pleasure to be working on the mother world of humanity."

"Yeah, well, here's the plateau we found. Eli, it's your turn now."

"My dad made his sketches right from that position between those two boulders." Eli pointed at the spot, twenty to thirty yards in front of the spacecraft.

Yow moved the shuttle ahead, hovering inches above the ground. "Any idea where the device might be?"

Eli peered at his father's sketches. "I think my dad tried to depict some kind of chamber. That's the torus—must be the device you've mentioned. It's in a cave or something like that."

"Any details? An opening? A sign?" asked Yow. "I don't see anything around here that could be an entrance."

Ash crawled to Eli and peeked at the sketch. "The plateau ends with a precipice. Could the entrance be below the edge of the cliff?"

Yow touched the shuttle controls, and the craft swerved toward the edge and moved down, so the cockpit faced the rock.

"Ash is right." Eli pored again over the notes. "We need to find something shaped like the letter Y on the face of the rock. Go down… lower… more…"

The shuttle descended quickly into the canyon as Eli watched the steep, almost vertical, rock face pass. "Nothing yet. Keep moving… more… Bingo!"

Yow abruptly stopped the shuttle, leveling it to make an outcrop of a lighter inclusion visible in the cockpit's window. A crystallized material trapped inside the grayish igneous rock formed a shape that indeed reminded one of a handwritten slanted Y, about five feet tall.

"So what do we do now?" asked Yow.

"If this is what I think it is, my dad had no time, no tools. Did he just touch it?"

"I have a telescopic docking system we can use to get to the cliff." Yow turned the shuttle and extended the dock. "Ash, the hatch is behind you. Can you please let me by? I need to disable the lock."

"Easier said than done." After some clumsy maneuvering, Ash clambered out of her seat, and Yow disappeared into the dock entrance.

After a minute or so, he was back. "I touched it. I tried to scratch it, rub it—nothing. I have tools, but it seems like a monolith."

Eli shook his head. "I don't think so. It must have been something simple. I want to try."

Another hustle in the cabin and Eli squeezed his way into the dock. Its tube was narrow and didn't fit snugly to the cliff. Wind gusts rocked the shuttle, and the end of the metal docking ring was scratching the rock, leaving deep furrows where it touched. Eli reached the end of the dock and leaned closer to examine the surface. Nothing unusual, except for a barely noticeable airflow fluttering along the contours of the Y-shaped inclusion. He stretched his hand toward the rock and pictured the desperate situation his father would have been in, trying to save his life against all odds. But it was more than that—it wasn't his dad, but he *himself* hanging on the parachute lines in the middle of the violent storm, with the wind butting him against the cliff. It felt real. A cold sweat broke out over Eli's body. He jerked his hand away, and the sensation disappeared.

"Eli!" he heard his mother's voice. "Eli, are you okay?"

"I'm fine. I'm just—"

"It's been five minutes... What are you doing out there?" interrupted Yow.

"Ah, I see..."

Without hesitating, Eli touched the middle of the Y. Part of the cliff in front of him vanished, revealing an immense cavern. At its bottom, he saw a large, flat metal structure, like a landing platform, extended outwards below the shuttle. Eli jumped onto the platform and took several steps to test the metal under his feet. *This thing can hold a whole fleet, not just Yow's flyer.*

He turned around. Yow stood inside the shuttle's dock, staring in disbelief at what was happening. "Did you see that?" yelled Eli, waving his hands. "You can land here. I'm going into the cave."

The hole in the cliff was narrowing, leading deeper into the rock and transforming into a wide, tall tunnel. Eli looked back—the shuttle was still in the air, and he could see Yow in the cockpit. *What's he waiting for?* Eli waved his hand again, inviting Yow to proceed inside.

The shuttle finally moved in and slowly settled on the metal platform, as if testing it. While the ship was gently rocking on its landing shock absorbers, the open space behind it became cloudy. Then it darkened and quickly solidified, isolating the cavern from the outside world.

Eli, used to the daylight, stood in pitch darkness. When the wall closed the opening, his sense of time and the surrounding space changed. His mind was telling him he was on Earth, that the sky and the dreary desert landscape were still close. However, he felt like all those familiar things had moved a million miles away, and a new, unknown world was within his reach.

As his eyes adapted to the dimness, Eli noticed a faint light coming from the depths of the cave and decided to keep moving. He took a couple of steps forward and almost tripped over something soft. That's when lights from the shuttle illuminated the immensity of the cavern. A pile of parachute cloth with tangled lines lay under Eli's feet. A jet fighter's pilot helmet was nearby. He picked it up. The paint of its signage was flaking in places, but it was readable.

U.S. AIR FORCE

STINGER
David S.

Eli looked back to where Yow, Ash, and Sarah were getting out of the shuttle.

"Mom! This is Dad's helmet. He was here!" shouted Eli while raising the helmet triumphantly. He untangled himself from the parachute lines and rushed forward. Nothing could stop him now.

Energized by his find, Eli quickly walked along the tunnel, pressing on deeper into the mountain. The passage turned slightly to one side, and the faint light Eli had noticed before was growing stronger with every step. Several more, and he found himself on the threshold of another enormous cavern.

A few ghostly glowing lights looming in the distance illuminated the vast space, but they were barely enough to alleviate the gloom of the chamber. They were dancing in a slow, weird pattern, casting soft, moving shadows and providing few clues about the actual size and shape of the place. The ethereal mist filling the space added to the mystery, making the light seem to wrap around the stone's sharp edges. Rocky walls sprayed here and there with crystalline clusters of various shapes and colors rushed up, converging at the apex of the barely visible ceiling of the chamber. There was a strange combination of chaos and harmony to the place. Was it a human-made creation, or a quaint whim of nature?

The torus, the alien artifact sketched by his father, took center stage of the chamber. It stood there vertically, with its lower part sunk into the rocky floor—oddly like an inviting portal. By itself, especially at first glance, it didn't seem anything extraordinary. However, the dim lighting of the cavern and the torus' quiet glow gave the impression of power and eternity—a startling connection with the universe, far beyond the realm of human conscience.

Overwhelmed by the display of beauty and might, Eli stood gazing at the strange surroundings. Then he approached the torus. He couldn't know it, but the movement of his body, the position of his head and hands, were the same as his father's twenty-two years ago. And as his father did before, Eli went around the artifact and stopped behind it, leaning with his hand against the torus. Eli smiled as he touched the device, and a sweeping feeling of happiness flooded through him.

Ruke was the first after Eli to enter the chamber. He went straight to the torus, inspected it from all sides and, for reasons known only to him, knocked on it and listened to the sound it made. Satisfied with his findings, Ruke pulled out his flask, took a good gulp, grunted, and wiped his mouth with his sleeve. Then he passed through the torus and patted Eli on the shoulder. "All righty then, what do we do now?"

Ash, Sarah, and Yow were the last to enter the chamber. Like Eli, Sarah and Ash were mesmerized by what they saw. Yow was not. He stalked around the cave's perimeter, seeming more interested in the cave itself than anything else.

Eli was going to join the others when, in the darkness of the tunnel, a young woman loomed, holding a hand weapon aimed at Eli. "Stay where you are!" she shouted. But it was too late—Eli was already moving through the artifact.

"Aura! Don't shoot!" screamed Yow, while Sarah seized Aura's elbow and pushed it aside, anticipating the weapon's discharge and deflecting the blast.

All of Aura's attempts to shake Sarah off were in vain, as Eli's mother held her arm with a death grip. Aura deftly grabbed her gun with her other hand, but Eli was already pointing his new pistol at her. "Stand down!"

"You will stand trial for violating the Intergalactic Game Treaty," threatened Aura, her gun still aimed at Eli.

With the slight movement of his hand, Eli shot one of the chamber's lights hanging in the air near Aura's head. He returned the gun instantly to its previous position even as the bang still echoed, and shards of glass-like material scattered over Aura. "Last warning! Stand down!" Eli was calm, but it was the calmness of a man who wouldn't hesitate to act.

Aurabella (Aura) Thaleia

Yow rushed over to stand between Eli and Aura. "This is Eli Stroud, Aura. He knows nothing about the Gamer or the treaty. He's a native and on our side."

Eli growled, "In the past two days, I've been assaulted three times. Enough is enough. Lower your weapon!"

Aura softened a bit. "Ignorance of the law is no excuse." Without moving her gun, she admitted, "You're a quick draw."

"I hope you remember me this way." Eli shook the muzzle of the gun in a clear sign he was still waiting for Aura to stand down. "Are you one of those people who always want to have the last word? For your sake, I hope not."

Aura holstered her weapon and turned to Yow. "And I hope I

won't have to clean up his mess." She moved forward and, passing Eli, who still held the gun on her, walked up to the device and touched it. With the sounds of a smooth air release and a faint thud, the torus rose above the floor. With no apparent effort, Aura turned the alien artifact around on its vertical axis. "Yow, I need you come here and push the Gamer toward me."

A couple of minutes later, as they were carefully moving the device through the tunnel, Aura asked Yow, "How did you enter the sanctuary?"

"Eli opened it."

She stopped and looked at Yow, her face startled. "Eli? How?"

"I couldn't reach you with my communication system and decided to act on my own. Ab's closing in. So—Eli had sketches made by his father. You know that story, right?"

"I do."

"He followed his father's footsteps. We used my shuttle to get to that Y thing."

"That's the Gamer's emitter."

"Whatever it is, all he had to do was to touch it. I also tried, but nothing happened. Yet it responded to Eli. Why?"

"I don't know."

It didn't take long for Aura and Yow to move the Gamer to the entrance chamber. She led the way, walking backward, guiding the torus through the tunnel with both hands. Ruke, Ash, and Sarah followed, with a somber Eli bringing up the rear.

The bright lights of several docked spaceships flooded the chamber. Yow stopped. "Which ship you want to load the Gamer onto?"

"Well, your shuttle is too small," said Aura.

"I know. I guess the cargo ship, then."

"You brought more ships?"

"No. I thought the space fighter was also yours."

Aura abruptly turned around and gaped at the heavily armed, bulky fighter. "That wasn't here before. Who else is with you?"

"Nobody." Yow approached the ship. "Look at these cannons!" The entrance hatch was open, docking ramp down. Yow peered inside. "Anybody there?"

No one responded.

Eli came forward. "I have a strange feeling I've seen this ship before. She's a beauty, isn't she?" He circled the fighter, looking up and admiring her shape. He touched the heavy landing gear and patted it. A wave of overwhelming sensation caught him completely and unexpectedly off guard, so he closed his eyes and took a deep breath.

It was the same weird feeling of watching the world through someone's else perspective he'd felt when standing in the docking tube before touching the Y—what Aura called the Gamer's emitter —and opening the cave. This time, the inexplicable awareness of everything around him was coming from the space fighter.

He saw Aura. *She's so beautiful when she's not angry...* He saw his mother, her worrying face, and felt his throat constrict. *My dear mother, what can I do to make you happy?* He saw himself standing in front of... himself. *I look like an idiot staring like this.*

But now the awareness was more than a visual perception. Eli felt and knew a lot of things he didn't know before, like the temperature inside the cave and the barometric pressure outside. He felt each and every bit of the ship separately and united, functioning as a living system ready for his commands. *Wow, this ship can be fierce... or gentle, if I want... and she loves me.*

"Eli, are you okay?" asked Sarah.

"Oh, yeah..." Eli hurried to his mother—he could feel her becoming alarmed. "I love you, Mom. Not to worry, everything will be fine. I promise."

Sarah smiled, clearly embarrassed by this unexpected declaration of affection from her son.

Eli continued, "Guys, I know how to fly her."

Aura spat, "You'll answer before the law for what you've done!" Her eyes blazed with fury.

Wow, she's passionate. What a woman! "And what exactly have I done now?" Eli squinted at Aura, and then it dawned on him, *Ah, so that's what the device—the Gamer—does!* Eli resumed his walk around the space fighter, ostentatiously ignoring Aura. "I'll call her *Night Stalker.*" Ash sniggered, and Eli put on the smuggest face he could find in his repertoire. "Cheesy, but I like the sound of it."

"Aura, we must move on," worried Yow.

"Yow, do you know where Ab took Nox?" chimed in Eli.

"Most likely Pat'zan, the Elder Keep's home planet. Why?"

"She was kidnapped. That's a capital crime. At least on Earth." Eli fell silent, contemplating something, then went on, "You know what? Come with me."

"Are you seriously thinking you can take on Ab?"

"I'm thinking a lot of things. But I have to start somewhere. We can do it together."

Ruke intervened enthusiastically. "I'll go with you. I'm gonna get that scumbag!"

Yow gave Ruke a sidelong glance. "Sorry, Eli, I have to take care of the Gamer. About Nox, though, start with Korango. It's a neutral territory that Ab and his goons might want to use."

"Thanks for the tip, man."

Yow hesitated before continuing, "How about helping us to a safe space? Can you handle your new toy?"

"Sure, I'll help," responded Eli.

Sarah said worriedly, "Eli, stop. You don't even know where this Korango place is."

"I do. Mom, it's a space station. Let me show you something." Eli raised his hand, and *Night Stalker* started vibrating slightly, filling the cave with the powerful drone of her engines.

"Neural interface... interesting. Yow, let's finish the job." Aura pushed the Gamer toward her ship. "Hold it—I need to hoist it to the cargo bay."

Eli turned to Sarah and Ash. "Who else wants to fly with me?"

Sarah stepped back—she definitely didn't. Eli looked at Ash.

"I don't know. Honestly..."

"Ash, things have changed. I have a wild calling to be where I'm not. Let's get outta here!"

"Should I tell my boss I'm not coming to work tomorrow?"

Aura climbed into her cargo ship. "Okay, everybody, let's move! I'll raise the barrier as soon as I lift off."

Ruke patted Eli on the back. "Good job! Can I get in?"

"Sure, go ahead. Ash, get inside! Mom, you too. I'll take you to your car as soon as I'm done helping Aura."

Yow was already standing on the docking ramp of his shuttle, and Eli was arguing with his mother about entering the fighter when the wall separating the sanctuary from the outside world vanished. Sunlight fell on the landing platform. Gently rising, Aura's cargo shuttle shone under the desert sun.

Suddenly, the silhouettes of four space strikers emerged from below and above the edge of the landing platform. One of them looked familiar. Ab was back.

The menacing look of the strikers and their careful maneuvering left little doubt what would happen next. The attackers chose to use sonic weapons to inflict damage without the scorching and obliterating effects of energy beams. The sonic blasts pounding the sanctuary were powerful. Fragments of rock flaked off and flew around the cave like shrapnel.

Aura had to move deeper into the chamber to avoid the first wave of the attack—a sonic charge mutilated Yow's space shuttle. One wing, along with the engine, was torn away and propelled into the cave wall, narrowly missing Eli and his mother, who still stood near *Night Stalker*.

Eli screamed, "Mom, for God's sake, get inside! I'll be back!" and ran to help Yow. He leaped into the shuttle and quickly returned, dragging Yow under his armpits. Ruke rushed out of *Night Stalker* to help Eli. Fortunately, despite clear tactical advantages—their positioning against the sun and blocking the exit from the sanctuary—the enemy strikers had a hard time coordinating their movements in such a limited space. Ab's ship barely avoided a collision with another attacker.

Sarah Stroud

Eli looked back. Ash got out of *Night Stalker*, trying to yell something to his mother, who was paralyzed by the mere thought of what might happen to her son. He yelled, "Ash, *do* something!"

Meanwhile, Ab changed tactics. One of his strikers moved forward, targeting Eli's fighter. The sonic blasts didn't affect *Night Stalker*, though the showering debris became a real threat to everybody on the landing platform. Ash was still trying to make Eli's mother get inside the ship when a chunk of flying rock bashed Sarah hard on the head. She faltered and collapsed unconscious on the ground. Ash's efforts to drag her inside the fighter failed—Sarah was too heavy for her.

Eli, halfway to *Night Stalker*, left Ruke to take care of Yow and ran to his mother. Incoming energy pulses rocked his ship—*they've given up on the sonic attack*. A blue glow shrouded her with each blast, making his space fighter impervious to enemy fire. *Shields are up*, realized Eli. *What if Ab shoots at us instead of the ship?* A terrifying fear overwhelmed him. *How do I get the connection to her I felt before?*

He panicked, helplessly turning his head left and right, not knowing what to do. Then Eli saw his father's helmet lying on the ground. He picked it up and put it on.

"Eli... Eli! What are you doing? We need your help!" Ruke shouted.

Composure came as quickly as the panic had. And with calm, the connection to *Night Stalker* came back. *Aha, so that's how it works.* "I have a better idea!" exclaimed Eli. The whole chamber filled with the roar of his fighter engines, and all four of its main caliber cannons moved into the weapons-free position. The sight was not for the fainthearted.

A hell of a big *bang* from the cannons muffled all other sounds of the battle. One of the enemy ships disintegrated. The others stopped firing and moved out of sight.

"Ash—my mother! Quickly. Ruke, you pull Yow!"

With everybody finally inside, Eli rushed to the cockpit. He nodded at the co-pilot seat. "Ruke, come here, sit."

An enemy striker showed up again, spraying *Night Stalker* with everything she had. Eli touched the navigation controls. As his ship rose, Ab's and another surviving striker reappeared, making evasive maneuvers and shooting at Aura's cargo ship deeper inside the chamber.

Ruke yelled, "Look, Ab is shooting lasers at Aura!"

"They guessed where the Gamer is." Eli moved *Night Stalker* sideways, trying to position her between Aura and enemy ships.

Incoming blasts shook the fighter, but nothing got through the shields.

Ruke pulled out the flask. "Do you think her shields will hold?" He shook it, making sure there was enough liquid inside, swallowed a hefty swig, and smacked his lips.

"I'm positive. Enjoy the show." Eli focused, connected to *Night Stalker*, and directed his attention to the weapons system. *"TARGET ALL ENEMY SHIPS!"*

Night Stalker's response flashed in his head, *"CANNOT COVER ALL THREE AT ONCE. EITHER ONE OR THE GROUP OF TWO. SPECIFY PRIORITIES."*

"TWO DESTROYED BETTER THAN ONE. FIRE!"

Another salvo, and two of the enemy strikers were pulverized, giving Ab enough time to get out of sight.

"Fucking asshole... I'll get you—just wait." Eli cursed under his breath.

Aura appeared on the communication monitor. "Thanks. Those cannons, are they your creation, or the Game's?"

"I love projectile weapons if that's what you mean."

"That's not what I mean, and you know it. What's your status?"

"Yow is injured but will probably be okay, assuming he's as human as he looks. I believe my mother is in critical condition. On the bright side, the bad guys wouldn't dare try another frontal assault."

"Are there any other ships hiding outside?"

"Not that I can sense..."

"Let's be careful." Aura paused for a moment and then went on, "I must get to my battlecruiser. Does your promise to help still hold?"

"Your Honor, follow me," scoffed Eli and grinned. "I hope you'll appreciate my gesture of goodwill and shave several years from my jail time." Eli touched the ship's controls, and the landscape in cockpit's window changed as *Night Stalker* soared into the sky.

FIVE

AURA

Aura's battlecruiser, *Sheleucia*, a large disk-shaped craft, was hiding behind the Moon. The shelter was mostly a precaution for the cruiser equipped with the most advanced cloaking system known in this part of the Milky Way. At first, Ab's ship tried to shadow the cargo shuttle and *Night Stalker*, though keeping too far away for the naked eye to see her. But with *Sheleucia* in sight, Ab gave up and disappeared from *Night Stalker*'s sensor array.

The journey to the battlecruiser was short. Eli and company made it in well under ten minutes. Both Aura's and Eli's ships safely set their landing gear in the cruiser's hangar. The subsequent trip from Earth to Coatera, an exoplanet fifty-three light-years away and Aura's final destination, wasn't marked by any interesting events. Eli didn't even notice when they entered and exited faster-than-light speed. Aura joined an injured Yow in his quarters, discussing something behind closed doors. Eli spent most of the time sitting in a medical bay, watching his mother and hoping she would come out of the coma. Ruke hung around, not knowing what to do with himself, until he and Ash came across a food synthesizer and experimented with tasting its menu at random.

Their touchdown was so smooth that Eli, Ruke, and Ash missed it. They learned about their arrival only when Aura welcomed them to Coatera Cela, a space station and research facility in stationary orbit close to Coatera.

"I thought we would land on the planet," Ruke drawled with disappointment.

Aura shrugged. "Not much there—it's basically a nature reserve. Besides, we need to take care of Sarah immediately. *Sheleucia* isn't equipped to deal with her injuries. The station has excellent medical facilities."

Ruke squinted. "I'm watching your mouth, and you don't seem to be speaking English. But I understand everything you say. How's that?"

"Neural translators," explained Aura. "They're everywhere and understand most languages in the galaxy. We also have translation implants. Almost everybody has one."

The battlecruiser rested in the middle of the colossal spaceport. Aura, Eli, Ash, and Ruke stood on the upper platform of the cruiser's gangway. Aura's cargo shuttle was already in the parking area, with two robots moving the Gamer to a different location. Several more bots buzzed near the cruiser. Four medical droids scurried around Sarah and Yow's stretchers.

Aura caught Eli's eye and pulled him aside. "Eli, your mother is my highest priority. I already have a preliminary report. Sorry, there's nothing consoling—it's bad. But we'll start surgery immediately."

"Can I go watch?"

"No—it's an automated robotic surgery. I can provide an audio-visual feed, but it's not useful. I'll let you know as soon as it's done."

"Thank you... How's Yow?"

"He has serious injuries, but he'll be fine. Let's join the others."

Aura waved her hand. "Come on, everybody—I'll show you to your quarters. Make yourself at home. Meanwhile, enjoy the view."

Aura felt good in her role as host—a role she had never performed in her life. "Coatera reminds me of Earth... It's as beautiful, isn't it? The same size, and just as blue, but with more green," she said to Eli and the others.

Visible through the transparent dome of the station's port, which was about two hundred miles from the surface, Coatera loomed large. The first sight of an alien planet surrounded by the vast star-speckled darkness was, for Eli, Ash, and Ruke, an awe-inspiring experience.

"This was the first planet my ancestors colonized when they left Earth," Aura concluded proudly. "But our capital planet is now Gaia, almost thirty thousand light-years from here."

"How many years ago did they arrive?" asked Ash.

"More than one hundred thousand. During the first exodus from Earth."

"From *Earth*?" Ruke raised his brows. "What was wrong with Earth?"

"Nothing. I guess my ancestors didn't want to stay there forever."

"And you call yourselves Gaians?"

"We do. Outsiders call us Strangers."

"So Gaians and humans are all like sisters and brothers?" Ash gave Aura a soppy, innocent smile.

"We have the same ancestors, and we are *Homo sapiens*, humans like you." Aura beamed down at her Earth guests. "There are many Earth-descended peoples in this part of the galaxy—an area over fifty thousand light-years in diameter."

"Really?" Ruke sounded skeptical.

"The Exodus from Earth happened in waves. There were at

least three. But every wave laid the foundation for many human races." Aura stepped forward. "Okay, everybody, follow me! Let's take care of your accommodations. I also recommend translation implants, a one-second procedure, completely painless. Let me know if you want one."

Like everything on Coatera Cela, the sick bay was large. Lit in a quiet, pale blue, it was mostly empty, with few easily distinguishable medical devices and even fewer hospital beds. Only one of them held a patient, Yow.

"Sorry for the delay." Aura entered with the medical datapad in her hand. "I have mostly good news for you. You'll be good as new in a day."

"What did they find?"

"Four broken ribs, a broken arm. One rib punctured your right lung—that's why the delay."

"That was the bulkhead. I don't get how Eli managed to pull me out."

Aura jolted as the datapad in her hand lit up and buzzed. She feverously swiped across the screen. "Oh no…" She looked at Yow, her eyes haunted. "Eli's mother passed away during surgery… it's all my fault. What am I going to tell him?"

"Don't blame yourself. You were doing your job. Blame Ab. By the way, he knew about our next move on Earth. Every time."

"It all went wrong, and I'm responsible. No other way to look at—"

Several thuds came from someone stomping outside the sick bay, and, finally, a heavy blow to its doors interrupted Aura. The doors swung open, and Ash appeared, with a scared face and wild hair. Moving backward, she held her hands up, palms forward. "Go away! Leave me alone!"

Following Ash, a big cat slowly and majestically entered the room. It had a stocky body, a long tail, massive paws, and thick, smoky-gray fur covered with beautiful patterns of dark-gray and black rosettes. The cat stopped in the middle of the bay, calm and curious.

The unexpected appearance of Ash eased the gloomy mood raised by Sarah's death. Yow laughed and groaned at the same time —any movement of his body caused pain.

Aura couldn't help smiling. "Don't be afraid. This is Hippa, a female snow leopard and Nox's alter ego. You haven't met Nox, my colleague. She's not on the station right now."

Hippa Ell

Aura turned to the cat. "Hippa, this is Ash, our guest."

Hippa lazily approached Ash and butted her head against the Earth girl's hand, making her blush. "I was on my way here, and she stalked me!" she blurted.

"Once, Nox was scouting the mountains on Earth—that was before she found the cave in Nevada—and encountered the snow leopards. She fell in love with these cats and decided to bioengineer one. Hippa is intelligent and sociable with her friends," explained Aura.

"Can I pet her?"

Aura didn't respond, and her face darkened. "Ash, Eli's mother passed away. We couldn't save her."

"Oh my God! Does Eli know?" cried Ash, tears springing to her eyes.

"I've just learned about it. Could you… talk to Eli and tell him?" It was Aura's time to blush. She knew it was her responsibility and duty to take this grim news to Eli, but she couldn't. Even the thought of looking into Eli's eyes while telling him about his mother's death gave her the jitters.

"Why me? I don't know if I can do this…"

Aura kept silent.

"Right *now*?" Ash frowned and looked at Aura.

"I'm sorry for what happened, but I don't think it's a good idea for me to talk to Eli about this. Please?"

Ash sighed. "I'll do it." Ash leaned over to Hippa. "Nice to meet you. I'm Ash. I wish we'd gotten to know each other under better circumstances."

Ash found Eli on the observation deck watching Coatera. She came nearer and stopped behind him.

"I can't believe how wonderful this planet is," he said, without taking his eyes off the majestic spacescape.

She touched his arm. "Eli…" She stopped, not knowing how to proceed.

Eli looked back at Ash. "Whassup? Are you—" He noticed her unsettled expression. "Something happened?"

"Yes." She paused, then said in a rush, "Your mother passed away during surgery a few minutes ago. I'm so sorry. We're all…

My condolences." She paused again before continuing, "Let me know what I can do to help, in any way I can."

Eli didn't react, but his stern face seemed turned to stone.

Ash didn't know what else to say. The truth was that Sarah's death had touched her in many ways. She'd known her for a long time and had always been happy to talk to Sarah over the phone or see her when she was coming to visit Chris, especially during the last several years before he died. Sarah was almost a part of her family. Although Ash had never met Eli, she was always happy to hear Sarah's stories about her son and how he was growing. With time, in Eli's absence, she included him in the circle of her closest friends. Ash had realized long ago that it was a one-way feeling, and that for some reason, Sarah didn't want Eli to meet her or her father.

Being a perceptive child, she felt it all related somehow to the circumstances of Eli's father's death and to the notes Chris kept in their home. So Ash accepted things as they were without asking questions. But recent events had shed light on many issues she couldn't understand before and had only amplified her sympathy for Eli's loss. If Eli had said something, perhaps she would have known what to tell him, how to comfort him. But he was silent, and Ash was just standing there, desperately trying to find words to explain how sorry she was.

Finally, Eli came to himself. "I'm glad it was you who came to tell me about my mother, Ash. Sorry, but I can't talk about it right now. So much is going on in my head..." His eyes filled with tears, and he didn't wipe them away as they spilled over. "Remember I told you I suck in life? There was so much to talk about with my mother and tell her... I never did."

Ash gently took his hand, squeezing it and releasing. "Let's find some food. Do they have a galley here? I can cook something for you—"

"Hey, buddy! Sorry about what happened. Hang in there!" Ruke blared in a deliberately cheerful voice as he entered the observation deck. "Just wanted to tell you I'll stick by your side no matter what!" Ruke pulled out his flask. "Here, it'll help."

Eli took it and stared at his hand, still far away in his thoughts. "What is it?"

"The best moonshine in the world. From my personal wine cellar."

Eli swallowed, and his eyes nearly popped out of their sockets. He couldn't breathe. With his throat squeezed by a spasm, he opened and closed his mouth noiselessly like a fish out of water. Finally, Eli uttered, choking, "Oh God... You gotta be kiddin' me!"

"Do you now have that nice, warm feeling in your stomach?" Ruke shot Ash a gleeful look. "Someone mentioned cooking? What are we waiting for?"

Aura was nervous. It had been already twelve hours since she'd sent her report to Ronda Klaretah, the Commissioner of the GAME, and now she was anxiously awaiting her reaction.

Under the Gaian *Corpus Ludus Juris*, the GAME Laws, any illegal use of the Game was considered a serious criminal offense. According to the statute, Eli's action on Earth violated its most important provision—unauthorized access to the Game. That was precisely what had happened when he'd passed through the torus in the cave. Ronda wasn't Aura's boss. But Aura, the Governor of Coatera and head of the GAME Institute on Coatera Cela, a leading facility on all things related to Game technology, had an obligation to report the violation she'd witnessed.

Despite the aggravating circumstances—the unexpected materialization of *Night Stalker,* a powerful space fighter armed to the teeth—the case she submitted to the Commission of the GAME looked pretty straightforward. The fact that Aura, an influential authority on the Game in both government and scientific circles, had observed the violation directly only made the legal action against Eli easier and stronger.

The link between Eli's action and *Night Stalker* remained to be proven, but it seemed so evident that its legal proof was a mere formality. Multiple systems monitoring Game activity could easily substantiate the relationship. Even so, Aura saw many things in the case that defied anything she had seen or known about the Game. A true professional, she added extensive commentary to the report, making a case for Eli's innocence.

Aura's anxiety and the Gaian government's involvement with the Game would be hard to understand without knowing the history and details related to the underlying science. Its emergence had been a long and challenging process.

It started when Gaians still lived on Earth. Their scientists discovered pioneering methods of manipulating atomic and elementary particles in order to change their quantum properties, forming atoms and molecules at will. Any transformation of matter on a subatomic level was called *quantum conversion,* or *QC.* At the time, and for millennia since, their QC research had focused on two areas—building or altering objects and transforming one type of energy into another.

However, because of the quantum transformation complexity, the initial scientific discoveries hadn't been useful for real-life applications. To manipulate physical substances—with or without mass—and transform them at will into specific objects or forms of energy, the Game had to know their exact composition and properties. Also, a mechanism to manage the conversion process had to be added to adapt the science for practical purposes.

For example, to create a pork chop, the Game would have to start with the exact specification of all components of the final product. Knowing its makeup, it could manipulate the atoms of carbon, hydrogen, nitrogen, and everything else required to fabricate the organic materials present in pork. Eventually, all structural units would have to be assembled to fulfill the user's wish.

The real technological breakthrough had occurred nearly ten thousand years ago, when scientists developed the first artificial intelligence stable and capable enough to control the process of rearranging matter and energy following users' requests. With the new AI, the Game took its conceptual shape.

As the application of scientific knowledge for everyday purposes grew, the need for more sophisticated AIs became obvious. Their role was expanded to help the Game communicate and better interpret users' wants and needs.

Once a tiny subfield of quantum physics, the technology became an omnipresent commodity used by everyone without even thinking about it. Very few knew that originally the Game was the GAME, an acronym from *Generic Augmentation Molecular Enhancer*, a fancy terminology that appeared when the scientific breakthrough took place. Virtually nobody ever heard about the GAMERIN, another acronym—the term initially used to refer to the GAME Remote INterface.

Still in use in official government documents, in everyday life, even among the scientists, the GAME became known as the Game and the GAMERIN as the Gamer, words in their own right. That the names converted readily to languages in the Milky Way quadrant stemmed from sophisticated translation algorithms capable of matching the meaning of concepts and constructs in ancient Gaian language to the phrases and words of the same connotation in other languages.

The change also included an altered perspective on the technology, now perceived as something amusing and recreational—like a regular game. However, the commodifying of the Game wasn't as smooth as most might think, knowing about its current pervasive use. The problem lay in the nature of the technology with the almost unlimited power of manipulating matter. By adding to the

Game databanks gazillions of bits of knowledge on anything Gaians encountered and discovered, they created a God-like monster capable of working miracles and destroying the fabric of the universe, not to mention smaller things like stars and planets.

Even the first technically successful experiments after the initial application of the breakthrough AIs revealed enormous social and ethical problems. The most immediate one was a potential for an evil mind to easily manifest its biddings when exposed to the Game interface. Gaians countered the dilemma by adding security protocols to the AI controlling the Game. However, as they quickly discovered, that didn't guarantee the eradication of the problem.

The issue was the dual nature of right and wrong. Like any other sentient beings, Gaians struggled with the question *Who determines what's right and what's wrong?* or any simple variation of it, like *Who's saying whether skinny people are more attractive than fat ones?* Gaians had always dealt with such questions by relying on their social and cultural institutions, philosophies, religions, and traditions—they didn't want to give up their moral principles to a piece of hardware.

To make matters worse, inaccurate interpretations of people's desires by the Game's AI resulted in several mistakes with horrible consequences. One such blunder was a project to update the Gaian power distribution systems, the first challenging task to take advantage of the Game's capabilities. Because of an inaccuracy in the use of the terminology related to the system, the machine misconstrued the request. Instead of getting rid of its obsolete components, it destroyed all small celestial objects in a nearby star system. The error caused the deaths of over three hundred Gaian scientists stationed on one asteroid destroyed by the Game.

Despite the best intentions and problem-solving techniques added to the AI, the communication barriers—in particular, perception, language, and cultural differences—turned out to be insurmountable. At the time, multiple technical and ethical complications had led to a strong societal push to prohibit the technology. However, Gaians didn't want to forgo its potential benefits. After much debate, their answer to the problems was to literally and figuratively hide the Game from the public view and regulate it as heavily as possible.

To implement the plan, a new secretive Commission of the GAME was created within the Directorate, the Gaian executive branch of power. A set of rules regulating the Game and its access was developed and codified in the *Corpus Ludus Juris*, or the GAME Laws. The commission also became the investigative authority responsible for ensuring compliance with the legislation. The leading Gaian law enforcement agency, the DRC—the Bureau of Development, Research, and Contacts—was entrusted with the associated prosecutorial powers.

According to the official history endorsed by the government, the final version of the Game was rebuilt in a secret place. The GAME Laws drastically limited the number of people authorized to access the machine. Initiating QCs without authorization became a crime of high treason, with capital punishment being the statutory maximum.

To administer the Game, Gaians created Nox Ell, a synthesized human female. By special law, she became a fully-fledged Gaian citizen. Officially, Nox was the first and so far, the only Game Administrator and human being who knew the machine's location and could directly access the Game's AI.

The Commission of the GAME was charged with issuing QC permits. Nox could also issue such approvals on the grounds of a clear and present danger to Gaian society. However, the law prohibited the Game Administrator from initiating QCs and instructed her to report her authorizations to the Directorate.

Many design constraints were added to the machine to safeguard its use. The major ones didn't allow the Game to affect directly other sentient beings, to fulfill solicitations having emotional goals, or to consider requests involving recurring actions.

The Gaians devoted great effort to solving the problems of communicating with the Game, one of the weakest elements in the practical use of the technology. To address technical aspects of the communication process, Gaian scientists developed the Gamers, relatively small and simple interfaces and relay devices. One Gamer was hidden on Gaia, the capital planet of the Gaian Domain, with others scattered in undisclosed locations in the galaxy, including one on Earth.

To address semantic aspects of the communication, a neural interface was developed to tap directly into the user's brain activity, bypassing the need for interpretation of the linguistic constructs. Verbal communication and various input devices were deemed to be the least reliable.

Neural communication modules eased the problem but didn't solve it. The remedy was found in limiting the number of such interfaces and restricting their access. With time, the only remaining neural interfaces became the ones built into the Gamers. Gaians also developed dedicated terminals and autonomous facilities serving specific purposes—for example, converting and generating energy, transporting goods or people, or providing authorized medical procedures. Such terminals with permanent connections to the Game couldn't be repurposed.

At a higher level, *molecular conversion*, or *MC*, was added to the Game. MCs couldn't deal with energy. They could only produce tangible results by manipulating *existing* atoms and molecules. Similar to the QC, all MC interactions with the Game were conducted via dedicated devices—food stations, retail dispensers, manufacturing facilities, and first aid stations, to name a few. Gradually, many functions requiring MCs became supported by autonomous devices without any need for the connection to the Game.

Direct neural communication with the Game was strictly limited to licensed users certified in mental imagery. To meet the growing demand for QCs, in the Game's lingo called *implementa-*

tions, and ensure their safety, the Commission of the GAME created the Game Safety Ward with the Game Wardens as its members. With time, the Ward became the primary avenue for processing custom implementation requests.

Although Gaians remained a somewhat isolated race, preferring not to mingle with others, the conveniences of life on Gaia and its seemingly unlimited access to energy attracted the attention of other inhabited worlds. Gaians became a source of envy in an extensive area of the galaxy. Many species showed open hostility, fearing the mysterious source of the Gaian power. Fortunately, the Gaians' reputation as a peaceful race helped convince others that they didn't have any evil intentions. Not without pursuing its interests, Gaia initiated the Intergalactic Game Treaty, joined by many species in the quadrant of the Milky Way occupied by Earth-descended peoples. The agreement prohibited the research and use of the QC technology and designated Gaia as its sole perpetual guardian and guarantor. An advisory steering committee was created to monitor compliance with the treaty.

A successful career woman, Aura maintained relationships with a wide circle of colleagues, scientists, and government officials. Always kind and pleasant, she was respected and welcomed by many. But no matter how amicable such personal connections might be, she hadn't found anyone with whom she had a bond of real mutual affection. In other words, Aura didn't have any real friends. Practical and pragmatic, she knew what she wanted and walked through life with her head raised high. Strong and independent, she was always capable of taking care of herself and felt no need for help.

Aura found what had happened on Earth disturbing, especially when Eli put himself under enemy fire to shield her. Nothing like that had ever happened to her before. She was even more unsettled by the fact that the person who did it was a stranger, and someone she had threatened with a gun. This had occupied her thoughts since then. The more she thought about it, the more she liked how Eli had tried to protect her. It meant that someone in this universe worried about her.

Aura sighed and cupped her face in her hands. No matter what happened, she didn't want Eli to be found guilty by the commission. She didn't doubt that Eli's passing through the Gamer and triggering the implementation process was unintentional. After all, he had no clue what the Game was. But the GAME Laws didn't discriminate between intentional and subconscious or accidental requests.

Having seen Eli in action, she understood how he might dream about a space fighter, but not *that* fighter, which seemed amazingly complete in all details. And she had already checked—the Game had possessed no prior knowledge it could rely on to deliver such a ship. *Night Stalker* was the only one of her kind in this part of the galaxy—a space fighter of a type unheard-of. She had projectile cannons that fired antimatter shells, a neural interface allowing for complete integration with the pilot, and a propulsion system with no need for refueling. The latter was a clear sign that *Night Stalker*'s engines used a Game-like technology as a source of energy.

Aura was ready to swear that the Game itself had created the whole ship using parts of its own design. If such a thing were possible, that would show Eli's innocence. But was it? The thought tormented her. She felt that a veil of mystery covered everything that had happened on Earth.

"Incoming call from Commissioner Ronda Klaretah," announced the long-range communication system.

Aura was pulled out of her thoughts. "Take the call."

A holographic image of Ronda, an imposing woman in her fifties, appeared in the middle of the control room, Coatera Cela's nerve center, where Aura spent most of her time. "I hope I'm not disturbing you," Ronda began.

"I've been waiting for your call."

"Your report is troubling. I wanted to invite Paxt Zorg to our conversation. Do you know him?" More than anything else, Ronda was an experienced and shrewd politician. Involving other government bureaucrats to sense the winds and build support had been her usual tactic.

"Never met him in person," Aura admitted. "Don't you think it's a little premature to invite the DRC Director?" She maintained a steady gaze, staring directly into Ronda's eyes. "This is a complex case."

"Your report is clear. You witnessed yourself what happened. All we need to do is to check the activity logs, and that'll be the end of our investigation."

That was an attempt to exert pressure on Aura. *I described in my report all the unusual circumstances and details of what happened. What does the bitch want? A quick political gain by showing her resolve and political correctness? Is she trying to probe me? I'm not that stupid.* She put on an impassive expression to hide her true feelings. "So what do you propose to do?"

"Strange question. We have probable cause, don't we? Paxt wanted to send his team to Coatera to impound the ship and take... what's his name?"—Ronda grimaced— "Estroud, into custody."

"Elias Stroud. Did you read my report?"

Aura and Ronda eyeballed one another for a few seconds.

She believes she can squash me. Aura smiled graciously at Ronda— perhaps too graciously, like smiling patiently at a child who has difficulty understanding a straightforward concept. *Okay, let's see how it goes.* "First off, Eli—his use-name—doesn't appear the type ready to surrender. He's responded with deadly force at my attempt to stop him. It's in my report."

"We're talking about the DRC. They know how to handle this."

"Secondly, I assume you remember the part of my report where I described the ship's tactical specifications, including readings I took from my ship sensors. His *Night Stalker*, as he calls her, makes use of antimatter weapons and neural interface technology. It will pulverize anything DRC is likely to send—and probably half of my space station along with it. He can do all this without even leaving his quarters on the station." Aura kept smiling. "Paxt should pray that Eli hasn't learned more about his ship in the last two days, though I doubt that his prayer would be answered."

"He'll be a fugitive, and eventually, he will be caught. You're in the best position to explain to him that his resistance is pointless."

"And you, Ronda, will be a punching bag the whole Directorate will laugh at while you and Paxt Zorg scramble all over the galaxy, trying to catch Eli. Did you explain that to Paxt?"

"It's disrespectful to speak like this!" Ronda raised her voice. "You know who I am and what I can do!"

"I'm simply taking my time to explain to you things you should already understand. I wouldn't do that if I had no respect for you, especially when I hear thinly veiled threats in your words."

"If you try to warn him, you'll become an accomplice." Ronda pushed her shoulders back and her chest out, but her voice got squeaky, belying her menacing posture.

You're ready to backpedal, thought Aura, and said aloud, "You insist… I regret that. What the Game did, in this case, has never happened before. As the Commissioner of the GAME, you have an opportunity to show wisdom and leadership, maybe even take the next step in the Game's saga. As a practitioner and a scientist, I want to understand what happened, and I invite you to do the same."

"Well, that's not what I got from your report. And that's why I decided to talk."

"I'm sorry." Aura erased the smile. "I'm glad we cleared the air." *It's time to change the subject*, she thought. "You know, Eli's mother died yesterday."

"What happened?" Ronda raised her eyebrows.

"While Eli was helping me protect the Gamer from the Elder Keep, she was wounded by a rockfall, and we couldn't save her."

"Poor thing... Aura, don't think I'm personally against this young man. The law is the law, and we must uphold it."

"I believe no wrongdoing took place. We need to understand what happened so it doesn't happen again."

"Nox can help. You say in your report she was kidnapped. How do you know?"

"Based on Eli's account. There was also another earthling who witnessed her abduction."

"It's hard to believe she was abducted at all."

"We'll see. I'm not too worried. If I were a Pazon, I wouldn't mess with the Game or with Nox."

The Commissioner visibly relaxed. "Aura, I'm glad we talked. I count on you as the lead investigator in this case."

"Thank you, Commissioner. I'll keep you posted."

The hologram disappeared—the call was over. Aura breathed a sigh of relief. *That went much better than I expected. I wonder what exactly made Ronda change her mind...*

The high-security detention center where Nox was held happened to be in the basement of the Elder Keep Security Chancellery. Abaddon supervised all the details of the prisoner placement. Although he tried to exude confidence and produce an impression of an infallible special-ops official, deep inside, he knew he was dealing with the unknown. His bragging report to Xiir Zanrod had been little more than a bluff. The circumstances of the kidnapping were still giving Ab concern. It had seemed too easy, and he was playing through different scenarios in his mind, trying to prepare for all contingencies.

He even advised his boss, Asphalis, the head of the Security Chancellery, to activate Pat'zan's defenses in case the Strangers decided to retaliate and free Nox. This suggestion didn't sit well with Asphalis, who called Ab an idiot and told him to use other facilities next time to minimize the risk of an attack on Pat'zan.

Ab didn't regret his decision to house Nox at the Chancellery. He knew that no matter how foolish it seemed to expose the planet to a raid by Strangers, there was no other choice. Only the detention center at the Chancellery could support the research and experimentation with the Game technology. Instead of arguing, he enlisted the support of Xiir Zanrod, his influential patron, and stopped thinking about the issue.

The cell where Ab had put Nox was armored with a particular material and shields capable of withstanding an antimatter blast should one occur in the proximity of the Chancellery facilities. The room itself was full of equipment, with more added in the past several days. A chubby, middle-aged bearded Pazon wearing antique spectacles rushed along the rows of racks loaded with paraphernalia, making final adjustments and fine-tuning this and that.

Ab entered the cell and headed to a hexagonal cage with transparent walls in the center. Nox sat on her knees inside, silent, motionless, her eyes closed—a figure that reminded him of a meditating Buddhist monk from Earth.

He walked around the cage. "My dear, I trust you find our detention center and your treatment not too unbearable for your taste?"

Nox didn't move.

Ab made a sign to the Pazon technician. "Ready, Killiel?"

"Yes, sir!"

Ab went on, "But since you're involved in the Game, it would be logical to find yourself in a predicament like this sooner or later."

Nox opened her eyes. "You cannot harm me..." she said, showing no emotion.

"Oh, no. That's not my intention. All I need is some information regarding Coatera's defense system."

"Don't be cocky, Ab."

"You know my name? I'm flattered. You see that man?" asked Ab, who resumed his circling and scrutinizing of Nox. "He's determined to hack your brain and get what we need, anyway."

Ab nodded to Killiel, who touched controls. A hood with nobs, lights, and a bunch of wires attached to it moved down from the cage ceiling and slipped over Nox's head. A low hum filled the cell. For a second Nox remained still, and then her body went limp, with her whole weight sagging against her legs. Killiel cursed and tapped a series of controls.

Concerned that things had gone wrong despite his best efforts, Ab worried. "What happened? Is she dead?" he barked at Killiel.

"If I may say so, sir, I suppose she is," the technician said shakily. "For all practical purposes, that is."

"She turned herself off? Like a kill switch?"

"There was a sharp spike in her neuron activity, and then she was gone!"

Both men stood there, open-mouthed, as Nox's body began disintegrating. First, it transformed into a pile of tiny, black, shiny cubes. After a second or two, the black heap began to evaporate, shrinking until any trace of what had been Nox disappeared.

Aura had been looking for an opportunity for a one-on-one talk with Eli at a time when they would be uninterrupted and in a place where Eli would feel at ease. Such an occasion presented itself when she sat in Cela's control room and felt a slight vibration. A swipe at the holo monitor to check on the spaceport showed *Night Stalker* detached from the safety clamps and slowly rotating to face the port entrance. Eli was inside the cockpit.

When Aura came down to the docking compartments, Eli had

already finished maneuvering, and the automatic safety controls had disengaged the security barrier. The docking ramp of his ship was open, showing her wide entrance bay. A separate ladder leading to an open hatch rose near the cockpit. Aura came nearer and lifted her head. *Thirty feet or more... Why do we call her a fighter? A destroyer would be more accurate.*

She climbed the ladder and found herself in a small airlock leading to the cockpit. She squeezed through the hatchway—Eli was inside. "There he is!" That came out too deliberate, too optimistic—not a friendly greeting as Aura wanted it to be.

Eli glanced over his shoulder and mumbled glumly, "Hi."

Not much enthusiasm. Well, I'll say it, anyway. "I saw you in the cockpit window of your fighter. I wanted to thank you for your help. I don't think we could have made it without you."

"I promised." Eli shrugged and kept fiddling with the ship's controls.

Aura didn't want to give up. "So, how have you been?" she asked in a light, casual tone.

"How have I *been*? Are you fucking kidding me?" He turned around to look at Aura, eyes blazing. "For starters..." Eli paused for a moment and continued boiling with rage, "my mother is dead, and, skipping some minor details, I may as well have killed her!"

In a gesture of disagreement, Aura raised her hand, trying to say something.

"I haven't finished yet!" he barked. "What else? Oh, I broke a law I had no clue about. Then the woman I saved, when instead I should have been saving my mother, is going to turn me in, and now I face criminal trial fifty light-years from Earth. Also, there are some minor things like you almost killed me, and then bad guys nearly killed Yow because, somehow, I helped them find your Gamer. And by doing so, I'm now involved in some kind of interstellar war which is not mine, and altogether makes me believe that in a flash I have many enemies eager to harm me in many possible and impossible ways, whereas a week ago everybody loved me!"

Aura stared at Eli. "Quite a speech…"

"Guess I wasn't prepared for this talk," snapped Eli.

"Most of what you said is true. But you're forgetting something."

"Yeah, I was shot. Granted, not by you. You missed."

They looked at each other, Eli with challenge and annoyance, while Aura held off saying more in an attempt to understand what was going on in his mind.

Eli's rage dissipated quickly. He turned his back to Aura and started messing with the control panel again.

Surprising herself, Aura exclaimed, "What do you *want?*"

Eli glared at Aura. "If you want to take my fighter away from me, that won't be easy. Understand?"

That's exactly what I thought. Nothing can stop this guy.

Aura smiled, and that was probably the first smile she had given Eli, at least the first kind one. Eli noticed it, but either because of the lack of life experience or the need to fight off an imaginary menace, he interpreted it in his way. "Don't patronize me."

"Please don't be difficult. Nobody wants to hurt you." Aura chose her words carefully, trying to get through to him. "I guess, at this point, you know what the Game does?"

"Something like the Midas touch?" Eli became interested.

"What's a 'Midas touch'?"

"An old legend on Earth where a king who loved gold was given power by the gods to turn everything he touched into gold. But there were unintended consequences."

Smart guy if he understands this… Aura readily picked up the topic. "This is one of the reasons wise people prohibited the use of the Game. At least in the way you used it."

"One of the reasons?"

"There's enough evil in the universe that would want to use the Game to its advantage."

"Oh, I get that part. Anything else?"

"Those who created the Game didn't realize the difficulty in interpreting the wishes and desires of sentient beings who often don't even understand what they want." *To say or not to say...* Aura hesitated, and then added gently, "You'd be a good example."

"What did I have to do with this?"

"Were you thinking about your spaceship when you passed through the torus?"

Eli looked at Aura. "No! I was thinking about..." He hastily broke eye contact and stopped.

"The Game is designed to detect a person's strongest wish even if it stored in the deep recesses of the mind, in unconscious memory."

Eli sat, overwhelmed with what Aura was saying. She patiently waited for him to take it all in. Finally, he asked, "Can the technology be improved? Can we make ourselves better?"

"All attempts to do so have been mostly disastrous. What happened to you is an exception... Nice ship, by the way. Congratulations!" When Eli didn't react, she peered at his disappointed grimace and added, "Well, there's always hope, so we keep the Game..."

"I want to be a believer," he murmured.

Aura couldn't help it. "Oh, blessed are the believers..."

She waited for a moment, but again, Eli didn't react. "One more thing. We have a sacred burial site on Coatera. If you want, that can be your mother's final resting place. You'd be welcome to visit at any time, now and in the future."

Eli didn't say anything. He looked at Aura blankly, as if unable to figure out what she was talking about.

"Well, it's your decision. I've got to go."

Aura had mixed feelings about her first attempt to reason with Eli. By nature, she was an adventurer, always in search of the truth, exploring the world to unravel its mysteries and find her place in it. Despite her youth, she had proven to be an astute person, usually in control of a situation and accustomed to getting what she wanted. Ambitious and sometimes mischievous, she loved the thrill of the chase to escape boredom and broaden her horizons. So the recent events with Eli didn't bother her at all.

On the other hand, Eli himself remained an enigma to Aura. She couldn't understand how such a simple, obviously naive young man had managed to stir powerful people and things to action and survive. *Is he still alive after the trials and tribulations of the last few days because of his unknown abilities or skills? Or sheer luck? His* Night Stalker *helped him live. But he embraced her, the Game's deadly and ingenious creation, at first sight, knowing nothing about the ship, willingly and enthusiastically. And what about his connection to the Game? Yes, it exists, no doubt! But then how is that possible?* The conversation with Eli hadn't clarified anything at all.

When Aura returned to the control center, Yow was already waiting for her, wearing an envelope sling on his right arm. "You wanted to talk?" he asked.

"How are you?"

He waved his right arm. "Better."

"What do you think? How is Eli holding up?"

Yow was noncommittal. "Difficult to say. His life took quite a spin recently."

"You know him better than I do... There are some strange things about him."

"What do you mean?"

"I looked at *Night Stalker*. This implementation is like nothing I've ever seen. The level of details is amazing. The Game always tries to stick to the basics—except in this case."

"I'm no expert. My concerns are different. I wonder... Is he going to try to resurrect his mother?"

"I spoke to Eli. He understands what the Game does and its limits."

Yow grinned. "Did you at least use your softer self? He's afraid of you, no matter how cool he's trying to look."

Aura shrugged. "I wanted to do something for him as a sign of my gratitude for his help with the Gamer. I allowed interring his mother's body on Coatera. According to our law, that makes him a Coatera resident." She frowned. "What bothers me is that since Eli became involved, events have developed at an alarming rate."

"That crossed my mind too. Since Eli—"

"You think he's working for the Elder Keep?" interrupted Aura.

"No. But I'm certain they tracked him somehow. Perhaps they're still tracking him, and I can't fathom how Ab did it. I checked everything. The only possibility is that they somehow implanted an undetectable tracer in his body."

"The Gamer is safe on Coatera," she stated flatly.

Yow nodded. "I suppose. You know your station better than I, but honestly, I'm not sure about that. In any case, I collected biologics from Eli to determine whether there was anything foreign to his body. I must go to Korango to analyze the samples."

"Keep me informed. One more thing—the Gamer on Earth. Did Ruke or Ash pass through the gate?"

"I was the last to enter the sanctuary, so I missed the first ten or fifteen seconds of what was happening in the chamber. And it was my first direct encounter with the Game technology. I don't know. It's possible, though unlikely."

"Don't fret about it—I'm pleased with your service and commitment. You'll get a better space striker to replace the one you lost. I've also transferred funds to your account on Korango. Untraceable, as usual."

Yow brightened and bowed slightly. "Thank you. Staying true to our customers is what we do on Korango."

～

The funeral procession—Eli, Ash, Ruke, Aura, Hippa, and four drones acting as pallbearers—stopped at the entrance to a magnificent temple in the middle of the planet's green wilderness. The design of the building bore no features to remind anybody of the highly advanced Gaian technology. The architecture was much like something one might encounter on Earth. The facade, with its mighty, polished columns, looked like the tall portico of an ancient temple. Rich figural reliefs and sculptures depicting strange creatures covered the walls. A broad staircase sitting on a massive foundation led up to the entrance. There were traces of coloring everywhere, though time had taken its toll on the original refinements.

Through the wide entrance, one could see a large cella, and more cameras disappearing deep inside the dimly lit interior. Faint sources of unsteady light, apparently floating in the air in defiance of gravity, emphasized the grandeur and the mystery of the place.

Sarah's body was in a closed stone casket that resembled an ancient Egyptian sarcophagus, adorned with a sculpture of her recumbent form and the English inscription of her name. Aura made a sign to the drones, and they lowered the coffin and moved away.

She stepped forward. "I don't know Earthly traditions," she began, "but I wanted to say I'm honored that Eli has accepted my planet as the burying place for his brave mother. I bow to her courage and selflessness, and I will always remember Sarah as someone having those two great virtues. Eli, dear guests, welcome to the Temple of Emerala, the Gaian Goddess of Shadows."

Eli stood silently with his head down, staring blankly at the toes of his boots. He didn't weep or try to hide his emotions—it didn't look like he had any. Instead, Eli had the strange feeling he had died with his mother, and the person standing in front of the casket was someone else. For that person, the funeral was a final farewell—not only to his mother but also to his old self. New Eli was grieving for both lives that had ended too soon.

Not knowing how to interpret Eli's silence, Aura felt awkward. Nodding at the drones, she clarified, "If you want to be alone with your mother on her last journey, to her final resting place in the Temple, they will help with everything."

Eli came back to life, lifting his head. "Aura, thank you..." He looked around and saw friendly faces. "You know, I've realized that I'm not going back to Earth. Nothing for me there..." Eli stopped and then timidly added, "Guys... can we go to the Temple together?"

Aura beckoned the drones and stepped away, letting the others join Eli.

"Aura, please join me. Unless you have reasons not to..." He trailed off and approached her, looking miserable and lost.

She glanced at him and unexpectedly felt so sorry for Eli that her chest tightened, and her heart wrenched. *How could I not understand who he is?* "Here. Let's go!" Aura offered Eli her hand.

He took it, and his heart began to beat faster at the gentle touch of her skin.

SIX

KORANGO

Yow didn't like his new space striker. In the first place, it was too big, and Yow preferred small things. Small things attracted less attention, and Yow didn't like attention, either. In his private eye job, being invisible, undetected, and covert was essential.

All such qualities were in his blood. When he was still a boy, he'd often dreamed about cloak-and-dagger operations where he would play an important role, an intergalactic man of mystery. With almost fifteen years of experience as an investigator for hire, his appetite for adventure diminished, and the need to pay bills and rent transformed him into more of a hole-and-corner guy. Still, his fondness for remaining out of sight never abandoned him.

It wasn't that Yow didn't appreciate Aura's generosity when she presented him with a sleek, armed-to-the-teeth spaceship. There were many advantages to keeping a new space striker. Dealing with sharks ready to defend their interests required a display of fire-power and a respectable spaceship. Yow suspected that, with Aura and the Gaians as his important customers, encounters with powerful players might become more frequent. But for Yow, the new ship was mostly a sign of his client's acknowledgment of his good work—a sign that might ironically cause many problems.

For example, he couldn't help but be concerned by how much the mooring of such a vessel would cost him on Korango. Everything was expensive on the space station, the major business hub in this densely populated region of the Milky Way.

The size of a small moon, Korango was home to about one hundred thousand Korags. Many of them belonged to the Hunters, an independent conglomerate of loosely associated social groups. Traders, financial dealers, mercenaries, and outlaws—their rejection of government control and rule united them. They had their ethics code, emphasizing loyalty to the customers and even higher commitment to themselves.

Korango was Yow's birthplace, and he'd spent most of his life on it building a successful investigation business. As his job required more and more space traveling, he was always glad to return to the station. Whenever he saw its domes as he approached Korango after a long trip, he felt an overwhelming warm feeling in his heart—the anticipation of being home.

Oh, the station domes! Visible from thousands of miles away, cyan or royal blue depending on the local hour, they had become Korango's hallmark in the galaxy. Since the space station's construction many thousands of years ago, they'd represented a successful, daring, and untouchable enterprise free of any obligation other than maximizing shareholder returns.

The traffic was always heavy in the station's vicinity, and today was no exception. Spaceships of many sizes and configurations swarmed in and out of Korango's multiple docking bays. To Yow's disappointment, he wasn't allowed to dock in his usual parking platform—his new striker was too big—so the traffic controller sent him to a remote docking area away from Korango City.

Luckily, a space taxicab immediately latched onto the ship's lock. In a matter of seconds, Yow was inside the flyer, departing for the metropolis. After passing the vast industrial zone, the cab entered the city limits. Following a winding path among the skyscrapers, it proceeded to an old but clean and tidy area close to downtown. The taxi descended into a dark, deserted street and landed near a brick-and-stone building. Yow got out of the cab and raced to its entrance.

Reynard Fliek, nicknamed Rey the Fox, and Rey to friends, sat at a computer, fixing his gaze on the screen. Hawkish eyes with bags underneath, deep wrinkles, and a prominent forehead amplified by the total loss of hair at the front of the scalp made him look to be in his late sixties or early seventies.

He was a man of many talents, with high intellect and secret knowledge of things—a scientist, a businessman, a computer specialist and, above all, the ranking member of the Hunters Society. With such credentials and reputation, and with his motto, "I make it happen," Rey was an excellent specimen of a Korango man.

Matching his luminary prominence, Rey's lab was crammed with electronic devices, computers, and other sophisticated equipment whose purposes were secret for the uninitiated. Even so, judging by various pieces of furniture usually found only in living quarters, along with dirty dishes, clothes, and even shoes scattered around the place, its owner used it not only for work but also for living.

The sound of a doorbell distracted Rey from his work. He glanced at the wall monitor—a push of a button, and Rey turned in his chair to face the door. Yow came in smiling.

Rey rose. "Glad to see you back, my friend. How's your business?"

Yow looked around, still smiling. "It's like I was here yesterday. I missed Korango." He paused for a second, then answered the question. "Nothing special. Messing about with some usual stuff. How have you been?"

"Surviving. I'm sure you've heard what happened yesterday."

"Yesterday?"

Rey squinted. "Ah, too small for you now? VIP clients?"

"Seriously, what happened?"

"Gavryn Jax was killed yesterday."

Yow's jaw dropped. "What? You mean he's dead? Like, dead-dead?"

"Yep. Dead. No more."

"And who's the new big boss?"

Rey grimaced and shook his head.

"Come on! You're a ranking member of the Hunters Society. You know!"

"Okay, okay... only to you. It's still a secret. According to the will, his riches go to some fellow named Rurik Cavell. Because of this, Korango laws make Cavill our next president and the chief executive officer of Korango Enterprises."

Yow made a supreme effort to hide his surprise. But Rey, who at first enjoyed the effect the news had produced on his friend and partner, was a keen observer. "What? You know him?"

Yow hesitated, unsure of what to say, and decided on a half-truth. "I've heard the name somewhere. He's a human, from Terah, right?"

"I don't know. The Korango Law Offices of Ournor and Co. are trying to locate him."

"Don't you find it strange that Gavryn Jax suddenly left everything to an obscure individual nobody knows?" asked Yow.

"Not *that* suddenly. Korango Enterprises' bylaws require the owner-president to file the will immediately upon entering the position. Besides, we can only speculate about people Jax knew." Rey patted Yow on the shoulder. "Let the rich guys play their games. What brings you to Korango this time?"

Yow reached into his pocket, pulled out a small metal box, and opened it. Inside was a test tube filled with a dark liquid. "That's the blood of an individual with a hidden tracer somewhere in his body. The thing is, I can*not* find the damn bug! My only guess is that it could be some kind of organic material that blends with his tissue. Can you look at the sample?"

Rey took the box with the tube.

"I'd appreciate your discretion in the matter," Yow said worriedly.

"Sure."

Rey moved to a hefty apparatus in the room's corner and opened a small hatch. He took the tube from the box and inserted it into his device. With the tap of a finger, it began humming. Rey remained glued to the small monitor, watching the data spat out by the machine.

It took a while before Rey looked up from the screen. "Well, the blood is that of a Stranger. Nothing unusual so far... Wait a minute... Interesting... It's Terahn." Rey continued to monitor the analysis. Finally, he stated, "Indeed, this person has a tracer implanted. Elder Keep technology, highly advanced... So advanced they keep it under wraps. It's used only when they can't do without it. Few people know it exists." He looked at Yow. "It means you're working on something special."

"Well, it's gotten more serious, then. How can I remove the tracer?"

"You can't. It becomes part of the body. But ionizing radiation can easily destroy it. It's like an old-style cancer treatment. I can send you instructions."

"Thanks. How do I know when it stops working?"

"When the tracer generates power from bodily fluids, a particular combination of blood components shows up in the molecular profile. You need to know what to watch for. I'll add that to my instructions."

"I have to ask you to destroy all traces of the blood sample and your analysis."

"Absolutely." Rey put the test tube in the incinerator and reset the analyzer.

"Old buddy, thank you. I'll double your share for work done on such short notice." Yow patted Rey on the shoulder. "I'd love to have a glass of Oaken Hopper with you, but I have to report back to the client." Yow hugged Rey and rushed out of the lab.

Rey watched Yow go before reaching for his commsys.

Yow entered the cockpit of his striker and plopped himself down on her pilot seat. He flipped several switches, and the ship came to life. Another button and the monitor on his right lit up, showing Rey's lab. A partial view on Rey speaking on his hand communicator appeared on-screen. Yow rewound until he found the point where Rey started talking.

> Drach? Rey here. I wanted to let you know that one of your operations has been compromised.
>
> ...
>
> No, I don't know which one. I don't have the list of people you've bugged. All I can say is that I just had a visit—
>
> ...
>
> My partner, Yow—
>
> ...
>
> I'm not an idiot—
>
> ...
>
> You know who he is? Good. That's all I have for you.

The screen went dark, but that wasn't the end of the recorded transmission. Yow fast-forwarded it so as not to miss anything. At the end of the recording, he saw a close-up of Rey, who seemed to be talking to something in his hand. According to the background noise, he was outside his lab, probably on the street.

> Yow, I knew you'd do something like this. Anyway, sorry. I didn't

have a choice. My lab is bugged, and they're watching me. So, I hope you'll get this. I'll destroy your transmitter.

The screen went dark again—this time it was the end. Yow grinned and pushed the throttle, rocketing away from the space station.

SEVEN

RUKE

Ruke was lost in the labyrinth of Coatera Cela's corridors, a series of dimly lit passageways all painted the same pale-blue color. He was struggling to find the conference room Aura had mentioned in her morning message. Memorizing door signs displaying the names of the facilities in English when he was passing them didn't help. Confused by the scientific gibberish, Ruke was ready to give up navigating the maze, but right then he bumped into Yow.

"Nice to see you!" Korag greeted him cheerfully. "Ready for the meeting?"

"I wish I were. Can't find the damn place," grumbled Ruke. Realizing he'd forgotten to greet Yow back, he blurted, "Hi, haven't seen you recently."

"Yeah, I returned from Korango an hour ago. Can I ask you something?"

"Shoot."

"Do you know someone by the name of Gavryn Jax?"

"Why? You know him?" Ruke stopped walking and looked at Yow suspiciously.

"Knew. He died recently. I learned about his death when I was on Korango."

"So, old Jax kicked the bucket? Well, I spent time with him in the same cell when Ab and his thugs abducted me. What happened?"

"He was killed... Do you know who he was?"

"We used to take care of each other. Never heard from him after."

"He was a big shot on Korango. As a matter of fact, so big that he practically *owned* the space station. He was the majority shareholder of Korango Enterprises."

"Good for him."

Rurik (Ruke) Cavell

"It appears to be good for you, too," said Yow. "The Korango Law Offices of Ournor and Co. are searching for one Rurik Cavell of Earth as Gavryn Jax's sole successor and rightful heir. Is that you?"

Ruke went pale and still, stunned by the news. "That's... uhhhh... a miracle," he croaked after a long moment.

"Let's keep moving—we don't want to be late."

Aura and Ash stood at the panoramic window, enjoying the view of the planet. Hippa sat nearby. It was noon on Coatera. Its orb was glowing green and blue in full glory, reflecting the cold light of Alderamin, the local star.

"Most of my people are scattered across the Milky Way. Few inhabitants are living on Coatera," Aura explained to Ash and pointed to a blue area on the planet, occupying about a third of its surface. "That's our only ocean."

Yow came in, and Ash turned. "Your arm? No sling?" She blushed and hugged Hippa. "We hope you feel better!" Ash treated Yow to a coy smile.

"I'm fine. Thank you for asking." Yow broke into a smile too.

Ruke, who had entered the room behind Yow and seen the exchange, smirked. *There she goes. She barely knows him...* He stared with scorn at the big oval table surrounded by a dozen chairs. The conference room seemed little different from the corridors—the same dull industrial design. *Aliens! Could they make it less attractive?* Ruke sank into a chair. *Huh, feels better than it looks...*

Eli was the last to show up. "Hi, everybody." He noticed Ruke and flopped into a chair next to him.

Aura looked around the room. "Hippa, Ash, please take your seats."

Ash headed to the seat next to Eli. Unexpectedly, Hippa made a long jump from the window across the conference table, at least thirty feet, and plopped herself down on the chair next to Eli, leaving Ash behind.

"Wow!" Eli yelped in surprise. "You're a real leaper. How about a warning next time?"

Hippa settled herself more comfortably in the chair and looked innocently at him with her languorous, smoky eyes.

"She likes you," Ash said jealously and sat next to Yow.

Aura patiently waited until everyone calmed down. "I asked you here to discuss recent events before you decide what to do next with your lives. Yow, please…"

"Two things. First, I'm certain that Abaddon planted a tracer on Eli. That's how he's been following us."

"But you checked and found nothing," Eli protested.

"It's an organic implant introduced into your body. We have to remove it."

"The Band-Aid!" exclaimed Eli.

"Band-Aid? What's that?" asked Aura.

"It's an adhesive bandage. Ab treated a cut on my forehead after I tangled with a gang of juvenile delinquents." Eli touched his eyebrow. "Here."

Yow examined his forehead. "That's plausible."

Eli's eyes lit up. "Maybe we shouldn't remove it. At least for now."

Yow shook his head. "Why? It's a simple procedure."

"I mean, I guess the Gamer is safe on Coatera, but they know it's here. I can go to another planet to make Ab believe we have moved the device."

Ash put up her hand. "I have an even better idea. We can fight back and tarnish Ab's reputation."

"What do you mean?" Aura raised her eyebrows.

"We do what Eli says. Then, we suggest covertly to Ab's boss that the Gamer is on yet another planet, *not* the one Eli would travel to. So, when they don't find it where Ab says it is, they'll blame him. It'd be his second major failure, the mission on Earth being the first." Ash ignored everyone's stunned gapes. "Seeds of mistrust can sometimes have greater power than cannons, my dad always said."

Ruke clapped his hands. "I love it."

"Wow… You're far more devious than you look," noted Eli.

"Is that good or bad?" Ash's face brightened with a smile.

Yow stepped in. "Hey, people! Let's not get carried away. I hate the fact that the Elder Keep thugs know where the

Gamer is, but with all due respect, all these ideas are fantasies."

Ash insisted, "We need to think outside the box."

"Do you know where the box is? Ab is a high-ranking official of the Security Chancellery, but he maintains his allegiance to Xiir Zanrod, Lord Guarantor, one of the most powerful people in the Alliance. How do you propose to deliver this information to Xiir?"

"We can pass it off as a fake document, or... tell him. I can do it. When Ab does not deliver what his bosses want because it's not there, they'll remember what I said."

"Aura, this is crazy." Yow had reached the limit of his patience. He turned to Ash again. "And how are you going to approach Xiir?"

Ruke intervened, "Oh, that's the easy part. Off the top of my head, I'd say she can make a juicy donation to whatever His Lordship is in charge of."

"And where do we get the money?" Yow didn't back down.

Ruke puffed out his chest proudly. "I'll give you the smackers!"

"*You* have money?" Aura glared at Ruke.

"He"—Ruke jabbed his finger toward Yow—"says I have plenty."

"About that..." Yow grew uneasy. "Evidently, Ruke is rich." He looked Aura in the eyes. "He inherited a fortune and the Korango presidency from an old friend who recently passed away."

"Man, I'm happy for you!" Eli shouted, raising his hand. "Give me five!"

While the buddies were sliding and slapping their palms, Aura stood up, massaging her temples. Ruke's and Eli's enthusiasm died down, and silence fell in the room.

"Is this true?" Aura remained calm, but steel hardness broke through in her voice. She turned to Ruke. "Did you go through the Gamer?"

Eli shook his head. "No, he didn't. I was there."

"I'm Rurik Cavell. A Norseman! A man from the North. I did. I have nothing to hide!"

"Then I'm sorry, Mr. Cavell. I have no choice but to declare you *persona non grata* on Coatera. You have to leave. Immediately."

"Lots of wucking furds, but not much story there, lady. I don't believe in your sorcery." Ruke looked at Eli. "Hey, chief! Can you give me a ride to my new home?"

Eli hesitated.

Ruke went at Aura, "And stop bitching. You really need to work on your social skills." He stood up and left the room.

"Sorry Aura, I have to go." For a moment, Eli's voice trembled, but he got it under control. "If you need my help, let me know." He stood and left without looking back.

Hippa gazed askance at Aura, leaped out of her chair, and skittered out of the conference room.

Aura bit her lip but quickly regained composure. "Ash, about your idea. I have no right to put you in danger. That's all I have for today." She gave Yow a look. "We need to talk."

"Can we meet in the bio lab? I have something you need to see."

"About Eli's idea. Chances are, Ab's people know we discovered the tracer."

"Are you certain?" Aura frowned.

"No. But I used my sources. It's only a matter of time before they link me to Eli and you... And now to Ruke."

"I see. Anything else?"

"Yes. I want to show you something." Yow led Aura to a large machine. "You have some good biometric stuff here—I like your blood analysis system." Disdaining direct voice input, he jabbed several keys. "Here is the composition of Eli's DNA. As usual in Earth-descended humans, he has these four nucleotide bases." He pointed to the screen. "But he has more. This one appears only in Gaians' DNA."

"Are you telling me Eli's one of *us*?"

"Moreover, he has the sixth nucleobase found in some humans but not in Gaians… Or so I was told. Now watch this." Yow tapped a key to display more DNA molecules on a second monitor. "These are from the Gaians of 75,000 years ago. That nucleobase was in Gaian DNA then but is not anymore. About ten thousand years ago, Gaian DNA started mutating, and your Gaian ancestors lost it."

"But there have been no major mutations in our species in—"

"I found Gaian papers that claim otherwise. The role of this nucleobase has never been fully understood. Speaking of mutations, one of every 500,000 Gaians still has this type of DNA."

"Uh… Are you saying that Eli is genetically an ancient Gaian?"

"Kinda. I analyzed his father's blood on the helmet Eli found. Same result."

"Did you tell Eli about all this?"

"Not yet. Don't you think it's disturbing that the Game became widespread during roughly the same period when the mutation appeared? A coincidence?"

The lab trembled, and the gentle rumble of disappearing thunder filled the lab. Aura and Yow stared at each other. Both knew what that was.

"Just let it go. He'll be back." Yow looked at Aura and added, "He's a nice guy…"

Aura shook her head stubbornly. "I played this as I should have, but Ab may try to target them on Korango. I'll send Nox to help."

"Nox has been captured!"

"We have a few tricks of our own." Aura's voice sounded triumphant. Perhaps too triumphant for the occasion, but that was what she needed right now to maintain a calm state of mind.

Korango appeared as a tiny disk visible from *Night Stalker*'s cockpit.

"STC... LWBS *Night Stalker* Gaian SA, transporting Mr. Rurik Cavell. Requesting permission to enter the station space and dock."

"*Night Stalker*. STC cleared to dock, Bay 4 starboard ramp. Proceed zero-five-zero to enter Yellow Zone, watch for Number Four."

"Affirmative." Eli touched the controls to engage the auto-docking system and leaned back in his chair. "Hey, buddy, you'll be home soon."

Ruke took a deep breath and said nothing. He fidgeted in the co-pilot's chair next to Eli, licking his dry lips. Finally, he let out a deep breath. "Do you think they'll accept me?"

"Dude, it's gonna be monumental. Trust me."

Eli's fighter entered a gigantic rectangular opening in the outer shell of the space station, moved sideways, and landed softly on a docking pad. Eli slapped Ruke on the shoulder. "Let's go get 'em, Mr. President!"

As soon as they got out of the ship, two Korango spaceport officials approached *Night Stalker*. "Welcome to Korango! Please state the purpose of your visit," said one of them, while another walked around the space fighter, entering data in a palmtop computer.

Ruke squared his shoulders. "Homecoming."

"Are you a resident? Your ID card, please."

"Not yet."

The second officer interrupted Ruke, "You have military-grade weaponry exceeding the allowance on Korango. You'll have to anchor the ship one hundred and twelve miles from the station. Who commands her?"

"I do," Eli said, "No problem, offi—"

The rest of Eli's answer drowned in the sound of an energy weapon discharge. The spaceport officer fell, and a red spot spread on his uniform.

As Eli grabbed Ruke by the sleeve and dragged him behind

Night Stalker's heavy landing gear, another blast killed the second officer. Korango spaceport police poured into the bay. They began shooting at random in various directions, but the enemy wasn't visible.

Eli poked his head around the gear strut to see what was going on. "I don't think they're targeting us."

"You mean they want to take us alive?"

A small space fighter flashed into the bay area and shot her laser cannons twice in the direction of the attacking fire. Instead of taking on enemy soldiers one by one, her pilot obliterated part of the bay. The enemy attack ceased.

The fighter glided across the bay and landed dashingly near *Night Stalker*, turning to face Eli and Ruke before touching down on the pad. The fighter canopy opened. A pilot in a military-style uniform swung over the side of the cockpit and landed right in front of them.

Eli and Ruke stood there, taken aback by what had just happened, and silently stared at their savior. The pilot was a middle-aged woman. She seemed to no longer care about her looks, preferring to live and dress plainly without burdening her life by trying to please anyone other than herself.

"Gentlemen, what seems to be the problem?" she asked.

Ruke looked around. Encouraged by the silence after a fierce battle, he proclaimed, "You've inflicted serious damage on my property, and, my lady-warrior, I'm wondering what you were thinking while doing so."

The stranger walked around Ruke, glanced at Eli, and burst into laughter.

"Are you Rurik *Cavell*?" she finally choked out.

"I usually go by Rurik or Ruke for friends." He pushed back his shoulders and jutted out his chin. "With whom do I have the honor of speaking?"

"I'm Shyster... Hunters leader and Gav's assistant." Shyster wiped the smile off her face. "Well, used to be his assistant...

Anyway, welcome to Korango! We've been disheartened by the untimely death of Gavryn Jax—your dear friend, I heard? But I'm relieved his heir and successor is here to bring order and balance, and stop the impending turmoil on Korango, our humble home."

Ruke offered his hand. "Nice to meet you, Shyster. Hunters... They'd be... Who?"

"A society of proud adventurers and outlaws, sir!"

Shyster shook hands with Ruke, who turned to Eli and said, "I'd like to introduce Eli Stroud, my friend and right hand in all things that matter."

Eli wanted to say something but instead nodded his head.

"Nice to meet you, Eli."

Eli gave a little bow. "Ma'am."

"My apologies, gentlemen. I need to make the arrangements." Shyster pulled out a commsys, a hand communicator resembling an Earth smartphone, and called someone. "I need a probate officer to meet me, Rurik Cavell, and his guest at the Red Sail as soon as possible." She grabbed both men by their arms, drawing them inside the station. "My new friends, Ruke and Eli, let me introduce you to Korango. I'm sure that gentlemen such as yourselves will be thrilled by our traditions and way of life."

The Red Sail screamed wealth and power. It was an upscale bar and restaurant, the envy of many Korango inhabitants who couldn't afford to spend time there. But among those who could, the establishment enjoyed an enviable reputation as the place to go no matter what the occasion—a secret business negotiation, a birthday party, or just eating and taking pleasure in savoring new tastes. In a few words, the Red Sail was the epitome of successful living on Korango.

Shyster, Ruke, and Eli sat in a cozy round booth with a deep-buttoned leather sofa and an elegant wooden table. Shyster was busy with Ruke and left Eli on his own—which Eli didn't mind. He kept himself busy looking over the Red Sail's interior, simultaneously sumptuous and archaic, trying to figure out whether his decision to come to Korango had been the right one.

On the contrary, Ruke was happy and slightly drunk. He was fiddling with a glass of light-brown liquid, examining it in the light of the wall sconces.

"We call it Oaken Hopper," explained Shyster.

"I like the taste. It's like our rye whiskey," noted Ruke. He took a long swig from his glass, then unexpectedly switched topics. "Who were those guys?"

"You mean the ones I killed?" Shyster puffed out her cheeks and exhaled. "No idea." She paused but deemed it necessary to add, "Law and order are important to us here."

Ruke grinned as he tried to fish out a piece of ice floating in his glass. "Sure. Uh... stubborn sucker." He finally got it with his fingers and sent it to his mouth.

"We're small but strong. We have friends everywhere, and they respect us."

Ruke crushed the ice with his teeth, finished the drink, and broke into a happy smile. "Love it. Ice with a tinge of your Hopper. Mmmm..."

Shyster didn't give up. "I hope that with our mutual leadership, we'll make our alliances even stronger. What do you say?" Her big amber eyes were quizzing Ruke.

"No problem. I like law and order."

Shyster was distracted as an unhappy-looking older man with a folder full of papers and a couple of datapads showed up and minced obsequiously to the table. "Tart Osso, Korango Law Offices of Ournor and Company. Do I have the pleasure of meeting Mr. Cavell?" Tart glanced at Eli—but immediately rejecting the idea the latter could be his customer, he shifted his stare to Ruke.

Shyster glared at Tart. "You're going to nag us with your questions, aren't you?"

"Oh no, Madam... um, Administrator. I need to ascertain whether Mr. Cavell is indeed Mr. Cavell. You know what I mean. Perhaps something... um, in his native tongue?" Tart opened his folder and laid out the documents on the table. "I have everything ready. It's a mere formality."

Ruke looked at his buddy.

"I have an idea," gloated Eli. He pulled his handgun out and turned it to show the manufacturer markings. The handgun muzzle pointed at the probate officer's crotch. "Can this help? It's in English, our native language. Here, the pistol and manufacturer names, caliber... Right here—see?" Eli moved the gun closer to Tart. "You have to admit there's nothing like it in this part of the galaxy."

Shyster burst out laughing as Tart reddened. Using his finger, the lawyer slowly moved the muzzle away from his crotch. "Very convincing indeed, Mister... Eh, we were not introduced. My apologies to Mr. Cavell. Unfortunately, I need something I can file with the rest of the paperwork."

Shyster got serious. "What do you suggest?"

"Mr. Jax was extra prudent regarding possible problems with his will. May I suggest that Mr. Cavell agrees to provide a sample of his DNA? Mr. Jax was in possession of something that belonged to Mr. Cavell. He called it a 'baseball cap.'"

"My old baseball cap! Right, I gave it to him. I love this planet!" yelled Ruke, giving Tart a slap on the back. Tart's papers flew into the air—he had to grab the table to stay on his feet.

It didn't bother Ruke too much. "Oh, I'm sorry, Tart, didn't mean to... DNA, no problem."

Groaning, Tart bent down and got on with collecting his papers. "My apologies, with my age... I'm not nimble on my feet anymore. May I suggest going to my office? My flyer is outside."

Ruke rose with the empty glass and yelled, "Garçon! Bring me and my dear friend Eli... two Hoppers!"

The bartender hurried up with the bottle as Ruke continued, "A toast! I propose a toast! You all... Eli, let's drink! Through the ass to the stars!" Ruke concluded his fiery speech and drained his glass in one fell swoop.

Shyster enjoyed the situation. "Ruke, Eli... That was great. Have fun. See you later!"

Shyster was still finishing her Oaken Hopper when Nox showed up and moved straight to her table. She stopped in front of Shyster, eyeballing the woman.

Shyster looked up from her glass. "Do I know you?"

Shyster

"Forgive me, that was rude. Sometimes I'm so involved with my duties I forget social pleasantries... But it's only because I want to serve my customer to the best of my abilities."

"And who may that be?"

"Forgive me again, as I'm not at liberty to discuss that."

Shyster produced her laser pistol, waggling it for Nox to see. "What do you want?"

"We could discuss it peacefully..." Nox snatched out her laser gun from behind her back and pointed it at Shyster. "Or not. Threatening me can only make things worse."

Shyster made a sign to the barman. He made a quick move, but in a split second, Nox whipped out her second gun and pointed it at the bartender. He froze.

"I guarantee that I'm much faster than you. Both of you. Probably faster than ten or fifteen of someone like you. Please don't confuse my desire to be polite with my resolve to serve my client. Now, slowly and gently put your weapon on the table and push it toward me."

Shyster wasn't fainthearted, but she had learned to tell a bluff from a real threat. She obeyed.

Nox went on, "About your question. I want you to think hard before you start plotting to kill Ruke. Add Eli to the list. We didn't care when you were plotting against Gavryn Jax. But we care now." Nox flung Shyster's gun away from the table. "To avoid any misunderstandings—any harm, physical or emotional, or any effort to conspire against either or both, will result in your quick termination, and that of those you may want to involve."

"Does your customer approve of your way of doing your job?"

"Not always. But customers are usually more concerned about results."

Shyster probed deeper. "I don't respond well to threats, especially empty ones."

"Your involvement in an attempt to kidnap the individuals in question, similar to what happened in the docking bay today, will be considered a transgression." Nox gestured at the barmen with her gun. "Turn on the news. Slowly."

A monitor on the wall lit up. It showed an enraged crowd protesting in the center of a shopping mall. The camera panned and tilted to show a dead man on the floor with Korango police investigating the crime scene. The news ticker displayed the headline:

BREAKING NEWS —— High-ranking Hunter murdered ——

"Turn it up," Nox ordered the barman. The voice of a reporter informed viewers:

Another victim of the brutal attacks taking place near Central Square. Xegul Fenyr, an individual known to be close to the Hunters' leadership, was shot dead in cold blood earlier today inside the Northwest Kirin Shopping Center. Currently, police haven't found anything to move forward on any individual suspect.

Nox turned to Shyster. "I knew you'd be reluctant to face reality. I'm sure you knew him."

"Enough! You've made your point." Shyster panted through clenched teeth. "So that you understand what's going on, I saved them both today."

EIGHT

FUN AND GAMES

Not a Korango native, Shyster had moved to the space station quite some time ago in search of a better life. She'd quickly earned respect and recognition in business circles for being practical and realistic, a person with no illusions or pretensions. With her wit, fairness, and tact in dealing with people, she also gained a formidable reputation among the Hunters and eventually became their leader.

The Hunters established themselves as a peculiar entity, somewhere in between a political party and social club. Officially called the Hunters Society, the organization had a loose structure. Nonetheless, it became a dominant force on Korango, influencing almost all aspects of daily life.

It would be fair to say that the way Hunters organized themselves reflected Korango's tolerance for things that many other societies would consider serious offenses punishable by law—or that would at least be frowned upon as not fitting moral principles that governed their behavior. The *Live and Let Live* maxim became the Hunters' motto, encapsulating the essence of the organization.

Its council gathered once in a while, under the auspices of the

Hunters Society's leader, to discuss things that seemed the most urgent to its members. Such gatherings usually took place at Shyster's office, a large and functional, if messy, room with pieces of worn-down furniture scattered throughout. Council meetings often came about almost by chance, but none of the important events or issues on the space station ever escaped the council's attention.

Gavryn Jax's death and the arrival of his heir and successor made many Hunters anxious. Rumors about Rurik Cavell's arrival and Shyster's improvised welcome at the Red Sail soon reached every corner of the space station. The Hunters assembled at their leader's office wanted to know details and to vent their frustration and grievances in light of recent events.

Always cautious, Shyster didn't want to get into details. She felt that Gavryn's death, Ruke's unannounced arrival, her encounter with Nox, and many other things happening lately on Korango were somehow interconnected. But she didn't know how and didn't know how such events could affect their lives. For the moment, Shyster was trying to soothe the gathering—all men, as it happened—without betraying her concerns.

Reynard Fliek, invariably shrewd and deft, pushed hard with his usual demagoguery. "We've become an appendage of the powerful! What's going on?"

Lofty and pompous, he paused for a second, then went on while glaring at Shyster, "I don't recognize the station. Beggars, thieves, drug addicts. Xegul Fenyr murdered. Korango City—slums and decay. Street gangs taking over where the Hunters' code of honor was the way of life!"

Shyster shrugged. "Why are you looking at me? The Elder Keep Alliance and the Intergalactic League—your customers—pay the money, and they order the music. You deliver it, don't you?"

Rey couldn't stop himself. "Who killed Gavryn Jax? The killer was one of us. Not the Alliance or League!" Rey bit his tongue. He realized he'd gone too far, but it was too late now.

Shyster's eyes sparkled. She smiled snidely. "And how do you know that?"

The buzz of the commsys interrupted Shyster, saving Rey from answering the question.

She stalked over to her desk and put the commsys on speaker. "Shyster."

A voice reported, "Ma'am, the subject with his friend is in the Veil and Smile, confronting a hostile group of patrons. The situation can get out of hand any second. I need your instructions."

"Shit! Hang on, I'm coming there. If anything happens to that man, the same will happen to you."

Shyster grabbed her handgun. "Gentlemen, I have to wrap it up for today, but we'll continue. You!" She jerked her head toward Rey. "Come with me."

Korags loved the Veil and Smile nightclub for its loose morals, discreet service, and, most importantly, cheap booze.

The front area of the club, dedicated to erotic shows, generally failed to attract the attention of many clubgoers. Performances featuring undressing and nude or semi-nude dancing were merely a convenience for the Veil and Smile customers. Patrons, mostly men, usually wanted only a fleeting glimpse of exotic dancers before returning to activities more essential for Korags—talking about business, bragging about making a killing, drinking, playing cards, and—inevitably at trouble spots like Korango nightclubs—brawling and even occasionally shooting at each other.

Needless to say, such important activities happened mainly in backrooms hidden from the outsiders. This wasn't to say that *only* select clientele could access such places. The Veil and Smile owners had a strict policy of keeping all club amenities open and accessible to anybody. But the labyrinths and enfilades of poorly lit rooms served as a natural barrier to prevent newcomers from discovering the hottest spots of the club.

The spacious game room, filled with the crème de la crème of the male Korag populace, was one such place. A Western-style paintball duel was progressing in waves, either swinging wildly with the loud booms of shots, yelling, and drinking, or subsiding for a moment to replace losers with new hopefuls eager to prove their shooting skills.

Without missing an opportunity to take a swig from his glass, Ruke actively participated in the game, cheering winners and booing losers together with the crowd. In contrast to his buddy, Eli got bored immediately. The game didn't interest him—he sat quietly drinking and bluntly inspecting the few scantily clad women fidgeting on their chairs.

Meanwhile, another round of shooting finished, and a disagreement broke out over the winner. A tall redhead with biceps bulging like two air balloons yelled, trying to outshout the crowd, "He was ramping!"

"That's not against the rules," Ruke roared and waved his hands. Booze inside the glass he was holding splashed out into the redhead's face.

"You fuckwit… Apologize!" He grabbed Ruke by his shirt and raised him above the floor.

Half-strangled, Ruke swung his legs and arms, trying to reach the guy. "Goddammit, I'm the one motherfucker you don't want to fuck with…"

"Whaaat?" snarled the redhead.

A second club regular, with just as menacing an expression, yelled at Ruke, "I've never seen you here before. Who the hell do you think you are?"

"There's a new sheriff in town, dickwad!"

"What's that?"

"Dickwad? That's you. I'm the sheriff, idiot!" Ruke could barely wheeze the words out.

By this time, a third man, cleaner and better-dressed but smaller than the first two, had made his way to the redhead and delivered a skillful uppercut to his solar plexus. The redhead never saw it coming. He dropped Ruke and bent in half, gasping for air. The smaller man didn't waste time and hit the redhead with the butt of his gun, knocking him to the ground.

Suddenly, Eli, who up until that moment had been watching the brawl thoughtlessly, broke out of his chair and dashed to Ruke. In one seamless move of the hand, he whipped his gun out of the holster, aiming it toward the entrance doors. Someone stretched out a leg—Eli tripped over it. Still in the air, he pulled the trigger twice.

The loud cracks of the large-caliber shots sounded like thunder in the confined space, drowning out the noise of the crowd. Frightened club visitors tried to find a safe place to be. Some ran helter-skelter for the exit, while others, including Ruke, crawled to hide behind pieces of furniture.

Several more shots came from the opposite direction.

Eli jumped to his feet. Unsteady, he aimed and shot through the doorway at someone outside the game room. The recoil of the big pistol jerked his body like an epileptic spasm. The gun fell out of his hand, and the dead silence that reigned in the room was disturbed only by an empty brass casing bouncing until it finally settled on the floor.

Eli swayed on his feet, ready to fall. Ruke and the man who had knocked down the redhead rushed to catch him.

"Duuude... You're alive..." Eli hiccuped, staring at Ruke. "I think I'm gonna puke..." He blacked out, sagging into the arms of both men.

Drunk and barely keeping himself upright, Ruke whimpered, "Somebody... help... help..."

The smaller man glanced at Eli, then said aloud to the air, "He's fine, no blood. Drunk as a lord, though."

Shyster chose that moment to appear in the game room. "Ruke, please come with me," she said calmly. "If you can, that is."

She turned to Rey and the smaller man. "You two, help both—I want them in my office, and I want a police squad here. Oh, there's a dead body outside. I need his name now, and a full report on what happened here later."

Ruke slept proudly in his newly inherited office, in his executive chair at his executive desk. He almost slipped onto the floor, but miraculously, his backside stuck to the edge of the seat. He unglued his swollen eyes. His mouth was dry, and a loud bell pounded in his head. "Ugh... can somebody get me an aspirin?"

At the sound of Ruke's moans, Shyster opened the door and entered. "What's aspirin?" She stuck out her jaw, and her lips whitened. "Are you fucking out of your mind? Those people after you could kill you! Which I don't mind, except that they would kill *me* after that!"

"There's no aspirin on this whole damn planet?"

"It's a space station. Ring a bell?"

"Right... It was fun until you showed up and ruined everything. Oh, crap, I need a drink." Ruke raised his head and winced, "Where am I?"

"In your office."

"I have an office?"

"Yep."

Ruke licked his chapped lips. "Since when?"

"Since yesterday. Ournor's lawyers cleared you, remember? Korango Enterprises? Hello! You're the boss now." Shaking her head, Shyster opened a bar fridge, retrieved a bottle of water, and gave it to Ruke. "Here. Not esprin, but you'll feel better."

"It's aspirin... thanks." Ruke grabbed the bottle from her, took a swig, and assumed a more stable position in his chair. "Right, I remember now. I was with Eli... Where is he?"

"In the closet. Sleeping."

"What? Move him out here."

"He's drunk, and it's a big closet. You should get used to keeping up appearances, even if it means some little sacrifices." She scowled. "You know, someone tried to kill you yesterday. Eli saved you."

"Yeah, I wouldn't mess with that guy."

"You need to take over the station, and I mean with a firm hand. Korango has become a train wreck in the past year! Worse, we may be losing our independence. Pazons from the Elder Keep act like they're at home here. Much longer, and they'll make it theirs for sure."

Ruke flinched. "I keep hearing the name. Do you know Abaddon?"

"You *know* him?"

"He kidnapped me, long ago—tortured me for no reason, for days. It seemed much longer. Gav Jax was my cellmate. He kept me from dying of thirst, and I stopped him from bleeding to death after Ab got too zealous once... I had recent encounters... That shooting in the docking bay—they probably wanted to kidnap Eli and me."

"So, you don't think *I* want to kill you?"

"What? I like you. Where did you get that?"

"I had a visit recently—a beautiful girl, a cyborg apparently. She threatened to kill me if something happens to you. Have I given anybody any reason for such harsh treatment?"

"Ah, that's Nox. I think. No worries. I'll take care of it."

Shyster sniffed her clothing, and then the air. "When was the last time you took a shower?"

Ruke stuck his nose in the armpit. "Oh... that's awful..." Embarrassed, he turned away from her. "You know what? Life stinks," he uttered with a sulky pout and went on defiantly, "I like

Korango. Its spirit and everything... Blah-blah-blah... Please, not now. Sorry, I feel like a shitbag full of fuckdust."

Shyster twitched her shoulders. "Pig..." she growled through her teeth, before turning and leaving the room.

Ruke leaned back in the chair and closed his eyes. *Oh, God...*

Asphalis, the head of the Security Chancellery of the Elder Keep Alliance, stood in the middle of a large office, which was more akin to a cathedral than a place suitable for bureaucratic work. The interior perfectly matched its owner, a superb specimen of a Pazon alpha male—slow and deliberate, never uncomfortable with eye contact, a manly chest, broad shoulders, and classic masculine features such as a massive, angular jaw, a square chin, and prominent brows.

The doors opened, and Xiir Zanrod walked into the room. He stared at the spectacular opulence with a sneer. "I never liked your office, Phal," he uttered after a dramatic pause. "A cathedral, not a government place. Are you trying to come off as better than me?"

Asphalis bowed obsequiously. "Have mercy, your Holiness. 'Tis only a tribute to our Creator from his humble servant. All that I long for and need is in the name of the Almighty."

"How nice... I wish it were true, to restore my confidence in your competence."

Asphalis' eyes flashed with anger as he straightened. "May I inquire what could have possibly led you to doubt my abilities?"

"You promised me a quick win—the Game. Yet I hear your operation on Terah turned out to be a complete disaster," Xiir Zanrod barked.

Asphalis kept silent, but his face and eyes turned red with a rush of blood.

Meanwhile, Xiir continued, "Your subordinates brag about capturing sources of valuable information and the knowledge of the Game's whereabouts." He switched to screeching at the top of his lungs. "Then, those sources *disappear without a trace,* and your surveillance operations are compromised!"

Asphalis

Asphalis started pacing back and forth. He abruptly turned to Zanrod, pointing his finger at the cleric. "People like you, Xiir, are in the habit of not appreciating all the hard work we do for the glory of the Elder Keep Alliance! You take for granted everything you get without even saying 'thank you.' But when things go wrong, and when people die, mindless men like you yell their heads off in their righteous indignation."

"How dare you? You know who I am."

"And you forget who *I* am. As the security chancellor, I have files on every one of you, and I can bury you in your sins! So shut up and show some respect to my office."

The silent standoff continued for a while, Xiir Zanrod with his right cheek twitching, against Asphalis breathing heavily with the air flaring his quivering nostrils.

"Be careful, Phal," the cleric warned at last, "I don't give a damn about your files." Xiir looked mockingly at Asphalis. "So that you understand, you have your files only because I don't mind you having them. Sit! Calm down!"

The Lord Guarantor waited until Asphalis obediently sank into the armchair behind his desk before continuing, "You are twenty years younger than I, Phal, so I'll spare you—for now. Why? Because I think we want the same thing. So what are we doing wrong?"

"I am sorry, my Lord. I can see you're upset, and I was out of line." Asphalis' expression softened. "Discreet operations won't work all by themselves. The Strangers are too strong and elusive. Even low-profile and covert black ops require firepower and assault teams. We didn't have them on Terah."

"Is the Game still on Coatera? Can we seize it from there?"

"We have patrol ships nearby. I believe it's on the planet. But I think we should target those who are in charge of the device to learn more about the technology. Does the name *Aura* sound familiar?"

"Yes. She's a real flesh-and-blood Gaian, isn't she? Unlike Nox?"

"Nox was our mistake. That's how little we know about the Game."

"You want to go for Aura? Do it. I'll ask the Supreme Leader for more resources."

NINE

YOW

Yow peeked into Cela's control center and saw Aura inside. "I was passing by, so I thought I'd stop in for a chat," he announced. "Is this a good time?"

Aura was reviewing the latest surveillance information. She sat in front of a holographic display projecting the recent traffic data in the vast region around Coatera. "Please, come in. I wanted to talk to you too." Aura waved her hand, inviting Yow inside. "Here's the latest telemetry. Sensor arrays show increased traffic in Coatera space. Some ships have the Elder Keep signatures."

Yow looked at the traffic patterns and shook his head. "I can see that. You should also know that the Alliance is very active on Korango. I believe they've infiltrated the Hunters Society, including its council."

"Anything in particular concern you?"

"I'd feel better if you closed the doors." Yow glanced over his shoulder.

Aura rarely saw Yow so worried. "It's that serious?" she asked, jabbing at the holo to close the doors.

"It is. I worry about Ruke. He's naive and inexperienced, and soon will be a Hunters Council member—an easy and tempting target for Elder Keep intelligence."

"What about Eli?"

"Pazons aren't in the habit of abandoning their plans. They want the Game. Maybe they don't understand how, but I'm sure they realize there's a connection between Eli and the technology."

"What makes you think so?"

"I bet you think about it yourself." Yow smiled. "Did you think they didn't notice who opened the cave? Most likely, Eli's also a target, perhaps even more so than Ruke. You should have kept him close."

"I wish I could, but Nox is making sure both are safe. I also asked her to watch for any contacts between them and the Elder Keep people on Korango."

"Does she know Reynard Fliek? He's a member of Hunters Council, prominent on Korango and easy to find. Also known as Rey the Fox, or Rey. Used to be my associate. Smart and manipulative—he may be a person of interest to Nox."

"I'll let her know immediately."

"Have you decided what you want to do with the Gamer?"

"I think—" started Aura and stopped. The sliding doors opened, and Ash appeared in the doorway, hesitating to enter. Hippa, her loyal companion for the past few days, sat next to Ash.

"Ash, I'll be with you in a minute—"

"It's okay—come in!" Aura interrupted Yow.

"I wanted to ask if I can be helpful. It's cool to be here, but I'm feeling lazy." Ash smiled shyly.

"Thank you, Ash. We're fine. I'm sorry for being such a poor host—"

Yow cut in, "If you don't mind, I'd like to show Ash the planet."

"Wonderful idea! I can imagine how disappointing it can be to stay here and watch Coatera, near and yet so far, day after day, instead of going there and getting a breath of fresh air."

"Can Hippa go with us?" Ash's pleading eyes moved from Aura to Yow and back.

"Why not? I'll meet you in the docking bay," said Yow.

Yow's space striker cruised at low altitude over Coatera.

"That's one of their old cities, abandoned now." Yow circled a green area with ruins barely visible among mature trees and kept moving. The green plush of vegetation, mostly gigantic trees, spread out below.

Yow Nayo

Ash was glued to the cockpit window. "It's beautiful. The trees are like the sequoias of Earth. Why did they abandon the planet?"

"I don't know. Gaians are reserved people. You know, outsiders call them 'Strangers.'"

"Are you working for them?"

"I'm a private investigator for hire, Korango-based. I'm working for Aura now, but she doesn't let me in—only tells me what I need to know. What happened on Earth was mostly as much of a revelation to me as to you and Eli."

"The Gamer?"

"The Gamer is an interface, a part of the Game, the Gaians' biggest secret. We saw it in action with Eli. He created a spaceship out of thin air. Ruke? Probably the same story—both passed through the Gamer, and both got something."

"That scares me," Ash breathed.

"What do you mean?"

"Does it grant wishes? What if somebody wishes for bad things? Or doesn't realize that what they've wished for could cause bad things?"

Yow pretended to be busy with finding a spot to land. "Oh... Here's a place we can stop by. You'll like it!"

The place Yow selected for the shore excursion turned out to be remarkable, a picture-perfect, park-like setting with an elegant building sited at the edge of the woods. Idyllic, romantic, and spiritually uplifting, it was one of those rare places that nobody could improve upon.

"That's a guest house." Yow pointed to the building. "Beautiful, isn't it?"

The life-affirming beauty of the setting seemed to transfer to Hippa. With her tail up, ears facing forward, curious and joyful, she ran across the lawn and disappeared into the woods.

Ash touched Yow's shoulder. "It was a serious question. Wishes can be evil. Purposefully or accidentally."

"Yes, they can," he admitted with a sigh. "It's no wonder Abaddon wants the Gamer."

"And he's a bad guy."

"He's also the Elder Keep Alliance's Chief of Special Ops."

"That's even scarier than I thought... the Gaians need to destroy the Game."

"As I understand it, there are reasons they keep it. Aura is in charge of that."

Yow kept walking. Then he abruptly turned to Ash, took her by her shoulders, and pulled her closer to him. "Promise me you'll stay away from this thing. It's dangerous. I've already risked my life more than once for it, and I've been scared to death the whole time." His eyes became hard, narrow, and focused. "I'm scared for you now, Ash. Leave! You have Eli. Go to Korango. Ruke will help you. Just go!"

Ash wouldn't let up. "But if bad guys get hold of the Game tech, they may kill a lot of people. Ab will probably start with us, anyway." As if sick of arguments, she paused and said gently, "But when you're holding me like this, it's not that scary."

Ash looked at Yow. Their eyes met and locked. Yow's head came down, hers up, and all of a sudden, they lunged into a kiss.

Purring, Hippa came quietly to them and butted Ash's hip with her head. Pulling slowly, carefully away from Yow, Ash squatted and hugged Hippa. "I don't care about Eli or danger right now," she told Yow. "But I do feel that it's time for me to move on. I don't belong here. So let's go to Korango. It's your home, right?"

Later that night, Yow found Aura in the mess hall grabbing a quick bite. He beelined toward her. "Is this seat taken?" Yow smiled, looking around—the room was empty. "I know, I know... sorry to interrupt your meal."

"That's fine. How was your trip to Coatera?"

"Very interesting. Ash was impressed. I wanted to ask about your plans for the near future. What else can I do for you?"

"We'll move the Gamer from Coatera to another location soon. I expect the Game Wardens to come and take care of it. No need to involve you."

"That's what I thought. Eli's idea is off the table now?"

"Yes. You should disable the tracer."

"I see... Well, that's it, then—I'll be on Korango until I hear from you. I want to take Ash with me. She has to find a new home, and it won't be Coatera."

"Agreed. One more thing—I'll need some weaponry, quickly. Can you take care of it?"

"Another reason to go to Korango. Send me specs. Take care of yourself, Aura!"

"You too!"

"Crime is on the rise here. Be careful not to veer off the main streets." Yow kept setting Ash on the right track as he opened the door and led her into his apartment in Korango City.

Ash looked around, wide-eyed. "So many paper books on a space station! Do you read them?"

Yow's apartment was a bachelor dwelling—simple, functional, and old-fashioned. It consisted of several spaces—a small cooking area Yow never used, a tiny bedroom with an en suite bath, and a modest rectangular room serving most of Yow's remaining needs. Its decor couldn't be simpler—a worn-out couch in one corner, an unusually low desk with a matching chair, a lamp, and a computer. A light fixture in the shape of a globe hung in the middle of the ceiling. Shelves full of books took up all the space along the perimeter of the room.

"I read, though not as often as I'd like to," he admitted. "Reading relaxes me. When I was younger, I used to collect paper books. I even have one from Earth, representative of the modern era of the current civilization."

"What is it?"

"*King Lear* by William Shakespeare. But let's not digress—decide where you want to stay. My place is all yours, but if—"

"Your place, that's all I want."

The doorbell rang, and Yow looked at the small screen on the wall. "Eli and Ruke. I told them we were coming. I thought you'd like to see some familiar faces. Shall I let them in?"

"I'd love to see them. I can't believe all this is happening to me. Can I open the door?" Ash rushed to the entrance. "It's this button, isn't it?"

"Right." Yow smiled.

Ruke entered first, and Ash threw her arms around his neck. "Hey, the rich guy! So, it's true. You've inherited money!"

Ruke, chuffed to bits, bragged, "And the station. Tomorrow is my inauguration, and you're all invited." Losing a lot of his enthusiasm, he added, "Unfortunately, I've also inherited responsibilities."

Ash couldn't help but try to get a rise out of Ruke. "Oh... You poor thing, where's your limousine?"

Ash's mischief didn't produce any effect on Ruke. Instead, he fixed his gaze on Yow and Ash. "Whoa. Are you two together now?"

But Ash had already veered away from Ruke and switched to Eli.

"Look at you! At both of you! A step through a hoop, and *voila*! A spaceship. Is that what you wanted?"

Yow stiffened. "Ash, let's discuss that later. I need to talk to Eli about the tracer."

"It's a simple question. What if you two wanted something else? Something bad? You, Ruke... Did this thing have to kill someone to make you rich?"

"What?" Eli bristled. "Are you accusing Ruke and me of something? Or are you jealous of missing the train?"

"I figure that any normal person wouldn't sleep well when it's like tick-tock somewhere, ready to kill you, and you don't even know about it."

Yow decided to intervene before the atmosphere got too hostile. "Please, Ash, stop. We have things to do. Ruke, you promised to help Ash get settled on the station, right?"

Ruke breathed a sigh of relief and twitched. "Yes. Right, right... Ash, let's go. So many things to do. I'll show you around."

"Please don't forget to buy her a commsys," reminded Yow. "That's what we call our phones," he explained to Ash.

After Ash and Ruke left, Yow gestured Eli to the couch. "How have you been?"

"Okay, I guess. Not sure what I'm doing here. I want to go back to Coatera."

Yow opened the drawer of his desk, took out a pack of ten pills, and gave it to Eli. "These'll take care of the tracer. Take one every day. You may be dizzy after each one, but it'll pass. About Coatera... Aura is moving the Gamer elsewhere."

"Where? Does she need help?"

"I don't know. I'm sure the location will be secret. She doesn't want me involved."

"I see." Eli thought for a second and continued, "What's with Ash?"

"She's worried someone will misuse the Game technology. She has a point, you know. There are rumors about this technology, about how it can be abused. I want to ask you—were you thinking about your *Night Stalker* when it happened?"

"No! How could I? I had no clue such a thing was even possible."

"That confirms what I've heard. It grants wishes, the strongest ones, even if they're subconscious. That could lead to lots of problems."

Eli shrugged. "Yeah, but it can also be useful."

"The Gaians are secretive about it. About everything, actually.

But if someone wants something bad… Or, even worse, people wishing good things might want bad things deep in their minds."

"They guard the Gamer… or is it the Game? I'm confused. But look, Aura tried to kill me for using it, despite me having no clue what it was. And Ruke—she kicked him out. Rather overzealous, but it proves that she's serious about guarding the thing."

"But the Gaians can use it to create or destroy anything they want. Don't you think this gives the Elder Keep reasons for seizing the Game? I don't think Gaians will ever do something catastrophic with it, but that's me."

"Are you saying it should be destroyed? Is that what Ash wants?"

"The Game, as it currently exists, is around ten thousand years old. I've heard there were incidents. That's why Gaians protect it."

"You know, five minutes ago I wasn't worried about Aura… well, I almost wasn't worried. Now, I am. Thanks, pal—"

The sound of a commsys buzz interrupted Eli. Yow checked the monitor—it was Rey Fliek. "Shhh…" Yow pressed his index finger to his lips and pointed to a corner away from the monitor. "Stay there!"

He waited for Eli to move and accepted the call. "What's up, Rey?"

"I've heard you're here and wanted to warn you about Abaddon. He knows who your client is and that all your Terahn friends are on the station."

"Thanks, Rey. Yes, I arrived yesterday. I'm in the middle of something right now—I'll call you later."

"Please do."

TEN

REY

Rey's hunched, shadowy figure didn't stand out against the background of the dark stone building located outside Korango City's downtown. Nervous, he was meandering, looking around and checking the time almost every second. Several more steps and Rey turned into a wrought-iron gateway and blended with the darkness under its arch.

Rey loved Korango nights—his best friends and allies. Bright signs of various establishments and occasional streetlights attracted passersby like magnets—some of them hanging around and others busy with various pursuits. But if someone like Rey wanted to find a quiet spot to check the surroundings while being hidden from others, Korango City could offer many locales similar to the one Rey had chosen to meet with his Pazon contact.

Rey cocked his ears—another dark figure, a man, was approaching the place. A black hood hid his face. As the man got closer, Rey sighed with relief. He recognized Abaddon and came out of the darkness.

With his hands in the pockets of his hoodie, Ab got straight to the point. "Anything new?"

Rey held out a small disk. "Yow Nayo and Ash Kline are on Korango. I think you may be interested in this recent recording."

Ab scowled. "Something special?" he asked, ignoring Rey's hand with the disk. He always wanted to delay the moment when his acquaintance with the contacts of dubious character would be impossible to deny.

Reynard (Rey) the Fox, also Reynard Fliek

"An intriguing exchange between Eli and Ash. The girl is unhappy about the Game." Rey swelled with pride.

Careful as always, Ab offered, "Go on."

"It may be a long shot, but I see a potential to exploit her reservations about the Game."

"You have my attention." Ab decided not to slight his mole anymore.

"I believe Ash may feel compelled to destroy it if she has the chance... and you know how resourceful these Terahns are. You want it in one piece, but we can make her think she's destroying the Game, while in reality, she'll only cripple the ship Strangers use to transport the Game. It'll make it easier for you to capture both the machine and the person who is in charge of it, Aurabella Thaleia. You mentioned you wanted her too, right?" said Rey, with high shoulders and a straight back. He'd done well.

Ab thought over Rey's plan. "Can you talk to Ash?"

"I don't think it's a good idea. She knows Yow. He's a smart guy. He'll see immediately what's behind it if he finds I've approached Ash. I'll lose his trust."

"If we go with your plan and it fails, that's fine with me. We have other options. And his trust? He doesn't seem to trust you now." Ab waited for a moment, and his voice softened, "Good job. To show our appreciation for your service, here is what I have for you." He took a tiny box out of his pocket and gave it to Rey. "The key to your new bank account, with access in most places in our part of this galaxy. When you check it out, I'm sure you'll be pleased enough not to worry about Yow's trust. Besides, I'll double the money if your efforts are successful."

Rey took the box. "Thanks." He heaved a sigh and stuffed the box into his pocket. "I don't doubt that your compensation of my efforts is fair. It always has been. I'll talk to Ash, but I can't promise anything until I understand how far Ash is willing to go."

"Fair enough." Ab stepped into the darkness of the night and soon passed out of sight.

Rey took the box out of his pocket. Inside was a small memory card. He raised it to his eyes to get a better look. Only the most prestigious private banks offered such high-security keys. Rey spun it in his hand like in the old coin routine, and the card disappeared. He turned the hand back, and the key reappeared. Rey smiled and walked toward the brightly lit city center. The time had come to relax and celebrate the deal.

Korango City Hall occupied a whole block in the capital's downtown. The Dome, as Korags called it, was the Hall's central and oldest facility.

As Korango City grew, its owners expanded the original building, adding more structures. But the Dome, with its enormous meeting and reception chamber, stood as a proud reminder of the pioneers who had dared to build the space station in the middle of nowhere and who'd founded Korango Enterprises. Renovated many times, the Dome was in excellent shape. It seemed untouched by the deterioration visible in many parts of the city.

The Dome was designed to symbolize the station itself. From outside, its similarity to Korango's external protective domes left no doubt about the source of inspiration for the city hall's architecture. From inside, the arch pillars supporting the dome and annular or spiral balconies at different heights had become a common design solution for many large buildings on the station. The Dome's interior was decorated with traditional rust, clay, and amber hues complemented by the obligatory streaks of gold.

Understandably, Korango presidential inaugurations didn't happen frequently. Thus, many Korags regarded Ruke's ascension to the presidency as a rare chance, or even a once-in-a-lifetime opportunity, to look at the powers that were. Others saw the event as a spectacle or an excellent excuse to hang around with the very best of the Korango society, perhaps hoping some of their geniuses might rub off on them.

Crowds of Korags flocked to the Dome, pouring onto its oblong-shaped floor and spreading alongside the balconies in anticipation of the inauguration extravaganza. The event organizers prepared to celebrate the occasion in a big way.

Presidential symbols commemorating the occasion adorned the walls and pillars of the Dome. A colossal flag bearing the Korango official presidential emblem hung down above the central platform, and baskets of flowers were everywhere—around the podium, beside walkways, and hanging from balconies. Korango's service industry didn't stint, either. Numerous stands, kiosks, and walking vendors with trays offered souvenirs, sweets, snacks, and beverages, filling the attendees' souls with joy and helping to kill time before the event.

A group of musicians on the central platform had finished playing, and they hurried to collect their instruments and leave. For good reason—the crowd's noise gradually faded away as Ruke, surrounded by corporate and city officials, prepared to take center stage to begin the ceremony. The "the king is dead, long live the king!" moment had arrived.

Korango's master of ceremonies—a chubby guy with a mustache who was dressed in a ginger embroidered caftan with gold decorations, a sash, and fringed hems—stepped forward. "Ladies and gentlemen, I hereby present unto you Rurik Cavell, the undoubted President of the Korango Independent Territory and Korango Enterprises! You who are come this day to do your homage, are you willing to accept him?"

The crowd roared its approval in response, though not without some booing.

"Your Grace, are you willing to take the oath?"

Ruke pulled a long face. "I am willing."

"Will you solemnly promise and swear to govern Korango and its Enterprises according to their respective laws and customs?"

"I solemnly promise so to do." Ruke swallowed.

"Will you, to your power, cause law and justice, in mercy, to be executed in all your judgments?"

Ruke proudly stated, "I will."

Usually, inauguration ceremonies continued for hours, but after the oath, the event's most spectacular part, the crowds thinned out. Ruke's inauguration was no exception. His acceptance speech following the oath didn't attract much attention. Korags, practical and cynical, didn't believe in promises. Talk about changes and plans for the future sounded boring. Besides, the second part of the ceremony included activities closed to the public—Ruke would be meeting city bureaucrats, shaking hands with the top business management, and signing countless papers.

Eli, Ash, and Yow, curious at the beginning, quickly lost interest in the spectacle. They congratulated themselves for declining Ruke's invitation to join his entourage. Instead, they stayed on the top balcony with few people around them. The location provided an excellent view of everything happening on the floor.

Ash leaned over the balcony parapet. "Look, Ruke again... and that woman in the green suit with a hair bun, dancing and dancing around him."

Yow glanced down. "That's Shyster, the Hunters' leader. She better dance before it's too late."

It surprised Eli. "Why? Does she want something from Ruke?"

"I don't know. Probably no more than anybody else. She's a good woman, if you ask me. It's all a big show today—the oath, the speeches, the handshakes, the hugs... Not my forte."

"Is this what happens every time the reins of power go to a new boss?" Eli asked Yow.

"Possibly—I'm not sure. It's my first time also."

Rey showed up and slapped Yow on the back. "Hey, buddy! Nice to see you." He stared at Ash and then at Eli. "Let me guess... our new friends from Terah?"

"Ash, Eli, this is my business partner, Rey." Yow didn't appreciate Rey's sudden arrival, but he played along as if nothing had happened. "Rey, Eli is a friend of Rurik's. And Ash is... well, Rurik's and Eli's friend too. Both are from Earth."

"Welcome to Korango! Terah, eh? The mother world isn't a planet we do business with here. But it's so nice to see new faces on the station." Rey turned to Eli. "To answer your question about inaugurations—no, today's not what usually happens. Organizers fell over themselves trying to please the new president. They borrowed all that malarkey from Terahn coronation rituals."

Rey looked at Ash. "And you, Ash…" He shifted position and wedged himself between Ash and Eli. "I've never seen a Terahn female, in life or picture. But must I say, it's so refreshing to meet such a beautiful woman."

Ash blushed. "Thank you! You're a real gentleman."

Eli rolled his eyes, and Yow tensed up. Rey changed the subject. "So, guys, how long have you been on Korango?"

Yow stepped in. "Two days."

"Yes, only two days, and I've enjoyed them!" Ash sounded apologetic as she added, "Korango is so exciting. I wish I had time to see more."

Rey forged ahead. "I volunteer to be your guide. For example, city hall. We have a great museum here, the best place to learn about the space station." Rey was clearly in his element, as he went on, "Truth be told, I helped put it together. Do you want to see it, guys? I swear—it won't take long."

"Now?" Ash asked.

"Sorry, man… I promised to join Ruke," Eli said. "Yow, are you coming with me?"

"Of course, *now*." Rey kept pushing. "We'll be back in time for the reception."

"Then let's go." Ash took Rey's arm and pulled him away.

Yow stood silently, making every effort to pretend nothing had happened.

Eli patted his shoulder. "Come on—they'll be back." He paused and decided to voice his opinion. "Honestly, man, why didn't you tell him to fuck off?"

Rey led Ash to the museum exhibit dedicated to Korango's early days. As he'd expected, they turned out to be the only visitors in the room. He stopped in front of a three-dimensional panorama of the city. "That's Korango as it was more than one thousand years ago. On a large scale, few things have changed. From this point, it looks almost the same now."

"You're a proud citizen."

"We're a tiny but powerful force in the Milky Way." Inspired by his own words, Rey continued, "Generations of people like myself accomplished all this. Few know that the station was built around a gigantic ice asteroid." Rey tapped the floor. "The core is still there."

"Your station is like a juicy tidbit for many in the galaxy, isn't it? Aren't you afraid that someone will find it irresistibly tasty?"

"I am." Rey fixed his gaze on Ash and decided to go *va banque*. "Unfortunately, the danger is even higher these days. More enemies, new ways of destruction. Stories about Strangers and their technology…"

"You've heard about the Game?"

"When someone can wipe you out by merely thinking about it? We would disable it if we knew its location, but the Game can be anyplace in our galaxy."

"It can be disabled?"

"Yes! We have a group of scientists who have developed a device to do so. It's small. Alas, its reach is limited."

"How far away?"

"I don't know exactly… probably within one Terrestrial mile."

Ash moved to another display and passed her hand through the holographic image. Streaks and smudges of light wrapped bizarrely around her hand. She swiped across the image, and the projection disappeared.

"Your city is beautiful. I wouldn't like it to be destroyed as I destroyed this image."

"Ash, this is a serious matter. Do you know something that can help us?"

"How does your device work?"

"Once in range, the device is triggered from the outside. It emits particles that render the weapon inoperable. Don't ask me what kind. It's beyond me."

Ash tapped her chin thoughtfully. "I think I know how to place it close to the Game. But I need to know that it won't hurt anything or anybody other than the weapon."

"You're a kind soul, Ash," Rey said gently. "I wish there were more people like you. People with heart. People who care. As for your question, I know for a fact that it was specifically designed not to hurt anything or anybody."

"I believe you. You should know that Yow expects a shipment of tessellate gravity mines here on Korango and will forward it to Coatera."

"Why are you telling me this?"

"You're invited to the reception today. It means you have connections. I'll help where I can. Use my information to track the cargo. If your emitter is small, you can hide it in the shipment before Yow gets it."

"Are you sure about the name of the bombs?"

"Yow mentioned that the 'tessellation' part makes the mines unique. I remember the word."

"Yeah... Probably we can intercept—"

Two visitors walked into the room. Rey leaned to Ash, and her hand slid into the comfortable crook of his elbow. "You have a brilliant mind, Ash. I don't know how to express my gratitude. This station will be indebted to you."

Rey and Ash moved out of the History Hall. Ash checked— nobody followed them. She pulled Rey even closer to her. "I'm doing what I believe is right. I'd like to keep this conversation between us. Coatera is one of Yow's customers, but he wants to close his eyes to how dangerous the Game is."

"His business sometimes clouds his mind. You can count on me!"

ELEVEN

FAMILY MATTERS

The inauguration reception didn't begin as Eli expected. A polite but adamant security officer stopped him at the checkpoint and ordered him to surrender his gun. Eli refused, and after a heated argument, the guards confined him in a detention cell at the city hall police station. It took half an hour and Shyster's intervention to resolve the issue. Zarfo Khoin, the security officer who had detained Eli, apologized sincerely but not profusely and explained that the latest ordinance prohibited guns at the reception. Eli didn't have any grudge against Zarfo, so they parted friends.

Ruke didn't want to start the party without Eli. Until the latter finally appeared in the banquet hall, the guests talked listlessly, wondering what was going on. When Ruke finally took a glass and tapped it with a spoon, they all looked at him with confusion on their faces. Glass-tapping was not something Korags did—they didn't understand that the real party was about to begin.

"Friends, colleagues, and partners! Please sit down," began Ruke. "To tell you honestly, I didn't want to start without my dear friend Eli, who's just come in." Ruke held out his hands to Eli. "My dear boy, please sit next to me."

Ruke clapped his hands, but only a few others responded, not showing any enthusiasm. The lack of fervor didn't bother him. "Now that we've gathered here in a less formal setting, I'd like to start this wonderful event by telling you all more about myself and by making some important announcements."

The guests squirmed on their chairs and grumbled.

Ruke put his hand up. "Don't worry, nothing dramatic. I hope you'll love what I'm about to say. First, I want to tell you that I like Korango. It has spirit! And my primary goal will be to uphold Korangan independence and its long-standing entrepreneurial traditions. Do you like my strategy so far?"

The room filled with cheers.

"I told you all you'd love it! We have many good customers, like the Elder Keep Alliance and the Intergalactic League. That's more than one thousand planets who want to work with us! But I'll not allow the powerful of the galaxy to dictate their will!"

"Long live the president!" someone yelled. The guests' faces beamed.

Ruke raised his hands, waiting for emotions to calm down. When euphoria subsided, he continued. "I'm a simple man, a Norseman, a man from the North... on my planet, that is. And I've seen a lot in my life. It was an honor to know Gavryn Jax, a great man with whom I once shared a prison cell when we were both kidnapped by rogue elements of the Elder Keep Alliance."

The gathering was dead quiet, with people hardly daring to breathe lest they miss a single word Ruke was saying. "And I want to share with you something not all of you may know. No sooner had I set foot on Korango than two assassination attempts were made on me. Good people saved me. One of them was Shyster. That's how I met her for the first time. Everybody knows her. Shyster, thank you!" Ruke looked at her and clapped his hands, and the room eagerly joined in. "The second time I was saved by Eli Stroud, my friend from Earth whom I already introduced. Today, both are here, sitting next to me, and I owe a debt of gratitude to each of them. Please raise your glasses to Eli and Shyster!"

All the guests stood up, drinking, cheering, and applauding.

Ruke again raised his hands. "Please, please... I promise—five more minutes, and I'll shut up." He paused, waiting for silence, then continued. "What happened tells me that we have a difficult task of rebuilding the rule of law in Korango. We want more business, but we must reject *unfair* business. We must also reject murder, theft, and fraud!"

Again, loud and lasting applause filled the room.

"Finally, I want to announce a few appointments. I hope you'll understand my reasons for making them. First, effective immediately, I appoint a new general counsel of Korango Enterprises, Mr. Tart Osso of the Korango Law Offices of Ournor and Company. Where is Mr. Osso?"

Tart Osso

"Sir... Mr. President, this is so unexpected. I'm flattered, but I have obligations. You see, my law company... Perhaps another time... I, Mr. President—"

"I thought you'd say that. Honest men like you always do. So I talked to your boss earlier today, and he doesn't mind. He said he'd

be honored if one of his leading men joins Korango Enterprises."
Ruke felt like a million bucks. "That's the good news for Tart. The
bad news is that he'll have to do all the paperwork quickly for
himself and my two other appointments!"

The gathering rolled with laughter. Tart Osso, a man who never
laughed, smiled shyly. "Indeed, indeed... Bad news like this...
That's good... Thank you, Mr. President. I won't let you down!"

Ruke continued, "Secondly, I've come to appreciate the role of
the Hunters Society. I think it's like a glue that holds Korags
together. To stress the importance of the Society, I appoint Shyster,
its leader, to the position of the Senior Vice President of Korango
Enterprises."

Shyster turned pale. Ruke leaned toward Shyster and offered his
hand. "I count on your help and wisdom, Shyster. Will you accept
the position?"

Shyster stood from her chair. "I don't know what to say... I
think... yes. I'd be crazy not to accept such an honor."

The banquet hall burst with frenzied applause. Ruke stood,
pleased, looking at his guests raving with joy.

"Guys, one more thing. Considering the recent attempts on my
life, and a series of crimes and other developments—classified for
the moment—I've decided to create a new executive office at
Korango Enterprises, the Korango Security Council. I appoint Elias
Stroud as its director, with authority to oversee the Korango
Defense Guard, Korango Police, and the Special Operations. He'll
consult with the senior vice president and will report directly to
me. What do you say, Eli?"

"Man, any time. I'm always glad to help you out."

Someone from the opposite side of the table shouted, "Is this
the guy who shoots without aiming?"

Eli frowned. "Whoa... Want a demo?" Eli got up and put his
hand on the pistol at his thigh.

"Eli, please, not here." Shyster was prompt to intervene.
"Remember, you still need to consult with me. At least once in a

while." Shyster laughed. She hugged Eli and whispered in his ear, "I'm glad Ruke has you."

"Just kidding, ma'am." Eli smiled. "The desire to improve myself never leaves me." He became serious and said under his breath, "Please take care of him."

Ruke decided to wrap up the formal part of the event. "Tart, we need to get together to discuss all the details regarding the new Korango Security Council. We'll begin with its structure and responsibilities. Please meet me first thing tomorrow at the corporate headquarters. And now, dear guests, let the party begin! Enjoy dinner. Let's have some fun!"

The second half of the banquet was even more successful, as Ruke showed an enviable ability to make a good impression. Participants enjoyed the relaxed atmosphere, and many of them approached Ruke, congratulating him and expressing their desire to work with him. Ruke greeted everybody with a firm handshake, smiling, making eye contact—projecting confidence and assertiveness.

Eli, who usually got bored quickly during events like this, felt perfectly comfortable among Korags—joking and even demonstrating his shooting moves to guests. Meanwhile, he kept an eye on Ash and Yow, who secluded themselves in a far corner of the room and talked without paying attention to anybody else.

After a few hours of enjoyment, the gaggle of guests finally dissipated. Only close friends and top city and company bureaucrats remained in the room. Rey was among them. He shook hands with Ruke and Shyster, glanced over at Yow and Ash still busy with themselves, and went up to Eli. "I've wanted to greet you the whole evening, but you're so popular... always surrounded by people."

"Yeah, I've been watching you too, Rey. So, what's the deal between you and Ash?"

"What do you mean, 'deal'?"

"You don't know what a deal is? It's an agreement, an arrangement, or a pact."

"I hear a disturbance in your voice, even aggression. Did I give you any reason for that?"

"You did. Do you think I didn't notice what you were doing on the balcony this morning?"

Ash pricked her ears up. Yow took her hand and said something in a low voice. She yanked her hand away and stood up. "That's none of your business, Eli!" she yelled from her corner. Yow immediately grabbed her by the shoulders and led her out of the room.

"Hear that?" Rey grinned and continued through his teeth, "I'm a free man. I do what I want. If you need a lesson in what that means, I can arrange it for you, boy."

"Boy? Hmm... That reminds me of someone. But I'll tell you this—if I see you one more time near Ash, the best that will happen to you is a long recovery in a hospital." Eli moved his face to Rey's, nose to nose as he uttered those words. Nobody could see him pulling his gun and sticking it deep into Rey's abdomen. "I'm not Yow. Remember this moment, and don't you dare forget it. All I need to do is pull the trigger, scum, and I will if I have to. Get out. Slowly. I want to see your hands at all times."

Rey spread his hands and stepped back. He was pale, shuddering with fear.

Shyster noticed the gun in Eli's hand. She took a handheld transceiver out of her handbag and held it up to her face, saying something. Then, quietly, she tugged Ruke's sleeve and nodded at Rey.

The expression on Ruke's face changed. He hurried over to Eli and Rey. "Eli, what are you doing? Is everything okay?"

"For the moment. No worries—I'm doing my job... boss." Eli waved his gun at Rey. "Get out of here!"

As Rey dashed out of the banquet hall, Zarfo Khoin burst in

with security officers, holding Eli at gunpoint. "Stand down! Slowly put your gun on the floor."

Eli turned to Shyster and pointed his gun at her. "Shyster, you're messing with things you don't understand," he explained in a calm voice. "I'm trying to be patient here. First, please try to appreciate my good will. Secondly, please tell Mr. Khoin and the other two to put their guns on the floor and slide them toward me."

Shyster didn't react. Nobody moved.

"Shyster, do as Eli says!" exploded Ruke.

"Zarfo, do as Eli says," she echoed.

The security guards slowly put their weapons on the floor and stepped back.

Eli moved to the guns and one by one kicked them into the far corner of the hall. "Shyster, I'm sorry to put you through this," he told the Hunter chief, "but I'm afraid this is the only way to straighten everything up once and for all. I want you to explain to the officers what happened."

Shyster remained silent. Eli raised his gun again, pointed it at her, and smiled. "Do you know why I'm smiling?"

She shrugged.

Eli holstered his gun. "Turn around."

Shyster looked back. Nox stood in the far corner of the banquet hall, next to the three guns on the floor, holding her at gunpoint.

"Okay, you win. Guys, Eli is your new boss."

"What about *your* actions, Shyster?" Eli insisted. "I'm not going to stop until we're on the same page."

"I overstepped my authority."

"Nox, thank you. Everything is under control now." Eli's voice sounded drab. With the same lack of excitement and interest, he added, "Mr. Khoin, and you two—sorry, I don't know your names —I hereby put you on paid leave. You'll be back on duty in two days. No adverse entry on your service records. It's a little time for you to relax and think about what happened here. Understood?"

"Yes, sir," the guards answered in chorus.

"Dismissed."

Ruke hurried to Eli and pulled him aside. "It probably wasn't a good idea to humiliate Shyster publicly."

"There was no public, if you noticed. Only people close to us. Be careful, Ruke. You don't know what happened to your predecessor, and Shyster is clueless about our involvement with the Game. Something odd is happening here. Do you remember what Ash told you about how she thinks you got the presidency? She's obsessed with the Game and its potentially bad effects. I don't like obsessed people. Rey spent two hours with her today while you were admiring the attention of your subordinates." Eli taunted, "Do you honestly think he's interested in her as a woman?"

"So he's a bad guy? For God's sake, he's a senior member of the Hunters Society Council!"

"I don't care who he is—I don't trust him. I want to stay alive, and I want you to stay alive too. I don't see Shyster as a bad person, but she comes across as ambitious and self-confident. She needs to decide where she is, whether that's with us or not."

"I'll talk to her. She's down-to-earth."

"I'm not her enemy. At least for now. Ruke, you know what to do. By the way, you were magnificent today, and during the dinner, you were a natural—impressive... and presidential. They loved you. I had no idea you could do all this."

"Thanks, I'm glad you liked it. Means a lot to me... So, what we are going to do with Rey?"

Eli looked around. Nox caught his glance and nodded in the direction of the door.

"Nox is waiting for me. I'm going to talk to her, and then we'll see. But I can tell you I'm going to Coatera, probably as soon as tomorrow. Aura's alone there. As far as Rey is concerned, he'll be under constant surveillance. All I can say."

"You want to ask Yow?"

"No. There's a chance Rey blindsided him. Besides, think about

Ash—Yow's biased, because he's developing feelings for her. Ruke, it's a game, the old kind. Nothing is what it seems."

"Okay, got it…"

"I have to run. I may not see you before I leave, but let's keep in touch. Use *Night Stalker*'s commsys if you need me." Eli left the banquet hall.

Nobody noticed how, after a minute, Nox also disappeared from the room.

Eli stood in front of Korango City Hall, on the other side of the street. As soon as he saw Nox, he followed her for a moment and caught up with her as soon as she turned the corner. "Finally, we talk," Eli said. "I'm glad to see you safe and in good health. How did you get away from Ab?"

"It's not that easy to explain. Briefly, Ab tried to bite off more than he could chew… Listen, there are some things I need to tell you, and it may be a long talk. Do you have time?"

They came out on a brightly lit square—the nightlife was in full swing in the city. A few passersby, barely glancing at Eli, stared at Nox. He couldn't help but notice as one of the men stopped and followed Nox with a long, salacious stare. "Nox, I don't feel comfortable with the way you look."

"Now *that's* a good way to start a conversation with a lady."

"No, no, that's not what I mean." Eli felt awkward. "You're an exquisite woman, but you attract a lot of attention."

"Ah… It's nice to hear that. On Gaia, men would never say that. Thank you!"

"That's not what I meant." Eli tried to clarify his statement but realized that it still didn't sound right. "Well, you *are* a gorgeous woman, and I'm sure… Okay, that's not what… The thing is, right now, that attention you're drawing isn't helpful." Eli's cheeks flushed with embarrassment. "I mean your suit… and everything…

Let's buy something for you. Something more, I don't know, Korango-like, you see? In the morning paper, they'll publish our pictures with comments. Maybe a sweatshirt and jeans or whatever the equivalent is here."

"I see. Interesting... Watching you ten minutes ago, I would never have thought you could talk like this. Come with me." Nox led Eli to a dark spot. "Tell me if you think this will be more appropriate." The contours of Nox's body blurred, and she almost disappeared for the moment, but soon materialized dressed in a black-and-white athletic jacket and gray sweatpants.

Eli gasped—he stood before Nox with his mouth agape.

"So?" Nox spun around.

"What the hell? Who are you? I've heard you're a cyborg, but you're flesh and blood, aren't you?"

"I am. There are no cogwheels or wires inside me." Nox grinned.

Eli pointed to the small implants on her face. "What about those two things?"

"Cognitive augmentation devices. They are common on Gaia, though most Gaians prefer to hide them. But I like the way they look on me. Like jewelry, aren't they?"

Eli stretched his neck to better see her face and confirmed cautiously, "Uh... Look cute..."

"Let's find a place to talk," suggested Nox, and moved ahead. Eli followed. She piped up, "It's not entirely true, but the best way for us to interact is for you to think of me as the Game itself."

"The *Game*?"

"It's complex, far more complex than a human body or any other organic or non-organic thing known in the universe. I represent the Game and control it, but right now, it's more important for you to understand who *you* are."

"What do you mean?"

"Have you ever thought about why you could open the Gamer sanctuary on Earth? And before you, your father?"

"You mean when Yow couldn't?"

"Did he try?"

"He did, but I thought I only found the right way to touch that Y thing..."

"So Aura didn't tell you anything?"

"Aura tried to kill me when I went through the Gamer."

"Aura is almost as good a shooter as you are. If she'd wanted you dead, you'd be dead, trust me. And now she's trying to protect you from the Gaian authorities, risking her reputation and more."

"My mom pushed her hand with the gun. I saw it."

Nox said flatly, "Eli, if she didn't tell you, I will. You are genetically a Gaian."

"Riiiight... And you're Marilyn Monroe because your space garb was merely a trick."

"I'm sure Marilyn Monroe is someone well-known on Earth. But you *are* a Gaian. Officially. Genetically and, because of this, also legally—by Gaian laws. Whether or not you want it."

"Well, what do you know?" Eli stopped, blinking dumbly.

"Yow was the first who found out, after analyzing your blood. He then told Aura about his discovery. Aura did her research and confirmed his conclusion."

"Wow... So I'm screwed now?"

"Screwed?" Nox sounded puzzled. "What does that have to do with what I've said?"

"The Gaians are after me. But at least *before*, they could cut me some slack cause I'm a fucking alien idiot who was at the wrong place at the wrong time. Now they'll prosecute me to the fullest extent of their law, even though my family has been on Earth forever, and we thought we were Earth human all this time."

"That's an interesting way of looking at this."

They passed a dimly lit, seedy tavern with few customers. Nox gave it a nod. "Let's go in—I'm hungry."

"You eat?" asked Eli.

"You think I feed myself with my own saliva? I told you I'm a human being."

Eli pouted sullenly.

"Sorry." Nox went on, "I can find other ways to get the nutrients my body needs, but I prefer regular food. I like its taste."

The tavern wasn't bad. The muted music, which sounded something like perky jazz played only on woodwinds, was loud enough to keep conversations private. Nox led Eli to an empty table in the corner. "I'm paying. What do you want?"

"A beer, a big one, if they have them here."

"Two beers, large!" shouted Nox.

They sat silently until the waiter plunked two beer steins in front of them. Eli sipped. "Go ahead—I'm listening."

"What makes you even more… special is that part of your DNA matches the one found in ancient Gaians. Some call it 'pure blood.' But because of a mutation, there are few Gaians who still have it."

"I'm an ancient Gaian? That's quite a different matter," Eli smirked. "Aren't *you* full of surprises?"

Nox ignored Eli's sarcasm and continued. "Actually, it is. There's a theory that the Game itself caused the mutation. The importance of such DNA lies in the fact that the machine checks for the 'pure blood' presence before granting access to make changes to its design. Some believe its creators implemented a feedback mechanism for the Game to influence its own evolution since it cannot modify itself. The change is slow. It takes thousands of years for the mutation to take effect. Still…"

Eli brightened. "You created a monster, and now it's getting rid of you. Nice!"

"It's more likely that the more time passes, the more the Game doesn't want to be changed. We can destroy it at any time. No special DNA is required to do that."

"Then what's the problem? Sit and enjoy the ride. When you get the itch, kill it."

"That's not Gaian nature—not much different from Terahn. We

rely on the Game—all the time, each and every Gaian. We'll never give up the Game."

"Sorry, I still don't see the problem."

"There are two. Some Gaians like the *status quo*. Others want to change the Game—either to make it more powerful and capable or, vice versa, less powerful, because even in its current form, it corrupts people."

"Does it?"

"It seems so. What do you think will happen to you with unlimited instant gratification, Eli? No doubt, there are still those who want to evolve, but the social changes, like the spread of apathy, are difficult to ignore at this point."

"Whatever... Look, I'm sorry, but I don't care. If there are problems, they aren't mine. What can I, Eli Stroud, do about Gaians? Who, incidentally, are after me."

"I haven't finished. I completed the full analysis of your DNA, and I found something else. I tested it and I re-tested it. Your DNA is not mutable. At this point, I'm not sure if this marker is inheritable. Probably, yes. I haven't seen anything like it before."

"I see... I'm the One. Shit!" he spat.

"I don't know what that means, but someone like you will always be able to evolve the Game. So those who don't want any change will try to get rid of someone like you. Those who want the change will try to make sure you're on their side. Inevitably, your life will be affected in some way. But there's one more thing... Earth."

"You think—"

"Both sides will fix their eyes on Earth. Those who will try to get rid of your kind will be most dangerous—they'll try to make sure there's no one else like you on Earth."

Eli sat dumbfounded. He didn't know what to say.

"If you have questions, ask," said Nox.

"So, everything you told me is true?"

"Good. I see progress."

"Who knows about it? I mean the 'One' thing."

"You and I."

"Now, you're the Game. What do you, the Game, think about all this? What do you want?" Eli demanded. "Though I have to assume that you may not be totally honest with me."

"I'm always honest with you. You may doubt it, but it doesn't matter. The Game can't harm anybody in and of itself. That's the heart of its design. This feature cannot be removed or disabled without destroying the Game. The machine can be used indirectly to harm people by creating weapons, but that's no different from many other things people do. You're from Earth—you know that. You know the ethical arguments associated with such things. But the Game leaves ethical considerations to the Gaian authorities. And there are laws—as you discovered recently—which make it exceedingly difficult for Gaians to misuse the Game."

"Authorities? Nice! But what about me?"

"I came to *you*, didn't I?" Nox pointed out.

"But that's today. What about tomorrow? Am I going to find you on the other side of the fight one day, if it comes to fighting?"

"Eli, I don't know what will happen tomorrow. I can't even conjecture. If it comes to a moral choice, the Game has an obligation to ask the Gaian authorities. Gaians with markers can change the Game. The stronger the marker is, the more significant that person's voice is for the Game. You have the strongest marker known. Hence, the reason I'm talking to you. It would be disappointing if you let me down."

"So, we have a kind of alliance?"

"Call it what you want. But don't forget what I said—only when it comes to a moral choice. Otherwise, the Game's job is straightforward."

"I understand. Is it okay if we keep everything that has been said today between us?"

"That's my intention. Well, Aura and Yow already know something about your DNA. But I won't tell anybody that your Game controlling marker is invariable."

"Thanks. For your information, I'm going to Coatera tomorrow. I feel that Aura is in danger. I don't like Rey... and this thing with Ash. I don't think Ab will give up so easily."

"You're not the first who's talked about Rey."

"Who else?"

"Interestingly, Yow. He told Aura about him. Aura told me."

"I feel better already. Thank you, Nox, for everything, especially for today's conversation. I need to think it over." Eli got up but immediately sat back down. "I have another question."

"Go ahead."

"When I met you the first time, on Earth, you said you knew my father. What happened?"

"I wanted to help him. But he wished poorly."

"What did he want?"

"He wanted to get out of the cave—literally. And I granted his wish. I saw something in him, so I provoked him into going through the Gamer, the remote interface. But I cannot tell people what to wish, nor can I trigger the implementation. That's my curse... or a blessing. Depends on how you look at it."

"I see... What about Ruke?"

"You mean his presidency of Korango?"

"Yes. He went through the Gamer."

"His presidency is legitimate. He saved Gavryn Jax's life in prison. The Game had nothing to do with it."

"But the Game did *something*..."

"Yes. It filled his flask with whiskey. Still a crime on Gaia, though."

"That's it? Huh. Your ancients knew what they were doing." Eli got up and left the tavern. *I wanted an interesting life... I should be careful what I wish for.*

TWELVE

FRIENDS AND FOES

E li's commsys chimed. "Hi, Yow. Whassup?"
"I've heard you're going to Coatera?"
"Amen."

"I have a delivery for Aura, but the freight is too bulky for my space striker. Can you do me a favor and take the crates that don't fit in my cargo bay? I'll take care of the rest."

"When do you leave?"

"This evening."

"Fine, what's your dock?"

"Yellow Zone, Bay 10."

"I'll meet you there with *Night Stalker*."

"Thanks."

"No problem, see you later." Eli disconnected the call and punched in another number. "Mr. Zarfo Khoin? Elias Stroud here… Yes, your new boss. I need to talk to you. Where do you live?… Good. Do you have a flyer parking nearby?… Then I'll pick you up. … How about half an hour?… See you then."

~

Eli hadn't previously visited the sector where Zarfo lived. He arrived early and flew over the area. Not affluent, but not a ghetto, it was one of those places where people just lived, getting by with their everyday routine—on a slow burn, without being noticed or punished or praised, and making little impression on other people's hearts and minds.

Eli noticed Zarfo Khoin from afar. Stocky, with a military bearing, he stood motionless, waiting in a parking lot. Eli landed in front of him and opened the door.

"Mr. Stroud, good afternoon."

"Please, get in."

Zarfo didn't hesitate. He looked sure of himself and sat down without asking questions. He glanced at Eli and buckled his safety harness.

Eli took off and put the flyer on autopilot to circle over a remote area of the city. He kept silent, and his passenger didn't seem to mind. *Can I trust this guy? I know nothing about him. But I need to start somewhere. Okay, whatever happens, happens.* He started with something entirely unrelated. "Call me Eli."

"Nice to meet you, Eli. I'm Zarfo."

"Are you a Korango native?"

"Oh, no. There are few natives here. I'm from Fliria, came here twenty-five years ago."

"Fliria?"

"It's a small agricultural planet seventy-five light-years from here."

The man was tight with his information, Eli noticed. "Tell me more about yourself."

"Not much to tell. We're mostly farmers. Fliria has good soil and plenty of rainfall, and we've learned how to produce various crops. That wasn't my thing, though. Parents died. One of my neighbors knew someone on Korango, so I moved. I quickly found a job as a police officer." Zarfo was calm and spoke with confidence, without any attempt to impress Eli or gain his attention.

"You've spent all your time here as a policeman?"

"Well, I first joined the city police force, but I was quickly offered a position as an investigator at the Enterprise's security office. It didn't last long." Zarfo smiled.

"What happened?"

"I took my job too seriously. Probably was overzealous. Went too far, I guess. Not what my bosses wanted. So they moved me to the security detail. It's all in my record." Zarfo clarified quickly, "But I'm not complaining."

Interesting. It seems he's telling the truth. I wonder, is there anything that's not in his record? "Did they want you to cover something up?"

"Something like that. Fliria isn't part of any alliance, and Flirians are like Korags, independent-minded. Not as rich, though. But I learned my lesson." Zarfo smiled again. "Nothing remarkable."

"I couldn't help but notice how readily you followed Shyster's orders yesterday. She isn't your boss."

"I'm sorry, sir. I acted as I would have, you know... Before the new president..."

"Please, no 'sir.' So, Shyster used to control the Enterprise?"

"If in black in white terms, then yeah, pretty much."

Eli cocked an eyebrow at the officer. "Do you know who killed Gavryn Jax?"

"No," Zarfo bit out. Eli gave him the once-over, and Zarfo continued reluctantly, "Well... There are rumors Shyster did it, but I don't believe them. No evidence, but there are people around here who stir up trouble, constantly muddying the waters."

"People like who?"

Zarfo hesitated before saying, "Like the fellow you put in his place yesterday."

"Rey Fliek?"

Zarfo nodded shortly.

He is a straight shooter. But afraid of Rey? Why? "Does Rey have much support among the Hunters?"

"I don't think so. It's more like they're afraid of him."

"Well, I don't want to play hide-and-seek with you, Zarfo. The reason you're here is that I want you to lead the investigative team at Korango Enterprises. Are you interested?"

Zarfo didn't respond. A healthy dose of skepticism appeared on his face.

Zarfo Khoin

"You'll report to me," Eli said. "I'll never ask you to cover up any wrongdoing. You'll have a team—it'll be up to you to propose candidates—you'll have plenty of funds and equipment, and most importantly, you'll have the authority to deal with people like Rey, and, if necessary, to use lethal force. Nothing more. As it's spelled out in Korango criminal and prosecutorial laws. Does it sound better now?"

"It does. I'll do it. But what about the cool-off leave of absence?" Zarfo deadpanned.

Eli sniggered. "It's a smokescreen. I want you to start immediately. The paperwork has already been filed and signed by Ruke Cavell. At this moment, only three individuals know about it—the president, you, and I. Oh, and Tart Osso. So four people. It's essential to keep it that way, at least for the moment. Is that clear?"

"Yes."

"For outsiders, I'd like you to continue with your current job—but much closer to the president, kinda like his senior bodyguard. Ruke knows. That'll give you some freedom and help conceal your new responsibilities. Your stipend will be much higher."

"What's my first assignment?" Zarfo's tone betrayed a touch of eagerness for his new job.

"To keep an eye on Rey Fliek."

Zarfo nodded, unsurprised.

Eli continued, "I want to know if he has any connections to the Elder Keep Alliance. I can give you a lead—Abaddon or Ab, Chief of Special Ops at the Elder Keep's Security Chancellery. I'll send you a photo. He may be currently on Korango. I'm assuming you have street cameras and facial recognition software, since we have them on Earth, and you're centuries ahead of us technologically. Go through all the new street surveillance footage. If you find something, let me know immediately, any time, day or night."

Eli paused, thinking for a moment. "Secondly, start monitoring shipments—anything originating from Gaia and other planets in its domain. You'll get all the assistance to do that—let me know what you need. Plus, keep an eye on anything going to the Elder Keep. Recruit agents and assets familiar with this type of job. For the moment, hold back from searching cargo, unless there's a legal basis to do so. Procure specialized equipment for scanning all the cargo I mentioned. Most importantly, study the Intergalactic Game Treaty. Korango is a party to it, and we have legal obligations to fulfill."

"I see where you want to go."

"Please make sure that your interest in the Game remains

unnoticed. It's top secret. Keep in mind, the job I'm asking you to do is dangerous. Questions?"

"How we are going to communicate?"

"For the moment, via your personal commsys and the commsys on my ship. I'll send you all necessary contact info. Get the system with the strongest encryption you can find—money's no object. For all money matters, talk to Tart Osso. I won't be on Korango for the next few days. But through my ship's commsys, you can get immediate access to me."

"Sir... Eli, I won't let you down."

"I hope you won't. I'm putting a lot of trust in you, so if you do, that would be disappointing. Remember, in my absence, you'll be the highest security authority on the station."

Eyes wide, Zarfo stated, "I didn't realize that. It's a great responsibility."

"Yeah, but please don't play police chief. I need a spy."

"I understand."

"Good. I'll take you to the spaceport. You'll have to take a taxi to get home—sorry for the inconvenience. I wish you luck."

The spaceport security and landing control systems on Coatera Cela immediately recognized *Night Stalker* and directed his and Yow's ships to the landing platform near *Sheleucia*, Aura's battle-cruiser.

The space station looked different than previously, with only a few lights and two drones active. The drones hurried to the docked ships and started pulling metal crates from cargo bays, stockpiling them near the cruiser. Yow's cargo, fifty large boxes sealed with metal latches, was unmarked. Hippa, who usually avoided Cela's spaceport, prowled between the containers, growling and sniffing around the shipment.

"What's inside these?" Eli came closer to a box and patted it.

The packing case responded with a hollow sound. "Wait, are they empty?"

"I'm sorry, that's privileged information protected under Korangan law." Yow pretended to be checking the latch seals to avoid Eli's eyes.

Eli scowled. "Yow, please understand," he began, trying to be gentle. "The cargo came from Korango, the jurisdiction I'm now in charge of protecting. If you don't want to tell me, I'll respect Aura's rights as your client. But for your information, all shipments to Gaian territories and of Gaian origin will be inspected from now on."

This galled Yow. "Tell that to Aura," he snapped. "You can ask her what's inside."

"Come to think of it, where is she? Shouldn't she have met us here?"

"Probably in the control room. What did you expect her to do? Come and throw her arms around you?"

"Ouch!" Eli shook his head in disbelief and left. As Yow had guessed, he found Aura working in Cela's control room.

Indeed, she didn't show any joy when Eli came in. She broke away from her work and said, surprised, "Eli! What are you doing here?"

I came to help you. What else? I worry about you! "I... I thought you might need help."

Aura swiped in the air with her hand, and a holoprojection of the spaceport sprang to life above her desk. One of the droids was visible on *Night Stalker's* ramp, slowly moving a crate onto the deck. The droid could barely keep the box from sliding down the slope.

Interesting. That one looks heavy as hell. I thought they were easy to lift.

"Ah, you helped Yow with the shipment. Thanks!"

"I've heard you're moving the Gamer somewhere. You know, I thought you were alone on the station."

"That's very nice of you, but I'm fine. I have everything I need. How have you been? Ruke?"

"Busy—he's the president now. Officially, I help him with security."

"Seriously?" She sounded nonplussed.

"Not a lot of confidence in your question, was there?"

"Sorry, I didn't mean—"

"Mean what? Aura, I'm concerned about your safety. What's in those boxes? Are you sure you can trust Yow?"

She frowned. "Are you trying to set me against him? I've known Yow for years—unlike you. What would it be now? A week? Two?"

"Think whatever you want. I don't doubt Yow, but he's not working in a black hole. There's Ash... Did you know that Ash is consumed with the Game? With how dangerous the Game is? And then there are his partners. Did he tell you that Rey the Fox is one of them? And that Rey spent several hours with Ash two days ago, and nobody knows what they talked about? Do you know that Yow fell head over heels for Ash and has apparently lost his ability to reason? They sleep together! And I'm his worst enemy now because I don't like this sudden Ash-Rey alliance!"

"Eli, stop—"

"I, for one, suspect that Rey is connected to Ab, and don't shush me, please."

"I appreciate your concerns, but Eli... Honestly, you sound rather paranoid. I'm aware of Rey. I even told Nox about him. I'm safe here. You can't even imagine what firepower *Sheleucia* can bring to bear. It's all new to you. Look, I understand your need to prove yourself—"

"Now, you stop! You think I'm paranoid, but I'm telling you something is going on. You don't need me? Fine. You don't want me here? Even better. I'll go back tomorrow. To prove myself." *What are things coming to? Wow... I came here because Yow asked me to help with the cargo?! I don't give a hoot about Yow!*

Eli took a breather and got hold of himself. "Sorry for the

outburst. I must be tired, but I'm done here. Can I stay at the refuge on Coatera for the night?"

"Yes. But Eli, you're misinterpreting—" Aura didn't finish, as Eli had already hurried out of the control room.

Eli threw *Night Stalker* into a nosedive. Plasma flashes wrapped around the ship, but the space fighter held her own nicely through the brutal entry into Coatera's atmosphere. Through *Night Stalker's* neural interface, he felt her particle intakes increasing their absorption rate and replenishing the reserve of what Eli called *dull matter*.

He had no clue about its physical nature. Eli perceived it through the neural interface as a gray, heavy, sticky mass in a state of constant flux, like a dark dough changing shape, swelling, and shrinking. The only practical thing Eli understood about the dull matter was that the Game used it as the primary raw material for its quantum conversions. Yes, the Game had created his ship as its own miniature, albeit with limited capabilities. But that was precisely the reason for *Night Stalker's* versatility and power.

Eli's rapid descent didn't leave much time for thinking, but he already knew he wouldn't stay at the refuge. Instead, he turned to the Temple of Emerala and landed nearby.

It was already late on this part of Coatera. At first, Eli wanted to illuminate the grassland in front of the temple with the fighter's searchlights but quickly changed his mind—it would be an abomination to violate the planet's purity by invading it with modern technology like that. *Night Stalker's* presence was bad enough. He got out of the ship with a low-tech flashlight in his hand.

The dark bulk of the temple against the background of the twilight sky seemed mysterious and menacing. Eli took several careful steps. After the enclosed spaces of Korango and Coatera Cela, the vastness of Coatera appeared intimidating. He shivered, hunched, and then turned off the flashlight.

Coatera rotated faster than Earth, and night had already descended on the Temple's continent. The light of Alderamin reflected by Cela flooded the meadow like moonlight on Earth. Eli noticed the sounds—the chirring and whirring of insects, the murmuring of the wind, the babbling of a stream... And the aromas—the gummy bouquet of the meadow and the woody smell of nearby trees rushed to his head like wine.

He looked up. A swarm of Coatera's version of fireflies fluttered around him. The stars—myriads of them arranged in unfamiliar constellations—flickered and glimmered, under a glowing, silver arch that swirled across the sky. It dawned on Eli. *It's the Milky Way. Beautiful!*

He stepped back in awe, and his legs tangled in the thick vegetation. Eli squatted, taking in the night-blooming grasses and plants that surrounded him. After a little thought, he picked a beautiful bunch of flowers. *Just what I need!*

The night and the temple became familiar and friendly. Eli squared his shoulders and walked inside. He found his mother's sarcophagus. To his surprise, flowers covered its lid. As far as he could tell, they were fresh, arranged merely a day or two before. *Who did this? Aura?*

Eli carefully cleared a place for his bouquet and put the flowers atop the tomb. He bowed his head and stood there, crying silently. As if worried that someone would see his tears, he turned around and rushed out of the temple.

A moment later, *Night Stalker* soared into the sky. She flashed like a bright star and disappeared. Eli was headed for Korango.

The next morning, Aura woke up with a vague feeling of guilt and remorse. Remembering her brief conversation with Eli, a wave of uneasiness washed over her, even more so after she asked Yow in passing about Eli's motivation to come to Coatera.

He was worried about me—justified or not. I could at least have shown some gratitude.

Aura glanced at a timepiece. *It's not even dawn on Coatera.*

She slipped from the bed and, in a matter of minutes, was on her way to the refuge. Five more minutes in her flyer and her face fell when she saw no traces of *Night Stalker* in the proximity of the building.

Aura landed. It didn't take long to realize that Eli had never set foot in the place. She established a connection to Cela's control center and fired up its sensor array. There was no sign of Eli's ship anywhere on or near Coatera. *Where is he? Did he leave in a fit of anger? Aura was saddened by the thought. How could I let him go?* She was suddenly petrified. *What's happening to me? Oh, my God... Am I falling for him? For this guy? A Terahn?*

She sat for a while, trying to understand her feelings. *I am... Actually, there's nothing wrong with this guy. Deep inside, he's like a helpless, cute kitten—especially without his gun.* Aura smiled. *Right... without.*

Her fingers ran through the flyer's control surface, and it darted in the air to make an almost hundred-mile jump and alight in front of the Temple of Emerala.

Make a wish. And if he was here... Aura checked the sensor array logs. *Night Stalker* had landed near the temple the previous evening —*yes, he was!* A new day was dawning, crisp and bright. Fresh human footprints leading to the temple through the tall grass without a doubt belonged to Eli.

Slowly, Aura followed his steps, treading on the footprints he had left. She played an innocent game in her mind. *Here he jumped through a gully...* she leaped, trying to mimic Eli's imaginary jump. *Here Eli crouched picking flowers!* Looking around at the blooming meadow, she stopped and took in the glorious sight.

Her simple game revived her confidence. She entered the temple and went to Sarah's final resting place—a new, fresh bouquet lay on the sarcophagus cover. Aura got down on a knee in front of the tomb. *I pray we'll see each other again soon. I know we can do better. Please—I know I can do better. Please, I need you.*

Aura stood up and looked through Eli's flowers. She chose a full bud of a beautiful *felarus* bloom, pinched off the stem, and put it in her hair. "Forgive me, but I'm taking something of yours. I hope you don't mind," she said, setting her hand on the sarcophagus stone.

When Aura returned to Cela, she was in for a surprise. Slun Ceabb, a supervising agent of the Bureau of Development, Research, and Contacts—and, most notably, Aura's ex-boyfriend—met her at the station.

Almost a year had passed since obscurity had veiled their relationship. They used to spend a lot of time together, and the many thousands of light-years between Coatera and Gaia hadn't impacted their desire to see each other. Things had changed when Slun joined the Bureau and began to advance in his career. He disappeared from Aura's life. He didn't even contact her occasionally to remind her of his existence. By then, Aura didn't care. She stopped thinking about him—nothing called Slun to mind.

When Aura saw his ship docked in Cela's spaceport, she refused to admit any possibility that Slun had come to restore their broken relationship. Instead, she immediately linked his visit to the recent events and, in particular, to her conversation with Ronda, the Commissioner of the GAME. *Did Ronda double-cross me and decide to take action on Eli? No, I know her. This must be something else.*

Aura found Slun in a mess hall. Full of dignity, he lounged in an armchair, talking to Yow. When he saw Aura, he jumped to his feet and threw his hands up. "Look at you! Damn, you're gorgeous!"

Aura managed an artificial half-smile and, instead of coming into Slun's wide-open arms, went to get a glass of juice at a food synthesizer. To fill the silence, Slun kept talking. "I missed you so much! Work, always work... The government! Truth be told, I finally said enough is enough. I told them, 'I'm going to see Aura, come hell or high water!'"

She didn't react. Why bother? To verify her feelings, she took her time to inspect Slun. He looked like his usual self—a face-man, about as dull as a shining pan can be—sparkling blue eyes, dazzling smile that showed rows of white teeth, a cheeky face, and the usual side-part haircut with hair long enough for side-swept bangs. Aura had always hated these bangs and the way he wore them, strutting around like a bantam rooster—the cock of the village.

As far as Aura could remember, Slun had always looked much younger than he was. Even today, well into his thirties, he projected something boyish and immature. His white toga with its red stripe, typical for a high-ranking Gaian official, couldn't give Slun an imposing appearance. The elaborate, massive brooch securing the toga and displaying the letters DRC—the official designation of the Bureau and the acronym for the words Development, Research, and Contacts—didn't add appeal to his callow image either.

"Aren't you going to say something?" Slun didn't want to give up.

Aura winced. *Why couldn't I see what he was?*

Yow stood up. "I have to go. I forgot—I need to check some equipment before tomorrow's test."

"No, please stay. And you, Slun—what are you doing on Coatera?"

"I already told you—"

"Stop it, Slun, just stop it. Go back home, okay?"

"I expected a friendlier greeting..." Not getting any reaction from Aura to his last words, Slun went on, "Can I at least help you?"

"With what?" smirked Aura.

"Well, you're moving the Gamer. I can help make sure that

everything… works."

Yow cut in, "Yes, Mr. Ceabb wanted to inspect *Sheleucia*. He said—"

Rage distorted Aura's face. "What? Inspect? You're not even allowed to be on Cela when I handle the Gamer."

"I can call my boss. He"—Slun pointed to Yow—"is here, and he's a nobody."

"How rude! Yow passed the background check, and the commission authorized him to perform certain work in connection with the Gamer. Speaking of which—does *Ronda* know about your visit to Cela?"

Slun avoided Aura's eyes. "Look, I'm a DRC agent, I—"

"Commission Directive 244GR, section 5, I quote, 'prohibits, without prior authorization issued by the Commission of the GAME, approaching the Gamer and/or any Game-related equipment closer than five thousand feet when the Gamer and such equipment is being transported. Lethal force can be used to enforce the directive.' Is that clear?"

Slun puffed out his chest, straightened his posture, and declared loudly, "I'll show you and your Eli who's who, and who's in charge here! I won't let this stand!"

Aura shot a stony glare at her former boyfriend and turned to Yow. "Yow, please escort Mr. Ceabb to his ship. You have my permission to use deadly force if necessary."

Selecting Zarfo Khoin as the head investigator of the newly created Korango Security Council turned out to be an excellent idea. Zarfo knew the job and, after the security guard's simple routine, eagerly went back to the thrill of investigating criminal activities, gathering facts, working with witnesses, surveilling suspects, wiretapping, and analyzing crime scenes.

At first, he was skeptical about Eli—too young, inexperienced—

Zarfo had had nothing but trouble dealing with people like him in the past. However, he appreciated the confidence Eli placed in him. Zarfo wanted to do his best to justify his trust. Besides, he liked the clarity and sense of direction in the first tasks assigned to him. After many years in the force and a good deal of life experience, he felt that Eli's requests had to do with serious matters. Zarfo zealously took up his duties.

He ordered a dozen fellow police officers he trusted most to follow Reynard Fliek. Zarfo also created surveillance posts with cameras and electronic equipment to monitor the data traffic near his home and lab and wire-tapped both. Results were not long in coming. The next morning, Rey was spotted meeting with someone whose true identity remained unknown for the moment. Zarfo deemed the individual's credentials to be faked, and their origins had not yet been determined.

On four occasions, Rey sent and received long-distance communications using his own equipment. They were encrypted with a code that Zarfo's team couldn't decipher. The whereabouts of the message senders remained unknown. Based on the properties of the transmission streams, Zarfo suspected that at least two locations were involved, with one of them moving—probably a spaceship.

Zarfo himself started inspecting all cargo and related documentation passing through Korango, and not in vain. The discovery of a mysterious consignment in one of the local warehouses turned out to be the most important event during Eli's absence. It all started with the type of bill of lading, a carrier's acknowledgment of receiving cargo for shipment, uncommon for Korango trading practices. It attracted the attention of Zarfo's watchful eye.

On Earth, such a document would be classified as the "order bill of lading" used to ship merchandise *prior* to payment, thus requiring a carrier to deliver the merchandise to the importer. As is often the case, there was no named consignee in the paper. But a closer look at the document revealed some disturbing signs.

Although the carrier had previous business with Korango, the actual shipper was unknown on the space station. The exporter was also an unknown party, located, according to the bill of lading, on planet Slorix in Star System CO645. Zarfo had never heard of either designation, but a quick search revealed that the planet was an independent territory. Feeling that he was onto something, Zarfo kept digging and found that Slorix had a free-association agreement with Gaia.

The bill of lading listed "The Candid Packer," located on Eyphus, the capital planet of the Intergalactic League, as the importer. Being true to himself, Zarfo immediately contacted the League's authorities, but except for the address, he couldn't get any information on the business. That discovery didn't surprise Zarfo. Korango had little incentive to follow even its own regulations, with loose rules regarding export-import operations. However, specific instructions from Eli made Zarfo put aside his analysis of the paper trail and visit the depot for personal inspection of the twelve crates listed in the documentation.

When he got to the warehouse and found the cargo, he had to verify the markings and codes twice to make sure that the crates were the shipment referenced by the documents. The boxes turned out to be much heavier than specified. Zarfo tried to move one of them, but the crate didn't budge—it weighed much more than the hundred pounds stated in the cargo's description.

He ran his eyes over the interior of the warehouse—it had multiple levels of storage spaces and various catwalks, staircases, and machinery for lifting and moving cargo. Electronic terminals to access cargo and shipment databases were scattered throughout the floor. Zarfo noticed one stand with firefighting equipment—an ax, a sledgehammer, block splitters, and a couple of firehoses. Thinking about what he was going to do next made him feel warm and happy.

He took the ax from the fire station, returned to the unusual shipment and, with two swift movements, hacked off the latch seals on the container he'd tried to move earlier. Several more strikes and the lid of the crate fell onto the floor, revealing something dark inside. Zarfo rechecked the records. It listed "laser cannons and related equipment" as the contents. He fumbled in the box and threw off the top layer of the packaging. What he saw was *not* a laser cannon.

All such weapons had a few recognizable common elements, but none had a barrel. The thing in the box boasted a prominent one. It reminded Zarfo of an old-style projectile cannon he'd seen somewhere in a history book. It was massive, made of black metal. *This thing alone weighs at least three hundred pounds!*

He took another look at the weapon. The walls of the barrel seemed unusually thick, and its material looked strange. It was definitely metal, but with an unusual oily and glittering texture. *That's like the cannon from Eli's ship,* Night Stalker. *She has four of them exactly like this!*

Zarfo put the lid back and cleaned up the debris from his break-in, then called one of his aides. "I need you guys at the Red warehouse... Spaceport... Yes, now. We need to watch the cargo in Aisle 420, Bay 6, twenty-four seven... Twelve crates... It's a precise job. If someone shows up for the cargo, detain them. I'll wait for you at the warehouse."

Eli received Zarfo's report about his unusual findings in the warehouse while still on his way to Korango. He checked his navigation controls—less than one hour until his ETA. He immediately opened a private communication channel to Ruke. "We need to talk."

Ruke, in Korango-style formal attire—a frock coat and amber shirt—looked presidential on the commsys screen.

"I'm in the middle of something. Can it wait?"

"I need a word with you in private. It's super-urgent."

"Okay, do you need Shyster?"

"Ahhh…" Eli hesitated. "You know… yes. She'd be helpful."

"I'll transfer your call to my office and get back to you." The commsys screen went dark and, after a minute or so, lit up again. "Go ahead," Ruke said. "This link's encrypted."

"I've received a report from Zarfo Khoin. He found contraband in a warehouse at the port, or, at least, I think that's what it is. Gaian stuff. Covered by the Intergalactic Game Treaty, I believe."

"It's that serious?"

"I suggest you see for yourself and make an executive decision on what to do with the cargo."

"When and where?"

"Warehouse Red in an hour. Zarfo will meet you at the entrance."

"Good. See you there."

As soon as Eli ended the call, a loud clamor erupted from the aft compartment of *Night Stalker*. He whipped out his gun and crept to the bulkhead dividing the rear section from the cockpit. To his surprise, the door to the ship's utility bay at the end of the aft section was ajar with several boxes of supplies scattered nearby. One of them was torn open, and a white powder had poured out of it and spilled all over the place. In the middle of that mess, smeared with the same dusty stuff, sat Hippa, trying to clean her forehead, eyes, and ears with her paw.

"What are *you* doing here?" demanded Eli, putting his gun back into its holster.

She growled and hissed. If he could read her mind or understand what she was saying, it would be something like, *"I wasn't sure you'd agree to take me with you. So, while you were arguing with Aura, I hid in that terrible place over there with little space to sleep comfortably. And then I patiently waited until it was too late for you to return to get rid of me. And now, so that you understand how humiliating all this is, I'm going to clean myself for real!"*

The end of her talk coincided with the moment Eli approached

Hippa. She stood up on all four paws, spread them for a better balance and, with the violent movement of her whole body, shook off the powder covering her. A good deal of the white substance relocated onto Eli. He yelled, "You stowaway! You did that on purpose! In the shower!"

"Now you're talking!" chuffed Hippa. She walked around Eli and meowed, *"Let's go together. Can you rub my back and belly?"*

When Eli and Hippa found the warehouse aisle and bay containing the Gaian shipment, Ruke, Shyster, and Zarfo were already waiting. Ruke was staring into the opened box with the cannon inside when he looked up and saw Eli approaching. "Uh, you brought Hippa with you?"

"No, she stowed away in *Night Stalker*. It was too late to go back when I found her. Zarfo, Hippa is my friend, so please make her feel welcome on Korango."

Zarfo tipped his cap. "A gorgeous beast, I must say."

"Smart girl!" Ruke grumbled, then added, looking inside the crate, "This thing looks like one of your *Night Stalker* cannons."

Eli came to the container and bent over its side panel. "Yep, that's what it is. Ruke, you have a problem."

"You mean, because of the weapon provenance? Like—"

"Let's talk about that later."

Zarfo's commsys blinked and let out a beep. "That's one of my men watching outside. I'll put him on speaker." Zarfo pressed a button. "Talk to me."

"Sir, a subject, male, thirtyish, tall and slim with a goatee, entered the warehouse. Doesn't look like a Korag. I ran facial recognition. He's not registered on the station."

"Thanks. Send his picture to the rest of the team. Keep watching." Zarfo ended the call. "Mr. President, Eli, I suggest we cover the box to make it look like it hasn't been touched."

"Please do," said Eli. "Let's hide and see what happens."

"Shh…" Ruke raised his finger. "I hear something."

The sound of locks opening and gates closing became audible in the silence settling over the warehouse. Soft steps were heard, getting louder and closer.

"Move," whispered Eli. "Shyster!" he hissed while helping Zarfo close the crate. "Be ready to stop him if he beats a retreat."

Shyster quickly moved away and hid behind a stack of containers nearby.

"Ruke"—Eli nodded toward another cargo bay about thirty feet away—"stay there!"

The footsteps revealed that the visitor was walking toward the crates containing the Gaian cargo. Zarfo, in a swift and easy move, disappeared behind the box with the cannon. Eli stepped away into a dark area hidden from the approaching person by a stack of containers. Hippa followed like a shadow.

Suddenly, the footsteps stopped. Eli waited for a moment, not knowing what was going on, and then peeked out from behind the boxes. The visitor, a man fitting the description Zarfo had received over his commsys, stood there quietly, a small electronic device in his hands. Busy scanning the cargo, he didn't notice Eli standing a couple of steps behind him. Abruptly, as if detecting something unusual, the stranger turned away from the Gaian containers and headed toward the cargo bay where Ruke concealed himself.

Ruke stepped out of hiding. "Identify yourself!" he declared with a voice full of drama.

The man drew back, and this time, he noticed Eli. Apparently feeling trapped, the visitor threw his gadget away and looked around, trying to find a way to escape. He spotted a crowbar on the floor, grabbed it, and adopted an aggressive posture.

Eli slid his hand down closer to his handgun. "Hey, you! Drop the iron!"

The stranger wriggled between Eli and Ruke, waving the heavy bar. The standoff didn't continue long, either because of the size of

Eli's gun or the understanding that resistance was useless. In any case, the mysterious visitor threw the crowbar away and took to his heels.

Unfortunately for the runaway, Shyster stepped out of her cover and tripped him up with a swift movement of her foot. He fell and saw Hippa still sitting silently in the shade of the containers. Looking in dismay at the big cat and four people surrounding him, he shouted, "You can't hurt me!"

"Sure, I can. That's my property, and you're trespassing," stated Ruke.

"*Your* property? It belongs to Korango Enterprises."

"Oh, yeah? Well, smartass, Korango Enterprises belongs to me."

"Then you must be Mr. Rurik Cavell!" The stranger tried to stand up.

Hippa hissed and moved closer.

"Easy. Easy..." Eli stepped on the stranger's shoulder, pinning him to the floor. "Let's start with your name."

"Right, sorry... I'm Jour Talphi. From Gaia. I'm investigating some highly illegal arms trafficking. Here!" Jour pointed to the crates. "Four antimatter cannons and shells."

"Wouldn't it be easier to come to us and talk instead of acting like a clown?" sniggered Shyster.

"I wanted to know more before raising a stink. It's not in your interest to be involved in all of this."

"Oh, so you care about *our* interests?"

Eli intervened, "Jour, are you acting officially?"

"It doesn't matter."

"It matters to us. Who are you on Gaia?" insisted Eli.

Jour didn't respond, lying pressed to the floor.

Eli turned to Zarfo. "Can you please check on this fellow?"

"Certainly." Zarfo took out his commsys.

"Okay, okay... I'll tell you. I'm the leader of the New Formation Movement. It's a political party."

"Sir, do you want me to verify that?" ask Zarfo.

"Look, Mr. Cavell, we're wasting time." Jour appealed to Ruke. "I'm begging you! What do you want to verify? Watch the Gaian news!"

"Eli, I leave it in your skillful hands. Keep me posted—this is your highest priority. Shyster, let's go." Ruke hurried away with Shyster close on his tail.

"See you, boss." Eli waited for Ruke and Shyster to leave, then continued with the questions. "New Formation? Hmm… And what are you guys forming these days?"

"It's a neo-Game movement. If that tells you anything."

Eli held out his hand to Jour. "It tells me more than you think. Get up!"

Jour grabbed his hand and got to his feet, perking up. "You have to trust me—"

"Don't get too excited. You have a lot of explaining to do if you want to get outta here a free man. Zarfo, cuff him."

Jour obediently presented his hands to Zarfo, letting him tighten the plastic handcuffs on his wrists. "I found four more anti-matter shells," he unexpectedly blurted out, eyes bulging with emotion. "Not here, but nearby."

"How do you know?"

"My scanner." Jour craned his neck. "Where is it?"

"The gadget you had before fouling yourself when you saw Ruke?" smiled Eli.

"That's not fair, and it's rude." Jour's lower lip protruded in a childish pout. "I resent it!"

Eli shrugged and turned to Zarfo. "I'll take it from here. Lock down the warehouse. Get more people to patrol the area. To make it clear—only I, you, and Ruke can get in and out. Our dandelion from Gaia," Eli slapped Jour on the shoulder, "goes with me. I'll be on *Night Stalker*. And please find his scanner. Keep it safe. Check all the cargo in the warehouse. Nobody else should know what happened here, and that includes your team."

THIRTEEN

ASSAULT

The executive docks were located not far from the warehouse. Eli led Jour by the elbow, gripping firmly. Hippa sauntered behind with the drama of a movie star. When the procession reached *Night Stalker*, she yawned and hurried inside through the slowly deploying ramp.

Jour froze in his tracks as he silently observed the ship. Finally, he raised his tied hands and pointed at the ship's cannons. "What's this?"

"You don't know?" Eli pushed his prisoner forward. "Keep moving."

"Who *are* you?" Jour stumbled, twisting his head back, trying to get a better view of the fighter's weapons.

"Wait... That's the source of the emission my scanner showed in the warehouse! Are you Eli Stroud?"

"You know my name?"

"People talk about you. I mean, on Gaia they do..."

"Is it my reputation, or my ship?"

"The ship, yes. But you... A quantum conversion of that magnitude... and on top of that—unauthorized. You know, government folks—they talk."

Eli and Jour entered the ship. Eli closed the ramp, cut Jour's cuffs, and nodded at the co-pilot's seat. "Make yourself comfortable." He lounged in his pilot's seat with his legs on the control panel. "So, what *exactly* are they talking about?"

"Different people, different things. But I like what you did."

"Of course you do. I violated Game law—you broke into someone else's property. You scratch my back—I'll scratch yours. Almost soulmates."

Jour bristled. "I am not your soulmate!"

"I see that sarcasm is not in vogue on Gaia."

"What sarcasm? I'm serious. Although we are against most crimes, what you did is in line with our political platform."

"And what's your political platform?"

"Well, we are against—" Jour stopped and riveted his eyes on Eli. "The hell with the platform!" His eyes glinted with excitement. "I know why the cargo is here!"

"Please, enlighten me."

"It's simple. Our government, the Directorate, doesn't like you. Well... some may, but most don't. They're afraid of you and your *Stalker*. They want to get rid of you. You violated the status quo." Jour leaned in and whispered, "I have sources. The DRC—"

"DRC?"

"That's the Bureau of Development, Research, and Contacts, a kind of our security service. I know they wanted to prosecute you, and then they backtracked. And rumors..."

"What rumors? And stop whispering, for goodness' sake. I brought you here so that we could talk safely. It's the only place on Korango where we can."

Jour spoke up. "Oh, sorry... Rumors, yes. That you're a Gaian, but not a normal one."

"What's *that* supposed to mean?"

"I don't know. I guess you're not like everybody else. Is that true?"

Eli snorted. "Now, that's going too far. You should write fiction. Anybody ever told you that?"

"Yes. More than once... And you know what? The most interesting thing is how that cargo turned up on Korango because the shipper in the documents has never been here. Crosscheck it. The crates simply popped up in the warehouse," Jour said excitedly. "That's what the Game *does*. Methinks your ship is part of the Game's network. So everything leads to you. They're setting you up! As if you did it!"

"That sounds like a conspiracy theory. Are you one of those... you know..." Eli rotated his forefinger around his ear.

"I don't know what that means," Jour said, primly crossing his arms.

"It means crazy, mixed up. Are you?"

Jour glowered at Eli and fell silent.

"Where's your ship?" asked Eli after a pause.

"... Why?"

"I need you to go back to Gaia. You can't stay here."

"You're making a mistake. I can help."

"Thanks, buddy, but I need you to go home."

"I resent such treatment. I don't yield to your logic—I yield to the brute force! She's on Leaky Kettle. I hitchhiked to Korango."

"What? Leaky Kettle? What the hell's Leaky Kettle?"

"It's a small stop two light-years from here. I'll show you. If you don't know, it's under Korangan jurisdiction."

Eli started his engines. "Looks like this isn't your first time on Korango."

Jour chuckled, leaned back in his seat, and closed his eyes as Eli requested clearance to leave.

～

The door to Shyster's office opened slightly, and her assistant's face appeared in the crack. She was trying to block the entrance with her body, but Nox stood impatiently behind her, shoving her forward. "Ma'am, you—ow!—have a visitor. She insists."

Shyster stood up, flicking a piece of lint off her suit. "It's okay. Let her in."

Too late. Pushing Shyster's assistant aside, Nox had already opened the door and entered the room. "I'm sorry to bother you with my unexpected visit."

"Do we have a problem?"

Nox looked at Shyster's assistant. "Thank you, dear. You may go. Please close the door behind you."

Shyster sighed and dismissed her aide with a nod.

"I don't consider you a threat anymore," said Nox, "If that's what you mean…"

"I have no hope of being so lucky!" Shyster tried to put on a brave face to match her sardonic tone.

"My apologies," said Nox with a poker face. "I need your help. I cannot locate Eli. He's off the grid, and it's urgent."

"I saw him recently at the spaceport. I'll check traffic records for you. Let me see… His *Night Stalker* left Korango about an hour ago."

"Can you reach him with your comm system?"

Quick swipes at the computer were followed by a dialing chirp, and Eli's face—or a glimpse of it between the soles of his shoes—appeared on a wall-mounted monitor.

"Hi, Shyster. Whassup?"

"Nox is here. Wants to talk to you."

"Hello, Eli. Shyster, can you please add Ruke to the call?"

"Sure."

The screen split, with one half showing Ruke in his office.

"Eli, Ruke—"

"Nox," interrupted Eli, "before you start, keep in mind, I have with me in the co-pilot seat one Jour Talphi, Gaian. You may know him. If anything sensitive—"

"I know Jour. Pain in the ass, but he's fine. Soon everybody will know the Elder Keep Alliance has attacked Coatera Cela in a massive military operation. They took Aura and the Gamer."

"What?" Eli quickly removed his feet from the control panel and straightened in his chair. "How could that happen?" Eli's face turned pale, but he promptly got hold of himself. "Coatera's defenses are impenetrable. I talked to Aura—she was confident about that."

Nox looked at the commsys screen, impassive and frosty. "Most of the defenses were compromised. It was an inside job. The leads I have point to Korango, to the last shipment of the high-power weaponry to Coatera."

Who else could learn about the shipment and tip off the Pazons? Eli couldn't help wondering. *I know Yow—surely he would never talk about his cargo, and he's loyal to Aura. Someone must have bugged his office or hacked his computer... or someone close to him overheard his conversation.* Suspicion sent shivers down Eli's spine. *Ash? Was that what she and Rey talked about?*

Meanwhile, Nox, who had been silent for a while as if collecting her thoughts, continued, "President Cavell, on behalf of my people and the Gaian government, I officially ask Korango's authorities to fully cooperate in our investigation and assist with all means necessary."

Jour wanted to say something, but Eli shut him up with a swift hand movement.

Another moment of silence passed before Ruke responded, "Excuse me... Umm... Ms. Nox... Do you know who shipped the weaponry?"

"The shipment of high-power tessellate gravity mines on

consignment was arranged by Mr. Nayo on behalf of Aura herself. He and Eli delivered the cargo to Coatera Cela. However, I suspect that the act of sabotage resulted from tampering with the mines before the delivery took place."

"Who is this Nayo character?" asked Ruke.

"That's Yow. Where is he now? Is he alive?" worried Eli. "He was on Cela when I left for Korango."

"I found him on Cela, wounded. Not life-threatening. He will arrive on Korango soon. I interviewed Yow. As I understand the situation, a third party sabotaged the cargo. The mines were detonated remotely, most likely from an Elder Keep assault ship."

"Abaddon!" exclaimed Ruke. He clenched his fists as his face turned red. "He's not going to get away with this! Eli, where are you? I expect action! All Elder Keep visitors on Korango must be taken into custody. No exception. I want a full investigation into all recent arms transactions."

"I'll be back in a couple of hours," Eli said. "You need to close all spaceports and docking bays immediately for departure and arrival until further notice. I'll contact Zarfo Khoin and have him mobilize all security forces. He'll also provide our tactical plan with the immediate and short-term activities."

"I'm counting on you, Eli," said Ruke. He pulled out a handkerchief and wiped the sweat off the back of his neck and head. Puffing, Ruke got up and started pacing. The commsys camera followed him. "Shyster, convene an emergency meeting with all top management personnel in two hours. Eli will join us as soon as he's back. Don't disclose the agenda. I intend to participate and give you my signed executive order. As far as arrivals and departures, do as Eli suggests. Please coordinate all your actions with Nox and Eli."

Ruke turned to Nox. "I'm fed up with the Pazons treating Korango as their backyard. We'll help you, Nox. You can bank on it! Anything else?"

"A question for Eli," said Nox. "What's Jour doing on your ship?"

Jour opened his mouth. Again, Eli raised his hand to stop him speaking. "Nox, I'm near Leaky Kettle, a small station, a half-hour's flight from Korango—"

"I found Gaian weapons, contraband, on Korango!" yelled Jour. "I wanted to help—he wants to send me back to Gaia!"

"Approaching Leaky Kettle. Awaiting further instructions," announced *Night Stalker*'s navigation interface.

"Contact local authorities and inform them of my arrival. Ask them to locate Jour Talphi's ship. Dock near it," Eli commanded *Night Stalker* and went on, "About Jour… We caught him when he tried to approach the cargo, the contraband my people found. He was interfering with our investigation."

"I don't know anything about it. We'll talk when you're back. But Jour"—Nox smiled—"he's on Korango. Your jurisdiction."

"Sure. I'll be back in about an hour. See you all later."

The hum of *Night Stalker*'s engines died down. She rested in a small, mostly empty docking bay. A spaceship with an unusual configuration lay with her belly right on the bay's deck, not far from Eli's fighter. "Is this your ship?" He nodded at the strange spacecraft visible through *Night Stalker*'s cockpit windows.

"Look, you're making a mistake. I want to help, and I can."

"So far, I can't see how. What do you know about the Elder Keep?"

"Elder Keep or not, I can assure you—you're dealing with Gaians here, and you have no clue who we are. Besides, I can offer other ways of fighting you don't seem familiar with."

"Like what?"

"Like less violence. And I'm good at it. I saw your face. I bet you want to do everything you can to save Aura. She's a Gaian. Don't you think that folks from Gaia are your best chance?"

"Nox is on it."

"Oh, she's strong and resolute, but what do you know about Nox? About her relationship with our government, political parties? Her relationship with people who matter? People who control the Game?"

"Well, whoever that may be, it was the Elder Keep who took Aura. Someone should go there and retake what's not theirs. By the way, what's in it for you?"

"You wouldn't understand. Have you ever watched our news? Have you ever seen or talked to a regular Gaian?"

Eli didn't respond and instead stared at a fixed point in the distance. Then he stood up, slowly approached the co-pilot seat, and leaned with his hand on the seat's back. "You're right about one thing. I want to save Aura."

Eli brought his face nose to nose with Jour's and stared at him. Eli's eyes hardened, and his gaze became terrifying. Jour jerked his head back, and his face went pale. "I'll do *anything* to save Aura," Eli spoke slowly, deliberately pronouncing every word. "I want their blood. They killed my mother. An eye for an eye—do you understand that concept with that Gaian brain of yours?"

With the same nerve-racking slowness, Eli returned to his seat. He waited and then, as if nothing had happened, said, "*Stalker,* please display Zarfo's file, last report, images of Rey Fliek."

A large holographic image formed in the middle of the cockpit behind them. Rey and a younger man stood on the street. The younger man held something in his hand, ready to pass it to Rey. "Look at these guys." Eli waved his hand at the image. "If you tell me who this young guy is, you go to Korango. If not…"

Jour fidgeted in his chair. "That, um, was creepy," he said shakily. "Anybody ever told you that you could be scary?"

"Once or twice. Well, it was nice to meet—"

"That's Slun Ceabb." Jour pointed to the guy holding something in his hand. "He's with the DRC. Remember I told you about it? He's a special agent with the Game Division," he said, with a bit of his previous arrogance.

"This man is a Gaian? Are you sure?"

"Ask Nox. She probably knows him personally."

"I believe you. I'll keep my word. Do you fly your ship?"

"Yes, but I need to find my girlfriend."

Eli's eyebrows went up. "You take girlfriends with you when you investigate something?"

"Well, she's also my 'weapon.' I told you, I don't like violence. I don't like guns."

"Who is she?"

"Her name is D'Obba, D'Obba Chyllep. She's a journalist with the *Gaian Observer*. She's good."

"A hack? That's going too far."

"Look, I fight with words instead of guns. On Gaia, words are the best way to kill someone. Figuratively speaking, that is. And not only on Gaia. D'Obba helps me—she's really good. She digs stuff up, and I use it to discredit people, to tarnish their reputations."

"That's disgusting."

"How is it not disgusting to kill people?"

"I do it in self-defense. To defeat bad guys," Eli protested. "It's wrong to smear people."

"I don't smear anybody. They smear themselves. I expose corruption and ruin people's reputations for the same reason you kill—if it helps you grasp the concept. I fight for good causes."

"I wonder if your definition of a 'good' cause coincides with mine."

"We'll see."

"Yes. We will. If you want to help... The second man here," Eli nodded at Zarfo's surveillance holo, "is a Korag and a prominent member of Korango's Hunter Society. His full name is Reynard Fliek. They call him Rey the Fox. I believe he's one of the key players behind the assault on Coatera. If you can find a clear connection between Rey and the Gaian DRC, that'd be helpful."

"Rey could be a DRC asset," suggested Jour.

"Could be, but there's little logic in that."

Shrugging, Jour stood up and headed to the exit.

"Hold on. One more thing. I don't want anyone to know you're helping us. Nox will know, and Zarfo, my right-hand man—Zarfo only to make sure you're not booted from Korango or killed. Ruke will eventually know, but that's fine. Oh, your journalist, she mustn't know about our contact. For her, you act on your own. Agree?"

"Yes, perfect."

"Then, go. Use *Night Stalker*'s commsys if you need to contact me."

The Korango Enterprises conference room was dark and gloomy. It had big monitors stationed around its perimeter and a huge mahogany-like table in the center. Shyster and a dozen senior corporate officers were waiting there for Ruke. With perplexed and puzzled faces, unsure what to expect, they murmured and whispered, trying to guess what had happened.

Ruke entered the room and headed straight to his president's chair. Still standing, he waited for the gathering to quiet down and announced, "Coatera, the Strangers outpost one hundred light-years away, was attacked three hours ago by the Elder Keep. Its space station, Cela, was nearly destroyed—aided by one or more collaborators from Korango."

Ruke scanned the gathering. The reaction of those present varied. Some were looking at him in shock, while others tried to avoid his gaze. He continued, "We are conducting an investigation. Our station's reputation is at stake. I have declared a state of emergency. All points of entry or exit have been sealed by our security forces. I invite officers with any knowledge regarding what happened to volunteer information. Shyster and Elias Stroud will lead the investigation. Any questions?"

"Any leads so far?" asked one of those present.

"My invitation expires soon. Dismissed," stated Ruke, and left the room.

It took Eli half an hour to return to Korango, but the flight back didn't provide him with any respite from his new duties as Korango's chief police officer. He called Nox as soon as he departed Leaky Kettle. He told her about the shipment of Gaian weapons found in the warehouse. Nox wanted to inspect the cargo, and he offered to meet her at the spaceport to discuss the latest developments. Eli had to end his conversation with Nox abruptly, as an urgent text message from Zarfo popped up at the bottom of the screen.

> We deciphered two seconds of Rey Fliek's communication ten minutes ago. A local party initiated the call. Its location is untraceable. Based on the signal strength, it was in Korango City. No audio in the decrypted part.

Eli opened the video file attached. The artifacts of the decryption process strongly affected the quality of the holo image, but Rey's interlocutor looked familiar. *That's one of Ab's guys I saw on Earth when they abducted Nox. Drach and Lobo. Drach was the guy who knocked Ruke down, so this is Lobo. Whoa, that's huge! Rey is working with the Keepers. Holy smoke! I was right!*

Eli responded right away.

> Detain Fliek immediately. The person in your video is Lobo, a Special Ops Pazon. Find and take him into custody too. When you finish making arrangements for the arrests, call me immediately.

His subsequent conversation with Zarfo turned out to be much longer than his discussion with Nox. Eli started by briefing him on the attack on Coatera. Without going too deep into the details, he explained Nox's role in the investigation. Then he told Zarfo about his decision to allow Jour and D'Obba to stay on Korango, passed on the information about Slun Ceabb, and warned him about the growing role of Gaians in the investigation.

Finally, Eli wanted to ask Zarfo to detain Ash. He opened his mouth but realized that what he was about to say didn't fit his philosophy of life. He had no problems with arresting Rey, but Ash was different.

From the time Eli picked up his first Batman comic at age six, the hero—the strong man with no superpowers stepping forward to do what ordinary citizens couldn't do for themselves—had never ceased to fascinate him. The wonderment of fighting against injustice thrilled his imagination. The human among evil foes, the one who never gave up, ready to wreak vengeance protecting the weak, was someone young Eli rooted for and identified with.

His childhood passed, but the romantic appeal of vengeance didn't go away. Eli believed in the power of human beings, not institutions. Deep down, he developed a strong aversion to anybody with the ability to control the behavior of others. His dislike included legal authorities, with their claim to legitimacy provided by social institutions.

There was nothing rational about his attitude. Eli respected law and order. He always strived to be a responsible citizen, living by the rules, respecting the rights of others, trying to be tolerant and forgiving for the sake of harmony and peace. He didn't feel any hostility toward the authorities or hold them in disdain. Yet, a distrust of the government was deeply embedded in his psyche. In Eli's mind, anybody with the power to influence other people's lives seemed unfriendly and objectionable—a necessary evil that had to be allowed only for the greater good.

He had never dwelled on the origins of his feelings, nor did he try to understand or analyze the relationship between good and evil. In his life, he settled on a more practical approach, admitting *ad hoc* that virtue and vice always existed and that the only important thing was to follow the ethics of reciprocity—don't do unto others what you don't want done unto you.

Not a lawbreaker, and never seeking protection from wrongdoers or unfairness, Eli had never had to deal with the law enforcement system. His unexpected ascent to the head of Korango Security had resulted in a tectonic shift in his attitude toward power. He had become an authority and now had to do things he'd instinctively tried to avoid.

When Eli accepted the position of chief law enforcement officer on Korango, he didn't think that far ahead. But his life, the stubborn thing, posed unexpected questions. Eli realized that without even noticing—*How could it have happened?*—he had become a man burdened by the power to determine the fate of others. Worse than that, he had to behave like those he didn't like—to decide what to do with Ash, not a stranger but a friend. Eli feverishly went over everything he knew or believed about her role in what had happened on Coatera.

He was confident the attack had become possible because she had tipped off Rey, who had collaborated with the Elder Keep. Eli didn't know what kind of information she had passed—probably something Yow had shared with her, or something she'd learned from overhearing Yow's conversations with someone else.

On the other hand, he firmly believed that Ash would never intentionally harm innocent people, including her boyfriend. It was a case of bad judgment, not evil intent. Most likely, she wanted to do something about the Game, a grave danger in her mind, and Rey had exploited her naive understanding of the technology.

Nevertheless, Eli saw that what Ash had done was wrong—she

had betrayed her friends and their trust. Her actions could lead to an interplanetary conflict, and she should have known that. Lastly, passing commercial secrets to a third party not involved in a transaction was illegal on Korango.

Eli often relied on his intuition about what to do—but not this time. Immersed in his mental gyrations, he almost forgot that he was talking to Zarfo. Instead, he stared blankly in front of him, not seeing anything and not knowing what to say about Ash. The silence dragged on.

"Sir... Eli, are you okay?"

"Ah? Yeah." Eli collected his thoughts. Zarfo's professional approach to his duties, his reasonable initiative, and attention to detail forced Eli to listen to his opinion and seek his counsel. Eli began in a roundabout way. "You're a law enforcement professional. Have you had moments—mind you, I'm talking about *with* people—when you felt you had to do things you didn't want to?"

"Well, as for law enforcement, I know what I'm supposed to do."

"But you're also a human being. And it's not math."

"I see... Then it's a matter of judgment. Moral judgment. What your heart tells you."

"Heart? Here's the problem. You know about Yow Nayo—a Korag citizen who sold and delivered weapons to Coatera. He has a girlfriend, Ash Kline, who came with us from Earth. I have reasons to believe she was involved in the attack at Coatera Cela. No evidence. And she's not evil. However, more than once she's spoken out strongly against the Game—the technology stolen by the Keepers. Plus, she had a long *tête-à-tête* with Rey several days before the attack. I don't understand what they could have talked about. Make of that what you will."

"Circumstantial, but it *is* evidence. I don't mean to pry, but since you asked, I assume she's your friend, isn't she? Both she and Nayo?"

"Both."

"Probably, she was exploited. But don't you think she might be in danger if that's true? Also, as a cop, I'd have to look at Yow. If you agree, I can send a team to their residence. This way, we'll protect both, and you can come and have a talk with them. They should understand."

Eli breathed a sigh of relief. "You're right. Good plan. Please do that, and don't delay."

"Right away, sir."

"Thank you, Zarfo. I'm sorry, I've put too much on your plate. I wonder if you have time to meet Nox and me in the Red warehouse, in the bay with the contraband you found. Can you make it in fifteen minutes?"

"See you there. No problem—it's refreshing to have so much to do after years of being a security guard."

FOURTEEN

NIGHT STALKER

W hen Eli parked *Night Stalker* at the executive dock, Nox was already waiting for him. She smiled. "Nice place. The perks of being the police chief?"

"Ah, I don't care. Saves time, though. Let's go. I'll show you the cannons." Eli led Nox through the spaceport complex to the warehouse. "I invited my deputy to join us—he discovered the cargo. His name's Zarfo Khoin."

The cargo gates to the depot were closed. Two heavily armed security officers stood guard. They saluted Eli and opened a small side door to let them into the warehouse.

"I'm impressed," noted Nox. "Not the Korango I knew. Your directorship?"

He shrugged it off. "More Zarfo's than mine. He's not here yet. We can start without him."

Eli showed Nox to the boxes. He walked around the cargo and threw off the lid of the previously opened crate. "That's the one we looked at. It seems nobody's touched it since my last time here. Anyway, it's all yours. Tell me what you make of it. We don't know who shipped it. Zarfo couldn't verify the receiver."

Nox jumped inside the crate and started meticulously inspecting the contents. "Do you have time? It may take five or ten minutes."

"No problem. Do what you need to."

As Nox rummaged through the cargo, the sound of soft footsteps from the direction of the entrance made Eli prick up his ears. *What the fuck? Jour again? Or his girlfriend-journalist? That really would be too much!*

He hurried quietly to the door across the aisle and stopped in the middle of it. A blonde belle, almost a teenager, thin as a stick, was creeping and poking about with her back to the rows of boxes. Bumping into Eli, she stopped and stood rooted to the floor.

"Let me guess," said Eli with a broad smile, "You're D'Obba, a newsmonger and Jour's friend." Her first impulse to run didn't work—Eli grabbed her by the hand and set her in front of him. "So-o-o?"

She wrenched her hand out of his grip. Eli didn't mind—there was no place to run or hide. "I'm D'Obba Chyllep, with *the Gaian Observer* media network."

"This is Korango, miss, not Gaia. Your press credentials, please?"

"My organization sent an application to your government. It should be somewhere there."

"I *am* the government, Miss Chyllep, and I haven't seen anything from Gaia."

"That's not my problem. I—"

"Oh, but it is!"

D'Obba looked at him for a moment, then turned around and wandered off toward the exit. Eli didn't stop her. He stood watching with interest, wondering what would happen next.

What happened next was Zarfo. He flew into the room and rushed to the journalist, blocking her way. D'Obba looked over her shoulder at Eli. It was the look of a trapped animal resigned to its fate. Zarfo said something into his commsys—the door opened, and the two security officers guarding the entrance jumped at D'Obba. One of them twisted her hands behind her back. While the second was attempting to cuff her, she kicked the guard behind her.

D'Obba Chyllep

The boot went right in his balls—the guard folded in half. Not wasting a moment, she rolled a strong punch across the face of the second. She didn't spare Zarfo either. Crouching on one foot and spinning on it, D'Obba swept his legs out from under him, sending Zarfo crashing to the floor. She didn't look back at the defeated opponents as she dashed away and disappeared behind the door.

The whole scene took two seconds, at most. Eli stood in astonishment and then burst out laughing. Zarfo and the guards rose from the floor, embarrassed and humiliated. "I'm sorry. We'll catch her. She'll be in custody in ten minutes," promised Zarfo, pulling out his commsys and giving orders.

Eli got serious. "It's all right. Please find her, though—she's D'Obba Chyllep, the Gaian journalist I told you about earlier. I need to talk to her. But be gentle, Zarfo. Nothing really happened. Where I come from, we respect the media. She was doing her job." Eli turned to the guards. "Now, tell me how you both let her in when you were supposed to keep everybody—see, *everybody*—out? And under no circumstances to allow anyone in?"

The guards remained silent, exchanging glances.

"Zarfo, please work with your people so that what happened here never happens again. You guys," he said, pointing to the guards, "there will be no consequences today. You had your lesson. But I need to know what she told you. Be honest. It's important."

One of the guards stepped forward. "You bet, sir, a lesson. We are so sorry. It'll never happen again. She seemed so harmless, a kid practically. She said she urgently had to talk to Elias Stroud— that's you, sir—and Nox. She said Nox was that woman with you."

"I know who I am. Did you offer to call me?"

"We did... but she insisted. She said she had to go inside to show you something in those boxes. She said they could explode if she didn't show you how to handle them. That's it."

"Okay, guys. Please go back to your posts, but *do your jobs next time*."

The guards clicked their heels and hurried to take their posts outside the warehouse.

"Eli, my apologies. I wasn't prepared for the kid." Zarfo looked up from his commsys, "You know... she was good." He shook his head in approval. "I have news about Miss Kline. She's in the hospital with Yow. When my people came to their apartment, Nayo had already arrived from Coatera and, as I understand, told her what happened. After that, she had grabbed his handgun and tried to kill herself. Evidently, she doesn't have much experience with lasers, and that saved her. Her wound is not life-threatening. I have a team at the hospital. We'll protect Nayo and Kline."

Eli's eyes widened. "You think she did it because of remorse?"

"That's the most logical explanation." He glanced at his commsys. "Sir, if you don't need me, I have to go. Rey Fliek is still on the run. We've spotted him twice and lost him both times. He knows the city well—there are secret passages, places to hide. I need to make sure everything goes as planned."

"Sure. But Nox is here. I want you to meet her—it won't take long."

Eli and Zarfo walked to the crates carrying the contraband, and Nox's grease-smeared face peered out of the open one. "What was all that noise?"

"That was D'Obba Chyllep. I suspect you know her."

"I do. Everybody knows her. She's like her boyfriend—two shoes make a pair. What's she doing here?"

"Well, evidently, our friend Jour let the Gaians know what's going on with the Game on Korango. Though I don't think he and his girlfriend care much for Korags. Incidentally, this is Zarfo Khoin, my deputy. I thought I'd introduce you to each other."

"Nice to meet you, Ms. Nox. Zarfo will suffice. Eli told me we'd be working the same case—the attack on your space station and Korango's involvement. I'll do my best to help."

"Thank you. Nice to meet you too. Please, no Ms.—call me Nox."

"Zarfo has to run," Eli told her. "His team is rounding up Rey Fliek."

Nox jumped out of the crate. "It's about time. I wish you luck, Zarfo."

Zarfo bowed slightly and hurried away. As he did, Nox said quietly, "Eli, I found something. Your *Night Stalker* is nearby, correct? I can use her to check some of my theories."

"Sure, let's go. I have a surprise for you inside the ship."

"What is it?"

"Not it, she. Your soulmate, or so I was told."

"Hippa?"

"Yep. Stowed away when I departed Coatera."

"Thank you, Eli! I've been worried sick about her since the attack."

As soon as Nox came aboard *Night Stalker*, Hippa, still sleepy, came out of hiding as if she could tell by some sixth sense that her mother was near. The reunion was noisy and joyful. Hippa rushed to Nox, rubbing and pushing her head against Nox's body. The connection between Nox and her furry creation was profound and strong. Nox kneeled, hugged her, and kissed her on the nose, filling Hippa with ecstatic happiness. "You look gorgeous, my sweet. I'm so glad to see you safe!" Nox patted Hippa on the scruff. "Can you show me around?"

Hippa eagerly responded with an enthusiastic, chirping meow and skittered inside the ship. Nox followed her, examining *Night Stalker*'s interior with great curiosity. "Wow!" she stroked her inner wall. "How did you get such a wonderful space fighter?"

"You're teasing me, aren't you?"

"Maybe..." Nox smiled. "But there's some truth in my question. I can find out how the Game interpreted your thoughts, but that would only be the interpretation." She kept exploring the ship as she entered the cockpit and sat in the pilot's seat. She looked over her shoulder at Eli. "Is this okay?"

"Yes, please. About what I was thinking at the time... Well, many things. For example, I was excited that I had found the place where my father had been before he died. It felt good, like a new life was starting for me. A more worthwhile one. But no—no dreaming about space fighters, sorry."

Nox stood and looked around. "There are few controls for a spacecraft of this complexity."

"I don't need them. *Night Stalker* and I... we understand each other. I like to fly manually, but when it comes to something serious, she knows what I want. And I know everything about her. Well, almost everything."

"Are you still learning?"

"A little. But it's more like when you recall things you've known and forgotten and find a new use for them."

"Nice metaphor. Never thought about it that way. Have you already recalled why there's so much space in the cockpit? These things are usually more compactly built." Nox stood and went toward the tail of the ship. "Or here? In the aft compartment?"

"I use it as a cargo bay. Why?"

"So, you haven't 'recalled' that yet. Try now."

Eli tilted his head to one side. "How?"

"The same way you 'recalled' other things."

"Okay." Eli followed Nox to the aft section of the space fighter. He closed his eyes and, for reasons clear only to him, held his breath. Nox didn't interrupt Eli, quietly watching his fumbling attempts at the neural interface. After trying for about a minute without success, he grunted, exhaled noisily, and complained, "I feel like an idiot. It's like walking around without knowing where I want to go."

"I came here because I needed something I thought I could find in your *Night Stalker*," Nox clued him in. "I can tell you what it is, but I don't want to lead you by the hand and walk you through the door."

"Can you give me a hint?"

"A hint? You have all the hints you need—look at me."

Eli stared at her. "I can pay you all the compliments you want, Nox, but—"

The rear of the ship, dull and stern before, all of a sudden transformed beyond recognition. Lights went off, and the walls, floor, and ceiling disappeared. Stars, nebulas, and galaxies filled the aft area which, whether an illusion or real, now seemed to have no boundaries. A glowing sphere, suspended in the air, appeared in front of Eli. The ball didn't have a clear outline. A liquid or gaseous substance, pulsing and flowing with continually changing patterns, drifted around the orb.

"Oh, my... It's beautiful!" gasped Eli.

"Good. I'd hoped you'd have a Game interface in your ship. The stars are its default state. Mind if I use it?"

"Be my guest."

"Thanks, I'll take it from here. Watch and try to learn."

"Watch? Is it a demo or tutorial?"

"No need or time for that." Nox smiled. "It'll be easy with your neural connection to *Night Stalker*. Try to feel the Game. You'll get mental representations of concepts and properties." She looked at Eli's skeptical face and added, "More complex but similar to how our translators work. No need for any abstractions."

Nox approached the nebulous sphere and put her hands inside it. "The sphere is an amplifier, since the Game is far from Korango," she explained. "I'm accessing its primary controls now. Don't be intimidated by its output—that's for techies like me. With time, it'll all become intuitive to you."

While Nox was speaking, the three-dimensional starscape and orb vanished. The boundaries of the compartment rematerialized, and a more conventional setup emerged in the middle of the room. In its center rose a circular instrument panel, about four feet tall and twelve feet in diameter. Right above it hung a structure similar in shape and size to the console on the floor. A cylindrical column of light shimmering with all the colors of the rainbow, it rotated and twitched between the top and bottom circles of the machine.

"Is it a hologram?" asked Eli.

Nox came closer to the device. "The middle part, yes. The rest is real. You can touch it if you want."

Her fingers ran over the surface of the console in a series of quick legatos. Once in a while, Nox would slow the graceful movements of her arms and wrists to complement them with distinct taps. She looked uninhibited and relaxed. Eli watched and couldn't take his eyes off Nox's virtuosity. Every movement of her hands resulted in new splashes of glyphs and designs flowing through the surface of the column. The gushes of data kept coming. For an observer unfamiliar with the Game, the streams seemed nothing more than an elaborate, albeit difficult to interpret, symphony of colors, shapes, and symbols.

For Nox, they were full of meaning, significance, and nuances. On more than a few occasions she stopped, and the stream of data on the light column would slow down, moving only vertically from top to bottom. With various gestures of her hands, Nox manipulated the data movement through the column any way she wanted.

She continued working with the Game for about ten minutes. Eli didn't interfere. Finally, she stopped and announced, "The contraband you found in the warehouse wasn't brought there—not in a traditional way. It was beamed in by autonomous transporter, used by someone who had access to such a device—hence, by a Gaian."

"But who built those cannons in the first place?"

"Good instincts. The Game didn't directly fabricate them. Someone used an autonomous remote device and built them based on designs and specifications stolen from the Game's database. I can identify the terminal, but it may take a lot of time, and I don't think it would be helpful. What's important is that it was done on Gaia."

"Is that considered a crime?"

"Manufacturing weapons by using a stand-alone device? No. Accessing the database? Maybe. Sending them to Korango? Hell, yes. Keep in mind, the person behind it knew about this weaponry, which is unique to your ship. Its design was classified on Gaia as soon as our government learned about your cannons. So this was an inside job."

"Why do all this?"

"I don't know. You mentioned you couldn't ID the recipient of the cargo. If it doesn't exist, I'd say this cargo was transported to Korango to be found here. Or to be transported to another party, which I don't believe."

"Why?"

"Because these cannons are fake. They're functional, but anybody who tries to use them will find their yield to be much lower than yours and similar to many other existing weapon systems. Why go through the trouble?" Nox nodded at the Game interface. "I spent most of the last few minutes comparing the designs. Korango's version has a minor but critical change."

Eli looked chagrined. "You know, what you say makes me believe Jour was right. I laughed at his crazy theory, but now I see how it might be true."

"What theory?"

"He said that it was an attempt to set me up."

"How?"

"You've just explained how. I have an interface to the Game. I don't know how to use it, but this and other details like whether the cannons are fake are beside the point. And even without such an interface, if someone wants to set me up, they could easily claim I'm the only one with knowledge of the cannon design. Since I've got *Night Stalker*—obtained illegally, according to Gaian law—I could equally get these cannons as well. A criminal who pulled out all the stops in his evil doings. They'd only need someone like D'Obba Chyllep to fan the flames. Could that be the reason she's here?"

Nox plunged deep into thought. Eli patiently waited until she replied, "I think it's a legitimate theory. Though I'm not sure about D'Obba's role, or Jour's for that matter. They stink, and they're noisy, but they're known for their principles, which aren't that bad. For one, D'Obba doesn't publish garbage. She investigates abuses, corruption, and crimes. No rumors, only facts. And Jour… You need to know more about him, but it's a long story. For the moment, keep an open mind."

"Could it be Slun? Slun Ceabb, from your DRC?"

"Slun? Where does this come from? How do you know him?"

"Jour recognized him in a surveillance image—Slun was giving something to Rey Fliek. I have documented evidence he met with Fliek recently."

"And you waited all this time to tell me about it?" Nox demanded indignantly.

"I wanted to do it earlier, but every minute, something new comes up. And I learned about it only a day ago, anyway. Look, over the past two days, I've slept only an hour or two. I'm only human. Not all of us can be like you," he replied, exasperated.

"Sorry, Eli. That wasn't fair on my part. Now, we should dispose of this contraband. If we need something, I have all the data related to it, even the inscriptions on its labels. How about destroying the whole shipment?"

"How?"

"I can do it with your quantum transporter. By decomposing it for a transport and never re-materializing it."

"I have a transporter on *Night Stalker*? Like the one you talked about?"

Nox rolled her eyes. "Just go back to the warehouse. Make sure nobody's there. Use your commsys to give me a signal. I'll do it from here. Unless your duties as the chief law enforcement officer—"

"No problem here. And after that?"

"I'll lock up *Night Stalker* and join you. Don't freak out—I'll do it my way. I'm dying to interrogate Rey. Slun Ceabb is a shady person."

"That's also my intention," said Eli, and headed to the exit.

"Eli, wait! Nobody should know what you have on your ship. Nobody—for your sake and for the sake of everybody you care about. Understand?"

"Believe me, I do."

FIFTEEN

ASSASSINATION

Ruke quickly grew accustomed to his new life as the CEO of Korango Enterprises. It fit him surprisingly well. Bored at first with reports, charts, and endless meetings, he soon learned to delegate and developed a taste for the corporate bureaucracy and its reliance on pundits and advisers. But the events on Coatera, Korango's involvement in them, and the Gaian contraband at his doorstep undercut his authority.

Unfortunately, the reports on the investigation couldn't comfort Ruke as much as he would have liked. Eli's message that the antimatter weaponry found in the warehouse had been destroyed reassured him—out of sight, out of mind. But the latest updates from Zarfo and Eli, reporting failure to apprehend Rey Fliek, made him uneasy.

Thoughts about Rey, almost a celebrity on the space station, didn't leave Ruke. He loathed the man. Rey's self-confidence and sycophancy, his air of an important person knowing everybody and everything, and his frequent talks about new business opportunities got on Ruke's nerves. He recalled how once, out of curiosity, he had wanted to understand the nature of Rey's business and income. Nobody could tell him anything specific. At that time, with Korango being Korango, Ruke didn't give a damn, but his possible connection to the latest events intensified Ruke's dislike for the man.

Ruke looked around his office. It was part of the penthouse of an old stone building restored some time ago to its original eminence when the stone and iron coming from a nearby asteroid were cheap and plentiful. He was proud of the place and for good reason. Real estate was a precious and highly desirable asset on Korango, and the size of the room, nearly six thousand square feet, defied the imagination of even the wealthiest Korags. Size aside, the most remarkable feature of the room was its panoramic window, or rather the sweeping, unobstructed view out of it onto an extensive area of the city and Korango's famous domes.

Ruke dreamed that someday he would change the interior design of his office, which was quite unremarkable at the moment. It held a large desk in one corner with everything that befitted the chief executive of a giant corporation, a conference table in another corner, chairs, armchairs, and sofas scattered around where appropriate, and finally, a couple of mundane doors. One led to the private digs of the penthouse. The second led to the rest of the corporate headquarters.

Ruke often watched both doors—the assassination of Gavryn Jax, his old friend and former Korango president, remained fresh in his memory. Jax had been killed in this room, and Ruke sometimes wondered which door the killer had used—and whether he would suffer the same fate as his friend. Scenarios for his assassination swarmed in his head.

He didn't expect any of them to materialize. That changed in an instant when, right before his eyes, the door of his private quarters slowly opened and someone entered the office. It was none other than Rey Fliek, slinking into the room as quietly as possible. Despite his fear, Ruke didn't lose his self-control. He pressed the alarm button hidden under the desktop. The loud howl of sirens rang out throughout the building, and armored blinds clanged down, blocking the panoramic window and both doors.

Rey didn't immediately realize he had been spotted. His moment of confusion was enough for Ruke to get to his handgun and point it at the intruder.

"Don't shoot!" yelled Rey. "I'm not armed!"

"Get down! Spread your legs. Hands on your head!"

Rey readily stretched out on the floor. "Mr. President, I want to cooperate!"

"Then tell me where you were the night Gavryn Jax was killed!"

"In my lab."

"Lab? Ha! And what are you doing here?"

"I told you, I want to help!"

"Sneaking through the door from the private side of the penthouse? How did you get there?"

Rey didn't respond. Ruke insisted, "Didn't expect to find me here? Wanted to steal something or plant a bug?"

"I cannot answer these questions without my lawyer."

Ruke's anger grew stronger. "Or did you want to kill me? Like you killed Gav? If you wanted to help, you'd have come here like everyone else does, openly."

Rey stubbornly kept silent. Ruke was losing patience. "Spit it out, man!" His voice ripped off into a scream. "I haven't got all day! Or you'll soon start talking to Security Chief Stroud!"

The armor blocking the entrance from the corporate side rose, and a security detail stormed into the office. Shyster followed the guards. "Cuff him!" she ordered, pointing to the man on the floor, and hurried over to Ruke. "Are you okay?"

"I'm fine." Ruke pressed the alarm button again. The sirens stopped, and the metal blinds ratcheted back up. "That's better. Contact Eli. I need him here now."

"I already did. He's on his way."

A corporate shuttle carrying Eli, Nox, and Hippa glided toward Korango Enterprises' HQ. From afar, Eli noticed a small flyer already sitting on the rooftop pad. Its pilot stood nearby. "The gnat is waiting for us," Eli grumbled in displeasure.

"What gnat?" asked Nox.

"D'Obba. She's the gnat."

"I don't understand."

"She's as thin as a rake... look at her from the side! No ass. Skin and bones."

Nox shook her head disapprovingly. "That language and attitude don't suit you, Eli."

"Okay, fine. You don't like 'gnat,' so how about 'nestling'? But she bites. Nestlings don't bite."

"I can understand if you don't like her, but—"

"As a matter of fact, I enjoyed her performance. She dealt with three bruisers, just like that!" He snapped his fingers. "But they were *my* bruisers, and I don't think you know her. Watch what's going to happen when we land."

Eli was right. As soon as the shuttle settled on the pad, D'Obba rushed to the craft. With her arms folded across her chest, she waited until all three of them got out. Then she transformed. Ignoring Nox and taking a squint at Hippa, she came to Eli, touched him lightly on the elbow with one hand, smiled, and offered a handshake with the other. "Nice to meet you, Security Chief Stroud. Can I call you Eli?"

Ignoring the journalist's extended hand, Eli said, "You can call me Chief Stroud. Have you met Nox? And Hippa? If not, I recommend it."

"We were introduced before," said D'Obba. "Mind if I ask you some questions?" A small ball appeared from behind the reporter's back and hung in the air near her head. "That's my camcorder," she explained.

"I can talk while we walk to the security checkpoint. After that, I'll have to leave you."

"Very good. If you want to say something off the record, let me know."

"Excellent," proclaimed Eli, "Let's go. Shoot!"

"We're live." The ball behind D'Obba darted forward toward him. "Your crime of high treason—using the Game without authorization—has caused quite a stir on Gaia. Can you tell my readers and listeners why you did it, and how it happened?"

Eli stopped. "Have I been accused of a crime? Is that what you're insinuating?"

"No, but there is talk about it. My sources tell me that the implementation was documented, and the Commission of the GAME is investigating. Nox's presence speaks for itself."

"Well, if your commission is doing something, I guess you should ask *them*. As far as Nox is concerned, she's here to officially represent the Gaian authorities in our investigation of the alleged involvement of one or more Korags in the recent attack on Coatera. What we know here, on Korango, is that an important piece of the Game hardware was stolen, and a distinguished scientist and specialist in the technology was kidnapped. Should I conclude that your listeners and readers are more interested in *rumors* than in actual events that look to me like a gross violation of the Intergalactic Game Treaty? I think without support from Gaia, our investigation may encounter strong headwinds. We are a small polity with limited resources compared to the other players, but the scale of attack tells me that the perpetrator is powerful."

Eli resumed walking. His brisk pace made D'Obba run to catch up with him.

"Your investigation is my second question. Have you found any connection between the events on Coatera and the shipment of Gaian high-powered weaponry to Korango, which is similar to that used on your space fighter?"

Eli smiled impudently. "Oh, you mean those antimatter cannons that your boyfriend, Jour Talphi, claimed he *happened* to find in our warehouse and was arrested while trying to tamper with? If memory serves me, he *is* the leader of the Gaian neo-Game movement? Am I right?"

The ball-camcorder disappeared, and D'Obba's face twisted with anger. "You want to be a smartass?"

Eli stopped at the HQ entrance. Its elevator doors opened. "I stated the facts as they truly are. Your time is over, honey. If I'm an ass, should I call you an asshole?"

As if nothing happened, D'Obba backpedaled as quickly as she'd gone on the offensive a minute ago. "Obviously, your interview won't appear on my show. But I still want to talk to you. Where can we meet?"

"Honestly, D'Obba, I'm disappointed. I thought that tens of thousands of years of Gaian civilization could produce something better than the trash tabloid tactics you threw at me. We're not apes on Earth, you know… So, what's it gonna be?"

"Okay, okay. No more shit."

Nox and Hippa joined Eli and D'Obba. Nox anxiously glanced at her, then at Eli, but didn't say anything and only pierced him with an intense gaze. Eli smirked in return and kept talking to D'Obba. "You'd better mean that—Jour knows how to contact me. And," Eli squatted next to Hippa and hugged her, "I'll be with the kitty. If you don't behave, she'll eat you. Right, Hippa?"

Hippa growled in response.

D'Obba gave Eli the bird and walked away.

Already in the elevator, Eli asked Nox, "Do you know what that gesture means, the finger? I wonder if your translator could pick it up."

Nox shook her head. "Never seen it before."

"It means 'fuck you' back home. I'm impressed she knows and came prepared." Eli yawned. "Okay, I'm tired. So, how did you like the interview?

"I'm more concerned than ever. It was risky on your part to talk like that. I thought it would have been better to decline to speak at all."

The elevator stopped at the penthouse level, and several guards hustled to its opening doors with their weapons carried at high ready. They saluted when they saw Eli. One reported, "Sir, Mr. Khoin is with Mr. Cavell, and Ms. Shyster in his office waiting for you. The suspect is also inside."

"Thank you, fellas—give me a minute." When the guards walked away, Eli said to Nox, "You say 'decline.' Let me ask you... Is the Gaian government going to do anything to free Aura or not? What happened up there with D'Obba tells me a lot. The gnat is on Korango, but there's no sign of the Gaian authorities. Has your government sent troops to the Elder Keep? Do they know something we don't?"

"Eli, our politics are complex. I don't have answers to your questions. But I do ask you to be careful."

"Wow! Politics? Complex? Are you *serious*? Don't you care that one of yours might be tortured? Might be killed? You don't care about the vaunted technology you're so eager to protect?"

"I didn't say we don't care," Nox snapped. "It's just that we have so many considerations. The Gamer is important, but that's not the end of the world."

"And Aura?" Eli shouted. "Her dying's not the end of the world either, I suppose?"

Hippa, ears down and back, hissed and showed her teeth.

"You! Don't spit on me, traitor," yelled Eli. "Our friend is in danger."

"Hippa, please stop—" began Nox.

"I'll tell you this. I'll do everything I can to save Aura. But the moment we enter Ruke's office, events will break into a gallop. So be ready. As far as your super-sophisticated politics go, I think you're all used to a glamorous, fat life. As soon as you have it, anything else isn't your concern. That's cowardly. Second, if you live like that, eventually, *you'll lose it all*. You'll be neither the first nor the last that's happened to."

Nox sighed. "You're right. Most of my people have lost many

abilities our ancestors had. But that's exactly my point, Eli. You have a special relationship with the Game. You can change that. Your role is more important than you think."

Eli looked at Nox with pity. "Have you ever loved anybody? Do Gaians still know what love is?"

Nox stood silently, avoiding Eli's gaze.

"Nothing to say? Why am I not surprised? I'm done here," said Eli, and headed to Ruke's office.

When Eli and Nox walked into the office, Ruke sat in an armchair, aloof and silent, staring through the now-unarmored panoramic window at Korango. Zarfo and a crime scene technician stood in front of Ruke's desk, mulling over a few items found on Rey Fliek during the search. One of them, resembling a small coin, seemed interesting enough to be scanned with an array of probes scattered right there on the table.

The forensic specialist concluded, "Sir, this thing doesn't emit anything."

"Keep watching. It could be a near-field buoy recorder and transmitter using short bursts. Can you scan what's inside?" asked Zarfo. "I'm sure it's a bug."

"We need our lab, sir. We don't have a tomography scanner here."

Eli approached the table and nodded to Ruke. "Heya, glad to see you in one piece, buddy. What's up?"

Ruke winced. "Not much…"

"We're still trying to understand what Rey was doing here," explained Zarfo.

"What does he say?" frowned Eli.

"He sounds like a broken record. 'I came to help you' and minor variations of it."

Eli walked back to Rey, who sat uncomfortably on a stool in the middle of the room. He was pale and breathing heavily. Beads of sweat covered his forehead. "Are you sick, Reynard? If you need a doctor, tell me."

Rey curled his lips and lifted his head as if something interesting had appeared on the ceiling. He tried to look indifferent to what was happening around him, but deep in his eyes, Eli saw it—the fear. He decided to reason with him. "Look, Rey, can't you see you're done with your capers? We have proof that you're in contact with the Keepers. You may claim that it was nothing more than regular business. The problem is—some of your contacts work for the Elder's Security Chancellery."

Rey's gaze intensified, and increased fear in his eyes told Eli that the tactic was working. *He's probably trying to decide if I'm bluffing.*

Eli walked around the stool and looked at Rey's hands, still restrained with a plastic strip like the kind police departments on Earth used. The restraints were tight, and bruises had already appeared on his wrists. Eli pulled out a pocketknife and cut the plastic. "Don't take this as a sign of weakness. Let's not waste time."

Eli moved back to face Rey and gave him a stony glare. "I may have more questions later, but right now I want to know three things—how you helped Abaddon attack Coatera, what you were trying to do here, and the nature of your cozy relationship with Slun Ceabb. You catch my drift?"

With his eyes, Eli found Nox—she and Hippa stood quietly at the far corner of the office, trying to stay away from the security personnel processing the crime scene. Their eyes met, and Eli, with a small flick of his head, invited both to come closer. Nox and Hippa trailed between the uniformed guards and approached close enough to hear the interrogation. Shyster, who so far had held back from any activities and stood quietly close to Nox, followed suit.

Meanwhile, Rey remained silent, and his gaze drifted away. Eli didn't rush the prisoner. Finally, Rey's eyes returned to him.

"So you know about Slun." He seemed resigned to his fate. "I could never figure out that one. All he wanted from me was to arrange a meeting with Ab. But there were things I couldn't understand. First, I'd never met Slun before, so logic tells me someone told Slun about me. Secondly, this person obviously knows Slun. Finally, this person knew about my contacts with the Pazons. That someone is the person you need. He or she knows a lot of things, and likely much more than we can imagine."

"Do you know anyone who fits that description?"

"No. But I thought back over my contacts..." Rey paused.

"And?" Eli scowled.

"I hope you won't start by shooting the messenger, because the only person in my book who had or could have the knowledge and the opportunity is your friend, Yow Nayo."

"Are you saying he knew about your contact with the Keepers? Since when?"

"Since he came to me to analyze your blood, and I helped him get rid of your tracer." Rey smirked. "Ask Yow if you don't believe me. Your face looks like he never mentioned that."

"Do you know what Slun wanted to discuss with Ab?"

"Ask Ab. He's returned to Korango."

"That's impossible! All our space terminals are blocked."

"That's what you think. He's hiding in the catacombs below the Qillof Center. Catch him, and you'll know the truth. Ab told me they only wanted to disable the device. I'd never kill anyone."

"Hey, boss! Can you come here, please?" Eli heard Zarfo shout. He glanced at him—Zarfo was waving his hand, inviting Eli to come to their improvised lab. He looked preoccupied.

"Something happened?" called Eli, rushing over to Zarfo.

"Keep it down, please." Zarfo poked his finger at the small device he and the tech had been examining earlier. He took Eli aside and whispered into his ear, "It sent a signal. About one millisecond long. Eli, I don't like it. We need to wrap this up as soon as possible. It's not safe here."

On instinct, Eli looked at the window, the pride of Ruke's office. A small flyer armed with a laser gun rose from below, and the presidential office started vibrating violently. A low-frequency hum transforming into a deep rumble filled the room.

Eli screamed at the top of his lungs, "Down! Everybody on the floor!"

The flyer opened fire. The laser discharges ripped up the office window and walls and everything inside. In a matter of seconds, the old-fashioned, shipshape workplace transformed into a hell of furniture splinters, obliterated decorations, shattered glass, and debris flying around the room. Loud blasts muffled the shouts and groans of wounded people.

Twisting on the floor, Eli opened fire at the pilot with his pistol. The flyer pirouetted and slammed through the broken window into the room. The rasp of metal against the floor replaced the sound of laser discharges. The machine struck the wall and came to a noisy stop.

Avoiding being crushed under the flyer by sheer luck, Eli popped up, leaped over onto its wing, and shot off the canopy. In the thick dust wafting around, he could see only the silhouette of the pilot, who didn't sit on his hands. The engine roared again, and the flyer dragged along the wall and rose above the floor. Eli lost his balance and fell into the cabin.

As the flyer struggled to turn around, Nox, with inhuman speed and power, sprang across the room and into the cockpit, right before the machine darted through the gaping emptiness of the window.

Groaning, Ruke crawled out from under his desk and looked around. His office resembled a war zone. In the silence that followed, people began to rise from the floor and emerge from the few hiding places they'd managed to find in the room, still not sure the attack was over.

Zarfo sat on the floor, leaning back on the desk. His crime scene investigator lay on the floor, motionless. Blood covered his face and chest. "Is he dead?" ask Ruke.

"No, he has a pulse, but he was severely injured by flying glass," answered Zarfo. "How are you, sir?"

"I'm fine. We need a medical team here. Can you move?" Without waiting for an answer, Ruke yelled, "Shyster, we need a medical team!"

"On its way!" Shyster bent over one of the security guards, whose body was sorely contorted. "We have two officers dead. Rey was also killed."

"Aw, fuck! Did Eli get anything from him?" Ruke beckoned Shyster over and said, "We need to help Zarfo."

"Sir, nothing serious—it's only my ankle, a dislocation. Please take care of my forensic guy."

Ruke slammed his fists down on the desk, "Shyster, where *are* you?"

Shyster was moving slowly through the room, organizing those on foot to help the wounded. "I'm here." She looked dour. "Calm down."

"Give me the info, dammit!"

"According to Rey, Ab is hiding below the Qillof Center. He also implied that Yow Nayo could be involved in the conspiracy. Rey confirmed that he met with Slun Ceabb, who asked him to arrange a meeting with Ab."

"Who is Slun Ceabb?"

"He's a Gaian, a government official. That's what Nox told me, anyway."

"Why would a Gaian official meet with Ab?"

"I don't know."

"Did they meet?"

"Don't know."

"Where's Eli?"

"He and Nox jumped into the flyer. It took off with them aboard."

"Oh, good. I'm sure they'll subdue the pilot. Hopefully, we'll have one of theirs."

"That'd be nice." Shyster waited for a moment, then asked, "Now what?"

A cruel smile appeared on Ruke's face. "Now we search the Qillof Center. Get the men moving and hunt Ab down."

SIXTEEN
LOBO

When Nox plunged into the cockpit while the flyer was steering out of the penthouse, she fell directly onto the pilot's lap. The man at the helm grinned lecherously as his hand came up to stroke her hair. As quickly as it rose, it went down, and the smile disappeared. The pilot knew how devious Nox could be —he was Lobo, one of Nox's captors on Earth.

For a second, Nox stared at the man with cold, fierce eyes. Then she butted her forehead into his face with all her might. Blood gushed from his torn lips and broken nose. His head drooped helplessly forward, touching Nox's chest.

"Uuugh…" Her lips curled up, and her nose wrinkled. With one finger, she pushed his head aside and slipped out of Lobo's lap.

Meanwhile, Eli groaned and stirred at the back of the cabin. He'd hit the headrest knob of the driver's seat with his head.

"Eli! Are you okay?"

"My head… I hit something…"

The crippled flyer was losing altitude rapidly. Nox glanced at the instrument panel. The machine, a modified commercial flyer like a thousand others in Korango City, had simple controls. She clicked the autopilot on, and the flight path stabilized, though the damaged machine still swayed erratically. "Can you move?" she asked Eli. "We have Lobo here. Remember him? From Earth?"

"I do," he groaned, wincing as he touched the back of his head. "What do you want to do with him?"

"You tell me. We're on Korango."

"Right, we should get him to the base." Eli slowly sat up and looked at Lobo. The safety belts held his lifeless body in the pilot seat. "Is he alive?"

"He is. We need to move him. Someone needs to pilot this thing."

"Wait, he's heavy. I'll help you."

"Don't stress yourself—I'll do it." Nox unbuckled Lobo and pulled him from the seat. "I haven't flown these flyers much. And I don't know the city. Can you pilot her?"

"If I can get to the chair…"

A deafening blast shook the craft. Her irregular movement saved the machine from a direct hit, but the energy of the shock wave slammed her forward. The flyer pitched up—the bow pointed at the sky and seemed to hang in the air. Everything and everybody in the cabin rolled down into its back. Incapable of maintaining the position, the engine roared. What was essentially a flying streetcar hung in a vertical position—something she wasn't designed for. Fortunately, the chaotic movement of the flyer saved everybody inside for the second time—the attacking craft, heavier and less maneuverable, overshot.

"Critical system failure. Attempting an emergency landing," warned the autopilot.

The flyer was descending steeply over an industrial sector of the Korango City. Eli rushed to the pilot's seat. "I'll take it from here. Do you see the assailant?"

"No. We need to hide somewhere."

"I'm going to crash-land this thing inside the… Hold on." Eli sent the flyer through an open roll-up door into an industrial building, an abandoned environmental treatment plant, a relic from Korango's early days. The engine failed several feet above the ground even before the flyer entered the building. She slammed onto the concrete floor, spinning and screeching, and finally came to a standstill.

Nox jumped out of the machine. In the ensuing silence, the sound of the approaching enemy craft resounded closer and closer. Eli peered out of the wreckage. "Okay, their flyer is too big to get in. They'll shoot through the roof or entrance. Help me move Lobo closer to the walls."

Nox sprang back into the flyer and, with one swift movement, pushed the bulky man out onto the floor of the warehouse. She then grabbed him by the collar of his jacket and pulled him aside, hiding between old distillation towers. Eli joined Nox just in time —a series of blasts left gaping holes in the roof, pulverizing what was left of Lobo's flyer.

"Call for reinforcements!" shouted Nox over the rumble of the enemy engine.

"Already done. Zarfo's guys are coming. Wait here for them. I have to run." Eli pulled out his commsys. "I need a taxi. Lock on my signal."

"Ohhhh..." Lobo moaned as he regained consciousness. "What happened?"

"Someone wanted to kill you. Now be polite and say to Nox, 'Thank you for saving me.'" Eli nodded at the smoldering remains in the center of the building. "If not for Nox, you'd be in that wreckage."

Lobo raised himself on one elbow and looked at the flyer. "Who did this?"

"That's what I wanted to ask you."

"Me? I don't know."

"Perhaps your comrades in arms tried to kill you after you killed Rey? I don't think that's a coincidence."

"We don't do such things... makes no sense." Lobo groaned.

"If not your guys, then who else could it be?"

Lobo shrugged. "Whatever. I'm not going to talk."

"That remains to be seen."

A taxi appeared at the entrance to the building, maneuvered inside, and stopped nearby. Eli turned to Nox. "Promise me that nothing will happen to Lobo before I get my hands on him. I'll order Zarfo to comply. I need the guy. Use *Night Stalker* if you need to safeguard him. Fuck Korango, I don't trust anybody here anymore."

"I don't like it—" began Nox.

"I don't want to hear what you don't like. Swear you'll do what I ask you to do!"

"Okay, okay… If it makes it easier for you, I swear."

"It does. One day, you'll understand."

When Ash returned from the hospital to Yow's little apartment, now her home, Eli's call caught her by surprise. She had no desire to see him.

Ash didn't regret that her attempt to kill herself had failed. But deep inside, she decided that dead or alive, her bid to establish a new life among these aliens would never come true. It didn't mean she wanted to be back on Earth. She didn't know what she wanted, and she didn't *know* what to do with herself. This realization disturbed her greatly. But, as people often do, she disregarded the idea that the root of the problem might lie within her. Instead, she began looking outside, blaming everything and everybody other than herself.

Ash sat on a couch with her feet tucked under her, woebegone and depressed. "What should I tell Eli?" she asked Yow, who sat in a chair across the room with a book in his hands.

Yow wasn't reading it—instead, he was sorting out his feelings. The process typically gave him comfort and purpose.

Immersed in his thoughts, he was mulling over recent events. Unlike Ash, though, Yow knew exactly what was bothering him. His experience and instinct were telling him that what had happened was only an opening act in a drama threatening their lives.

He'd used to think of himself as a voice of wisdom, a bastion of righteousness and fairness. Not this time. Yow felt he had lost it all, and it galled him. Also, unlike Ash, he blamed nobody else. Yow firmly believed that his own actions had caused his predicament. Yet, his girlfriend's stupidity irked him. And Eli, a boy still wet behind the ears, had unexpectedly become a thorn in his side. But he couldn't fathom how and when Eli's actions had undermined his composure.

"The truth," scowled Yow. "You have any other ideas?"

"I'm not going to apologize."

"Then why did you want to take your life?"

"An impulse I regret. The Game is *bad*. It needs to be destroyed."

"You're naive. A lot of people depend on the Game. Billions! Many billions. Do you realize that? The Game has become too strong—stronger than anything else."

"Okay, I was naive. I learned my lesson. Nobody will use me anymore. I'll use them."

"Them—*who*? To do *what*?"

"Anybody. To live and do what I want. And I want to destroy the Game."

"The Game is the devil! It cannot be destroyed. And I believe Eli is eavesdropping on our conversation. Not personally, but he has Korango's full force behind him."

"There's nothing he can learn that he doesn't already know."

"Wrong again. You live in a bubble."

The doorbell chimed. Ash jumped up, then sat back on the couch and adjusted her skirt. Not knowing what to do with her hands, she placed them on her lap and smoothed wrinkles out of the fabric. Finally, she folded her arms across her chest. Noticing Yow watching her, she blushed. "What?"

"Nothing. Hang on—everything will be fine." Yow smiled and pressed the button to unlock the door.

Ash and Yow were silent for the entire time it took Eli to get from the street to the apartment.

"Hi, guys!" Eli began cheerfully.

"What do you want from me?" Ash spat, staring at the floor.

"Ouch. Why such a pissy attitude?"

Ash didn't respond and instead surveyed the bookshelf on the other side of the room.

"Up to you. You were stupid, and you're still stupid—and pigheaded. Okay, I need to talk to Yow."

Yow winced. "I don't have secrets from Ash. And please, no need to be rude."

"Oh, you don't have secrets from her? All right, fine. Because if you did," Eli stated, his voice rising, "Aura would still be safe on Coatera! And Rey Fliek and two other Korags would still be alive!"

Eli's words cut right to Yow's heart, but they also infuriated him. *Who the hell does this pup think he is, insinuating that I talk too much? And what does he mean, Rey and two other Korags would be alive—where is this coming from?* "What do you mean, alive?"

"Alive—as in not dead." Eli sneered. "A flyer piloted by an Elder Keep thug attacked Ruke Cavell's office. He killed Rey and two security officers during the hit-and-run raid—all because of your loose lips." He paused for a second. "Ash can stay. I don't mind. I want to talk about your dealings with Rey. I also want to know about your contacts with... Well, first, let's see how it goes with Rey."

Seething with anger, Ash sprang from the couch. "How dare you come here and accuse us like this! Nazi!"

"Ash, please," begged Yow. *Why does she butt into everything? Don't stick your neck out!* "It's not that simple."

His feeble attempt to calm Ash didn't produce any result. She raged in earnest, "It's all lies and dirt! And if you"—Ash jabbed Yow with her finger—"want to play along with this circus, I won't!" With all the dignity she could muster, she walked to the door and left, slamming it for all she was worth.

Eli stood dumbfounded, "Uh... What's gotten into her? You know, I came here with peaceful intentions."

"I'm sorry, Eli. I know she didn't mean it. She regrets a lot. She's devastated. I'm asking you to forgive her."

"That's why I'm here, and why she's not at the police station. You need to bring Ash to her senses. If she keeps behaving like this"—Eli shook his head—"I don't know how it's going to end."

A heavy silence hung over the room until Eli said, "Can we sit and talk? I'm here to ask you about a man named Slun Ceabb."

How did he sniff that out? Yow turned pale. Eli waited. "So, you know about Slun," Yow said weakly.

"Well, I know something, but not everything."

"I won't talk about Slun."

"That would be a mistake. Until what happened on Coatera, your relationship with this guy was of no consequence to me or anyone else. But not anymore. You see that, don't you?"

Afraid to reveal his fright, Yow feverishly tried to come up with an explanation for his acquaintance with Slun. *What should I tell Eli? Damn it! I need more time to think of something.* "For the sake of argument, let's say I see. So what?" Yow reluctantly admitted.

"To make it easier for you, let's assume—also for the sake of argument—that Slun met with Ab."

"So?"

"It's not a secret who Slun is. Why would a DRC agent want to arrange a meeting with Abaddon or any of the folks at the Elder Keep's Security Chancellery? To discuss what? In what capacity? As an intelligence officer to develop a Pazon asset? By using Rey, a person he had never met before? Come on! That's not how spooks operate—spying is an ancient occupation. So it must be something that either the Gaian government wanted or that Slun personally wanted. Perhaps with the blessing of his superiors."

He's like a fucking bloodhound. Astonished and goggle-eyed, Yow stared at Eli. *What exactly are you driving at?*

"Don't look at me like that!" exclaimed Eli. "I *know* what Slun wanted from you. Read the Bible. 'There is nothing hidden that won't be revealed.' Anyway, how is my logic so far?"

"I don't have a Bible," Yow said dryly. "Your logic is fine."

"Good. To finish up, I have to discard the Gaian government from this equation—solely because of what happened on Coatera. Unless Gaians are total idiots or their government agreed in advance to close their eyes on the attack on Cela, which is unlikely. And that leaves me with the conspiracy theory involving Slun and possibly some of his colleagues. Are you still with me?"

"I am. So what?" snapped Yow. *This is the Gaian government, the DRC. Does he get it? I don't care.* "Slun wouldn't give a shit about your theories you can't prove. And neither do I! What do I have to do with all this?"

Yow sat sweaty and red, with shifty eyes. Despite his desperate rudeness, Eli continued to build his case. "I agree that Slun wouldn't care. At least, not as things are now."

Yow looked at Eli with horror. *The bastard is enjoying it!*

Meanwhile, Eli began his final attack. "He wouldn't, but you should. You know why? Because if this operation isn't officially authorized, as soon as Slun and his comrades learn about Korango's investigation of the connection between the DRC and the attack, they'll eliminate everybody who might link them to the Elder Keep. Moreover, I suspect they've already started. An hour ago, someone tried to kill the man who killed Rey."

Yow remained silent.

"You turned out to be in the wrong place at the wrong time and didn't know when to keep your mouth shut," said Eli. "My wild guess is that when you started working for Aura and went through the vetting process, Slun recruited you as his asset on Korango—it was his job. But then, when the attack took place, you, a Korag, turned out to be involved. I know—unwillingly. But that doesn't matter, does it? Your involvement is the reason we're taking part in the Gaian investigation. Am I right?"

Fear overwhelmed Yow, grabbing his throat with its iron grip. *He's right, absolutely right. I'm next—they'll kill me like they killed Rey, and then they'll kill Ash. What am I to do? If I cough it up, will it help me... and Ash? Is Eli powerful enough to help? Why do I think he wants to help? Can he close his eyes to what we've done? Yes, that's it! Otherwise, we'd already be in jail. Even without Slun, I broke Korango's laws.* The sound of Eli's words faded, and a wave of nausea welled up inside Yow.

"Are you okay?" Eli's concerned voice seeped through the haze inside Yow's mind.

"Ah... What? I'm fine."

Eli continued staring at Yow for a long moment. "I was talking about your relationship with Slun."

"Yes. What you said is true. One correction—Slun approached me because he already knew about the Elder Keep showing interest in the Game, and Korango was a convenient false flag to collect more information on that. He recommended me to Aura as an aide."

Yow, who had finally recovered from his panic, pulled himself together and gloomily went on, "But generally speaking, your guesses are accurate. It was my mistake to suggest Rey as a channel to contact Abaddon, and I'm sorry about that. But I thought I was doing the right thing. You know... Gaians, the most ancient human civilization... I couldn't imagine some of them might have ulterior motives."

"I didn't say you were a bad guy. The thing is, this story is far from over. I can't tell you more. Hope you understand. But I need you to do me a favor. If you agree, it'll also help you—at the very least, there'll be someone to witness your honest intentions in dealing with this complex situation. Though I hope it'll never come to that."

"What exactly are you suggesting?"

"First, tell me, did Slun try to collect information about me?"

So it's all about Eli! But I didn't want to harm him. "Yes, he did. He asked a lot of questions about you. Sorry, but I told him everything I knew. He even asked me to provide some of your DNA. I gave him samples of your blood. I didn't get what that was all about. Do you?"

"Another question. Did he meet Ab?"

"I don't know for sure—probably yes. The last time I saw Slun Ceabb, he was on Coatera, the same time you were there. He became angry with Aura. You know, they… well, know each other. The way he talked about you, and Korango, and Coatera… I recall he wanted to inspect *Sheleucia*, Aura's cruiser—we were loading mines onto the ship. In hindsight, Slun probably knew something about the impending attack. He got drunk, swore a lot, threatened —nothing specific, though. You know, he's a sleazy and pathetic guy, but that time he sounded more certain of himself. I thought it was because of Aura and you. You know, I think she loves you."

Eli glared at him. "The last question. Why didn't you tell Aura about Rey and Ab?"

Why is it so difficult to get? I don't think he understands who Slun is. "Why would I? He's the security man, not Aura. It's up to the Gaians to sort out their differences. But for the record, I told her about Rey and the danger he represents."

"Okay. What I'm asking you to do is simple. Don't show any initiative regarding Slun. Don't contact him unless he wants to meet with you. Don't ask questions—listen. Don't hide the fact that Korangan authorities—and I'm one—asked you questions about the assault on Coatera as a part of our investigation. But present it as a routine probe.

"Never mention that I'm interested and know about his contacts with the Pazons. You're not a novice, and I don't want to scare you. But if you do, I'm afraid your days will be numbered. Stay on Korango. If he or someone else asks you to leave the station, say that the authorities ordered you to stay here. If you have something new, contact me. Unless something serious happens, I won't contact you. Questions?"

"What about Ash?"

"The fewer people who know about our conversation, the better off we'll all be."

Weasel! He's slippery as a snake. Probably should be if he wants to take on the DRC. "But you said at the beginning you wouldn't mind if Ash stayed here when we talked."

"Good, you believed me. I hope she did too. Honestly, do I need to teach you what kind of bullshit you should tell her? I'm disappointed with Ash, but I don't want revenge. I wish she were less stubborn and admitted that she made a grievous mistake. If she allows others to take her for a sucker like that, she won't last long here and will drag you down, too."

Eli's commsys dinged softly. He pulled it out. "That's Ruke. I have to take this."

"Eli?" Ruke said into the commsys, barely containing his irritation. "Where *are* you?"

Judging by his face, Ruke didn't care much for Eli's lengthy response. He listened for several seconds, winced, and pulled the phone off his ear, waiting for Eli to stop.

Ruke looked around. Destruction and decay surrounded him. The abandoned underground facilities below Qillof Center had made a terrible impression on him. He stood amid a cleared area surrounded by pools of stinking water, strange crumbling structures, broken industrial equipment, remnants of flying machines, and passages lined with ducts and cables. He was losing any hope of capturing Abaddon, his sworn enemy, in this disgusting place. A melancholy took hold of him.

Ruke waited a bit longer, then sighed and put the commsys back to his ear. "Okay, okay… I get it," he interrupted Eli. "You have Lobo, nice. Crack him. Rey's tip about Ab hiding under the Qillof Center was a ruse. I'm counting on you." Ruke ended the call.

It had been already hours since two armored drop-ships had settled on the center's main square and unloaded dozens of the Korango Defense Guard. The guards, the closest thing to an army the space station had, launched the operation quickly and efficiently. Armed soldiers invaded the underground lair from all directions through the little-known nonpublic entrances and spread like blazes inside the musty, abandoned basements of the Qillof Center. But a whole day of searching had failed to produce results.

Shyster and Zarfo, dirty and tired, approached Ruke. "Sir, I don't think Ab is here," said Zarfo.

"Yes, we need to call off the search," agreed Shyster. "The Defense Guard can probably leave. But for the time being, I'd assigned police officers to patrol the area on foot."

"I like the foot patrol idea. Zarfo, please do call off the search. Shyster, inform the Guard. Even if Ab was here, he's not anymore." Ruke sighed. "Anyway, I talked to Eli. He and Nox captured Lobo— the pilot who killed Rey. Believe it or not, I know the guy." Ruke smiled wryly and added, "Eli thinks he can get something from him."

"Yes sir, my officers booked Lobo and took him down to the police station," confirmed Zarfo.

The swift justice and simple laws of Korango made prisons unnecessary. Law and corporate rule-breakers, if found guilty at quick court procedures, were banned from the space station—the only and most fearful punishment in the minds of Korags.

When Eli showed up in the city detention facility, only one of the five lockups was occupied. Two police officers stood guard on either side of Lobo's cell. "Hi, guys. You can go now," said Eli.

The guards exchanged nervous glances. "Sir, Zarfo ordered—" started one of them.

Eli frowned. "I know. I cancel the order. Before leaving, open the door to the cell. Give me the keys. Cuff the prisoner." Eli pointed to a video camera attached to the wall. "Also, get rid of that."

"Sir, it's attached to the wall."

"Dammit, I don't care! Break it out of the wall if you have to. Shoot it off. Whatever."

"Yes, sir!" The bewildered policemen rushed to carry out the orders.

Lobo lay on a ledge with closed eyes. Guards moved him onto a metal stool and cuffed his hands behind his back. He didn't resist and stared blankly at the floor as the guards left.

Eli sat on the ledge. "I'm Eli. Who are you?"

"Lobo D'Matroc, a member of the SOF, the Elder Keep's Special Operations Force."

"I remember you from Earth. You were with Abaddon on the mountain plateau. Abaddon is your boss, right?"

"Yes. But that's all I'm gonna say."

Eli took his time to examine Lobo. He had a weather-beaten face, wide cheekbones, inflamed eyes, a scar on his forehead. His lips and the bridge of his nose were bleeding. *This guy has been through plenty in his life,* Eli thought. "What do you want?"

Lobo turned slightly, showing him the handcuffs. "Can you remove them?"

"Do you want anything more than that? I can help you if you help me."

"What can you possibly offer?"

"Just about anything you want."

Lobo smirked. "I've heard about you. That's why you sent the guards away?"

"The Elder Keep took something from me. I want it back."

"The girl?"

"That's none of your business. So?"

Lobo D'Marroc

Under Eli's steadfast gaze, the smirk disappeared from Lobo's face, and a frown replaced it. "I know what you want from me. I won't do it. I'm a pawn. They'll crush me. They'll kill my family. Where do I go after that?"

"That's why I asked you what you wanted."

"Oh, I'll tell you what I want." Lobo's words sounded like gunshots. "I want all of you… to fuck off."

It was now Eli's turn to smirk. "I know the feeling. What else?"

"Listen!" Lobo chose not to avoid Eli's stare. "I killed one of yours. Maybe more. Do you think your bosses will close their eyes to this?"

"You'd be surprised. Besides, I don't have bosses. *I'm* the boss."

"And you'll give me what *I* want on a golden platter with a glass of wine to wash everything down?"

"Something like that. But not until I get what I want. It'll be a dangerous operation. Good news—the higher the risk, the higher the reward."

"And if you fail?"

"Then I'm dead. Most likely… In such an outcome, you'll die *before* me. But all in all, it's still better than certain death awaiting you now."

"Why should I trust you?"

He's talking about trust. Is he ready to give up his loyalty to his bosses? It doesn't seem there's more than that. "Because it won't cost me much to reward you, and because we're on Korango. So, why not help a brother out?"

Apparently, that English set phrase was translated as it should —Lobo fell silent as the fiery glance and challenge in his eyes waned. "Damn Ab, damn you," he muttered. His voice sounded tired and broken. "Damn that day when I agreed to work for Asphalis!"

"Who's that?"

"Abaddon's boss. I'm sure you'll have the pleasure of meeting him if you go ahead with whatever plan you have. Be that as it may, I'll work on my list of things I need. Safety for my family first."

Eli sized up Lobo's hunched figure. *He doesn't look like a thug, and I like the 'my family first' thing.* "I'm glad we've understood each other. Now, the guards will be back soon. They'll uncuff you. Be ready for the action. It'll happen quickly. Be wise—don't talk about what happened to you, for your own sake. Someone tried to kill you today. Do you know who that was?"

"No. That wasn't one of ours. I can guarantee that."

"Actually…" Eli pulled out his commsys. Three swipes and the hologram with Slun Ceabb hung in the air. "Do you know this man?"

"I've seen him."

"Do you know who he is?"

"No."

"When and where did you see him?"

"Just once. I was helping Ab with countersurveillance. I don't remember the name of the place. It was underground..."

Wow, I'm glad I asked. That's already something. "Does the Qillof Center ring a bell?"

"Yep, that's the place."

"Is Ab still there?"

"I don't think so. I think he left Korango. You probably don't know, but there's a tunnel to an abandoned space dock in the center's lower ground floor. That's what we've been using."

"Then a change in plans. Zarfo, my deputy, will be here soon. I'd appreciate it if you explain to him how to find the dock."

"Send him in. As you said, 'why not help a brother out'!" Lobo scornfully mocked Eli.

"Hey, I like the spirit. Can you tell me where your guys are keeping Aura?"

Lobo hesitated—Eli waited. "Ah, here goes nothing," muttered Lobo. "In the Chancellery's basement. I can draw a map."

"Good. What about the machine, the torus, you stole from the Gaians?"

"Also in the basement. In a different wing. I can add the location to the map."

"Final question for today. Who ordered the attack on Coatera?

"Asphalis. It was our operation."

"Can he sanction an assault of such a scale on an alien planet?"

"I don't know. Probably not..."

Eli stepped up and patted Lobo on the back. "I see we can work together. See you soon!"

SEVENTEEN

JOUR AND D'OBBA

"It stinks like a sewer pit in here," complained Jour, whispering in D'Obba's ear. "We've got what we wanted. Let's get out of here!"

Jour and D'Obba were standing in a dirty old shop in the Qillof Center catacombs. Their figures merged with the darkness, and the only light came from a small device in D'Obba's hand, which cast a faint silver glow over her face. "I want more. And don't spit into my ear."

"I'm not spitting. I'm trying to be quiet. The police are still here."

"The residual transport signature I'm getting isn't strong enough. If we can get closer to the materialization spot, we could ID the transporter type." D'Obba poked her nose out the door into a long underground corridor. "Nobody." She stepped outside the shop and moved her gadget in different directions. "This way. I'm going. Stay here if you want." With decisive steps, D'Obba headed to the left, where the underground corridor opened into a hub.

Jour raised his voice, "Wait! You'll ruin everything. I'm sure police patrols are still there."

D'Obba hissed, "Shhh... I don't care. The signature is getting stronger. One more good reading is all I need." She sped up her steps. "Hurry if you want to—" D'Obba looked back. "Oh, crap!"

A security guard showed up at the far end of the corridor, cutting off the path to retreat. Without hesitation, quick as a wink, D'Obba raced to the center of the hub, holding her scanner in front of her... and then she stopped. At least a dozen heavily armed men filled what had seemed to be an empty area partially cleared of debris. They blocked all corridors converging on the hub.

"Why, if it isn't my old friend D'Obba!" she heard a familiar voice call.

"Screw you, shithead!" D'Obba stomped closer to Zarfo.

"On the floor, now! Or you'll regret it, lady." A baleful smile passed over Zarfo's face.

Jour stepped in front of D'Obba. "Please, sir, we mean no harm. Please, let us go!"

D'Obba peeked out from behind Jour's shoulder. "Not before I check that spot!" She pointed at the middle of the hub.

Zarfo relented. "Both of you, what are you doing here?"

"Sir, it's vital that we evaluate certain, umm, spatial parameters around that spot," answered Jour.

"I've met Ms. D'Obba Chyllep, so you must be Mr. Jour Talphi. What parameters, and why is it so important?"

"That's right—I'm Jour, sir—"

"His name is Zarfo, dear," interrupted D'Obba, teeth tightly clenched. "He's Eli's stooge."

"Nice to meet you, Zarfo." Jour shielded her again with his broad shoulders. "We can't tell you what we're doing here, but if you could be so kind as to give us a chance to talk to Eli—after we assess the parameters, that is—he'll appreciate our help. And Mr. Rurik Cavell. I can guarantee you that. Please, also accept my apology. D'Obba is a little nervous right now. May I say, on edge. The... er... parameters we are looking at—they change quickly."

"I'll talk to Eli right now. Do you promise to stay calm and not do anything stupid?"

"Yes, Zarfo!" Jour answered readily.

"I also want to hear from your girlfriend. How much time do you need to finish all this?"

D'Obba showed her face again. "If you promise not to hurt us, and if you promise to give us five minutes to complete our evaluation, I promise not to hurt you and not to run away from you. Happy now?"

"Just my luck." Zarfo took out his commsys. "Stay here!"

He stepped away while talking and returned in less than a minute. "You've got it your way. But I have my orders to escort you to meet Eli as soon as you complete your... Well, whatever you do here. Do we have an understanding?"

"Yes, sir!" Jour breathed a sigh of relief while D'Obba began walking methodically around the hub, glancing down at the sensor readings.

She finished quickly, pulled Jour aside, and muttered under her breath, "It was a Gaian government standard-issue transporter."

"Slun?" whispered Jour.

"I think so," D'Obba whispered back.

Eli finished creating a simple, quiet ambiance with three armchairs and a cocktail table in the aft of *Night Stalker* just as D'Obba and Jour appeared at the bottom of the entrance ramp with Zarfo behind them. Zarfo shoved the two detainees gently, encouraging both to walk up into the belly of the space fighter, and left.

Jour felt at ease. He went straight to a chair and flopped into it, stretching out his long legs. "Finally. That was a difficult day!" He glanced around. "I don't remember the chairs. Did you redecorate?"

"I did." Eli chuckled and turned his attention to D'Obba, who still stood hesitantly near the now-closed ramp. "Please, sit down. Can I offer you something to eat? Korango menu? Or something to drink?"

D'Obba blushed. "Yes, please. An Oaken Hopper?"

"Sure!" Eli disappeared in the utility bay and returned in a second with three glasses and a bottle of the Korangan whiskey. He quickly poured the alcohol and raised his glass. "Nice to see you both."

D'Obba's barely noticeable shyness didn't escape Eli's attention. However, either because the time that passed did the trick, or the Oaken Hopper made a difference, but she quickly regained her aplomb, returning to her usual self-confidence and aggressiveness. She stood up, pulled out the gadget she had used in the catacombs, and walked around the room. "What the fuck? It doesn't work!" she exclaimed after a moment.

"No, it doesn't." Eli was calm.

"Then why this masquerade?" D'Obba kicked the armchair.

"It's not a masquerade. It's my ship, and I decorate it any way I want." Eli reached for the bottle, poured himself another drink of Hopper, and pushed it toward Jour. "Help yourself, buddy." He sipped the liquid from his glass, squinting like a cat after every nip.

An awkward silence hung among the three. Eli looked at D'Obba, and the flames of banked fury sparked in his eyes. "D'Obba... and Jour. I want to explain something to you. First, I don't appreciate your attitude, D'Obba. You're with me, and not in a prison cell, only because you promised to explain what you were doing in Qillof Center. Second, you are guests here on Korango, and guests should respect the laws and traditions of the place they're visiting. You are rude and obnoxious. Third, you underestimate me and don't appreciate my good will. Come to your senses, or you will regret it."

"Are you *threatening* me?" shouted D'Obba.

"I am, scrawny piece of shit. Do you Gaian pigs, really think I'll kiss your asses? If you don't apologize immediately for your behavior, bitch, I'll rot you and your rube in prison. Don't make me count to three!"

Jour sprang from his chair and dashed toward D'Obba. With a lightning-quick movement, Eli pulled his gun on Jour. "One!"

"Sir, there's been a misunderstanding!" shrieked Jour. "We'll keep our word! Slun Ceabb was there, or at least we think so—a Gaian government quantum transport took place in that catacomb!"

Jour Talphi

"Good! Now apologize!"

"I'll never apologize to the likes of you!" D'Obba flared her nostrils in anger.

"Two!" Eli pulled out his commsys.

"We want to help you, you bastard! Chauvinist!"

"That's pathetic! Do you think you can outswear *me*? I'm from Earth! No one outswears a motherfucking Earthman! Three!"

Eli began making a call as D'Obba burst out laughing. "Okay, okay! My apologies! It was insensitive, and it won't happen again."

He slipped the commsys into his pocket but kept holding Jour at gunpoint.

"Eli, please put away your gun," begged Jour. "It's scary. Were you really going to shoot me?"

"Not now, maybe later." Eli remained unperturbed. "Care to explain your change of heart?"

"No change." D'Obba kept giggling. "We like you, we always did. I know it was stupid, but still, we wanted to know more about you. My idea, my apologies again."

Eli holstered the gun. "So, what are your findings?"

"You know, sometimes you looked like a suit," Jour said. "That wasn't comforting—"

"But it was fun!" D'Obba cut in.

Jour continued, "Did you kill people?"

"Started recently. Anyway, what's the point of your exercise?"

D'Obba got serious. "We want to know where you stand regarding the Game. And whether—if you support our position—we can rely on you as a person?"

"I don't support any position. The Game seems like a cool thing, but to tell the truth, I know little about it. Why do you care about my support? I'm a guy from Earth—I'm nobody."

"Well, loose lips have been flapping..." Jour said reluctantly. "Slun Ceabb or not, some folks in the Gaian government are *very* interested in you. My theory is they're watching you and looking for ways to set you up."

"Why?"

D'Obba wrinkled her nose. "I'd guess to get rid of you. Or to coerce you into doing something for them. That's the government."

"I take it you guys are not big fans of your authorities?"

"Are you?"

"Excluding you, I know only two Gaians, Nox and Aura. Isn't it too early for me to decide where to place my sympathies?"

D'Obba didn't back down. "Nox *is* a government, and Aura is damn close to it."

"You don't get it. Not to go into details, but Nox... well, she knew my father. Even helped him. Aura... Aura is different. The Keepers kidnapped her, and I'm responsible for that. Her life is in danger." Eli bridled his tongue as his passion splashed out for others to see.

Jour and D'Obba looked at each other and exclaimed almost in unison, "Your father?" Then D'Obba squinted. "Are you romantically involved with Aura?"

Eli didn't answer, and Jour chimed in, "He is..."

"You knew about this, dear?" D'Obba opened her eyes wide.

"I did. So what?" Jour looked confused.

"Oh, man! Fuck! Sorry, Eli. I just... I don't know what this is. Just fuck!"

"No, don't worry, I understand. When it's fucked, it's fucked. And it *is* fucked." Eli's voice failed him.

"What difference does it make?" Jour resented.

"Shut up! Okay?" D'Obba yelled and started pacing.

"So hey, can you explain all that business about the Game and your government?" Eli asked.

"Jour, tell him!"

"Someone told me to shut up." Jour sounded offended.

"You can talk now! Happy?" snapped D'Obba.

Jour sighed. "It's complicated. Briefly, there are two sides. One wants the Game to be mostly the Game it is now. That's where D'Obba and I are. The other wants to expand the Game, to give it even more power. That's what our government wants. Not everybody, but a good part of the Directorate and the administration. And that's the scariest thing I can think of—to create a god and then attempt to control it. Surprised?"

"Not really. As they say, 'power is not a means—it's an end.'"

"Then you're more on our side, am I right?"

"Could be. I need to know more. Also, how do I fit in with all this?" Eli gave Jour a perplexed look.

"It is *always* about controlling the Game." Jour glared at Eli. "As I told you, some say you have something to do with it. Like having special skills, or access, or ability. Any of these true?"

"Evidently, the people in your government know more than I do. I learned about the Game only four weeks ago. I've been here next to no time."

"That's true." Jour looked disappointed.

D'Obba doubted that. "Then why guys like Slun Ceabb swirl around you? Incidentally, I saw that you weren't surprised when Jour told you about him."

"Very observant, but don't forget that I'm now in charge of security on Korango. I know things. As to why people swirl around me—ask them."

"I hope when you know more, you'll understand our concerns," D'Obba said. "We want to stay on Korango a few more days, specifically in space near the station. Do you mind?"

"I don't. Can you tell me if your government is going to do something about the Elder Keep attack on Coatera?"

Jour frowned. "If you mean militarily, I wouldn't be surprised if they don't. Diplomatically, yes. But we don't like to use force even if we can or should. Our place in the Milky Way is rather special."

"Are you *kidding* me? I know the guy who probably led the Keep's forces into the attack. He's ruthless. They torture one of yours! And the Gamer? I've heard Gaians are concerned about the crazy shit going on with the technology. Pazons stole a part of it. It could be a catastrophe if they figure out how to use the Gamer to connect to the Game itself. Anyway, they slap your cheek and what —you offer another?"

Jour spread his hands in bewilderment. "I wish I had a better answer for you. If I have something new, I'll let you know."

"Thanks. I'm relieved to see that your people—as attested to by you—still have many of the bad human qualities I thought could only be found in a few barbarous places, like Earth."

Jour gaped at Eli and remained standing with his mouth open.

"Uh... That's classy! Gives me confidence Gaia has a chance." D'Obba presented Eli with a smile. "Jour, close your mouth. It was sarcasm, dear."

Eli waited until Jour and D'Obba left and called Ruke.

EIGHTEEN

ELI'S PLAN

R uke took the call immediately. "Eli? What's up?"

"Hi, dude! Do you want me to kill Ab?"

"I do. Is he here? You found him?"

"Not yet, but I will."

"How? I believe we're at a dead end. We need a plan."

"I have a plan."

"What are you gonna do?"

"I'll fly to Pat'zan to free Aura. I think Ab will be there, so I can kill him for you."

"When?"

"I haven't decided yet. Probably tomorrow or the day after."

"You're not serious, are you?"

"Dead serious."

"Shouldn't the Strangers take care of Aura?"

"That's what I thought. But they won't, and I can't stand around and do nothing. They fucking used Korango. I knew that and did nothing to help Aura."

"That's not your fault."

"If something happens to Aura... I don't know... I love her. See?"

"I get it now. How are you going to do it?"

"If you help, my chances of success will be much higher."

"What do you want me to do?"

"Go to Pat'zan in your official capacity to meet their higher-ups to complain about Keepers meddling with Korango affairs. We'll hide *Night Stalker* in your cruiser's hangar and get into their space undetected."

"Ah, I do want to talk to the Pazons. I've had about all I can take from them. I want to find and punish all perpetrators."

"Good. Then I'll beam myself to their prison, free Aura, and beam back. Simple. Your hands are clean."

"Beam?"

"Yep, that's a *Night Stalker* thing—don't worry. Like in *Star Trek*."

"So it's real. I knew it! Do you know where they're keeping her?"

"I do."

"How?"

"Lobo."

"He talked?"

"Yes."

"Good. I'm in."

"Good. Then do your part. You probably have some diplomatic channels you can use to make the arrangements?"

"It's in the bag—I'll take care of the visit. You ready?"

"Almost. I need to work on contingency plans. I also need to learn how to use the transporter."

"You don't know?"

"It's not what you think. It's a brief session with Nox."

"She doesn't know about your plan?"

"Not yet. She'd nag me and try to talk me out of it. So I wanted to talk to you first."

"Right. She's nice, but annoying sometimes."

"All righty, sounds good. I'll call Nox right now. Talk to you later. Bye."

"See ya…"

"Nox? It's Eli."

"It's midnight!"

"Can you come by?"

"If you need to talk—"

"I'm in *Night Stalker*—I need you here."

"As my regular self? Or something special, a T-shirt?"

"I don't care. I want to know how to use the transporter."

"Right now?"

"Are you coming or not?"

"Give me a second."

Nox appeared right in front of Eli—he jumped up in fright. "I didn't expect you to show up like this!"

She walked around the living space Eli had created to meet Jour and D'Obba. "Did you do this yourself? Nice! Seeing someone? Or is it for me?"

Eli didn't respond.

"That was a joke. If you want to use a transporter, you should know what it looks like."

"I need to know how to use it, not what it looks like."

"I mean, you need to see how it happens. There's nothing to learn if you use *Night Stalker*—same deal as with everything else. You have the neural interface. But be aware, there are some limitations."

"Like what?"

"Like, the transport can fail. Or it can take a lot of time when you try to send someone or something to a place—for example, the Security Chancellery on Pat'zan—without knowing its exact coordinates and layout. And the transport range may vary."

"Why is that?"

"The transport process is based on Game technology, but it requires tremendous computing power to test the feasibility of the transferal and its safety before it happens. If the system determines that there are problems—and it's extremely conservative in doing so—the procedure is automatically aborted."

"How can I make it certain?"

"Use transport terminals. If a terminal isn't available at the place where the relocation ends, you'll need a beacon on you to get back."

"Where do I get one? What does it look like?"

Nox opened one of the compact devices attached to the belt of her spacesuit and pulled out a small disk. "Like this. It's standard issue on Gaia. *Night Stalker* will make one for you. But your plan to transport yourself to Pat'zan and then transport back with Aura won't work."

Eli's face showed disappointment.

"Did my explanations dash your hopes for a quick win?"

"Very cunning observation. So, how do I get to the Security Chancellery?"

"Use a drop pod, a small one. Get a verification code from Lobo if you haven't yet done so. And pray that the Pat'zan border patrols won't discover the ruse. See? Simple."

"I'm not in the mood to appreciate your sarcasm."

"Sorry. I thought you'd turn a deaf ear to my arguments and pleading."

"*Don't* tell me that Aura can take care of herself. Don't tell me I have more important things to do."

"It's a suicide mission. And you wouldn't listen, anyway. Can you explain why?"

"Because I want Aura to be... to breathe. To look at the sky. To smile. Or even cry. It's called life. See? Simple."

"Do you understand that even if you somehow deceive the Elder Keep and *avoid* getting killed, your actions will be considered a crime on Gaia because you'll be using *Night Stalker*, a part of the Game, without an authorization? Our government will be relentless. They will hunt you down, and I don't know in what prison your life will be better, on Pat'zan or Gaia. What's in that for you?"

"If you want to rot with your Game, I don't care. I'm neither a criminal nor an apostle, and I know it won't be easy. But if I survive, and if she loves me, I'm a lucky guy. If she doesn't, I may lose more than I find. Anyway, it's a pleasure to hit the mark without aiming. Got it now?"

"So there's nothing I can do to keep you from this crazy enterprise?"

Eli's face contorted with rage. "You people are *disgusting*! If you, in any way, represent what Gaians are, I'm *glad* to be a barbarian from Earth. I'll pull it off. Watch me gamble and appreciate the beauty of the deathmatch."

"All right. I go with you."

"What? Wait! No! No, no, no... You can't. I cannot allow—"

"Oh, try me!" Two sudden tears rolled down from Nox's eyes.

"You're *crying*? I'm so, so sorry!"

"Don't be. I don't know how you do it, but it's working."

"What's working? Please, please don't cry. I'm such an idiot!"

Nox, in tears, looked at Eli. "It's okay—it's life. You said it. I never thought much about such things before, but I envy Aura. She has you. That's what's working." She shook her head and wiped the tears with the back of her hand. "Who else is going with you?"

"Lobo agreed to help."

"You persuaded him to join you?"

"More like coerced and corrupted. Ruke is going to meet with the Elder Keep authorities. I'm planning to hide *Night Stalker* inside his cruiser. He wants to help."

"I'll work on logistics tonight. When do you want to get underway?"

"Tomorrow, if possible."

"You can count on me. I'll help you and try to keep you alive. Both of you. It's important to me." Nox held out her hand. "Give me your gun."

"My gun?"

"You'll survive a night without it. I want to make another one for you, with new ammo—a gift from the Game. Well, from me. You'll like it. Remember, we have Gaian technology and weapons. The Pazons are no match for us. We'll make it!"

NINETEEN
ACTION POINTS

R uke sat at his desk in the ready room of the presidential cruiser. He looked out the window—Korango, his space station, was floating in the darkness about fifty miles away, a shining jewel in a black velvet setting. A surge of emotion clutched at his heart. Until now, he hadn't realized how much he'd become connected to the place.

Oh, God... Will I ever see her again? Ruke licked dry lips and swallowed hard. Out of the corner of his eye, he glanced at his friends and supporters gathered to talk through the rescue operation on Pat'zan. *Anybody see what I did? It's never happened to me before. Am I getting old or something?* Truth be told, Ruke understood the risks of the mission he was about to embark on, and danger had never been his weak spot—he knew how to face it. *So what's different now? Is it anxiety? Nah... Everything will be fine! I owe everything to Eli. Plus, this is an excellent opportunity to see Leobla in action.*

The presidential cruiser ISS *Leobla*, an Imperial Star Ship according to the standard Galactic Spaceship Universal Classification, was drifting near Korango. She had been commissioned by

Gavryn Jax, Ruke's predecessor, and delivered to Korango shortly before his death. He had never used the cruiser.

The owners of the space station spared no expense when it came to their starships. Symbols of Korango's prosperity, they were sturdy and fast. There was no problem finding places between the Perseus and Sagittarius Arms of the Milky Way willing to deliver the latest in space travel technology and weaponry. *Leobla*'s builder, a shipyard near Eyphus, the capital planet of the Intergalactic League, had designed her as a light, heavily armed battlecruiser. Though the word "light" mentioned in her specifications referred only to her exceptional maneuverability and speed—the ship itself spanned almost two miles. Automation and redundancy allowed a small crew of twenty-two to operate the cruiser.

Ruke, as much an adventurer as his younger friend, relished the prospect of using *Leobla* in Eli's mission to Pat'zan. Nevertheless, he had to bridle his excitement about it. Shyster, his vice president —and a woman whose warmth and care Ruke had come to appreciate—expressed strong opposition to the idea, deeming it dangerous and risky.

But when she persisted in her attempts to dissuade Ruke from his involvement in the venture, he rebelled. Ruke hit the ceiling and called Shyster a traitor, and promised to throw her out of Korango if she ever tried to stand between him and Eli again. He was serious, but that didn't prevent Ruke from asking for her forgiveness when he calmed down. Still and all, being as wise as she was, Shyster understood the limits of her hold on her boss and partner. She didn't dare keep nagging and solemnly promised to support the risky undertaking and help Eli with everything she could.

Ruke looked at the members of the mission. Zarfo wiped the sweat off his forehead—he and Shyster sat together and talked in undertones. Eli was in an armchair with a datapad in his hands, moving his finger across the screen. *Funny how this technology isn't much beyond Earth's. What is he doing? Doodling? He's never done it before.*

Ruke noticed how Shyster furtively cast a glance at him. He smiled in response, trying to look confident. *Are we all going to die? Is that what they think? Or is it only me? I need to say something to them.*

Nox entered with a big duffel over her shoulder. She sat on another sofa, then put the bag on the floor and pushed it toward Eli. The move was precise—just strong enough to cover the space between the couch and his armchair and to clunk softly when it hit his foot. Ruke relaxed. Nox's presence encouraged him. *She won't let my boy down. She'll protect him. What's in the bag?*

Nox gestured with her hand, inviting Eli to open the duffel. He did and took out a handgun, his old pistol with a silencer attached. He dug more and smiled—there was another similar-looking gun. Eli gave her a thumbs-up and put the weapons back. Ruke smiled. *Wow, another bad boy! I hope she added some nasty Gaian stuff to make the guns more powerful.*

Hippa soon entered the room and curled up on the floor near Nox.

Ruke cleared his throat. "Ahem... Ahem... Can we please get started?" Everybody looked at him. "As you all know, we're going to Pat'zan today. Officially, to protest against the Alliance interfering in our relationships with other planets. The true goal of the operation, however, is to make up for the damages that resulted from the involvement of several Korags in the Elder Keep attack on a Gaian outpost."

The mood in the ready room grew dour.

Oh, crap... I need to say something nice now! "I want to add that it's a noble but risky mission. I don't force anybody to participate. Eli and Nox will carry out its most dangerous parts, but we're all in this together. The success of the operation depends on our collaborative effort. I'm sure we'll succeed and prove that Korango is a force to be reckoned with. Many worlds—our neighbors and business partners—have condemned the Pazons for their cowardly actions on Coatera and support us. Eli will brief us now on the details of the plan."

Eli stood. "We estimate that we should complete our operation in less than three hours. It starts when *Leobla* approaches Pat'zan and enters a geostationary position at about three hundred miles above its capital city. The arrangements for the meeting between Ruke, Shyster, and the Elder Keep authorities determine the timing.

"Here's the timeline of the operation. Assuming that the summit is scheduled to begin at time T, the orbital placement should be completed at T minus *sixty minutes*. At T minus *forty-five minutes*, Ruke and Shyster depart for the Lord Guarantor's official residence. They will use the shuttle. The timing is calculated to divert the Pazons' attention from our primary goal. At T or a bit later, when the meeting starts, Nox and I leave for Pat'zan, using two drop pods to land on the upper-level landing platform of the Security Chancellery building.

"Ruke and Shyster will use their diplomatic skills to drag the negotiations along for up to one hour. At T plus *sixty minutes*, they'll head back, and return to *Leobla* at T plus *ninety minutes*. We have two objectives—to rescue Aura and to destroy the Gamer. By that time, we should accomplish the first. The second part of the operation will be completed by T plus *one hundred minutes*. At that time, the Gaian technology will be automatically activated, and Nox and I will be instantly transported to *Leobla*.

"I should add that the success of the operation depends on the accuracy of information provided by Lobo D'Matroc, a Pazon recently captured on Korango. He's the former member of the Elder Keep Security Chancellery. He helped us in planning the operation. When Nox and I are on Pat'zan, he'll also provide real-time updates. Lobo is already on board *Leobla*. Zarfo is responsible for this part. Any questions?"

Shyster raised her hand. "What if something goes wrong? What if Lobo lied?"

Nox stepped in. "I have good memories of the underground facilities in the Chancellery building. Learning more about the

Security Chancellery was the reason I surrendered so easily on Earth. I also found some Elder Keep equipment in Lobo's flyer and recovered useful data. So his information is important, but we won't be in the dark without him."

"What if your transporter doesn't work?" Shyster didn't want to let it go. "What if the Pazons are smarter than you think, and they catch you?"

"Nox, I'll address these issues," cut in Eli. "Things can go wrong, but we have contingency plans. I don't want to talk about them for security and safety reasons. I'll mention, though, that Gaian transport technology is not the only tech we'll rely upon. Our options will depend on specific eventualities that may arise.

"My major concern is not the mission itself, where we expect to have a clear advantage based on the use of Gaian technology that Pazons can't match. It's the aftermath of our operation. For example, do we have the support of the Intergalactic League if we have to defend Korango because of our actions against the Alliance?"

"I don't think there's much of a threat there," said Ruke. "The Keepers won't risk starting an interstellar war over our operation. It's not much different from what they did on Coatera. But as a precautionary step, I'm waiting for the League's two battleships to berth at Korango. I talked to their prime minister. They are alarmed by what—"

Ruke's intercom buzzed. "Speak!" barked Ruke.

"Mr. President, Ybe Strib, *Leobla*'s shipmaster, is here. We've received a docking request from a Gaian ship, a small one with an unknown configuration and a crew of two. Their names are Jour Talphi and D'Obba Chyllep. They've asked me to contact Mr. Stroud if there are questions."

"Who the hell is Mr. Stroud?" Ruke raised his eyebrows.

"That's my last name, Ruke, remember? Shame on you," said Eli.

"Oh, sorry... Do you know them?"

"I do. They're a pain in the ass, but they could be useful. Let me take it from here."

"Sure. Deal with them," grumbled Ruke.

"Hi, skipper. Eli Stroud speaking. Let the ship in, but don't allow the occupants to exit the hangar. I'll be there shortly."

Eli picked up the bag with guns and headed to the door. Passing Hippa, he stopped. "Hey, gorgeous, want some fun? Come with me."

Hippa jumped up, looked guiltily back at Nox, and trotted behind Eli.

Eli and Hippa met Jour and D'Obba near their spaceship. About the same size as *Night Stalker*, she looked unusual, as if her hull wasn't quite made of solid matter. A slowly swirling substance covering the ship's outer shell resembled liquefied gas exposed to normal temperature. A plethora of appendages protruded through it in different directions.

Hippa walked around the ship on half-bent legs—she was tense, sniffing the air as if about to attack a terrible beast. The hair on her scruff stood on end. She bared her huge fangs at the ship and growled a soft but threatening warning.

Eli came closer. "Your ship wasn't like this when I saw her on Leaky Kettle," he said to Jour. "What happened?"

Eli was about to poke his finger into the smoky stuff when Jour stopped him. "Careful—that's liquid helium covering sensor arrays and transmission antennas. She's a weapon in her 'ready' state."

Hippa chuffed and walked away from the ship.

Jour went on, "Not deadly force, but effective—our way of doing things. I told you."

"Are you spying on us?" asked Eli.

"A little," boasted D'Obba and waved a boxy gadget in her

hand. "I like to delve into the essence of things, but if we have something on you, that's only an incidental collection."

"Incidental?" snorted Eli. "What's in your hand?"

"Just a scanner to check our equipment."

"Then why were you pointing it away from your ship?" Eli turned to Hippa. "Gorgeous, can you please take D'Obba's device and show it to Nox?"

D'Obba stepped back. She raised her hand with the gadget as high as she could. "Hey, you... Go away! I don't give it to you!"

"You'd better," Eli remarked. "Don't joke with Hippa. Her sense of humor is minimal with people she doesn't trust."

Hippa twitched her tail.

"D'Ob, give her the scanner! What's the point?" exploded Jour. "Let them check it."

Hippa raised a paw above her head and strained her hind legs. She was preparing to pounce.

"Okay, okay..." D'Obba handed the device to the leopard. "Just be careful. We'll need it soon."

Hippa's jaws carefully clamped on the scanner, and she turned and walked away.

As if nothing had happened, Eli asked, "What are you doing here?"

"We want to go with you to Pat'zan." D'Obba tossed her hair over her shoulder.

"We're not going to Pat'zan."

"Then why are *revenge* and *Pat'zan* written all over your face? Not to mention other signs of your intentions?"

"Okay, we *are* going to Pat'zan, but frankly, you guys would slow us down."

"Slow you down? *You?*" shouted D'Obba and stamped her foot.

"D'Ob, stop it!" Jour put his hand on her shoulder. "Eli, you consistently underestimate our desire and ability to help. We've found a Gaian government cruiser in Korango space. It's cloaked, but we've detected its signature."

"And if we don't go with you, I'll tell everybody about your mission to Pat'zan!" D'Obba made a step toward the spy ship while looking imploringly at Eli.

"Are you good guys or bad guys?" asked Eli, smirking.

"Good guys," said Jour, looking straight into Eli's eyes.

"Good guys don't blackmail. They explain things and try to convince."

"We won't tell anybody about your mission to Pat'zan without your consent," D'Obba said, a wounded innocence in her voice. "So, can we go?" She bestowed a look full of virtue upon Eli and batted her eyelashes, looking for signs of approval in his eyes.

"Why do you want to go with us? What do you mean, *with us?* Go by yourself. You don't need my permission to do that."

"It means our ship will be inside the presidential cruiser. The cruiser can assert diplomatic immunity if the Elder Keep patrol ships try to inspect her."

Eli remained skeptical. "But you're not going to stay inside when we arrive?"

"No, but we have a cloaking device too."

"I don't want to be difficult, but... why not use your device all the way to Pat'zan?"

D'Obba straightened, thrust out her chest, and put her hands akimbo. "Because cloaking doesn't work at faster-than-light speeds. At least, our device doesn't. Satisfied?"

"No. But I'll ask Nox. It'll be her decision. Please stay in your ship until further notice."

"Sure. If you need to contact our ship, use LWSS *Groerok*, Gaian SA."

Nox entered *Leobla's* hangar to find several military droids hovering around Jour's ship. Jour and D'Obba loitered inside the security perimeter, and from what she could tell, both were pissed off.

"Finally!" yelled D'Obba as she rushed to Nox. One of the droids blocked her way. "Fuck!" D'Obba threw up her hands and shoved the droid, only to be pushed back toward their ship.

"Calm down! Eli asked me to talk to you. Explain what you want," said Nox.

Instead of answering, D'Obba scoffed, "How did you weasel your way into his confidence?"

Nox cocked her head and stared silently at D'Obba.

Jour intervened, "If I may—we believe you're headed to Pat'zan. We don't know what the Korags plan to do there, but D'Obba and I want to observe."

"Why is your desire to observe events Eli's problem?"

"Our observing means collecting material—"

"Jour!" D'Obba yanked his arm. "Be careful. She might be a government stooge!"

"It appears Eli trusts Nox. That's good enough for me. We cannot do everything ourselves. So, what I wanted to say is that such material can be useful against... Well, evil minds. Do you know that a Gaian government cruiser, cloaked, is near Korango?"

"I do. What's your point?"

"The ship can follow you to Pat'zan without being detected. Since we don't believe Gaia will do anything about Aura and the stolen tech, the question becomes, what else might they do?"

"And what else *might* they do?" echoed Nox.

D'Obba chuckled. "They might block Eli's transporter."

"Is that so?" Nox looked at D'Obba with glassy eyes.

"That's up to you to decide. Besides, our ship is a monitoring and cloaking monster. We can help. Wouldn't you like to have something like it on your side?"

"Yes. You're going with us."

D'Obba gave Jour a knowing look and turned back to Nox. "So, we can stay?"

"Yes, assuming you'll keep your word to Eli not to publish anything about him without his consent."

"He tells you everything!" D'Obba's eyes bulged in frustration.

"I don't offer you any accommodations, though. Stay in your ship. We'll depart soon. And *Leobla* is fast."

Eli strode down the long corridor to *Leobla*'s brig, which had been transformed into an improvised mission control and communication post. This arrangement made sense for the mission to Pat'zan as Lobo, a prisoner in the brig, had become a valuable asset in planning the approaching operation.

Isn't it strange how so many people don't know what they want? thought Eli, recalling his conversation with Nox when she'd told him that the Game had only filled Ruke's flask with whiskey.

Time seemed to have slowed for Eli. The sense of impending danger became acute. Anxiety and apprehension filled him as he readied for the mission. *Whiskey—oh, my... Is that true? When hooligans in Las Vegas beat me up—it seems like an eternity has passed since then —Mom asked me, "Is that what you want from life?"*

And what do I want?

Eli didn't like to dwell on his feelings. *Evidently, I want what I want! Enough blubbering... It's time to release the moorings.*

He pulled out his commsys. "Ruke, we are ready to leave for Pat'zan."

Nox turned out to be an invaluable tactical expert. She sat in the brig bay on a case with the communication equipment and worked with the mobile replicator terminal to manufacture uniforms, comm devices, explosives, and weapons to use during the operation on Pat'zan.

At first, Eli hadn't appreciated the need for a separate dedicated terminal—*Night Stalker*'s Game interface could take care of everything they would need. But looking at the stuff piling up on the floor next to Nox, he realized that frequent direct requests to the Game could attract attention and compromise their mission. On the other hand, manufacturing terminals widely used on Gaia wouldn't arouse suspicion.

Zarfo and Lobo stood near Nox, with Zarfo mostly gawking at the device and the results it was producing. Lobo, still handcuffed, seemed to enjoy his role as a guide into the minutia of the Elder Keep's methods and equipment used in its security operations.

Eli walked into the brig. "Hi, everybody! How's it going?"

"We've almost finish debriefing Lobo. Maps are ready—" Zarfo began with enthusiasm.

"Sorry to interrupt you, buddy." Eli put his hand on Zarfo's shoulder. "Lobo, remember we talked about Asphalis?"

"Sure."

"Where is his office?"

"In the Chancellery building, why?"

"Yeah, but *where* in the building?"

"If you're planning to pay him a visit, that wouldn't be a good idea. He's a little paranoid about his personal security."

"I'll keep it in mind. Still...?"

"It's in the tower. His office and entourage have the three floors at and above the same level as the landing pad, though the windows look the other way. I've already explained the layout to Nox."

"Great, thanks." Eli turned to Nox. "We need to finalize our plans."

"I'm almost done here." She stood up. "You should try on your Pat'zan uniform. Pick your size." Nox kicked her foot into a pile of clothes on the floor.

"You mean *here*?" Eli became uncomfortable.

"I have several sizes." Nox noticed his embarrassment. "You

can try them on in your quarters. Choose whatever you think will fit you. I also have a gauntlet with a communicator and a holo-emitter."

Eli squatted in front of the heap on the floor and dug into it.

"There's also a pouch with more ammo. Be careful—it's extremely powerful."

Eli squinted at Nox and said nothing. *She cackles like a hen trying to protect a recently hatched chick.*

Eli liked his new Elder Keep look—the uniform was comfortable and functional. The sleeve of his jacket concealed the gauntlet. The holsters on both thighs fit the style of the outfit and didn't look foreign at all.

"May I?" Nox's voice came from outside the door.

"Sure, come in."

Nox appeared, dressed in the female version of the same garb. She walked around Eli, scrutinizing him. "You look good. What about me?" Nox spun in front of Eli.

"Um, if you don't do this," Eli twisted his finger in the air, "It'll do. I think."

"What does that mean?" Nox repeated the movement of his finger.

"Well, I don't know how the Keeper men react to women like you, so if you don't... You know..." Eli broke off.

"Sorry, Eli. I could change my appearance and shapes to your taste, but it might take the time we don't have. So, here I am—the best help you can get."

"Oh, you're quite to my taste already." Eli stopped pondering. "Actually, if you unbutton the top of your shirt, and they react as I think they may, it'll give me a few milliseconds to kill more of them."

"Seriously?"

"You look like a beautiful female villain from Earthly movies. You can try to test my theory and see what kind of men they are."

"So, you like me?"

"Nox, I'm done talking about you."

"What if we meet some women? Will you unbutton *your* shirt?"

"To test that theory, I should unbutton something else... Enough of that!" Eli stopped for a second and continued, "I should have asked you before. How will your government perceive your involvement in all this? Are you in danger?"

"Aw, you never want to talk about good stuff..." Nox sounded disappointed. She sighed but went on. "I don't know the answer. I act the way I'm supposed to act according to my duties as the Game Administrator. Many in my government don't know about them. Others don't know all the circumstances and don't see the connection. Some don't care about the Game and Gaia. Also, there are people who see me as an obstacle to their ideas of what the Game should be. I'm not a robot that can malfunction, you know. I'm a human being—I have free will, and I can quit if I want. It's my choice."

"Can they hurt you?"

"You mean by killing me? Not the way you think. Besides, that would disrupt for a long time the whole framework the Game is built on, and that'll be a problem for those who would love to get rid of me. Anyway, these aren't issues we should talk about now."

"Right. I'll talk about them when Aura is safe."

"Then let's go over our plan again. Good news... Lobo reproduced most of the layout of the building... if he's not lying. But what I know about it fits what the Pazon says. I talked to him more than once—he gives me the impression of someone telling the truth. I ran his responses through a lie detector. Looks good. Zarfo came to the same conclusion."

"Did Lobo tell you where Aura is?"

"The cell he pointed to is the same cell where they put me. Lobo didn't know where I was, but I recognized it immediately. I had a hood on my head, but Ab didn't know I could see through it."

"And the Gamer?"

"Let me show you everything on my holo display." A schematic diagram of the building appeared in front of Nox. "This is the Security Chancellery building—"

"How do you *do* that?" demanded Eli.

"A holo-emitter—it's in the gauntlet. You can control it with the contact lenses. Here." Nox gave Eli a small box. "You should put them in before we leave. They're input-output devices. You'll see a menu. Focus on the options to select them."

A series of images appeared in front of Nox. "Here's the landing pad on the roof where we'll land with drop pods. Then we'll use the stairwell to get to the building security center on the twenty-second floor. That's where it gets interesting. There are usually two guards. Lobo recommends we wait until the new shift comes on and kill both shifts."

"Ouch!"

"He says officers with the red circle and triangle insignia have the highest access. If we spot someone like that, we can use their eyes and body ID chips to get access to almost everywhere in the building."

"That's gross."

"I have a retinal scanner, so don't worry about cutting out eyeballs. Get a knife for the IDs, though. In case my transplanter doesn't work."

"What about our drop pods? Can Pat'zan's space control stop us?"

"About the pods... I recovered Lobo's transponder from his flyer. He has clearance to land in the city. I also removed his ID chip. I need to implant it into your abdomen—that's what they do. Okay?"

"Sure! Do it." Eli unbuttoned the bottom of the shirt and puffed out his belly.

"Just relax." Nox produced another box and pressed it against Eli's skin. "Done."

"I felt nothing."

"Why should you? Let me check."

An image with an intricate design replaced the diagram of the building security center. "It's working. You'll appear as Lobo on their monitoring equipment now. But let's continue. You need to decide where we go first, Aura or the Gamer?"

"Aura—human life is more important than any machine. We might leave as soon as we get her."

"I knew you would say that. Lobo thinks differently. He says our chances are higher to save Aura if we blow up the Gamer first —it's in the basement of their Technical and Research Division in a special armored vault. We won't have much time to get to her from there, because the prison cells are on the other side of the building. But the chaos after such a mighty explosion would create a diversion and make it easier to free Aura. Lobo says she's heavily guarded. Besides, we don't know her physical condition—how fast she can move and all."

"With *Night Stalker*'s transporter, we can beam all of us up almost instantly into *Leobla*. Or we can beam up Aura and continue without her. Right?" Eli raised his eyebrows, "That's what you told me."

"I did… But what if the transporter doesn't work?"

"Broken?"

Nox shook her head. "No, blocked."

"By whom?"

"By the mysterious Gaian ship shadowing us."

"Are you serious? Not only do your comrades *not* want to help free Aura, but they also want to kill her!"

"It may not be her…"

"Then who?"

"You."

"Me?"

"If certain people in the Gaian government realize the danger you represent for their plans, that's the cleanest way to get rid of you. It's brilliant."

"They won't stop me," Eli growled.

"That's what they may count on. A direct assassination isn't politically workable on Gaia. But if there's no other way, they might opt for that. After all, there were some mysterious attempts on yours and Ruke's lives—"

"Sounds like a conspiracy theory," said Eli aggressively.

"Look, the DRC learns about the Elder Keep plans to attack Coatera, to steal the Gamer and kidnap Aura. Instead of stopping it, someone like Slun Ceabb promises someone like Abaddon to close their eyes on everything the Elder Keep wants to do on Coatera. In reality, Slun is counting on your desperate desire to rescue Aura from Pat'zan prison, expecting or even encouraging Ab and company to kill you when you try to do it. Brilliant. Slun doesn't need to explain anything to the Pazons as soon as you take the bait."

"Yeah, Jour and D'Obba alluded to that too. Do you realize how insane that sounds? I left Earth—when was it, a month ago?"

"It may sound insane to you, but you don't know or understand how damaging you can be to them. I do. Moreover, I see now how the recent contraband case might be a part of the plan to neutralize you through the Gaian legal system. If the criminal case against you for using the Game's quantum conversion falls apart—"

"Wait!" Eli raised his hand. "A question for you. How do they know about our plans?"

"The DRC is the oldest intelligence service in our quadrant of the galaxy. They plan for contingencies and opportunities of every kind. They have sources. Besides, it's not that difficult to guess. Ruke's visit to the Elder Keep is no secret. *Night Stalker* is inside *Leobla*'s hull. Don't be so naive as to think Slun doesn't know about you and Aura. I'm sure they know your fighter has transport capabilities."

"Okay. Jour and D'Obba go with us, right?"

"I've decided they do."

"Perfect. If what you say is true, they'll help me get rid of those who want to get rid of me. But Aura first. And then we'll see who comes out on top. So, let's increase our chances and start with the Gamer."

"That's your decision?"

"Yes, it is." Eli tapped his finger on the head. "I've devised Plan B—if they block the transporter, we'll use *Night Stalker* to escape. We can place her on a lower orbit, cloaked. *Leobla*'s orbit is too high for the neural interface."

"How low?"

"A hundred miles will work."

"Cloaking like that in low orbit is risky. The traffic is too dense. Instead of trying to avoid a collision, you should focus on the action in the building."

"Then I need to talk to the skipper—" Eli's commsys buzzed. He looked at the screen. "Speak of the devil... Hi, Ybe. What's up?"

The more he listened to the skipper, the more sullen Eli became.

"Okay, I'm in my quarters. I'll be on the bridge as soon as I can. Hang in there. Don't allow them to approach the cruiser. I'll talk to them."

"Something happened?" Nox asked anxiously.

"We've entered Pat'zan space. A patrol ship wants to board *Leobla* for inspection. Nothing to worry about." Eli punched a number on his commsys. "Jour? You still there? Cloak your sloop, we have visitors... She's not a sloop? ... No? ... Does yawl sound better? Just fucking do it!"

Hippa walked into the brig, growled, and settled on the floor in front of the lockup, staring grimly at Lobo. The force field blocking the cell entrance was down, and he instinctively moved deeper, away from the snow leopard. Zarfo, who was setting up equipment in front of the cell, noticed Lobo's nervousness.

"That's Hippa, Nox's companion," he told the Pazon. "I asked Eli to keep the cell open so it's easier for us to work. He agreed, as long as we had Hippa here."

"She's gorgeous! And a killer? Look at her fangs and claws!"

"Oh, yes, she's fast. Her wild relatives are predators on Earth. But don't worry, she's intelligent."

Hippa yawned, put her head on her front paws, and closed one eye. The other remained open. Its yellow iris stared at the prisoner, following the slightest movements of his head, hands, and body.

"You should understand why Eli wanted her here. You'd do the same."

"That doesn't bother me."

"What does?"

"My future. Is Eli a good guy?"

"It depends. You probably thought of yourself as a good guy when you were part of the attack on Coatera, and before that, when kidnapping Nox."

"You know about that too? But that's different. That wasn't personal."

"It was sure personal to Eli, especially since his mother died because of Ab's attack on Earth."

Lobo swallowed hard. "Can... can I trust him?"

"Whoa, what a question! The question is, can _he_ trust _you_? He put a lot of faith in you. Too much, if you ask me. What if everything you'd said is a trap?"

"I'm not a novice. Clearly, you've already verified many of the things I told you."

Zarfo didn't react.

"I'm helping you, but what I really want is get out of this business. Eli promised me something. That's an opportunity. Will he keep his word? What will happen to my family and me when it's over?"

"Why not go to Fliria?"

"Never heard of it."

"It's a nice planet, seventy plus light-years from Korango. I was born there. Eli will help you."

"He will?"

"If the mission is successful? Of course he will. You shouldn't have any doubt about that."

"That's nice to hear. I'll pray for his safe return... because what he's about to do is crazy."

"Have faith." Zarfo was calm, and his face emanated confidence. "I'm sure he'll make it. He's bold and smart. He knows what he's doing and what he wants."

"Hmmm... Fliria... What do you people do there?"

"We're independent. We're farmers. We grow things to feed others. We don't like to kill."

"Farmers? Interesting..."

TWENTY

MISSION

E li found Ybe, *Leobla*'s shipmaster, standing in the middle of the bridge, sweaty and red-faced, in front of a big screen. He patted the skipper on his shoulder and plopped into the captain's chair with his leg over the arm support. "What seems to be the problem? Who's that guy?" Eli pointed to the screen.

"Sir, this is—" Ybe began, but the Pazon interrupted him. "I'm Kruak Xyv'et, patrol ship commander. Submit—"

"Whoa, whoa, whoa! I didn't ask *you*." Eli raised his index finger and poked it toward Kruak. "Where are your manners?"

Kruak insisted, "This is your last warning—"

"Shut up," Eli yelled, enraged. "Ybe, red alert! Or whatever color you use when you're ready to shoot! And you, punk"—Eli again pointed to the screen—"if you move your washtub even an inch closer to our cruiser, you'll be obliterated. Got it? Ybe, target the patrol boat. Shoot to destroy on my command."

"Sir, as commander of the Elder Keep patrol ship on duty in this sector, it's my responsibility to inspect your ship. Especially a heavily armed cruiser," Kruak protested.

"And I say that instead of threatening us, a diplomatic mission, you should have at least greeted us politely and assisted with our movements through your space. Rurik Cavell, the new Korango president, is making an official visit to Pat'zan to meet His Highness Lord Guarantor Xiir Zanrod."

"Sir, it does not matter, according to—"

"According to the Intergalactic Convention on Diplomatic Relations, the heads of nations and planets are given safe passage and are considered not susceptible to searches, lawsuits, or prosecution. Besides, all the *Leobla*'s tactical details, her flight path, and her orbit were communicated to the Elder Keep Foreign Affairs Office in advance. The last I checked, our ship has followed the protocol of the visit to the letter, including our trajectory and time of arrival. *Nowhere* was an inspection specified or agreed upon. So get your ass fifty miles off our ship and follow us in, as prescribed by the aforementioned convention. Our only other option will be either to defend ourselves with all force necessary or cancel the visit—which I wouldn't recommend, unless you want to embarrass yourself. The galactic mass media will not let such an incident go unnoticed."

"Sir, I need to talk to my superiors. Can I ask—"

"No, you cannot. I'm the head of Korango Security and see no reason to keep talking to someone at your level. You have ten minutes. If there is anything to discuss, you have Ybe Strib, the captain of the ship, to speak to. End the call."

The screen went dark, and Eli stood up.

"Sorry, skipper. I didn't mean disrespect to you or your chair. It was a show."

"Sir, it worked. They're moving away."

"Good. Now... Ybe, I need to talk to you privately."

The captain's stateroom was close, a short way through the automatic doors that closed softly behind Eli and Ybe. They sank into nicely upholstered chairs, and Ybe waited for Eli to start.

"You understand the nature of our mission, right?" Eli uttered.

"All I know, sir, is that it's dangerous. I'm not aware of the details, but I noticed that you lead the mission."

Ybe Strib

"Good. According to the plan, you should jump back into hyperspace as soon as Ruke and Shyster return from Pat'zan when you receive the signal on your commsys from Zarfo or me. I expect that the signal will come approximately ten minutes after the presidential shuttle enters the hangar. But the time can vary."

"I know that much."

"What's our current altitude?"

"Three hundred miles, per the protocol you mentioned."

"How much time do you need to drop to one hundred?"

"To be safe... Ten minutes."

"How about one?"

"One minute? Theoretically, it's possible. But there may be casualties, even with our inertia dampers. It's a big ship, sir."

"Can you prepare for the contingency? Will it help?"

"Yes."

"Then here's what we need to do. After Ruke comes back, you may get the signal we've talked about from Zarfo or me. But it may come with a variation—first, to drop the altitude, and then, without decelerating, to bear home. The one hundred miles is not a precise number—the moment when you should stop losing altitude may happen above that point. Watch the hangar. The moment you see *Night Stalker* disappearing, change course immediately, wait five seconds, and go into hyperspace. Use the time between the arrival of the shuttle from Pat'zan and the signal to prepare Ruke, Shyster, and your crew for the contingency."

"What do you mean, 'disappear'? Like taking off and flying out of the spaceport?"

"More like vanishing into thin air inside the hangar."

"The whole ship? Who'll pilot her?"

"It's complicated. The best way to describe it is to say that she's programmed to do certain things by herself."

"Does the president know about this?"

"No. Such a possibility has come up unexpectedly. Too late, as he's about to leave."

"There may be consequences, sir. You're asking me to violate the trust of the president."

"Sort of... But he won't mind if he knows the request comes from me. My life and the lives of other people may depend on that maneuver, Ybe. If I'm alive afterward, you'll be rewarded generously. If I'm not... Well, in such case, the subsequent events may affect the lives of everybody on Korango. Nobody will care about the drop in altitude. Trust me."

Ybe sat silent for a short time. Then he got up and saluted Eli. "Sir, I've heard about you. I saw you in action today. I'll do what you ask. Furthermore, if there's a chance, I'd love to work for you or serve under your command. I'd be honored."

"Thank you. I'll keep it in mind. But for now, let's get the bad guys. Remember, the changed signal is 'Plan B.'"

Two open-cabin drop pods rested on the hangar floor as Eli and Nox finished last-minute preparations for the three-hundred-mile drop to the rooftop landing platform of the Security Chancellery building. Eli cast a swift glance over his shoulder at the black opening gaping into space. The purplish shades of Pat'zan looked mysterious and intriguing through the faintly flickering force field blocking the entrance to *Leobla*'s docking bay.

The swarm of the Elder Keep patrol ships floating not far from the cruiser sent involuntary shivers down his spine. "Shit," he muttered to Nox. "I don't think I can ever get used to the idea we can see through the force field, and they can't."

Nox shrugged. "It'll pass. I'm thinking about the best way to sneak unnoticed out of the cruiser. You mentioned you want to use *Night Stalker* to cover us with her cloaking device?"

"Yeah, but that means keeping her outside *Leobla*. Then you brought up the possibility of our transporter being blocked. With the fighter outside, what are we gonna do? The neural interface won't work at this range. If we position her lower, where I can reach her from Pat'zan, the cloaking isn't reliable—too close to the planet's atmosphere. I now want to keep *Night Stalker* inside *Leobla*. The skipper is standing by to drop the cruiser two hundred miles lower if the transporter is blocked. Let's use your fellow Gaians to shield us."

"You mean..." Nox turned around. Jour and D'Obba puttered around their spaceship with gadgets in hands. "Did you talk to them?"

"No, I'm going to."

Eli went to the far corner of the hangar where Nox had slotted a place for Jour's ship. D'Obba noticed Eli and hurried toward him. She smiled coquettishly—the purring charm of the professional newscaster or raconteur. Eli could have sworn that if he hadn't moved briskly away from her, she would have rubbed his side like a kitten.

"What, you don't like me?" she purred.

"I do, but I need something else from you."

"Oh... Your heart belongs to only one—only one, and she's not me... What am I to do? But don't worry, I'll do everything I can to get the object of your desire into your fervid embrace!"

"I need your and Jour's help, that's all."

"Of course you do. You want us to hide you and Nox with our cloak. We'd be delighted to lend a hand." D'Obba danced around him and curtsied.

"Why are you doing this?" Eli mocked her curtsy.

"Because I like you, and because I want to make what may be the last moments of our lives brighter than they are now. Because these guys up there—to be more cogent and persuasive, D'Obba poked her finger somewhere upward—"want to kill you or, even worse, to vivisect you. I'm certain the DRC wouldn't spare Jour or me either. They'll have an open season on us soon."

"So, they're there?"

"You bet they are. Whenever you're ready, we'll start the cloak here and use our tractor beam to keep you under our ship. I'll try to find a Pat'zan military cruiser on a lower orbit and release you nearby—a ruse to deceive patrols about your point of origin."

"We start in three minutes. Go ahead as soon as you see the pods in the middle of the port."

"Aye, sir!" D'Obba saluted Eli and hurried to her ship.

When Eli came back to Nox, she handed him a flat box the size of a big book. "Standard Gaian spacesuit. Put the box on the floor and step on it. It'll fit you automatically."

"Nifty... D'Obba and Jour will pick us up from the middle of the port." In his contact lens display, Eli saw the time. "Ruke should start the meeting with the Elder Keep authorities any minute now. The die is cast!" He set his feet on the spacesuit deployer.

Nox didn't communicate to Jour and D'Obba her decision to abandon the cloaking shield and to plunge directly into Pat'zan's atmosphere. She asked Eli to do so as soon as the drop pods reached Pat'zan's Kármán line—the imaginary boundary between the planet's atmosphere and outer space. On Pat'zan, it lay at around one hundred miles above the surface.

The speed of their descent, about one mile per second, didn't produce much heat and didn't present any danger. The drop pods' thermal protection system easily absorbed its flux. Conversely, passing through Elder Keep space security was one of the riskiest steps of the operation. The success of that phase lay beyond Eli's control. His doubts didn't leave him, despite all Lobo's assurances.

Eli knew he had to rely on a combination of circumstances and events where even a minor detail could spell disaster and derail the whole mission. That was the hardest thing for him to accept. Yet none of the contingency plans he'd developed seemed a better alternative for moving through Pat'zan border controls.

Eli and Nox counted on Lobo's security credentials and his ID chip to sneak onto the planet. But one security chip wasn't enough for two people. To make them look like a single space object to the border control authorities, Nox insisted Eli keep his pod as close to hers as possible.

Pat'zan Space Control's facility didn't stand out as a particularly sophisticated installation. It was a circle of enormous stations surrounding the planet. A long-awaited upgrade was necessary, but for the moment, Space Control personnel relied on a vast net of satellites sending exabytes of data, ending up mostly on two-dimensional output devices—the telemetry overwhelmed the station's screens. Trajectories, orbital lines, scrolling texts, identification data, interfaces to databanks, and images of spaceships were everywhere and required significant human effort to process.

Most of the passing traffic received quick approvals, and for a good reason—travelers tried to avoid dark, isolated Pat'zan, the capital planet of the mighty and aggressive Alliance. Tourism was virtually unheard-of, and typically only those with an actual need to interact with the Elder Keep's concerns would appear and request permission to approach the gloomy planet.

Violations and hostile attempts to enter Pat'zan space didn't happen frequently. Pat'zan's isolation had a soothing effect on Space Control operations. To keep complacency from dulling the edges of the personnel inured to the absence of serious border violations, the higher-ups at the Security Chancellery had established an obligatory personnel rotation. Nobody knew, though, if this and other policies aimed at increasing the effectiveness of the border control accomplished the goal.

Space Control personnel were aware of all the details of the Korangan visit to Pat'zan, even as they allowed the border patrol to harass the diplomatic ship. In their bureaucratic minds, the *Leobla* fit the profile of a typical visitor perfectly. Meanwhile, no sane Pazon could link a small object that appeared out of nowhere on one of the security monitors to the Korangan Imperial Spaceship. Nobody would think of anything sinister either. It was probably debris. Nevertheless, the traffic control system detected an irregularity, and the alarm sounded.

The officer on duty assigned to the sector reported, "Sir, we're receiving a transponder signal with a lapsed code coming from low orbit. It belongs to Lobo D'Marroc, Special Affairs Unit."

The supervisor, busy drinking a dark beverage, immediately reacted. "Initiate contact."

The officer pressed several buttons on his control panel and stared at the screen, waiting. "Sir, no response." He pressed another button. "Standing by to intercept."

The supervisor put his mug aside and made himself busy with his set of screens. "Belay that. It checks out. His ID chip data matches what's on file. He's been on a deep space mission. Probably couldn't update the system while he was away."

The drop pods approached the capital city of the Elder Keep Alliance. Both machines swept around the towering building of the Security Chancellery and settled on its landing platform. The whole descent, from leaving *Leobla* to deceleration and maneuvering, had taken about fifteen minutes. Not bad, but the clock was ticking.

Eli and Nox knew that by now, Ruke's meeting with Xiir Zanrod, the Elder Keep Lord Guarantor, had already begun. According to the plan, they had an hour to complete the mission. They exited the open shells of the carriers, removed their spacesuits—which self-folded into the deployment boxes—and threw them into the pods.

Eli bared part of the gauntlet hidden under the sleeve of his uniform and turned the device on by rotating and locking a ring at one end. Then he closed his eyes for a second. "Okay, good. *Night Stalker*'s transporter is in range."

The contours of the machines trembled and began to blur.

"The transfer is in progress." Another second and both pods disappeared. "Transfer complete. However, I can't access the fighter's neural interface—her orbit is too high," stated Eli.

Meanwhile, Nox fired up her gauntlet, and her face lightened. "I have a stable connection to our communication and control system in *Leobla*'s brig. Choose the input source named 'Zarfo' to join. Do you see it?"

"I do." Eli intertwined his fingers and stretched his arms out with the palms facing forward. His knuckles cracked.

"What are you doing?" asked Nox.

"What do you mean?"

Nox repeated the movement of Eli's hands. "Something you do before going into a fight?"

"Ah... No. The first time... Probably, because I'm itching to lay my hands on the Keepers. But it's always a good idea to stretch regularly your fingers, hands, and arms—improves your blood circulation."

"That's what you're thinking about right now?"

"No." Eli turned his face to the building entrance. "Ready?"

"Ready."

"Then let the party begin."

Asphalis, lost in thought, sat in a deep, comfortable armchair opposite Xiir Zanrod. The security chancellor didn't like the invitation to take part in the meeting with Korango's president. He saw no need for his involvement and considered it another tactical gambit on the Lord Guarantor's part—a new ploy to undermine his authority as the Elder Keep's chief security officer.

Bored, he looked around. The reception hall in Xiir Zanrod's residence, where the meeting with the Korags was about to begin, confused him. It looked and felt like a stark contrast to the Lord Guarantor's office. It yielded, however, the same result—the impression of greatness and might—but by a different means.

The opulence and elegance of the residence struck Asphalis no less than the grandeur of stone and cathedral ceilings of Xiir's headquarters had. Fine art here highlighting the beauty of life replaced the few ascetic decorations added there with the sole purpose of stressing the power of their owner. The twilight of the Lord Guarantor's workplace combined with bizarre patterns of light beams coming through stained-glass windows differed strikingly from the soft light of chandeliers, sconces, and table lamps scattered throughout the reception hall.

It was Asphalis' first time at Xiir Zanrod's residence, and he didn't know what to make of it. Asphalis examined a bucolic painting on one of the walls. *Who the hell is this creep?*

Many people in the Elder Keep Alliance, especially in its upper echelons, would have gone out of their way to find the answer to that question. Alas, it remained a mystery even if the Lord Guarantor didn't try to hide the origins of his magnetic power—the ability to spark a fire on a global scale, to conquer minds, to inspire people and bend them to his will. However, Xiir's natural behavior was probably the most confusing thing about him—something those around him could never understand.

Those who met him in person would say that he didn't boast a lightning intelligence or charismatic personality. He seemed friendly, simple, and without a trace of haughtiness.

Those who had more frequent interactions with the head of the Congregation of Tyanis, the official Elder Keep religious institution, would recognize that, first and foremost, he was a political warrior who left all human qualities out of politics. He'd proven to be decisive and ruthless from the beginning of his adult life and knew that loyalty, gratitude, and respect for past achievements had no place in political games.

"Why do you think the Korags wanted to come?" asked Xiir.

"Conceivably, they think they're in the crossfire. They soiled their pants when they found out that one of theirs had helped us on Coatera," answered Asphalis.

The Lord Guarantor laughed, nodded approvingly, and fell again silent.

What are you sniggering at? Asphalis got suspicious. *Can't you see that this is an unexpected visit? Or is it another attempt of yours to stab me in the back?*

Xiir's hearty laughter would appear rather grim to those who met him frequently and noticed his cunning ability to suppress outward emotions. But the latter didn't mean that he couldn't occasionally show his anger or pique, or pleasure and good humor.

However, even for those who knew him well, such manifestations of pure human feelings would only impede attempts to understand Xiir Zanrod's true nature and decipher his political moves. Watching his bold and singularly unscrupulous deeds and deals, they would never concede that Xiir's strength came from his unwavering religious faith in the Tyanis gospel. The *realpolitik* pursued by the Lord Guarantor seemed to stay far from the holier-than-thou platitudes aimed at high moral principles proclaimed in the official Elder Keep religion.

In the irony of relying on practical considerations in politics, Xiir Zanrod was remarkably devoid of selfishness, believing in his fate and divine providence. That made him strong and his life simple—he was convinced that the wisdom of Tyanis would ordain nothing without a purpose. Gradually, that led him to despise many people. In his mind, he became an intellectual aristocrat—his vanity grew even greater than his affinity for power, an instrument to achieve his goals.

"You know," Xiir began again, "as much as I am pleased with our victory, we cannot ignore Korango. They have a lot of supporters in this part of the Milky Way."

"We won't, my Lord. Those supporters are equally concerned about the Strangers' technology."

The door opened, and the Pat'zan's Protocol Doyen, or PD, appeared in the doorway. He announced, without looking at anybody, "The Korangan delegation has arrived!"

Xiir stood, smoothed out his shiny black coat, and asked the PD, "How do I look, my dear?"

"Your Excellency looks perfect!"

Asphalis stood up and stepped behind Xiir, who rubbed his hands and cheerfully said, "Then let them in."

The Protocol Doyen disappeared for a second, showed up again, and slowly walked into the room, now holding a tall staff in his right hand. Ruke and Shyster followed, looking around in amazement. The Lord Guarantor smiled, satisfied with the impression the room had on his guests. Meanwhile, the PD raised his staff and banged it hard on the floor. Xiir winced, looking for damage to the expensive parquet, but quickly assumed a pious appearance, listening to the PD's presentation.

"His Excellency, the President of the Korango Independent Territory and Korango Enterprises, Sir Rurik Cavell!" After again banging with his staff, the Protocol Doyen continued. "Her Excellency, the President of the Korango Hunters Society and the First Deputy President of the Korango Independent Territory, Lady Shyster Walruse Agargara Della Plansutsea Dalmad!"

With a quick gesture of his hand, the Lord Guarantor sent the PD away and came close to Ruke and Shyster. "Lord Guarantor Xiir Zanrod—or Lord Zanrod. Let's make it less formal," he said with a barely noticeable bow and turned toward Asphalis. "My security chancellor."

"Please, call me Rurik. Or Ruke. I'm a Norseman, a man from the North!" uttered Ruke.

Shyster followed suit. "Shyster will suffice."

Xiir felt right at home. "I recognize the Korangan spirit! Thank you for letting me use your shorter names. I'm an old man, as you can see, and would be embarrassed to make a mistake, no matter how innocent it may be." The Lord Guarantor moved closer to Ruke and held out his hand. "You're from Terah, I was told, and it is customary there to shake hands. Am I right?"

"Absolutely, sir... Lord Zanrod, it's very kind of you," said Ruke, shaking Xiir's hand.

"Thank you, Ruke." Xiir smiled and pointed to a cozy area in the room's corner to sit and talk. "Let's get more comfortable.

Allow me, please..." The Lord Guarantor led the way, half-turning to the guests. "I'm glad to meet with you, Ruke, as Korango's president. I've heard some terrible stories about one of your trading partners. How can I be of assistance to you?"

Asphalis stepped aside to let Ruke and Shyster go ahead. Uneasy feelings swept over the chancellor—despite the appearance and naiveté of the guests, the first moments of the meeting with these Korags made him seriously consider, perhaps for the first time, the purpose of their visit. *Are they total idiots? Looks like. Or they know more than we think? What do they expect? Our promise not to snoop around Korango?*

The last thought, for reasons the Pazon master spy would have difficulty to articulate, reassured him. *Ha! Don't hold your breath.* He straightened his shoulders and went to join his boss and the guests.

TWENTY-ONE

SECURITY CHANCELLERY, THE GAMER

The upper floor of the Security Chancellery complex, with its dull interior design, felt like déjà vu to Eli—gray walls, long empty corridors, closed doors—rather traditional and even Earthly for a government building on a technologically advanced planet. The floor seemed to be deserted—empty hallways, corridors leading to elevators, and even unfinished spaces. Only on one occasion did Eli and Nox hear someone's voice. They prudently waited until the sounds died down before moving on.

Nox turned on her holo display. She started walking, keeping her arm with the gauntlet in front of her.

"I see nothing," said Eli.

"Let's wait. It needs time to verify its position." Indeed, the building schematics created by Lobo appeared in front of Nox, showing her location.

"Oh, mine's also working now." Eli listened to the earbud and awkwardly turned, staring in front of him with unseeing eyes. "This way." He pointed. "Lobo says to use an escape stairwell to get to building security. That's fifty floors down."

Because of the identical anatomies shared by human species settled in the Milky Way, flights of stairs in the building turned out to be close to what someone would expect on Earth—exactly twenty steps per floor. Running down and jumping over two or three at once, it took Eli and Nox about five minutes to reach the twenty-second floor. It was impossible to miss it—the floor landing was the last one.

"It looks like that's the end of the public area," noted Eli, who was approaching the exit door.

"Wait!" hissed Nox. "Don't open it!"

"I only wanted to open it a little to look through."

"Not safe—we have something better." Nox walked to the door and moved her gauntlet closer to it. A holo image showed a picture of an ample space filled with electronic equipment, gates, and two guards behind a bar.

"How do you do that?" asked Eli.

"I'll show you later. But look, Lobo didn't lie. Do you want to wait for the next shift? He said the change occurs each base interval of their time, which is about an hour on Earth."

"Yes, if we're close to the top of their hour."

Nox fiddled with her gauntlet. "About fifteen minutes left."

"We'll wait."

The security shift came on schedule. Eli and Nox stood behind the closed doors on the staircase landing, waiting for the shift change. It seemed to take forever. In the dead silence of the security center, the building threw back the echoes of the guttural commands and reports of the guards. The translators couldn't pick up their meaning. Eli and Nox waited patiently for the old shift to move out.

At last, everything got quiet. Eli slowly pulled the heavy door as

Nox put her hand on his shoulder and whispered, "Let me take care of them."

"Are you sure?"

"Yes. I want to try your idea." She unfastened the two top buttons of her uniform. "Is it enough?"

"Are you out of your mind?" sputtered Eli. "Now's not the time!"

He looked at Nox and lifted his chin, trying to look deeper in the opening of her shirt. "It won't work, go deeper. At least two more."

"Two more? Do you want me to go without my shirt?"

"I don't want you to do anything." An indignant tone cut through his voice. "I regret mentioning this."

"I don't. If it works, then why not?"

"It was a theory, remember? And... don't forget to pull apart both sides of the shirt. What's, um, inside should be visible."

Nox quickly completed the alteration of her garment. "Better now?"

He gulped. "Just go! We don't have time. I'll stand by."

Eli opened the door wider, and Nox slipped out into the security center hall.

At first, she crept silently, trying to use any opportunity to hide. Then she stepped out into the middle of the hall and walked straight toward the guards with a jaunty gait. What happened next confirmed Eli's theory. Both oafs stepped toward Nox, gaping and staring at her ample cleavage.

She smiled invitingly, raised her hand, and gently touched the cheek of the guard closest to her. With a stealthy movement, she shifted her hand to his neck and did something to it. The guard's knees bent, and he dropped to the floor like a sack of potatoes. The eyes of the second man widened, but it was too late. Nox jumped at him, grabbed his head with both hands and, with one quick twist, snapped his neck.

When Eli approached closer, she warned him, "The first guard is still alive. He'll probably be unconscious for ten or fifteen minutes, but he'll wake up. Do you want to kill him?"

Eli shook his head. "I can't do it like this, sorry. I'm not a killer. But I have to say you were great—took care of them quickly and quietly."

"I understand. We may also need him. Can you pull both guards to the staircase? I'll search for handcuffs or restraints." Nox buttoned up her shirt. "I still haven't thanked you for the tip. It worked well."

Nox returned to the stairwell landing with plastic handcuffs and a roll of adhesive tape. She dropped everything on the floor and bent over the unconscious guard. "How is he?"

"Breathing. Why didn't you kill him?" asked Eli.

"You'll see in a second. It's probably a good idea to cuff and gag him first."

While Eli was busy with the guard, Nox pulled the small box where she had kept Lobo's ID chip previously and stuck it to her gauntlet.

"He has the red circle and triangle insignia. You noticed that, right?" asked Eli.

"I did. That's why he's still alive." She kneeled in front of the guard and made several swipes with her arm above him. "His chip is okay. Let me check the other guy."

Nox repeated swiping over the dead guard. "His chip's dead. That's what I was afraid of. It died with the body."

"Did Lobo tell you about this?" asked Eli.

"He warned me it could happen—a feature of the new generation of IDs. Did you talk to Lobo about our next move?"

"We have two options—either to use an elevator or find another stairwell that goes to the basement. The former is faster but riskier. He thinks it's better for us to avoid any contact with the Chancellery personnel as long as we can. I think it's a prudent thing to do. He explained where the stairwell is."

"Do we have time?" asked Nox.

"Yes, Ruke and Shyster should still be on the planet. Plus, we need to give them some extra time to get to the cruiser."

"Good. I need your help to do a retinal scan. Can you hold his head vertically?"

"Sure. What about his ID chip?"

"It's already inside me. The gauntlet has a mini-transporter for small non-organic objects. That's how I sent a miniature video camera to the security center."

The staircase to the basement led to a small landing with a steel door. Eli approached it cautiously and peeked through its clear glass insert. Behind the door, there was a small room with ducts and utility boxes attached to its walls. He rolled his sleeve up and looked at the holo display to identify the location of the room. "I believe we're right on target. There's a corridor behind the chamber. I bet they put the Gamer in a cell there. I wonder if Zarfo and Lobo can read our position?"

Nox looked at her gauntlet. "I'm picking up the Gamer's beacon—we'll be fine without Lobo now. We must be in their Tech and Research facilities."

"Good." He tugged at the door handle. The door was unlocked. "Ready to go in?"

"Let me check something." Nox looked through the glass insert. "Terahertz laser beams there—you can't see them. I go first."

"Okay." Eli attached silencers to his pistols. "My guns are too loud. Can you take care of the Keepers with your laser piece if they show up?"

"Sure."

Eli opened the door and let Nox enter the room. She moved forward, carefully circumventing the beams and helping Eli navigate to the exit.

They entered a long, empty corridor. Its thick wall panels and massive bulkheads, made of machined stainless steel, clearly explained the purpose the place was built for—maximum security and protection from attempts to penetrate or destroy the Elder Keep's holy of holies.

Nox moved her forearm with the gauntlet from side to side. "This way!"

"Shhh... I hear voices," whispered Eli. "They're coming from that direction."

They froze in place, straining their ears to understand what the Pazons were talking about.

"Let's get closer," suggested Eli. He crept forward, hardly making any noise. Nox followed.

The voices became more distinct. "... have you tried... the intensity evolution... torus... it's around four microns... multiphonon transition..."

"They're trying to crack the Gamer," Eli whispered, "How many voices can you hear? Six?"

"Six," Nox purred in his ear.

Eli shook his head and tapped a finger in his ear. "What are you doing? It tickles."

"Sorry, you turned your head and—"

"Okay, okay... Let's move closer to the door. Are you sure about six?"

"Trust me."

"Right. Mine are the three on the left. The rest are yours. On the count of three."

With guns in each hand, Eli crawled on his knees to the edge of the door. He looked back—Nox was behind him, ready with her laser guns—and slowly stood up.

"Three!" yelled Eli and jumped inside.

The high-level meeting between the Korag and Pazon officials had moved along toward its end. The conversation would, at times, grow brighter, then subside, and then liven up again later, but its tone, at least on the surface, remained friendly.

Ruke and Shyster, who felt uncomfortable at first, soon overcame their insecurity. Asphalis remained silent, while Xiir showed a real talent for making conversation. His courtesy and regard for his guests was an infallible strategy to win their sympathy. Deep down, however, he remained cold and manipulative, amusing himself with the awkwardness and inexperience of his visitors.

Yawning inwardly, Xiir glanced at an elegant mechanical clock resting on a lovely small table and decided to round off the conversation with polite and meaningless promises, a suitable amount of thanks, and friendly leave-taking phrases. "It all sounds like unfounded allegations. But I'll keep an open mind and will conduct a thorough investigation. If there's any truth in it, I'm sure we'll settle the matter."

Ruke bowed slightly in his chair. "I'd feel much obliged if you go to the bottom of it."

Something must have gotten into Asphalis, for he unexpectedly uttered, "My Lord, if I may?"

Xiir squinted at him in displeasure for a split second, but quickly got a grip on himself. "Please..." Then, with a good-natured laugh, he continued, "But don't bore our guests to death with the details of your standard operating procedures."

"About that. I'm curious," started Asphalis. "From what we know, Coatera is the Strangers' outpost responsible for the development and maintenance of this so-called Game, a stealthy and lethal weapon capable of eradicating not only armies but entire worlds in an instant. Or so we hear. Aren't you afraid of it?"

Asphalis stood up, turned around his chair, and put his hand on its back. Combining the right amount of poise and pathos, he went on. "Would it be a responsible thing to cooperate with the Strangers if it's true? I understand that business is, well, what you do. In fact, you admit that one of your subordinates was a supplier to Coatera." The closer to the end of his tirade Asphalis got, the cockier he sounded. "May I ask you what exactly your associate was selling?"

Ruke hesitated to say anything. Shyster fidgeted on her chair. Her lips twitched, and she snapped back, "If you're implying that military equipment was involved, I cannot accept this as a valid argument. Yes, we sell arms. And we sell arms to the Elder Keep too, among many others. We don't ask you why you buy them or how you use them."

Asphalis tried to say something, but Shyster stopped him. "Excuse me, I haven't finished yet. As far as what you call the Game, may I remind you of the Intergalactic Game Treaty? We comply fully with all its provisions. Do you?"

Xiir Zanrod frowned and looked at Asphalis with unconcealed disgust. "Let's not be overzealous—on either side. I think our discussion was productive, and we identified the next step. There's no need to overshadow it with fruitless verbal attacks."

The Lord Guarantor rose from his chair and turned to Ruke. "Mr. President—Ruke! I want to assure you that we value our good relationship with Korango, a vibrant society of free people. And I'm confident that no cloud will cast a shadow over our relationship."

Ruke and Shyster rose too, and Ruke stepped forward. "Lord Zanrod, thank you for the opportunity to discuss our concerns with you. We value our relationship with your Alliance. I'm sure that our mutually beneficial cooperation will survive any headwinds if there is goodwill on both sides."

The doors opened, and the Protocol Doyen appeared in the doorway. He patiently waited for Xiir to finish his handshaking routine with Ruke and led him and Shyster out of the room.

The Lord Guarantor watched the backs of the departing guests.

As soon as the doors closed behind them, he pointed to the chair and said, without looking at Asphalis, "Sit."

A regular explosive handgun bullet striking a human in the torso would take out vital organs located at the point of impact, shredding them beyond repair and opening multiple wound channels. Such a projectile gained a new meaning with the ammunition and pistol modifications made by Nox. With her improvements, Eli's weapon turned out to be a real war machine. Not only would it kill, but depending on where it hit the target, it could also rip the body to pieces, decapitate the victim, or tear limbs away, completely demoralizing and demobilizing the enemy upon whom its wrath was directed.

Quick cracks of Eli's silenced .50 calibers, sizzling blasts of Nox's laser, and thuds of bodies falling on the floor merged into one loud bang. The flying body parts and splashes of blood were not for the fainthearted. In a split second, five people were sent to a better world. Their disfigured remains lay on the floor in puddles of blood. The sixth, a uniformed guard, stood terrified in the middle of the room.

"He's alive. What happened?" Nox asked.

Eli pointed at the guard's insignia. "Red circle and triangle... This is an antechamber. I'm sure the Gamer is in the main compartment."

The room was rather big, with the same stainless-steel design as the corridor. One wall of the place looked like a vault entrance with a heavy metal door. Eli nodded at the armored safe room. "Open it."

"I can't," the security guard implored, stepping back from Eli to the table in the middle of the room.

"Do it, or we'll do it our way." Eli waved his pistol menacingly. "I'll count to three. One—"

Without further delay, the guard rushed to the vault. He put his hand on a wall panel near the entrance, and its large metal door panels slowly parted. Behind, there was the Gamer, hovering above the floor.

Nox acted quickly. She unwound a belt full of explosives wrapped around her waist, attached it to the Gamer, and turned to the guard. "Close it!"

"It'll c-c-close by it-itself when we l-l-leave," the guard stuttered.

"If you don't close it now, we leave—you don't," Eli threatened. "Two—"

"I'll do it. Please don't shoot!" The guard touched the panel with his hand again, and the door slowly closed. Nox immediately burned out the control board with her laser.

Meanwhile, the guard darted to the table, trying to reach for a small gadget lying on it among food leftovers and half-empty plastic cups. Before he could touch it, Nox shot him dead. "Well, he knew we'd kill him anyway. We need to get out of here. The clock is ticking."

"How long did you set it for?"

"As planned, fifteen minutes. The countdown is on our gauntlet displays. You and I can tap it five times for immediate detonation."

"Thanks. Now what? Central Yard?"

"Lobo said it's the best way to get to the wing with the prison cells. I'm more comfortable now with his tips."

"Okay. Wait..." Eli gave Nox a blank stare and raised his hand. "I'm reading a text from D'Obba. They've found a Gaian cruiser shadowing ours. 'Her energy signature is the same as that detected near Korango. She's moving closer to *Leobla*. So far, no transporter dampening field deployed.' That's the end of the message."

Nox shrugged. "We have our Plan B. I wouldn't worry."

TWENTY-TWO

SECURITY CHANCELLERY, AURA

So far, Eli and Nox had muddled through their operation, avoiding close encounters with the Security Chancellery personnel. The offices of the Technical and Research Division were not particularly crowded, let alone the emergency stairways and escape routes. The Prison Central Yard was a different story. It served as the major gateway for entering and exiting the detention center. That's where they ended up.

"I recognize this place," said Nox, gazing anxiously around. "We need to get to the other side of the yard."

Except for a huge opening for daylight to enter, it looked more like a military stronghold—all concrete and metal, massive columns, with trusses and beams supporting the roof. Two lanes in the middle could accept trucks with prisoners going to the admission and processing facilities at a lower level. Heavy bars and railings divided the yard, forming a highly secure area with the enforceable traffic separation scheme. Several armored vehicles with guards in and around them blocked the roads. Groups of heavily armed personnel patrolled the area.

Accustomed to the relative ease of moving through the building's staircases and corridors, Eli and Nox hesitated. They didn't notice the guard supervisor coming up from behind.

"What's this?" Menacingly swaying from his heels to toes and back, he called Eli out.

Eli turned around.

The Pazon aimed his index finger at Eli's guns. "I'm Eots Xohq, the shift supervisor. How many times do I have to repeat that non-standard-issue sidearms are prohibited here?"

Afraid to speak, Eli saluted Eots Xohq, mimicking the gestures he'd seen before.

"Or you think because you're Special Ops, you can get away with anything you want?" Xohq sneered.

Eli recovered from the surprise and regained his cool. "Sir, that's a custom-made projectile gun approved by the chief of special operations, Abaddon! Sir!"

The shift supervisor clung to Eli like a leech. "You aren't local. Where did you come from?"

Eli gave Nox an eloquent look and cast his glance at her arm with the gauntlet.

"Sir, our rules prohibit us from disclosing any personal information to unauthorized personnel."

Even sitting in front of the old statesman, Asphalis couldn't tell whether the Lord Guarantor was thinking or dozing. His eyes were closed. The mighty head of the Congregation of Tyanis sat silent and motionless for a long while. Asphalis hesitated to disturb him and waited patiently.

Finally, Xiir showed some signs of life. He took a deep breath and stared with his pale, piercing eyes at the security chancellor. "Where are we with the Gaian woman you got? Anything interesting?"

Asphalis knew that, eventually, he would have to answer such a question. But he didn't have anything to swank about, so he calmly admitted, "Nothing, my Lord."

"What about that torus you mentioned?"

"Nothing to brag about either. It appears to be a communication device. We believe that it connects somehow to the Game's primary component. The torus is probably what Strangers call 'the Gamer.'"

Xiir closed his eyes again and, after a long pause, resumed. "And the Strangers? Any sign of their retaliation?"

"None, my Lord."

"Is it because they don't care about the Gamer?"

"Our analysts have always believed that the Strangers would not engage in any military conflict unless a loss were critical to their survival. That's why we chose our target as we did."

Xiir gazed intently at Asphalis. "Have you heard of a Korag called Eli?"

"Your Excellency, even the slightest detail cannot escape your attention. What can be so interesting about him that made you heed such an empty barrel?"

Unexpectedly, Xiir burst into laughter. "The lack of answer to my question is more sensational than Eli himself. Still, it looks like the Strangers care about him if they agreed to close their eyes on our assault if we deliver them Eli. Didn't they?"

"Remarkable, my Lord. Why do we even need the Security Chancellery if you know everything?"

Reverberations of steel cut through Xiir's voice. "We need it because I *don't* know everything! For example, I don't know what's so special about this Eli—do you?"

"Slun Ceabb, our contact on Gaia and a high-ranking official in the Strangers' intelligence, explained that he proposed the deal for personal reasons. Aura, the Stranger we collected, used to be Slun's girlfriend. When Eli showed up, Aura backed out of her relationship with Slun. Slun thought Eli might want to attempt a rescue operation if we kidnapped her. That would be our chance to keep our side of the bargain."

The Lord Guarantor jumped from his chair and paced around the room with the ease of a twenty-year-old boy. "Do you even understand what you're telling me?" he asked excitedly.

"Your Holiness, I'm only trying to be honest."

"So, the Strangers *knew* that we would attack Coatera? Did your bozos leak information about the attack?"

"The Strangers knew about our plans long before we approached Slun, sir. For the record, the chief bozo you're talking about is Aspirant Inquisitor Abaddon, our Chief of Special Operations."

"You think I care?" returned Xiir scornfully. "Should I remind you that we didn't approach Slun? He approached *us*."

"It was a good opportunity to diminish the risk of their retaliation, sir. Plus, we learned that they have a mole in the Security Chancellery. We're looking for it now. That's a dirty business, my Lord."

"Have you at least checked to see if those love stories are true?"

"We tried. There's no direct evidence, but Eli Stroud could develop a relationship with Aura. During our attack on Earth, he tried to shield Aura's shuttle with his space fighter."

Xiir shook his head doubtfully. "Hard to believe all this. Since when has our Holy Alliance become so pathetic that we're asked to solve someone's romantic issues? Because there's another explanation for all this. There has to be."

The Lord Guarantor turned to Asphalis and patted his shoulder. "Are you sure you kidnapped the right person? I trust you know that Eli is on board the presidential cruiser?" Xiir returned to his chair. "Incidentally, where is he now?"

While the supervisor's eyes were filling with blood, and his face reflected a tense thinking process, Nox, like a cat, leisurely squinted her eyes and activated the explosives.

The sidewalk behind the shift supervisor swelled up. Flames and blazing gases burst out of the gaping hole forming in the yard, swallowing armored vehicles and guards. The deafening roar of the explosion and crumbling structures resounded over the prison yard and farther throughout the Security Chancellery complex until it died away somewhere in the city.

The noise of devastation and chaos absorbed the sound of Eli's point-blank shot. The supervisor's knees buckled, and he began to sag. Eli picked him up under his armpits and carefully lowered the body to the ground. He looked around—in the commotion across the Central Yard, the killing of the supervisor had gone unnoticed.

"So much for Mr. Eots Xohq..." Smiling spitefully, Eli stepped over the dead man. "I have a message from Zarfo—did you get it?"

"Yep. Ruke and Shyster are back. We must hurry. Follow me!"

The floor shook slightly, and the crystals in Xiir's chandelier jingled. Xiir Zanrod looked at Asphalis.

"I guess he's here, our friend Eli." Asphalis stood up and came up to the window. "It seems he's at the Chancellery. My Lord, I have to go."

"That's your fucking problem, Phal... I want this Eli. Alive! Is that clear?" Xiir leaned back in his chair. "Get out! Tell my butler to come to see me."

Eli and Nox ran through the prison aisles. They moved fast—Nox knew where to go and didn't hesitate to turn on a dime.

Floors and walls shook with other blasts strong enough to cause pieces of ceiling to fall and lights to blink out. Most of the guards they met were moving in the opposite direction, evidently going closer to the epicenter of the explosions.

Eli and Nox caught up with a group of six armed guards, also moving in their direction. They slowed and followed them.

"A message from D'Obba—our transporter likely disabled," Eli muttered under his breath. "How long till the cell with Aura?"

"Almost there. The aisle behind the corner..."

The guards turned right. Eli stopped. "Are they going to the same place?"

"Could be. How would *I* know?" hissed Nox.

"If I'm right, we kill them when they enter the cell with Aura. I activate Plan B—you follow the Pazons. I'll join you as soon as I send a message to the skipper."

What Eli saw, when he'd sent the message and turned the corner, were the guards standing in front of the entrance to a cell. Its armored door was sliding aside, and Nox, within thirty feet of them, was slowly catching up. She looked back and nodded.

The guards started entering the lockup as Eli's hands tightened on the pistols' grips. He darted forward, overtook Nox, and flew up to the door as the last soldier of the group was about to enter the prison chamber. He drew his guns, opened fire, and stormed inside.

When Nox bolted into the cell a second later, her laser pistol in hand, the show was over. An eerie scene opened to her gaze. The reinforcements, all six guards, lay dead on the floor, almost blocking farther access into the place. She looked closer and realized that more than six had died.

Nox scanned the room. It was the same interrogation cell

where she had been kept and tortured. Abaddon, the only enemy left alive, stood still near the transparent hexagonal cage with Aura inside. Both hands up, he appeared resigning himself to his fate.

"I was afraid to shoot at him. It could have hurt Aura," said Eli.

"It's okay. We may need him to open the cage."

Nox gaped at the floor—she stood in a pool of blood. And the worst part of the picture was the limbs and even parts of torsos scattered around, still oozing. She moaned and instinctively covered her mouth. *I thought I'd seen it all...*

Nox looked at Eli. Wispy rills of smoke were still trailing from the barrels of his handguns. He twisted his head in bewilderment and shifted nervously on his feet. It seemed he hadn't expected such effects from his shooting. *Who is this guy? I worried if he was up to the challenge. And now I fret... about what? But I don't want him to change.*

From the corner of her eye, Nox saw Ab slowly lowering his hands. "Eli! Ab!" she yelled.

Another crack of the gunshot made Nox flinch. This time Eli had aimed at a spot on the floor close to Ab's foot.

Wow! He's fast. Almost as fast as I am. How does he do that?

The bullet left a hole in the concrete floor of the cell. Because of the angle of the blast, most of the debris hit Ab's legs, tearing apart his boots and the cuffs of his pants. He buckled and fell to his knees.

"Open it!" yelled Eli, pointing his gun at Ab.

Ab tried to get up from the floor and failed. "My boy, I've been expecting—"

"Don't be an idiot, Ab. Open it!"

Ab threw a keycard to Eli. "Swipe it."

"He's stalling, don't you see?" worried Nox.

"That being so..." Eli kicked Ab in the abdomen as hard as he could. Ab wheezed and collapsed on the floor. "Aura, stay away from the glass. Turn around. Protect your head!"

Aura dashed to the far corner of the cage and squatted there, bending her head as low as she could between her knees.

Eli detached the silencer and shot at the glass. The bright blue flashes of powerful explosions accompanied each hit. The first two rounds produced a small chip. After the third, a long crack ran through the glass.

"Aim at the dent!" shouted Nox.

He carefully aimed and pulled the trigger. The last bullet caused a series of starburst cracks with a small hole at the point of impact. "Shit—I need to reload," said Eli and kicked the glass. The wall disintegrated. Eli jumped into the cage and helped Aura out of the hexagon.

"You came for me," she said. Her eyes filled with tears, and she hid her face on his chest. "They tortured me, but I didn't shed a tear."

Eli took her head in his hands and gently moved her face away. He looked into her eyes. "I love you. I'd do anything for you—you should know that!"

We did it! Well, he did it… I wish I had someone like Eli in my life, thought Nox, trying not to miss a single moment of the reunion. The reality of the situation, though, made itself felt. *We're not done yet.* "Eli, we need to go. Aura, can you walk?"

Aura moved away from Eli and wiped her tears. "Yes." She walked to the pile of dead bodies on the floor and, without hesitation, picked up a laser carbine.

"Hey, ladies… The skipper released *Night Stalker*," announced Eli while reloading his guns. "I have a connection to her interface. She's cloaked, drifting in low orbit. A lot of traffic there."

"Eli, don't kill Ab… yet. We may need him," said Nox.

Suddenly, the door slid wide open, and a smoke grenade flew into the cell. Eli booted it back into the aisle, waited four or five seconds, and leaped out into the smoke. Then, he opened fire.

The last stand is on! flashed through Nox's mind. She shouted to Aura, "Eli must live, no matter what! Understand?"

"Yes."

"Follow me. When you can, help him reload."

The Pazons took Xiir's order to catch Eli seriously. They deployed forty troops in the aisle near the high-security cell containing Aura. Divided into two squads, guards blocked the corridor in both directions. It seemed Eli's bold plan to free the captive was doomed. The overwhelming force and the lack of retreat should have guaranteed the Pazons a success.

Unfortunately, those who'd ordered the capture of Eli and his friends made four devastating tactical mistakes. The "Prison Battle," as the Security Chancellery operating manuals would reference it later, resulted in a slaughter in which the assailants killed all first responders.

The blunders started with the smoke grenade. It was launched into the cell as a screening device to conceal the movement of the attacking force. But when kicked back out, it obscured the view of the room entrance and let Eli exit unnoticed. Besides, it turned out to be too powerful—it spewed enough smoke to screen the whole area around the torture chamber.

Secondly, the attackers approached their operation presumptuously, relying on what they believed to be a tremendous firepower advantage, with no clue about the opposing side's weapons and its resolve to fight. Eli's and Nox's shooting and tactical skills came as a shock—ghosting through the smoke clouds, they killed half the attacking troops in the first four seconds.

The decision to block the aisle in both directions turned out to be the third blunder. The tactic would have worked if those on the defensive had surrendered when facing the seemingly overwhelming force. But they didn't. Having dealt with the fierce resistance, the Pazons found themselves in a predicament where shooting at the intruders could kill some of their own. It did.

Finally, the Gaian weapons technology, unknown on Pat'zan, played a decisive role. With the remarkable accuracy of the shooting, each shot was a kill. Combined with the destructive power of the Gaian laser pistol and Eli's upgraded American handguns, they completely demoralized the assailants.

Eli's shots resulted in the obliteration of all targets. Moving lightning fast and barely discernible in the smoke, he emerged from the cell spinning, guns in both hands. There were fourteen rounds in the pistols—fourteen dead Pazons. While he was reloading, Aura covered him by spraying the aisle with blasts from the laser gun she'd picked up in the cell. What Eli was doing with two weapons, Nox accomplished with one. Burying her scruples, she set the laser to maximum, increasing the impulse power and its duration. It meant not only making bigger holes in bodies but also cutting them apart.

Dismayed by exploding comrades in arms, severed heads and limbs, the smell of burned flesh, the thunder of shots cracking across the aisle, and the bleeding bodies of the dead, the remaining attackers threw down their weapons and tried to find cover. The corridor they had thought of as a trap for the intruders ended up the trap for the Pazons—there was no place to hide for those not killed in the first several seconds.

Running away didn't help. Eli and Nox took no chances, meticulously eliminating those who fled. They knew that each enemy still alive could return and kill them.

The fight ended in less than twenty seconds.

TWENTY-THREE

SECURITY CHANCELLERY, ESCAPE

The smoke dissipated quickly, and a new group of troops appeared at the far end of the aisle. They didn't dare to come closer, hiding instead behind the corners of the intersection. Several scurried around, building some sort of contraption.

"We need to get to the surface," called Eli. "Any suggestions?"

"Keep moving," answered Nox. "There's a cargo elevator nearby. Follow me."

"Wait! What happened to Ab?"

"I shot him when I left the cell," said Aura.

"Is he dead?" insisted Eli.

"If the bastard's alive, then it's his lucky day!" shouted Nox. "We have to run." She nodded at a growing lot of guards in the distance. "See them?"

"Okay, lead the way." Eli put one of his guns into its holster and reestablished his grip on the other with both hands. "Aura, follow Nox. I have your backs." He carefully aimed at the structure being built, which looked more and more like a weapon, and released a volley of shots.

A series of explosions danced across the device, tearing it apart.

Pazon troops jumped away from it and threw themselves behind the corners of the aisle. Eli emptied the magazine and ran after Aura and Nox while reloading the gun.

Nox and Aura stopped. The aisle began to turn, and they didn't want to lose sight of Eli. He looked back—the Pazons had resumed their attempts to build the device. He started shooting again, this time carefully targeting each shot. The last bullet brought success—an explosion tore the weapon to pieces and, judging by the screams and falling bodies, took the lives of several guards.

Eli joined Nox and Aura, and they resumed running. "This way." Nox gestured to the right. "The elevator is about a hundred feet away." They swerved around the corner.

"I bet they know where we're going." Eli ran his eyes over the walls and the ceiling.

"Probably... What do you propose?" asked Nox.

"Nothing. I wondered whether we could knock out their surveillance system..."

"And?"

"Too late, and a waste of time. They have eyes everywhere here."

"Then what do you want to do?" Nox scowled, and her eyes narrowed.

"What I said—to get to the surface."

"You have a plan?"

"Nox!" he shouted, exasperated. "Where is your fucking elevator?"

The buttons on the aisle wall next to the elevator entrance had only two options—two arrows, evidently a universal symbol to show directions. Pressing the up arrow brought the elevator to their floor. The doors slid aside, revealing an interior lined with metal panels, dirty and scratched, all bruised from prolonged, hard use.

"First floor!" ordered Eli.

Nothing happened.

"Lobby... Upper level... Main entrance... Main floor. Up!" Eli kept trying, but the car stood still. "How the hell are we supposed to control this thing?" He looked bewildered.

"The Chancellery building is not compliant with the Intergalactic Linguistic Convention," said Nox, as if it were the most obvious thing in the world. "Use the damn buttons."

Eli looked around the inside of the beast. "There's a panel. One button is highlighted. I assume that the buttons above it are to go up. How many levels are we below ground?"

Aura cut Eli off, "Guys, whatever you do, do it fast. The Pazons have shown up and are closing in."

Nox jumped to the doors. "Aura, get inside. I'll keep them at bay. Eli, five levels."

"Enjoy the ride," said Eli and pressed the button.

The doors closed, and the elevator jerked, moving up. The buttons on the control panel blinked, indicating the elevator's movement.

ONE LEVEL UP.

Eli raised his hand.

"Hey, I have a message from D'Obba. 'The Gaian ship moving to a lower orbit toward *Night Stalker*.' I don't like it."

TWO LEVELS UP.

"Nox, can you check your holo map to find out exactly where the elevator goes on the ground level?"

THREE LEVELS UP.

Nox turned her holo display on.

FOUR LEVELS UP.

"Transportation deck, some kind of main entrance."

The car jerked up, then down, and stopped.

"Damn! They blocked it. As I expected." Eli examined the ceiling. The lines on it seemed to indicate the contours of an emergency trap door, although it didn't have a handle or any obvious way to open it. He jumped, trying to push the door up with his hand. It didn't budge. Eli pulled out his gun. "Stay back!" He targeted the center of the outline and shot. The detonation of the bullet blew away the entire hatch, leaving a hole in the ceiling. Eli moved underneath the center of the opening, holding his hands together to give Aura a leg up. "You first, quickly."

Boosted by Eli, Aura disappeared into the hole. "Nox, now you."

"No, you go. They cannot harm me."

Eli sprang up, catching the edges of the hatch, and pulled himself up and out of the elevator. Almost immediately, his face showed back in the hatch. He held out his hand to help Nox.

"Give me a minute," she said and took something out of her pocket. "I stashed away an explosive charge. I'm setting it up."

"Get out of here! They can move the elevator at any moment. We shouldn't split."

The elevator shaft looked remarkably low-tech—a frame and its brackets, guide rails, a counterweight, cables—all elevator things familiar to Earthlings. Eli touched the steel beam, and disgust distorted his stern face. "This tech is like what we have on Earth. Can't help filching anything that isn't nailed down. Freeloaders…"

A noise came from above—someone was trying to open the elevator door panels one level above. Slowly, with a screech, they began to move apart.

"Nox, Aura, I'll be busy moving *Night Stalker* closer. She's our only hope." Eli jabbed his finger at the doors. "Be ready to take care of them."

"No problem." Nox threw the explosives she was working on into the elevator car and trained her gun at the door. Meanwhile,

Aura aimed her carbine at the widening gap between the door panels and shot. The noise at the door stopped. However, the car jerked again and slowly moved higher.

"Where is your ship?" Nox gasped anxiously.

"Twelve seconds to get her above the deck. Aura, move off the shaft center, closer to the side walls." Eli gave her a reassuring smile. "Nox, you too. Hang tight..."

The car slowly crept higher as a strained silence hung in the air.

When the top of the elevator car was about level with the deck floor, the walls of the elevator shaft vibrated, and a harrowing screech rattled the building.

The purplish light of Pat'zan Prime refracted oddly as it passed through the transparent material of the terminal's dome. It was late afternoon on Pat'zan. Usually, at this time, the employees would wrap up their dark deeds before calling it quits for the day and showing up en masse on the transportation deck, a vast covered area on the ground floor. But that wasn't happening today.

The higher-ups at the Security Chancellery learned their lessons quickly. Faced with the power of Gaian technology and its military applications, the Elder Keep authorities didn't want to take any more risks and decided to do everything possible to ensure the capture of the assailants. The evacuation of regular employees had been in progress since the first explosion—all nonessential personnel were exiting the building through emergency routes. The heavily armed Security Chancellery Special Forces replaced the regular guards and completely cordoned off the building. It didn't take them long to figure out the intruders' escape plan—most of them concentrated around and inside the transportation deck.

Twenty armored vehicles and two surface-to-air missile batteries were on their way to the Chancellery, and two battle-cruisers were hanging over the capital of Pat'zan. Security Chancellor Asphalis had commandeered one of them. Immediately after meeting with Xiir Zanrod, he'd gone aboard the cruiser and taken control of the whole operation.

When *Night Stalker* unexpectedly appeared in the sky above the Chancellery building, she didn't cause much concern. But the Pazons' anxiety quickly grew when a salvo of missiles launched at the space fighter produced no effect, and she continued her rapid descent. The actual awareness of the trouble coming from above occurred when, without stopping, the space fighter crashed into the dome and sent a shower of sharp transparent material down onto the people rushing around below, seeking safety. Yet many members of the Special Forces, particularly those near the entrance to the freight elevator, stayed where they were, carrying on with their jobs, preparing to capture the enemy entrenched in the elevator shaft.

Meanwhile, *Night Stalker* turned inside the dome. The columns supporting the structure and other architectural elements didn't stop the ship. As she was readjusting her position to move closer to the elevator, her hull rammed through the deck, pulverizing everything in her way.

But the worst was yet to come. A pair of high-speed laser guns popped up on the bottom of the ship and opened fire, killing everybody within proximity of the elevator.

The blasts of *Night Stalker*'s laser guns and the screams and groans of dying people echoed toward the elevator shaft. One of the Special Forces commandos pushed his body through the narrow opening in the elevator door panels, seeking salvation from certain death on the transportation deck. Aura, who had her carbine ready, pulled the trigger. The Pazon shrieked and fell into the shaft.

The laser blasts stopped. "According to *Night Stalker*, there's nobody near the elevator—time to get out." Eli peeked through the gap between the door panels.

"Not for you." Nox pushed him away from the doors. "Don't try to be a hero!"

"*Night Stalker*'s transporter is still offline. I have to see the ship to move her and shield us better," protested Eli, but Nox had already sneaked out of the elevator shaft.

"Seems okay… Go!" Nox leaped back into the shaft.

Eli popped his head outside. The space fighter turned and moved closer to the elevator, obstructing the view of its entrance from the rest of the transportation deck. Her loading ramp slowly descended. He turned to Nox. "We can go now."

"I'll join you in a second. I need to set the detonator for my parting gift. You and Aura run. Ready?"

Eli looked at Aura. She nodded.

Nox pulled out her laser pistol. "Go!"

"Aura, stay close to me!" yelled Eli as he dashed to *Night Stalker* with Aura following close behind.

Only twenty yards remained when a salvo of laser blasts danced on the deck, blocking their way. "Damn! Sniper fire!" Eli stopped. With a pistol in his hand again, he feverishly glanced around in search of the source. Aura also stopped—until suddenly, she leaped ahead and pushed Eli. He fell, and the shot intended for him slashed across her neck instead.

This time Eli spotted the sniper's location and discharged the whole magazine into their enemy. When he turned to Aura, she already lay on the ground, pressing her hand against the wound. Blood gushed through her fingers.

"Nox, cover us!" Eli screamed at the top of his lungs. He glanced at the wound. The sight chilled him—the laser beam had lacerated her neck badly. Aura was breathing heavily and began sweating. She was going into hemorrhagic shock.

His heart sank. *That's the carotid artery!* "No, no, no," he muttered, grabbing Aura by the collar of her jacket and dragging her to the ship while frantically shooting back at their enemies. Nox was running toward them, spraying laser-fire at anything that seemed suspicious.

Eli reached the ramp and took Aura in his arms.

"I'm sorry you've risked your life for nothing..." she murmured under her breath.

"We'll take care of you. You'll be fine!"

"I let you down..."

Nox reached Eli and Aura inside the ship.

"Do something!" Eli looked helplessly at Nox.

Nox froze for a second—and abruptly, as if by magic, the aft end of the ship transformed into a surgical ward. Eli carefully lowered Aura onto an operating table.

"Listen to Nox... She'll help you..." Aura closed her eyes. Her vital signs were deteriorating rapidly.

Nox approached the table where two robotic arms hung over Aura, quickly connecting devices and tubes to her body. Eli took Aura's hand and kissed her forehead.

"Hey! You aren't helpful here! Better blast the elevator entrance. It'll send the car down and set off the charge."

Eli rushed to the cockpit as a wave of cold fury overwhelmed him. "I'll level this fucking place!" he vowed.

As *Night Stalker* took off, hovering above the ground, the muted rumble of a remote explosion transformed into thunder. The doors of the elevator bulged, then sprang free as the blast propelled them into the middle of the deck. A huge fireball followed the doors, bringing with it metal shrapnel debris and shards of glass. The entire floor sagged, and the transportation deck began to implode. An enormous hole appeared in its place, devouring everything and everyone on the deck.

Nox entered the cockpit—her face stricken. "I'm so sorry, Eli... but

Aura passed away. There was nothing I could do. She lost too much blood before I could stabilize her. Too much, even for our technology."

Everything went cold inside Eli. He got up and walked aft to the improvised surgery. He stood still, stony-faced, looking at Aura's body. "Please take care of her... her body..." His voice failed.

"I will... Eli, enough fighting. Listen to me!"

Eli dragged his eyes from Aura's body. "I'll listen. That's what Aura said." The muscles in his face tightened. "But not now." He stalked back to the cockpit.

"Our response is becoming disproportionate to what they did." Nox followed him. "Do you realize that we've already killed hundreds of Pazons?"

"Ah, enlighten me... How do you calculate the proportion? How do you calculate the value of one life over others?"

"It's not a calculation. It's just... Enough! I thought you would understand this more than anybody else."

"Are you trying to shame me?" Eli pierced Nox with his eyes and turned away from her.

She didn't respond. The sound of the ship's commsys interrupted the silence.

Eli looked at the monitor. "It's Jour—*Stalker*, open the channel."

D'Obba's face appeared on-screen. She looked nervous and tired. "I'm glad to see you back in your ship. How'd it go?"

Eli winced. He didn't want to answer. "What's up, D'Obba?" His face gave nothing away.

"The Gaian cruiser is still here. Also, if you don't know, there are two Pat'zan battlecruisers in low orbit. They're maneuvering—probably up to something."

"Thanks, D'Obba. I appreciate the heads-up. See you guys later."

Eli ended the call and turned to Nox. "Here's what I'm going to do. I'll lift off slowly. If they don't shoot at us, I'll go away. If they do, I'll respond."

"You're deliberately provoking them."

"That's a little dramatic, Nox," Eli snarled. "I didn't know that was your style. But paraphrasing a wise man from Earth, they've got to know their limitations, don't they?"

"Do you know *your* limitations?" she asked worriedly.

"I feel lucky!" Eli grimaced. "I have some tricks of my own."

Nox shook her head in doubt.

Eli looked at her, and his eyebrows rose in surprise.

Nox felt confused. "What? Why are you staring at me like this?"

"Nothing... Déjà vu. The way you shook your head... It reminded me of my mom—she used to do it exactly like you just did."

"Sorry, I didn't mean—"

"A little while ago, I wouldn't have liked it. Now..." Eli clenched his fists. "I keep losing people I love!"

"Eli, if it's any consolation, you're not alone—you have friends. I'll help you any way I can."

A massive discharge shook *Night Stalker*.

"You see? They can't help it!" Eli said with grim satisfaction.

"That's why you were sitting here, waiting?"

"Yep. You didn't want me to shoot at them. I didn't. *They* started it."

TWENTY-FOUR

REVENGE

Night Stalker soared, leaving behind the ruins of the transportation deck. Eli took a deep breath and let the fighter bond with him to the hilt. Her might and power resonated in every cell of his body.

Laser blasts lightened the ship's hull. The sensation of energy converters topping up *Night Stalker*'s power reserves with the energy from the enemy fire swept over Eli. A heavy burden fell from his shoulders. For the first time in days, since the Elder Keep attack on Coatera, he realized how edgy and fearful he had been. He felt free now... even as he felt deep sorrow.

What am I going to do now that they've killed Aura? She saved my life...

The loss of his love overwhelmed him. Eli had never thought much about his future with Aura. But from the first moment he'd seen her, the mere thought she was somewhere, doing something, breathing or walking, would warm his soul and fill him with joy. He would fall asleep thinking about Aura, her voice, her smile...

Why did I never tell Aura I loved her? Why? Was I afraid? Of what? I'm not a kid. And if I'd told her, then maybe, just maybe, she would have listened to me when I tried to warn her about the Keepers and their attack on Coatera. Instead, I got angry. Oh God, I thought I was a man! Who am I?

A powerful blast shook the space fighter.

Eli broke away from his thoughts and focused on the targets detected and submitted by *Night Stalker*. Three small warships on the topmost landing platform of the Chancellery building were blasting his space fighter.

Ha! She marked them "no threat." Idiots, don't they understand they're dealing with weapons beyond their comprehension? Didn't they see what we've already done? This is a kindergarten! What about their bosses? Do they care? Or these poor saps are cannon fodder? Nox doesn't want me to kill them… Do I? Okay… Lobo said Asphalis' office is behind the solid wall on that side of the pad… I hope they'll get the message.

"Nox, I don't want any damage to Aura's body. Is everything okay down there?"

"Yes."

"Fasten your belt. The ride will be bumpy. Hang on—I only want to destroy the weaponry they've deployed around the complex and the central building. By now, after what we've done, it should be empty."

Eli focused on the wall. *"STALKER, MAIN CALIBER, TWO SHOTS, FIRE!"*

The ship obediently complied with Eli's command. Two anti-matter cannon shots obliterated not only the wall but the entire top of the tower. The shock wave from the blast blew one ship away from the platform. Pazons dashed to the remaining two, and in seconds, the landing pad was clear.

Good! Eli looked down—armored vehicles surrounding the Chancellery building were moving away. The two anti-missile batteries kept shooting. *"RELEASE A VOLLEY OF LASER SHOTS AROUND THE SURFACE-TO-AIR INSTALLATIONS. AVOID CASUAL-TIES. MAKE IT SCARY. FIRE! DAMAGE REPORT ON SCREEN."*

A three-dimensional representation of the area hit by the fight-er's weapons fire appeared in the cockpit. Fountains of dirt, stone debris, and fire cavorted around the two weapon systems, and now more Pazons were rushing away from the building. The space fighter made a few steep turns, choosing the best firing angle, leaving little more than piles of ripped-apart, jagged pieces of metal on the ground.

Eli made the ship fly around the Security Chancellery compound, discovering that its grounds were deserted. "*STALKER, DESTROY THE BUILDING. MINIMIZE THE DAMAGE BEYOND THE PERIMETER. MANEUVER AND FIRE AT WILL!*"

Night Stalker rose higher and tilted almost vertically, turning its nose toward the building. A crashing salvo of her four guns leveled the complex. Mesmerized, Eli stared at the ruins as the eerie feeling of emptiness crept over him again.

"Eli!" Nox's voice yanked him out of the darkness he was sinking into.

"What?" Eli flinched at her soft voice.

"It's time to get out of here."

"It's horrible…" Eli whispered and paused, finding it difficult to choose words. "I-I wanted to kill them all… But I tried not to, right?" He turned to Nox as if seeking validation of his words.

The sound of the commsys cut through the silence in the cockpit, and the screen came alive.

"Eli, don't take the call, I beg you," Nox said.

"That's a Pazon." Eli straightened up. "Sorry, I have to. I believe I know who he is. *Stalker*, open channel!"

A relaxed and smiling face filled the screen. "My boy, while I acknowledge your determination to destroy our property, I also advise you to stop immediately and surrender. There are two battlecruisers above you. So that you understand the situation."

"And you are?"

"Asphalis, the head of the Elder Keep's security."

Eli didn't respond. Instead, he began to scrutinize the man in front of him. *One hell of a pompous ass,* he concluded.

"Did you hear me?" demanded Asphalis smirking.

"I did. I'm thinking you guys have a nasty habit of addressing people as 'my boy.' That's rude. You know who else does that?"

"I don't. And I don't have time for this. Last warning!"

Eli sighed. "I wouldn't be so presumptuous if I were you. But I'm not. So, you want me to come to your ship?"

"Yes."

"And what will happen to me after that?"

"*I'd* kill you immediately. But some important people want you alive, so don't worry."

"Two cruisers. Which one is yours?"

"The flagship has distinctive red sigils. I'll be waiting for you." *Likewise.* "Okay, see you later. *STALKER, END CALL.*"

Eli closed his eyes and sat still. A series of symbols appeared on the screen, and a familiar female voice announced, "To enable this feature, I need your manual confirmation."

"She's speaking with my voice?" Nox was astounded. "What feature?"

"I could change the voice, but I like it this way." Eli smiled. "As far as the feature... You'll see. If they shoot first."

Eli put his hand on the keyboard and typed a long sequence of keystrokes. A mighty drone shrouded the cockpit.

Night Stalker looked ridiculously tiny in front of the two Elder Keep battlecruisers, bristling with weapons. They hung motionless against the backdrop surrounding Pat'zan—a picture-perfect cosmic landscape that would make any war or marine artist green with envy.

Eli's intentions seemed straightforward—he was approaching the flagship. As Asphalis promised, the purplish light of Pat'zan

Prime made the circle with the triangle inside easily visible on the hull of the cruiser. However, *Night Stalker*'s trajectory abruptly changed. Turning away from the flagship, the space fighter darted to the second cruiser, passed her, and rushed toward open space.

The Pazons reacted immediately. The warning salvo from the second cruiser brushed against the fighter's hull and brought her to a halt.

Excluding Eli, nobody expected the speed and the way in which ensuing events developed. His ship spun around, shrouded in a blueish glow, and emitted a barely visible beam of energy. Like a hot knife through butter, the blinding streak cut the battlecruiser into two halves. They started slowly drifting apart, leaking smaller debris. Then, probably because of the internal damage to the ship structure or systems, each exploded in a myriad of fragments, flying in all directions.

By sheer luck or Eli's intention, the flagship avoided the stream of energy—but the wave of shards and shrapnel sleeted hard into Asphalis' cruiser.

"What was that?" screamed Nox. "I didn't know your ship could do such things."

"I can't explain it. I discovered it accidentally—never used it before. I perceive it as a bunch of tiny Eaters."

"Eaters?"

"I used to read horror stories when I was a kid. Eaters ingest matter. All types. It's a mental image *Night Stalker* understands."

"It seems like a special case of quantum conversion. It bears a resemblance to the Game's Quantum Core."

"The Game fundamentals are not my forte." Eli dismissively waved his hand and nodded at the cockpit viewport, where the Pat'zan flagship was growing bigger. "You'd better tell me what to do with Asphalis."

"You want to kill him?"

"My hands are itching. He killed my mother and Aura, and he abducted you. He destroyed Coatera Cela. Gaia doesn't care. Someone has to stop him."

"I understand how you feel. There's probably someone above Asphalis who gave the order, though. Don't you think?"

"Good idea. I'll ask him."

Asphalis took the call immediately. He appeared on-screen, looking frightened, lips trembling. Eli sized him up with disgust. "So, you wanted Gaian technology? You got some."

Asphalis' ears went red as blood rushed to his face. He shuffled nervously in his chair.

Eli waited for a moment and continued, "Cat got your tongue? Anyway, who's your boss?"

"I don't have bosses."

"Don't try to find someone more stupid than yourself. Who ordered the assault on Coatera?"

Asphalis kept silent.

"I'm losing patience. I don't even need to press a button to kill you, understand? Last chance—*Who* ordered the assault on Coatera?"

"Well, we have a Supreme Council—"

"It always comes down to one person. I want to talk to this motherfucker."

Eli saw Asphalis beckoning to someone. "Connect me to the Lord Guarantor." Asphalis turned back to Eli and said, "You'll have to wait." The chancellor fell silent and sat, staring at his fingernails.

Eli patiently waited until, finally, he saw Asphalis raising his head. "My Lord, I have... someone here who threatens to kill me and destroy my cruiser if I don't tell him who ordered the attack on Coatera."

"I want a conference call," demanded Eli. In a second, the commsys screen divided in two, the new section showing an austere man with a scowling face.

"Who is *he*?" Xiir's face showed thin-lipped displeasure.

"I'm Eli Stroud, the head of the Korango Security Council. Right now, I represent Coatera *and* Korango."

Asphalis broke in with a shriek, "See the Chancellery building burning? My other cruiser destroyed? He did all this!"

Xiir's face puckered with ill-concealed disgust at Asphalis. Then he looked at Eli and raised his eyebrows. "Are you threatening me?"

"Not yet. Would you care to give me your name and explain who you are?"

"What do you want?"

"Your name and title, to start with."

"Xiir Zanrod, the Lord Guarantor of the Congregation of Tyanis."

"I demand full compensation for the space station your people destroyed at Coatera. The Korango Law Offices of Ournor and Company will prepare the bill. Secondly, make a public apology and affirm your commitment to refrain from any hostile acts against Korango and Coatera and their interests in the Milky Way."

Xiir frowned. "There must be some misunderstanding. We've agreed with the Korangan president on the course of action regarding Korango's involvement in the incident. Do you have any letters of credence to attest to your claims?"

"What a coincidence! So if you don't mind, I'll be hanging around to see the Korango presidential cruiser's safe return to the station. In case you decide to intercept her while she's on her way home."

"Mr. Eli... I need to address some issues you mentioned. First, your request for the compensation. It appears you have inflicted quite a lot of damage to our facilities and—"

"What else could I do with the Gaian technology I found in the basement of your Chancellery—in violation of the Intergalactic Game Treaty? And freeing the Coateran governor, one of the leading researchers on the Game, from your maximum-security prison. I also recall your goons who killed my mother on Earth. So, to your point... I've realized that I forgot *punitive* damages. For, you know, malice, fraud, distress..."

Xiir pouted. "Can we consider the matter closed, then?"

"When we get the money. And your formal apology. I understand that you were ill-advised by Asphalis. I reckon such actions amount to the crime of treason punishable by death on your planet."

Eli stopped, wrinkled his nose, and shook his head as if reluctantly deciding on something inevitable. "This is getting annoying, Xiir—I didn't plan for this, but you, guys, crossed the line. A little demo of our power for your pleasure. *STALKER, DESTROY THE BATTLECRUISER. FIRE!*"

Night Stalker filled again with the rising drone and vibrated slightly—the part of the screen with Asphalis rippled, and the picture disappeared.

"What happened?" yelled Xiir.

"Asphalis is no more. Together with his washtub. You condemned him to death, right? I carried out the sentence."

"That was an assassination!"

"Did you think I'd wait until he followed through on your order to capture me?"

"Asphalis told you about this?"

"It's all documented..."

Xiir gasped and remained sitting with his mouth open. He slowly regained control over his emotions.

"I think I finally understand what's happening. And you are..." Xiir shook his finger, pointing at Eli, and burst into laughter, "you're something. You really are!"

"So?"

"First, I'm sorry for what happened. I truly am. It was a mistake, my fault. I didn't correctly assess the information I had. Please accept my apology."

"I want a public apology and not only to me. Here is Nox"—Eli turned to her—"Nox, please, come closer. She was abducted too."

Nox got up and came to Eli's chair.

"Is that really Nox? My apology extends to her and everybody else affected. But I cannot make it public. I have my reasons, but it's also in your interests, Mr. Eli, to keep everything we talk about private."

"Why is that? I have no secrets from Gaians or Korags."

"There is a difference between the 'Gaians' and 'the Gaian government.' I know something about Gaia. I have to."

"You mean like the Gaian government battlecruiser hanging around, cloaked close to my ship, considering what to do with me?"

Xiir looked taken aback. "You picked up that too?"

"I take your question as your acknowledgment of the fact. Which makes me wonder how you know about the cruiser?" Eli silently cocked his head. "Ah, I see... A trusty Gaian, possibly one of those who is commanding the ship, told you?"

"You think I'm trying to deceive you? Politics is the art of the possible—are you familiar with this phrase?"

"Sounds familiar..."

"It should. You're from Earth, as I recall. But I digress. I made an error. I wanted the unattainable. The cost of my mistake turned out to be too high, and I regret that—"

"Xiir, I appreciate your enthusiasm and interest in Earth politicians, but I'm not in the mood to talk politics. I have urgent matters to attend to. I don't insist on a public apology, but I expect compensation for the damages and your commitment I mentioned. Do you agree?"

"I do. I'd like to invite you to Pat'zan as my guest of honor. I'm ready to make up for my reluctance to go public."

"You want me to volunteer to lead my own interrogation in the rebuilt Security Chancellery?"

"My interest in Gaia and its technology has changed. I'm

prepared to close my eyes to everything you did today on Pat'zan."
Xiir chuckled. "Moreover, I'm prepared to say that if you ever have
problems with your Gaian brothers and sisters, you'll always find a
safe place on Pat'zan, if you need one."

"Your Serene Lordship!" Eli bowed slightly, pressing his right
hand across his chest. "I don't trust your change of heart, but I'm
glad we talked. Say 'Hi' to Abaddon—if you managed to pull him
out from under the rubble before the building collapsed—your
next security boss, yes?"

Eli's mockery didn't produce any effect on the Lord Guarantor.
"You don't like him?"

"That's the problem with your invitation, Lord. If I see Ab
again, I'll kill him, make no mistake."

"I envy you, Eli. Where are my twenties?"

"See you around. *CLOSE CHANNEL.*"

The screen went out, and Eli leaned back in the chair. "Fucking
Xiir..."

Nox stared disapprovingly at him and shook her head. "I told
you, swearing doesn't suit you."

"At times, it helps me think." Eli nodded at the blank commsys
monitor. "What was that supposed to mean?"

"He probably believes that instead of dealing with Slun, he'll be
better off with you. He's a long-distance runner."

"You believe he's not lying?"

"I don't do crystal ball gazing. The future will tell."

"Whatever... We're going home."

"To my home, Eli—to Kierus."

"What's Kierus? Why Kierus?"

"Aura wanted to be buried in the place where the Game is
located. That's Kierus, a brown dwarf."

Eli froze. "I'm getting a message from *Groerok*..." He raised his
finger. "D'Obba warns us—'The Gaian cruiser has changed orbit
and is closing on your location at speed. Beware its tractor beam
technology.'"

"We can easily outrun them," said Nox.

"I may have a better idea. I need to ask D'Obba something. *STALKER, OPEN CHANNEL TO LWSS GROEROK, GAIAN SA. SEND MESSAGE, 'CAN YOU HACK THE GAIAN SHIP'S DATACENTER? ARE YOU INTERESTED? YOUR TECHNICAL REQUIREMENTS FOR THE CONNECTIVITY?'*"

"*YES, AND YES. NEED A PROXIMITY TO THE SHIP'S HULL TO GUARANTEE DATA TRANSFER. WHAT'S YOUR PLAN?*"

"*I WANT TO SEIZE GAIAN CRUISER. STAND BY. OUT.*"

"I want to take control of the Gaian battlecruiser. Or at least to try," Eli said to Nox.

She stared at him in amazement. "I'm speechless. How are you going to do that?"

"By offering *Night Stalker* as bait. We'll wait until they nab us, then I'll seize their ship."

"But how?"

"Eaters. I can control them any way I want."

"Have you ever used them this way?"

"No. But my idea is sound."

"Are you out of your *mind*? That's a Gaian battlecruiser!"

"I made a decision, Nox." Eli's tone left no doubt he would follow through. "We wait here, pretending we're about to leave Pat'zan space. I'm counting on their tractor beam."

The Gaian battlecruiser wasn't long in coming. She fell out of cloak abruptly and positioned herself above and behind *Night Stalker*. Eli was waiting for the cruiser—still, the sudden appearance of the huge ship caught him off guard. "Wow! What a beast!"

"You still want to take her on? Gaian cruisers are far superior to whatever the Elder Keep has."

"The ship's fabric is soft. I can feel it. The Eaters can handle it."

"I know nothing about your Eaters, but I know something about our government battleships, and I worry."

"Don't."

Eli and Nox swung in their seats. The stars visible in the cockpit window shifted, and *Night Stalker* changed direction—the space fighter moved backward toward the Gaian cruiser.

"I think I need to show some resistance. I don't want them to have even the slightest idea about our intentions."

The space fighter vibrated and slowed her movement to almost a complete stop. A high-frequency hum filled the cockpit. The vibration grew into short, jerking swings from side to side.

"I can't shake them off!" Eli looked puzzled.

"I told you. Don't repeat the Pazons' mistakes. Don't be cocky."

"Well, I can still try some tricks, but let's pretend that we've given up."

Night Stalker twitched back, accelerating toward the cruiser. In a matter of seconds, the invisible hand of the tractor beam pulled the space fighter inside the Gaian ship and put her in the middle of a large hangar.

An old civilization like the Gaians had surely learned how to manage instinctual responses to primal emotions. However, that didn't mean all Gaians had assimilated the methods of dealing with the negative aspects of strong feelings. Many thousands of years of cognitive development clashed with the permissiveness and easiness of life and resulted in significant shifts in the perception of reality. A small bump in the road, ignored in any other place, could easily lead to a disproportionate reaction on Gaia, causing frustration and the desire to disengage from anything not wanted or appreciated.

And why not? After all, Gaians had never experienced any lack of material goods and services, which were always in abundance, always readily available. Why deal with real life when you could build a cocoon and isolate yourself from the inconveniences of mundane existence? But it turned out isolation couldn't eliminate all problems. Even interacting with each other often ended in minor or major complications, leading to negative emotions. Those in Gaian government service, like Slun Ceabb, a rising star in the DRC, were especially vulnerable in this regard.

What started as an investigation into Eli Stroud's alleged violation of the *Corpus Ludus Juris*, usually a quick and sure thing, didn't go well for Slun. A supervising agent in the Gaian chief law enforcement agency, he'd gotten spoiled by his swift victories. But the more he plunged into the details of Eli's case, the more baffling and mysterious it turned out to be.

Slun didn't like mysteries. Life, in his mind, followed simple rules. Complexities irked and frightened him, and when a complexity escalated into a daunting task, he reacted angrily, as if someone had deliberately harmed or mistreated him.

Slun had learned to deal with frequent anger by hiding his physical and physiological responses whenever he talked to the people with whom he usually interacted. Even when rage overwhelmed him, most of his friends and colleagues didn't have the slightest idea that under his mask of calm, a tempest raged. But hiding his anger didn't mean rationalizing or, even less, suppressing or calming it. Such firestorms, as with any other feeling of displeasure or hostility, needed a vent, an escape, a target.

At the first sight of problems with the *Night Stalker* investigation, Eli Stroud became such target and Slun's foe. As all attempts led by Slun to find or create a pretext for Eli's arrest and prosecution failed, his invulnerability infuriated Slun further—he became obsessed with this person he hadn't even known existed a month ago.

Today, Slun felt good. He moseyed about in his private quarters and gloated, anticipating the moment when Eli Stroud, captured under his command, would stand trial—not only for the direct violation of the GAME Laws but for using the Game technology to attack a foreign nation.

Slun Ceabb

The sound of an incoming call brought him back to immediate matters. "Speak," ordered Slun.

His personal assistant was on the other end of the line. "Sir, *Night Stalker* is secured in our hangar."

"Excellent. Proceed as usual."

"Anything else, sir?"

"Yes, I need to talk to the Elder Keep authorities."

"Anybody in particular?"

"Abaddon." Slun chuckled. "If he's still alive. If not, Asphalis. Anybody in charge. It's urgent."

Slun sat patiently and waited while his assistant attempted to find someone for him to talk to.

"Sir, I'm sorry. I cannot get through—Abaddon and Asphalis are not available. Others seem uninterested."

"What? Go to the top! Tell them a high-ranking Gaian official needs to speak about pressing issues related to the Elder Keep's security—the terrorist attack on Pat'zan."

"Should I try Xiir Zanrod? They call him Lord Guarantor. He's the religious leader of the Elder Keep Alliance."

"Try Xiir."

The anger in Slun was rising. He felt deprived of his rightly earned attention. He clenched his jaw and sighed in disappointment.

"Sir, Mr. Zanrod has agreed to take your call."

"Put him through."

A holographic projection hung before Eli and Nox, showing Gaians and drones closing in on *Night Stalker*. Over a dozen armed troopers surrounded the space fighter, under the cover of drones hovering above the floor.

"They probably want to break in. Can't allow that..." murmured Eli. He squinted at Nox. *Let's see who's cocky here!* "STALKER, RELEASE EATERS. MAINTAIN SAFETY BARRIER AT TWENTY FEET AROUND THE SHIP. DISINTEGRATE INORGANIC

MATTER ON CONTACT. ABSORB ALL ENERGY BLASTS BELOW TEN EXAJOULES. REFLECT HIGHER ENERGY IMPULSES."

Eli and Nox sat in the cockpit with bated breath—the drone closest to the fighter, equipped with menacing-looking tools sticking out of its front, approached the imaginary defense sphere visible on the holo image. At first, the safety barrier seemed not to affect the heavy machine. It kept ambling slowly beyond the demarcation line.

Nox kept her eyes peeled for any damage to the drone. "It didn't work!"

"As I understand it, when an object comes in contact with the Eaters, they don't exert a force on it—Newton's Third Law doesn't apply," Eli explained. "It'll stop when its engine is destroyed, and other reaction forces slow it down. If they're not strong enough, the drone's inertia will push it forward until nothing remains of it. Hey," Eli pointed to the holoprojection, "check it out!"

By this point, it had become clear that the front part of the drone had disappeared. Instead of a jumble of protrusions, fittings, and nozzles, a concave surface was forming on the front part of the machine. Without encountering resistance, the pile of vanishing metal continued moving. Two robotic arms orientated backward lost their connection to the drone and fell motionless to the deck. The remnants of the drone, dragging stubbornly ahead, left behind a thin trail of thick liquid.

The Gaian advance, both people and machinery, stopped. One of the Gaians pointed his weapon at Night Stalker and pulled the trigger. The blast of energy disappeared without reaching its target. The Gaians started shouting and gesticulating frantically.

"Turn the external mics on," demanded Nox.

"Sorry, I forgot about them."

"… Force field immediately!… need to get rid of… we can also try… quantum conversion, there's no… it's as if—" came over the cockpit loudspeaker.

"What did I tell you!" Eli lit up with impish glee. "Now, phase two."

"We aren't going to kill them, are we?" asked Nox.

"No, I'm a Gaian. At least, you say so. How can I kill my compatriots? I only want the ship and everything they have on me. *SET INITIAL EATERS DENSITY FIVE TIMES TEN TO THE TWENTY-SEVENTH POWER PER CUBIC FOOT AND START INCREASING DENSITY TO DESTABILIZE THE STRUCTURAL INTEGRITY OF THE CRUISER UNTIL THE FIRST VISUAL SIGNS OF UNSTABLE MATE-RIAL APPEAR. INCREASE THE FIELD SPREAD BY FIFTY FEET PER SECOND UNTIL IT CONTAMINATES THE WHOLE SHIP. DESTROY WEAPONS AND PROPULSION SYSTEMS IMMEDIATELY. MAINTAIN LIFE SUPPORT, EVACUATION, AND COMPUTER SYSTEMS INTACT. GO!*

"*OPEN CHANNEL TO LWSS GROEROK, GAIAN SA. TRANSMIT MESSAGE, 'STAND BY TO APPROACH THE CRUISER ON MY MARK OR SIGNS OF HER CREW'S EVACUATION. AVOID ANY PHYSICAL CONTACT BETWEEN GROEROK AND THE CRUISER.'*"

The stern face of an elderly man appeared on Slun's communication monitor. "How can I oblige you, Mister…" Xiir spoke in a small, tired voice.

"Slun. Slun Ceabb."

"Mr. Ceabb."

"I'm a ranking member of the Gaian intelligence service. We've captured a terrorist who unlawfully appropriated the most sophisticated of Gaian weapons technology. We witnessed him using the weapon, resulting in the deaths of your people and significant damage to your military and civilian assets. This would be a good opportunity for your government to participate in our criminal case against this person. I have an attorney on board my ship who can work with your legal representatives."

"A terrorist?" Xiir's bushy brows rose in genuine astonishment.

"Yes, his name is Eli Stroud. He is on our Most Wanted list. He claims to be the head of the Korango security apparatus."

"This must be a mistake. I just finished talking to Sir Rurik Cavell, the President of the Korango Independent Territory and Korango Enterprises. Mr. Stroud is a member of his delegation. He had a separate discussion with my security people on details of our cooperation with Korango. I assure you, he didn't destroy anything or kill anybody."

Xiir spoke leisurely, and his eyes seemed to probe into the depths of his interlocutor. He stopped for a moment or two and then smiled—his rather fleshy lips stretched out into a thin thread while the eyes continued scrutinizing the DRC agent. "You cannot have possibly captured Mr. Stroud. I talked to him minutes ago."

The more Xiir talked, the stronger Slun's anger grew, until his usual control over his emotions failed. The Lord Guarantor's last words were the last straw. "What?" shriek Slun. "You know that he has destroyed two of your battlecruisers! I saw it! You cannot deny this!"

"Mr. Ceabb." Xiir, who until now seemed to stick to the screen, leaned back in his chair. "I don't know what goals you're pursuing by making these spurious accusations against Mr. Stroud, but yes, we detected the energy spikes and the fluctuations in the space fabric near Pat'zan, resulting in the loss of our two spaceships. At the time, he was here on Pat'zan." The Lord Guarantors voice was haughty. "Please don't tell me I'm lying, as that wouldn't go well if you want to deal with me—"

"Your Lordship, I'm not accusing you of—"

With an imperious gesture of his hand, Xiir stopped Slun. "My people told me about an unknown energy source presumably coming from a military spaceship. We tentatively identified her as a Gaian cruiser based on its size and configuration—the only ship in the area capable of generating such insane amounts of energy without defying the laws of physics."

"That's absurd! Are you claiming *my* ship destroyed your battle-cruisers?"

"Not at this moment. The assaulting ship was using cloaking technology, so some uncertainty remains regarding the assailant. But the coincidence is suspicious, and only Gaia possesses the cloaking tech." Xiir's arrogance suddenly gave way to boredom and apathy. "I don't believe in coincidences, Mr. Ceabb. I can see a motive for what you may be trying to do—to blame others so that you seem innocent."

The door to Slun's quarters opened without warning. His assistant, this time with disheveled hair and eyes dilated with horror, burst into the room. "Sir! Sir, you've got to see this. We've experienced some kind of spatial fluctuation. It's affecting ship systems... And it's spreading!"

"What's the source?"

"The source?"

"Where does it come from, moron?"

"We don't know. Judging by the progression of system failures, it started in the docking hangar!"

"Are you experiencing problems?" Xiir intervened in the conversation as a spark of interest flashed in his eyes.

"You still don't get it, idiot!" yelled Slun. "That's Stroud's ship in our hangar!"

"In your hangar?" Xiir's eyebrows shot upward. "How did she get there? You're still in our sovereign space. Unless you have proof of a clear and present danger associated with the ship you captured, we must consider it an act of piracy."

Slun opened his mouth but wisely shut it.

"Anyway," insisted Xiir, "what are you doing in our space? Are you acting in an official capacity on behalf of the Gaian government? I expect you to clarify your intentions here immediately."

"That's not your fucking business!" snarled Slun.

"But it is, Mr. Ceabb."

Slun's assistant hurried to the wall panel with the system

controls. "The ship's structural integrity is at a critical level, sir. The destruction of the ship is imminent!"

"How much time do we have?" Slun turned pale.

"Ten, fifteen minutes at best."

"Evacuate the ship. Set the self-destruct for fifteen minutes." Slun turned back to the screen. "You rat! Trying to play a double game?"

Xiir's eyes lit up with a blazing fire. "You are a criminal and an imposter, Mr. Ceabb. We'll file a complaint with the Galactic Inter-planet Organization!" he barked and turned his back to the screen.

"Jour, we've moved too far from the cruiser," complained D'Obba.

Jour sweated over the flight control panel. "Remember what Eli said?"

"Yeah, but getting closer helps increase the data transfer rate. Keep her at not more than ten feet."

"Easy to say, hard to do—the autopilot isn't reading the distance correctly."

"Why?"

"The cruiser's hull isn't stable. It's shifting or... wavering."

"Go manual."

"I *am* on manual!" bellowed Jour. "Do you think this is easy? The cruiser's surface is rippling like water in a storm."

"Don't be angry, sweetie. Do your best."

Jour's job of piloting *Groerok* while D'Obba hacked the Gaian battlecruiser's computer system turned out to be a balancing act. His small ship floated near the enormous spacecraft, trying to stay as close as possible but avoiding, per Eli's warning, physical contact with the cruiser. It was a difficult task as the cruiser's hull was undergoing strange metamorphoses—continually changing shape, swelling with humps and ridges, or forming recesses and valleys. Sensors bristling from *Groerok* made piloting even more difficult—the visual assessment of the distance between the sensor nodes and the Gaian ship was unreliable.

Adding to this, Jour tried to hide his ship from the swarm of escape pods that were leaving the cruiser and entering hyperspace. Considering the panic among the Gaians desperate to save their asses, putting *Groerok* out of sight probably wasn't the highest priority. Still, he preferred to find a cozy spot between two weapons housings while doing his best to maneuver the ship out of view.

"How is it going?" asked Jour. In their small team of two, he usually played the role of a wise, weather-beaten captain—an old space dog whose primary responsibility was to maintain the order aboard and to ensure the safety of the crew. "Any progress?"

"I'm in. Already started data transfer. Do you know what Eli did to the cruiser?"

"No idea. I haven't seen anything like this."

"I think *Night Stalker* has some of Game's capabilities. No other explanation."

"What data are you getting?"

"Everything. It looks like part of the DRC archive is in here."

Jour whistled in surprise. "We could go to jail for that!"

"We could, but it wouldn't be the first time—would it, darling?" D'Obba purred.

"Any ship navigation and operational data?"

"I opened another pipe. Getting it."

"Can you check to see if they enabled self-destruct?"

"Checking... Yes, they did. About twelve minutes left. Can you contact Eli? We need to warn him."

Eli's face popped up on the monitor. "Hey, what's up?"

"Self-destruct is enabled—we have about twelve minutes," said Jour.

"How much time do you need to finish the data transfer?"

D'Obba glanced at the screens. "An hour."

"Can you cancel self-destruct and complete the transfer?"

"I think so…"

"Do it now."

D'Obba surrounded herself with the wall of holograms, sorting them and canceling most of them. Her face darkened. "Sorry, I lied. It's hardwired. I can't control it through the hack."

"No problem," Eli reassured D'Obba. "Can you tell me where the charge is?"

"Sure…" D'Obba selected several holograms and swiped them out, "There are multiple charges. Sending schematics. What are you going to do?"

"I'll destroy them."

"How?"

"That's my problem. Finish what you're doing. I hope it's useful."

"Eli, it's a trove." D'Obba beamed with joy. "You won't regret it!"

"Hey, buddy!" Jour cut in. "Should we expect Pazons here soon?"

"Don't think so. Listen, I'll be busy disabling the charges. I'll let you know if I have any problems."

"Are you going to stay until we're done?" asked Jour.

"Yes. When you complete the transfer, leave. I'll take care of the cruiser."

"Are you going to destroy her?"

"She will… disappear."

"Eli, it's important for us to know what will happen to that ship. We can't leave any traces—hacking government systems is a grave crime on Gaia."

"I've got this covered. There'll be no traces. At all."

TWENTY-FIVE

KIERUS

Night Stalker approached Kierus, the location of the Game and the most thoroughly guarded place in the Gaian Domain. The secrecy surrounding it was a well-understood and accepted necessity to safeguard Gaian society from the unintended consequences of their pervasive use of the technology. But if someone wanted to make sense of the early history of the Game, including the decision regarding its location, that would be no easy thing to do.

The official history, as blessed by the government and the scientific community, didn't exactly lie. But as often is the case, it didn't tell the whole truth. Nobody tried to obscure the events on purpose, but the circumstances surrounding the Game, especially its early days, were so convoluted that the explanation of what had happened and why would take many volumes.

A streamlined, abridged version of the Game's history emerged, and it gradually became the mainstream record, eagerly accepted by most Gaians. The details of the Game's olden days couldn't boast much attention and familiarity, as if Gaians didn't want to be proud of them and preferred to forget. And all for nothing. It was a good chance missed by Gaian civilization to put the history to use for a better understanding of the present. Kierus, as a secret location for the Game, turned out another palliative with which Gaians approached the ubiquitous use of the technology, plagued as it was with numerous setbacks and major mishaps.

What Gaians called Kierus was a substellar object, a binary brown dwarf about six and a half light-years from the Sun. The proximity to the origin solar system was not accidental.

Kierus entered the history of the Game when it wasn't even the GAME, and Gaians were still on Earth—the planet they called Terah. It was a humble endeavor by a small group of Terahn scientists to better understand the fabric of the universe... An attempt that prompted a vicious reaction by the public and the government, outlawing all related research and activities deemed as dangerous not only to Terra but to the whole solar system.

The prohibition, a futile attempt to keep humanity from learning the true laws of nature, failed. The Terahn policymakers underestimated the resolve of the researchers and the fact that space travel had, by that time, grown to be the norm, and that Terahns had already harnessed the gravitational forces, with gravity and anti-gravity devices in wide use. A group of unrelenting physicists secretly moved all their facilities from Terah to Kierus B, the smaller and the cooler of the associated brown dwarfs. In choosing the place, they counted on its environment. With surface temperatures often exceeding one thousand degrees Kelvin and crushing gravity where an average Terahn would weigh over five tons, the dwarf could hardly attract attention with any practical purpose in mind.

Kierus became a secret guarded carefully by the founding scientists. With time, their group expanded into a secret organization called the Cabal and grew into something between a clique, a sect, and a cult. Meanwhile, their relentless push to learn more about the interactions of matter and energy did not subside.

The colonization of space resulted in a changing perspective on

Game research in places where Terahns were settling. The most significant shift took place when the planet Gaia had already become the center of the burgeoning Gaian Domain. Feeling more comfortable with the forces of nature, Gaians legalized and revitalized Game science. But the Cabalists, having little trust in the new policy, remained faithful to the secrecy and intellectual brilliance of its founding fathers. The Cabal lived on, and its independent scientific pursuits flourished.

The Gaian government, aware of the Cabal's clandestine activities, tried many times to find the research location and penetrate its facilities. Eventually, such efforts were challenged successfully in the court system and condemned as a witch hunt. The Supreme Court of Gaia ruled that *any* attempt to persecute or ban scientific and technological research of any kind violated the constitution by interfering with the free will of Gaian citizens.

When the Game transformed into reality and its practical use increased, the Kierus group agreed, after lengthy negotiations, to hide the Game technology from the public eye and host it in their secret place. The new laws entrusted the Cabal with the relocating of all significant parts of the Game to Kierus. Its members agreed to an attrition process whereby, in a matter of one generation, the group would cease to exist and Nox, at least on paper, would remain the only custodian of the Game with the knowledge of its location.

The law also blocked all modification of Game design—its status quo became the law of the land. However, the equilibrium remained ambiguous. Nobody knew for sure if, and to what extent, the last surviving members of the Cabal had implemented the latest agreements. Nox might know, but she kept silent as prescribed by the *Corpus Ludus Juris*.

Most of the journey from Pat'zan to Kierus Eli spent in seclusion in

Night Stalker's cockpit, experimenting with the ship's manual controls. Nox kept herself busy in the aft of the fighter. Eli showed no interest in her activities, and she preferred not to bother him.

At the end of the trip, Nox replicated a hamburger and offered it to Eli upon joining him in the cockpit. He accepted the food, but when Nox tried to fill him in on the story of Kierus, he paid little attention to what she was saying.

In all fairness to Eli, he tried to be polite by making an effort to follow the narrative and never interrupt her. Only when she stopped did he ask a question. "So, if it's against the law, and it's a secret, why are you taking me to Kierus?"

"I'm in your ship, and I must fulfill Aura's last wish. I told you."

"Right. I'll close my eyes when we land."

Nox didn't respond. Her glance at Eli was clearly meant to tell him the conversation about Kierus wasn't yet over.

"You took care of her body, right?" Eli asked solemnly.

"I did... Eli, what happened, happened." Her words sounded tough. "In another day, we may all be dead. But today we are alive, and life goes on. You have to come to terms with it."

"You told me you can't die."

"I can be killed under certain unlikely circumstances. I don't know what will happen to me when our adventure on Pat'zan becomes public knowledge."

"I'm sorry, Nox. That was selfish of me. I'm in eternal debt to you for what you've done. Without you, I would be dead. Do you think I don't understand that?" Eli stopped and smiled bitterly. "I know, not much of a promise."

"It means a lot to me, no matter what. But for now, prepare for landing. Open your eyes and learn. One day you may find this knowledge handy. Start with the Game's exact location." Nox nodded at the instrument panel in front of the co-pilot seat. "May I?"

"Sure."

Nox sat and typed long strings of data. "Eli, please direct your ship to these coordinates and prepare to compensate for the gravitational forces. Enjoy the view."

The spaceship turned and plunged deeper into Kierus' atmosphere. What came into view in the cockpit windows defied imagination. Magma of all shades of red shooting off from the openings in the dwarf's crust, poisonous gases, and rocks of odd shapes—there was nothing else to see on this gloomy and dangerous creation of the universe.

Night Stalker proceeded to an enormous sea of sizzling lava and set out from the shore. The coast had disappeared, but the ship kept flying over the molten rock—a terrible, monotonous landscape that stretched in all directions as far as the eye could see. Finally, the space fighter stopped and hung over a spot. Nothing distinguished it from the rest of the flaming ocean.

Nox turned to the instrument panel, and her eyes opened in surprise. "Your space fighter knows the location of the Game. I was supposed to unlock the entrance. I changed its code recently, but she knows it!"

A megastructure emerged from the depth of the fiery magma. Streams of hot lava draining from the surface of the strange construction rushed down, flopping heavily back into the boiling sea and raising fountains of melted material.

"And that means what?" asked Eli.

"It means a lot. It means that everything that's happening is no accident. We have a long talk ahead of us."

The front wall of the structure vanished. Nox jutted out her chin. "Enter the elevator."

"You call it an elevator? It's not the Game?"

"No. The Game is deep inside the magma. Go ahead and let the Game control the ship."

Night Stalker slowly disappeared into the belly of the human-made beast. The wall closed, and it submerged again. Nothing on the surface of the ocean of magma indicated what had happened there.

The elevator was big, with enough space for at least several dozen more spaceships like *Night Stalker*. Its floor, dark at the beginning, blossomed with many lights like those of airport runways and parking areas. Eli looked at Nox, waiting for further instructions.

"Follow the blinking lights to your assigned spot. It won't start the descent until you comply."

The lights led Eli to a corner where he had to place the fighter's landing gear inside circles on the deck. As soon as the shock absorbers dampened the landing impact and the bouncing of the ship after touchdown, giant pincers moved from under the floor and seized the undercarriage struts.

Eli winced. "She doesn't like it."

"She?"

"*Night Stalker*. She doesn't like to be pinned to the floor."

"Sorry, it's a safety measure. There are strong magma currents below. Tell her to be patient."

The descent took half an hour. It was monotonous—only random amplitude rocking and the occasional slight shudder even suggested the gigantic machine was in motion. Finally, a blunt jolt signaled the end of the descent.

"So, we went through Hell. The first step in the soul's journey to God... What's next, Purgatory?" asked Eli, with a sullen expression on his face.

"What do you mean?"

"It's from a book on Earth. It says we go through Hell to Purgatory and eventually to Paradise, where we're supposed to live in bliss with God. So, I thought that if the Game is God, and the magma ocean is Hell, where's Purgatory?"

"I don't understand the concept of Purgatory."

"Think of it as a penitent life of suffering and spiritual growth."

"Fascinating... No, we don't have anything like that here."

"I'm relieved." Poisonous sarcasm bubbled over inside Eli. Then he looked at Nox, and her confused look pulled at his heartstrings. *Why am I doing this? She risked her existence to help me. I need to run away from all this. Run away... Without looking back.*

The terrifying thoughts throbbed in his mind, obscuring everything. For a second, Eli lost all sense of reality and time. He looked around him and licked his dry lips. Then he felt a touch at his elbow and, in fear, jerked his hand away.

"Eli, Eli..." He heard a muffled voice. His senses seemed shrouded in a dense fog. "Are you okay?"

He turned to the voice. "Ah? What?" Nox's sympathetic look pulled him back to reality. "No... Yeah, I'm fine. It's just..." Eli closed his eyes and immediately opened them, frightened by the visions that appeared again in his mind. "I'm scared, Nox. What happened on Pat'zan torments me. Aura died, and I went crazy. I killed people... A lot of people. I have to make peace with myself."

"You need a break. Let's go. I'll show you the guest rooms. I can give you something to unwind. A relaxant? I have whiskey here, from Earth..."

"Get drunk? An excellent idea!"

"Good. Ready for transport?"

"Where are we going?"

"Inside the Game sanctuary. There are no doors. Transporters on the arriving ships are the only way to get inside."

TWENTY-SIX

KOND PHYNS

The transporter beamed Eli and Nox into a vast hall with bizarre architecture. The floor struck Eli the most. Its polished stone, lit by red light, reflected stylized columns and walls designed to display natural rock. Most remarkably, the light thrown back by the near-perfect mirror of the floor didn't seem still. It moved, fluctuating as if liquefying the outlines of the objects it reflected, reminding Eli of the surface of the magma ocean. The effect seemed to spread beyond and above the floor, playing havoc with the light passing through the air, making it shimmer.

The movements were subtle but affected Eli when the transporter materialized him in the middle of the hall. "This place makes my head reel!" he exclaimed, instinctively grabbing Nox by her shoulder.

"Sorry. The Cabal people were rather creative. It'll pass in a minute."

"What's Cabal?"

"The Cabal—those who built the place and the Game prototype. I wanted to keep it the way it was when they were alive."

"Who killed them?"

"Nobody. They passed away when their time came. Sometimes we call them Ancients."

"They lived here?"

"Mostly. Some traveled, though. The Cabal kept their part of the bargain to conceal the Game location when we decided to keep it on Kierus. They stopped accepting new members and died out... I'm planning to hold Aura's burial ceremony tomorrow. We'll visit the cemetery. You'll see."

"You want to inter Aura there? She won't be alone? I like that... You know, Kierus is a depressing place."

"You can come here any time you want. You can live here. It may be gloomy, but once you get to know it, you'll see how beautiful it is."

"I doubt it." Eli shook his head. "But if there's a place near Aura... The city of the dead... When did the last Cabalist die?"

"Ten years ago."

"Ten Earth years?"

"Yes. Surprised? You shouldn't be."

"You mean this somehow relates to me?"

"It does. Look, you wanted to get drunk. I need that, too. Let me show you the Game—its interface, the only part you can see—and then we can start."

The path to the Game went through three long corridors, each ending in massive arches and elaborate doors. According to Nox, the passages and arches served as a security feature to collect certain information on those who wanted to access the machine's controls. Eli understood that the Game needed no physical protection, as it could thwart any attempt to destroy or damage it.

The last corridor opened into a room that seemed small

compared to the other monumental structures related to the Game. At the end of the room, in an alcove, a large sphere hung an inch or two above the floor.

A myriad of symbols ran along its surface in strange patterns. Originating somewhere at the sphere's top, they descended and slowed their movement near the equator. Many of the symbols stopped, formed clusters, and moved sideways, changing positions, rotating, and even disappearing. Like huddles of living organisms, having fussed around the equator, most of the symbols would rush down, fading at the bottom of the sphere.

"It reminds me of the Game interface you used in *Night Stalker*," Eli told Nox. "But that was a cylinder."

"This is the primary terminal, much more complex than what you saw."

"Where is the Game itself?"

"We're standing on it. 'Seeing the Game' would be a misnomer. You cannot see the Game itself. It goes many miles deep into Kierus. Besides, any direct exposure to most parts of the Game would kill you."

"Who maintains it?"

"Nobody. To put it simply, the Game is a reactor. The trick is in controlling it. Once you know how, it becomes a self-healing entity that takes care of itself. So, when we refer to 'the Game,' we always mean its control facilities and the interface in particular."

"Is it self-aware?"

"No. At least, I hope not. To make sure it's not and never will be was one of the most contentious issues in the history of the Game."

"Can we get closer to the controls?"

"Please do."

Eli stepped forward and slowly approached the sphere. It lit up —the movement patterns became more complex, and the symbols' gallop accelerated.

"Elias Stroud, welcome to the Game interface," a mellow computerized voice stated out of nowhere. "It is ready for your input."

"What input?" he asked curiously and reached out.

Nox yanked him by the sleeve. "Get away from the console!"

Eli recoiled from the sphere as if it had scalded him. "For God's sake, don't scare me like that! This thing is weird enough without you doing scary crap."

Nox shrugged. "Sorry, I didn't expect the Game would recognize you. But don't freak out. You're at home here, just not ready for it. It may not be ready for you either—a dangerous combination."

Eli stared hard at Nox. His mind was churning. *I'm not ready? Did I ever say I was? What am I doing here? I should leave... go see Aura for the last time and leave!*

The more time went by in silence, the stronger the creepy, implacable impression grew on him. He glanced back at the sphere. It felt cold and distant. *Dammit! It looks almost like a farce!* "What happened?" Eli again fixed his eyes on Nox.

She avoided eye contact.

"You know... I should probably go," said Eli and headed to the exit.

"Don't... Please!" Nox's eyes were brimming with tears. "I know it turned awkward, but I didn't expect its greeting either!"

She seemed sincere, and her words disarmed Eli. He stopped walking. Struggling to stay calm, he said, "Just tell me for once—no talk about how important I am, my DNA... What do you *want* from me? Please don't avoid my question. Talk to me!"

"I-I don't want anything in particular. I never wanted."

"What about in *general*?"

"Just for you to learn about Gaia, about the Game. To be ready."

"Ready for what?"

"I don't know *what* could happen. Anything... Want it or not, sooner or later, with or without me, you will be drawn into the Game's games. Why is that so difficult to understand?"

"I'll consider the possibility that what you're saying is true. But for now, there's nothing I can do for you, right?"

"You can learn."

"I learned up the wazoo already! Okay? Can I get some rest now?"

"You can—"

"Then, if you don't mind, I'd like to see Aura, say my final farewells, and leave."

"You don't want even to go with me to perform the burial ritual?"

"No. Aura doesn't belong here. Kierus and the Game are everything she is not."

"But it was her last wish…"

"I can't argue with that. Thanks for following through."

"Are you leaving… forever?"

"I'll be coming here occasionally—if you don't mind, that is. Aura will always be the only one in my heart. But I don't like Kierus."

"That's good to know. Before you see Aura, I want to show you something in our Pantheon. It won't take long. I thought we could do it tomorrow, but since you're leaving—"

"What's in the Pantheon?"

"It's our graveyard. Not all the Ancients are there. Some wanted to rest on other planets. Several are even on Earth."

"Don't expect too much from the Pantheon architecture," said Nox while getting out of the capsule of the railway connecting various parts of the Cabal complex. "Mostly, it's a simple adaptation of what nature created."

The Pantheon, the most remote destination in the Kierus transportation system, looked nothing like the rest of the Game facilities. The rail came to a dead end at the bottom of a concave chamber formed by the natural rock. A small platform around the terminal led to stairs carved in stone.

Nox led the way, and Eli followed. The pale red reflections flickered on the dark surfaces of the rocks. Eli's fertile imagination, already set on the theme of death, immediately associated the place with a boiling cauldron of sinners. *A true underworld. What did Aura know about Kierus? I bet not much if she wanted to be interred here.*

As they proceeded upward, the air got hotter and began to smell of sulfur. It seemed there would be no end to the steps meandering between the piles of rocks. Trying to escape from the painful thoughts, Eli trailed behind Nox, almost treading on her heels.

She stopped and turned back. "Want to take a breather?"

"I'm fine. So, where's Satan?" He grimaced. "The sinners need the guy!" Seeing the stern face of Nox, he quickly raised both hands. "No disrespect for the dead meant. It's a joke!"

"A joke on whom?" She showed no emotion. "Seems disparaging. Or is something on your mind?"

"Do you keep Doctor Freud on your nightstand?"

"We don't have nightstands. But speaking of Satan... Remember me mentioning the last of the Cabal members, who died ten years ago? I'm certain now he was your great-great-great-grandfather."

Eli looked thunderstruck. "You can't be serious."

"He was an old fraudster, a genius, and an egotist of the highest order. One of the original Game developers, Grand Pilgrim Kond Phyns—remember his name. Some Ancients used to call him The Great Satan."

"How long did he live?"

"Honestly, I didn't look it up. Ten thousand years? Maybe more?"

"It's impossible!"

"One of the perks of living on Kierus, Eli. The Cabal didn't give a damn about the GAME Laws. Complete rejuvenations on molecular and atomic levels, prohibited by the law, were common here."

"How long have you known about Kond Phyns and me?"

Nox smirked. "Not long. I figured it out on our way to Kierus. I had to keep myself busy—dead bodies and blood were chasing me. You hid in the cockpit—"

"So, you too? I thought—"

"That I'm a certified assassin?"

"Honestly, the thought crossed my mind. Yeah. Watching you snuffing out Pazons, I learned something from you..." quipped Eli. Then his eyes sparkled with interest. "Can we go back to Kond? Why did people call him The Great Satan?"

"As I remember, you didn't fall far behind me on Pat'zan. Plus, you blew up two battlecruisers without batting an eye. Was that necessary? Many would call you evil." She flashed him a charming smile. "Are you?" Nox resumed climbing the stairs.

Eli frowned, puzzled by the question. "It's not that simple."

"When it comes to you, it's never simple." She sized Eli up. "You think The Great Satan was simple?" She sped up the pace. "I want you to look at Kond first. Then I'll try to explain."

The Pantheon rail terminal was left far behind and below. Eli and Nox stood on a raised platform that enjoyed an austere but magical view of the eerie landscape. Around three hundred tombs were scattered over the cemetery. At first glance, their placement seemed haphazard, but Eli quickly identified a subtle pattern and the reason for the design.

The tombs rested on a spiral causeway built of hexagonal columns formed by slowly cooling lava, contracting around almost equally spaced spots, and eventually solidifying into prismatic pillars. The burial ground itself represented a peninsula—a cliff at the edge of the sea of lava.

Eli jumped from the platform and stepped onto the nearest monolith. Cracks separating the rock formations gave off unpleasantly hot fumes—the dark red glimmers of magma boiling deep inside the crevices filled the gases with a wavering light. Some fissures were covered in solid clinkers that floated on top of the lava flows pushed around the rocks.

Hopping from one pillar to another, Nox quickly reached the center of the graveyard. "The spiral symbolizes our Milky Way. Kond Phyns is in the middle."

Unlike the other Ancients buried here, the Satan lay in a transparent casket. On full display, the body lying in repose seemed remarkably well preserved, though most of it was draped in white cloth. The sunburnt shiny skin on the old man's bald head and face reflected the shimmers of lava flowing along the perimeter of the Pantheon.

Eli joined Nox. He walked around the pedestal with the glass sarcophagus. "So, that's the guy?"

"Yes."

"Remind me, why should I remember his name?"

Instead of answering, Nox pointed to Kond Phyns' holographic image as it formed behind Eli. The holographic Satan paced slowly back and forth, stopping and turning his face to the camera occasionally, and then resuming sauntering, as if carefully thinking over what he would say.

Finally, he began.

I'm Kond Phyns, one of the founding fathers of the Cabal movement, and the principal developer of the Game in its current form. I'm recording this message for Elias Stroud, my great-great-great-grandson. Eli, if you hear this message, it means that the sensors have identified you by your unique DNA markers and triggered the playback.

Listen carefully, for this message will be played only once. At the end, you will be able to ask questions. I'll try to anticipate them with pre-recorded answers. Since I cannot foresee everything you may want to know, I'll focus on issues I consider important.

I'll begin with saying that if you, Eli, are standing in front of my body, it means that you've done something important— something that revealed to you the existence of the Game and its location.

I'd love to meet you personally, but I know now that this is not meant to happen. You're too young, and I'm very old. Unfortunately, I have to terminate my life—people on Earth sometimes complain about aging bodies still having young spirits. In my case, it's the opposite. As long as I stay on Kierus, my physical existence could continue almost indefinitely. Unfortunately, my mind is losing coherence and is on the brink of full collapse. I cannot continue to live without jeopardizing the existence of many people and civilizations.

When I found that the end was coming, I took steps to find my replacement to take over my last mission—to save the Game from my people and save my people from it. I started doing this long ago and focused on Earth, the closest planet to Kierus and the cradle of humanity. I wanted to limit the set of people who can modify this monstrosity to only those who fit my criteria and have some of my abilities.

To achieve this, I added a unique subroutine to the Game that recognizes particular parts of my DNA. Then I realized that at that time, in post-Civil War America, people wouldn't be able to even comprehend the concept of the Game.

But I didn't waste time. I altered my DNA and planted my seeds on Earth, hoping that the moment would come when a worthy replacement was born. I continued to follow my descendants—your father became the first with whom I tried to implement my plan. It turned out a total failure, and I take full responsibility for what happened. Yes, I knew him personally, and my actions resulted in his death.

I realized that I needed a stronger person and, more importantly, one who was much more ambitious—your dad wasn't one of those. I had my eye on you. Look at my body, my face... Remember your substitute teacher in the Science 5 class? Did you notice I'm speaking English?

Kond Phyns

Eli looked back at the sarcophagus, and his eyes nearly popped out of his head. Meanwhile, the hologram kept going.

The DNA markers mean little unless you're able and willing to take the path I want you to choose. It won't be easy. We overcame many of Game's setbacks, but most people don't see that it corrupts our minds. The Gaians are degenerating, and the Game is to blame.

I need someone who can bring fresh blood to our society—who can shake off the human froth that thoughtlessly enjoys the blessing of science and technology. Someone who can turn upside down the majority who has lost interest in challenging the status quo. Someone who can fight those who, under the pretext of making life better, in reality, want to use the Game to exercise their power, who are no different from the dark side of the Game. Yes, it's there!

If we don't start soon, the process of societal decay may consume us quickly. I want Gaia to be great, a role model for others, a leading force in science and technology, a protector of the oppressed and the defender of the humanity... Because there are things in the universe that can destroy Gaia, no matter how strong we are.

The person I'm looking for has to be immune to the dark side of the power, which is the most serious danger sentient beings will ever face. Someone who can walk the thin line, the razor edge, between right and wrong. As your Bible says, "for every one to whom much is given, of him much will be required, and from him to whom they entrusted much, they will demand the more."

I'm optimistic. If you're here, it means you've done something worthy that gave you the right to be here. Along the way, you probably screwed some things up—who didn't? But I'm not looking for a saint. I'm looking for someone who, sooner rather than later, can distinguish between the idols and the ideals.

My advice. At the beginning of your journey—that is, if you accept the challenge—you will be alone. But alone, you won't accomplish much. Devote time and attention to the people you meet. Learn to appreciate and trust your friends. Be devious with your enemies. Some need to be killed. Some need to be handled with kid gloves. For now, you have Nox. Trust her. She is a good human being.

Finally, take my gift, your spaceship, if you haven't done so already. A simple pass through the Gamer or near the Game interface will deliver it to you. Don't listen to stupid speeches praising the GAME Laws. Many of those who the most cite the Laws have violated them more than once. I know several whose necks deserve a noose. I do not encourage you to break the law— it's merely an observation about us, human beings, and our hypocrisy. My gift has nothing to do with the Laws.

With time, you'll learn more and understand your ship better. She is your protector and your friend. She is unique, and nothing and nobody can stand against her in this part of the galaxy. You'd better remember that your first lesson will start with learning when and how you should use the power of my gift.

So, what's it going to be? Do you accept the challenge? A simple "yes" or "no" will do.

Eli silently scrutinized the avatar. *Do I want it? No... I've had enough of it!* Then he turned to Nox as if seeking support. "I'm not looking for gifts. My encounters with the Game... You know, it started riding my ass. Can I think a moment?"

Nox found it hard to resist the plea in his eyes. "Take your time. He said you can ask questions."

Questions? Questions... What should I ask? I don't want even to think about questions. I didn't come here for all that nonsense. The feeling of entrapment overwhelmed Eli.

"Why am I here? I'm not going to program my life and commit to the choices this freaky guy"—Eli nodded at the hologram —"wants me to take. For the record, I don't like these mushy talks about responsibilities, the future of humanity, love, and world peace. The only reason I'm here is to fulfill Aura's wish. Instead, I'm trapped and have to face moral challenges. I'm not a fruit fly to watch and dissect under a microscope. Besides, this selling tech-nique—a one-time offer—never worked on me. I'll make my deci-sion, if I make it, when I want!"

Eli fixed his piercing gaze on Nox and shook his finger at the hologram, "This guy basically confessed to killing my father! Was it with *your* help? And now he has the nerve to try to recruit me?"

Eli sprang up to the hologram and smacked it, giving it every-thing he had. His hand went through the image without meeting any resistance. He lost his balance and fell to the stone floor. With a groan, he rubbed his bruised arm. "Oh, that hurts... Still feels good. Thank your lucky stars, asshole, that you're a bunch of photons!" He climbed to his knees and then sat on the ground.

Nox said irritably, "If you have issues with Kond, that's your problem. But what you implied about my role in your father's death is unfair. I'll meet you at the rail terminal. I'm done here."

"Oh ho ho!" Eli yelled after Nox, "Innocence itself!"

He waited until she disappeared down the stairs and turned to the Ancient.

"So, I can ask questions. Here is the first. Why do they call you The Great Satan?"

After a long pause, the hologram uttered,

I don't have a pre-recorded answer to that question. But another answer I have could be helpful. "People rarely understand what they want or need. People often confuse wants with needs and vice versa. Sometimes, I helped them make a choice."

"Huh! What are the options? To sell or not to sell my soul? Next question. What if I say no?"

That would be a great choice, and it would save you from many troubles. My gift, though, won't be available. And if you already have the ship, she'll be instantly pulverized into a bunch of particles. Hopefully, Nox will be kind and give you a lift to the next place you want to go.

"And if I say yes?"

Then I'd say I've corrupted another ninny and once again affirmed my lifetime observation relating to the nature of people. Plus, if you ever betray me and turn away from the promised path, I'll curse you, and you'll burn in Hell. Which you probably wouldn't care about anyway, and it wouldn't make any difference, because I'm already dead.

"Got it. Here's what I have to say." Eli switched to singing. "Fuck you very, very mu-u-u-u-uch!" He raised his finger and clumsily danced on one foot, hopping to the rhythm of his syncopated delivery.

"Join the quest, and I'll reveal to you an important secret," came The Great Satan's voice as Eli was already descending the stairs.

"Shove your secret up your ass!" shouted Eli from below.

When he was already inside the capsule, Nox asked, "What was your final response?"

Eli laughed. "I sang him 'Fuck You'—its first verse seemed appropriate. I even danced a little."

"You *clowned around*? Eli, this was a unique opportunity. Your response was rude and unreasonable!"

Eli began to sing softly, "'Look inside, look inside your tiny mind...'" He glanced at Nox and winced. *Ah, a lost cause. She'll never understand it.* "You know what? *You* are unreasonably reasonable. In the first place, it was a job, not an opportunity. For reasons I still don't understand, you and Kond need me. Not the other way around. Secondly, it wasn't unique. Want to bet?"

"A bet?"

"I'll see The Great Satan again. If it happens, I'll take Aura to Coatera where she belongs, and you won't say a word."

"Kierus was her last wish."

"Your Kierus is a fraud, figuratively speaking. She had no clue what the real Game is—how cold it is. Now, take me to Aura."

"I don't bet on things like this," she said, nervous now.

"You know, if the Satan wants to change Gaia, he should probably start with you!"

TWENTY-SEVEN
FAREWELL

Aura's body lay on a pedestal in a dark room. Pale-blue light barely illuminated her face, and her legs were lost to the inky blackness.

Nox stepped aside, letting Eli approach Aura.

"The kip is covered by a force field. It's customary on Gaia to preserve the remains as much as we can. If you want to get closer to Aura, you can turn the field off briefly."

"Thank you, Nox. That's okay. I want to spend some time with her."

"I'll leave you here. Take all the time you want. I'll be with the Game." Nox looked deep in Eli's eyes. "I'm truly sorry for your loss. I'm so sorry..." She raised her hand to touch him, but something stopped her. "I wanted you to be happy and... I let you down." Nox quickly left the room.

Eli approached the kip. Except for Aura's head, tight clothing covered her. Her face exuded calmness and humility.

He looked at her neck. The burned flesh left by the laser beam had vanished. A clean scar marked the place of the mortal wound.

Even dead, she's beautiful. The thought made Eli shiver. Struck by awe, he stood transfixed in grim despair. *You've shown to me what it means to love. How am I going to live without you?*

Nox didn't notice Eli when he entered the Game control room. For a minute, he stood silently watching her. As if feeling his presence, she turned around. "Oh, you scared me! How long have you been staring at me like that?"

"Not long. I'm leaving now."

"Already? Still want a glass of whiskey?"

"Suddenly, I'm not thirsty anymore. I wanted to ask you something. Are you busy?"

"I noticed an unusual spike in the Game activity. It probably reacts to your presence. I wanted to figure out what was going on, but go ahead."

"Your Satan, what he said regarding my father. Did you know that he planned to lure him into his Game schemes?"

Even in the darkness of the room, Eli noticed how her face blushed scarlet. "If you think I'm fond of that son of a bitch, you're wrong," she said bitterly. "That's what he does, even dead. Using others to his advantage, insinuating, worming his way into—"

"Nox, I'm not saying you're like him—"

"I had no clue! I was a pawn, like your father. I violated the Laws by letting your father go through the Gamer. *I* invited him to do that!"

"Nox, I believe you. I saw my dad's drawings with you and your hand encouraging him to go through the torus. But I wanted to hear it from you before I leave."

"Where are you going?"

"I don't know. I'll be off the grid. I need to spend time with myself. I still have my ship—she gives me freedom. I'll travel. I want to see the galaxy. I want to spend time with *Night Stalker*."

Eli's face brightened. "You can't even imagine how different she is from the Game. Friendly, warm—she likes me!"

"Are you going to come back? What Kond said about Gaia and the Gaians was true."

"I will. I want to say that you matter a great deal to me—you're my friend, Nox. After what we did on Pat'zan, I worry about you. The Gaian laws... Are you—"

"Since the Ancients created me, my most important mission was, and still is, to maintain the balance between human idiosyncrasies and the technology. That's in our laws, and that's what I'm doing. The GAME Laws are on my side. But despite all our prosperity, there's still one thing not available to everybody on Gaia—power. Unsurprisingly, some hate me when I'm breathing down their necks. Come back and help me! It's something worth doing."

"So, you think your decision to bring me here is in line with your law?"

"I do. It's in the best interest of the Game. Don't worry, I can prove it easily. It even knows you. With your *Night Stalker*, you could find it without me." Nox stepped toward Eli.

He stepped back and bowed slightly. "I'll be back, I promise."

She looked down and then right into Eli's eyes. "Don't go away. Do it for me..." There was no plea in her glance, but an attempt to find an answer to a lingering question.

Eli didn't break eye contact. Instead, he smiled and said softly, "I can't. Sorry..." He turned around and moved away from the room. Then he stopped. "If you see D'Obba and Jour, ask them to wait to publish everything they saw on Pat'zan. It's not the right time yet. Also, I won't tell anybody about my visit to Kierus. Agreed?" Eli gave Nox a knowing wink and pointed at his eye. "You know what that means, right?"

"I do." She smiled at him. "I agree. I understand."

TWENTY-EIGHT

SIX MONTHS LATER

The climate on Coatera was unusually mild, even for an Earth-like planet. Warm seas washed its poles and, except for a few highlands and mountains, the temperature never fell below freezing. The planet's vast regions between the polar circles knew only one season, summer.

To tell the truth, Gaians who harbored a weakness in their souls for spending vacations in this paradise would disagree. According to them, the second half of the summer on Coatera was a separate "low" season characterized by skies often covered with dense clouds, stronger winds, and longer periods of rain or, more precisely, drizzle and mist. Temperatures dropped during the "low summer," resulting in the patchy hues of red and orange appearing here and there in the planet's all-green palette.

It was this gloomy time of year when bright splashes of light flashed above the dense layer of clouds covering the night sky. They were followed by a roaring thunder rolling across the vast area around the Temple of Emerala. The strange atmospheric phenomenon scared wildlife. Birds took off—leaving their night-time roosts, they circled above the holy place, loudly flapping their wings and uttering guttural cries. Noisy insects paused their never-ending songs to restart even louder when the rumble in the skies stopped. The shock wave coming from above, albeit weak, shook the tree manes and bent the grass.

The early morning had already claimed itself when it happened. The gray strip of the coming day was barely visible on the horizon. The dwellers in a small house on the hill among the woods surrounding the temple were sleeping. Not anymore. The front window of the house lit up, but there was nothing to see outside.

In a moment, everything seemed to go back as it was before. Then the dark shadow of the starship, slowly and warily, as if terrified of her intrusion into the undisturbed nature below, slid out of the clouds and hung fifty feet above the ground.

Our consciousness always throws at us images, thoughts, ideas—some of them vague and fleeting, some stubborn and haunting. They are our memories and wishes, hopes, daydreams, and ambitions. Some are our deepest secrets, tucked away forever in the darkest corners of our souls. Some scream to be known by the rest of the world.

As Eli approached Coatera, unknown emotions bewitched him. He peered inside himself, but no matter how hard he tried, he could not grasp the nature of the feeling. It had no name and no words. He tried to convince himself, *Just wait. I'll see... I'll know...*

But that couldn't help either. In the feverish movements of his mind, everything was alive, lurid and incoherent, as if in delirium. His heart was beating in anticipation of the unknown inescapability.

Fed up with the uncertainty and the hesitation that caught him off guard, Eli sharply turned his fighter, hovered above the ground, and flopped her down onto the same spot where he had landed the last time on Coatera, close to the Temple of Emerala. He opened the landing ramp. Fresh, moist air rushed inside the ship, and with it, the sounds of nature and the tranquilizing scent of a place mostly untouched by civilization hit Eli with long-forgotten sensations.

He got out of the ship, and the mud beneath his feet squelched. He looked down and then back at *Night Stalker*. When the bulky space fighter hit the ground, she had scattered the water-soaked soil all over the place—a thick layer of dirt covered her belly. But that didn't upset Eli. On the contrary, he smiled, and his anger with himself and the exasperation from the uncertainty he felt vanished as if they hadn't besieged him seconds ago.

He sighed deeply and burst into laughter with abandon. *I'm home!* Eli loved the thought so much that he yelled, "I'm home! I'm ho-o-o-ome! You all out there, do you hear that?"

A flock of birds, having calmed down after the starship's noisy landing, rose again into the air in response to Eli's wild shout. They whirled around him, circle after circle, as if uncertain whether to greet the unexpected newcomer or fear him and run away.

Eli waved to them. "Hey, you! Calm down—I'm your friend!"

Still watching the birds, his gaze skid lower and stopped at the small house on the hill. The lighted window in the middle of the cottage stood out against the gloomy morning. *Shit! I fell out of hyperspace and woke them up. But I don't remember anything on that hill. Hmmm… Nice place. Beautiful views. I'd love to live in something like that.*

Eli's twinge of envy for the owners of the house quickly passed. *I bet there are millions of similar places here.* He headed for the temple, the main reason for his coming to Coatera.

As Eli climbed the stairs at the temple's entrance, he began to understand how much he had missed Coatera, the planet where his journey and the new chapter in his life had started, where he met his love and where his mother had died.

He passed the entrance cella and walked deeper into the long hall with its multiple cameras and niches. His footsteps echoed in the silence of the temple. With the naiveté of a young person who'd just come into life, but who had already passed its first tests, Eli felt old. There was something elusively satisfying in this feeling—he couldn't resist and gave himself to the warmth of the emotion. His bearing changed. His face stiffened, his eyes darted forward, his steps became wider and more confident.

He reached the niche with Sarah's sarcophagus, and the illusion passed. He noticed, with some surprise, fresh flowers on the cover. He didn't know what the flowers were called, but they resembled Earth daisies, tulips, and moss roses... the same wildflowers he had picked for Sarah on his last visit here. He touched the carving of his mother's face—with both hands on the cold stone, he reminisced about his life. *It happened recently, but it seems so long ago. Could I have thought—could I have believed then I had parted ways forever with my previous life?*

He closed his eyes, and the vivid sights of recent events came back to him. The image of the mortally wounded Aura lying help-lessly in his arms sprung to his disturbed mind, and he groaned with fury and impotence. He dug fingernails into the bas-relief of the sarcophagus. His knuckles turned white, and fingers scraped over the stone.

Eli still stood, leaning with his hands on the sarcophagus and breathing heavily, when he heard a sound. Although faint, it resonated in the deathly silence of the temple. Steps—someone is coming... *Dammit! I can't find peace even here.*

Eli turned his head slightly—the steps were approaching. He straightened. The niche with the sarcophagus wasn't deep. From his position, Eli could see the top of the stairs at the beginning of the hall. Someone's head, then shoulders, then the whole female silhouette appeared from the depths of the staircase. *A woman?*

As the figure came closer, a streak of light fell onto her face. Eli froze in fascinated horror, watching Aura coming closer and closer. "Who *are* you?" he asked in a strangled voice.

No more an unwavering warrior, a lass—tense and unsure of what would happen next—stood before him a few steps away, not daring to come closer.

A lump rose in Eli's throat. "Aura?"

"I knew you'd come to this place," she said in a low voice.

Eli approached Aura and touched her face. "How?" He looked into her eyes.

Aura only smiled shyly and didn't respond.

"Nox?"

"No. Only you could do it... And you did. You wished me back."

Eli kept silent.

"I wanted to see you." She held out her arms to him. Another pause. Aura stepped back. "But I won't stand in your way."

Eli winced and turned pale. "Oh, God... Aura!" Carefully, not believing in the miracle that had happened in front of his eyes, he went up to her and took her head in his hands. "Please don't say such things. When you died, my life ended. I'm terrified now! If I lose you again... I... I..." His eyes welled with tears.

"You still love me?" Her eyes shone with hope.

"I fell for you the moment I saw you. I love you, Aura. I don't want to live without you!" Eli kissed her forehead and hands.

Aura caught his hands in hers. "I love you too! Where have you *been*? I needed to tell you so many important things. It was so stupid to pull the gun on you on Earth."

"I was angry, too. You seemed so out of my league."

She wrapped her arms around his neck. "Kiss me!" she whispered and immediately became frightened of her demand. "I know, I want too much. Sorry..."

Aura and Eli pulled away from each other for a moment, and

then they came together and their lips locked in one overwhelming desire.

Aura came to her senses first. "Not here! I have a place nearby!" Without saying anything more, she took his hand and led him away from the temple and into the house on the hill.

TWENTY-NINE

ELI AND AURA

E li opened his eyes. He was alone in the bed. The clink of dishes came from the kitchen.

"Aura? Is that you?"

The sound stopped, and Aura fluttered into the bedroom. "Yes! Sorry, I woke you up. I'm making breakfast."

"Breakfast?" Eli gawked at the dress she was wearing. "What's this? I didn't know Gaian women wore dresses."

"Hardly ever." Aura waltzed around the bed. "I put it on for you. Do you like it?"

Her moving, expressive face glowed with wild happiness. Her blue eyes shone with joy and tenderness. The spinning skirt rose, showing her legs. She abruptly stopped at the edge of the bed—the silky thin cloth rolled around her, revealing the curvy shape of her body.

Aura kneeled down before the bed. A timid concern replaced her gaiety. "Say something..."

"I love it! I was watching you—your eyes... Blue? With the white dress—you look amazing. And your dress, it's gorgeous!"

"Really? Thanks! Blue are my natural eyes. You saw hazel."

Eli crawled on the bed closer to Aura and touched the scar on her neck. "You still have it. It's exactly how it was when I saw you lying—" Eli hesitated for the right word and hid his eyes from Aura.

"Dead." She finished the phrase. "Now that you're back, I'll get rid of it."

"You never seemed like a superstitious woman."

"I changed." Aura sighed. "You also changed. Long hair? With an eagle-eye all-pervading glance. The sign of those who make history."

"Whoa! Please don't. I'm just a guy. Don't embarrass me."

"Not my intention. It's true. Something is different about you. Maybe a sad look?" Aura kept her eyes on Eli. "Well, it doesn't matter. So, what do we do now?"

"Someone mentioned breakfast?"

"And after breakfast? Tomorrow? In a—"

"We'll live. At least, I'm not going anywhere. I'll cling to your apron strings and stay here. I'll beg you not to drive me out. And even if you do, it won't be easy to get rid of me. What about you?"

Aura took Eli's hands in hers. "You're not the one who clings to apron strings. And I... If you choose me, I want to share my life with you. Till I die. For real."

The bedroom door opened with a loud bang—Hippa broke into the room and leaped onto the bed. "Hippa?" Eli yelled, "Don't do it!"

Hippa grabbed the blanket in her mouth, slid off the bed, and ran out of the room, dragging the bed covering behind her. Eli jumped onto the floor in his boxer briefs. In the daylight, Aura saw a long scar crossing his lower torso. The wound was recent. Wide keloid marks on his skin terrified Aura. "What's this?" she asked.

"Uh... Long story."

"Can I hear it? We have time."

Eli turned his back to Aura and quickly put his shirt on. "Hippa is with you now?"

"Nox asked me to keep her company."

"Where is she?"

"She tried to contact you. She'll be on Cela tomorrow."

"I'll call her today. I was too far away to reach."

"Where?"

"Nowhere special. After you died, I had to be alone. I went wherever my ship took me. I'll tell you everything. Not now, though. Tell me, who knows about your death?"

"Nox said nobody. I woke up in the refuge here on Coatera. The official story is that she healed me while you and Nox were on your way to Coatera. Actually, I didn't even know I died. I was mad at Nox when she couldn't explain why you disappeared. But she finally gave up and told me the truth. I suspect that what she told me wasn't the whole truth. Am I right?"

"Let's stick to the official story. I don't have secrets from you, but what I learned… Well, I better keep it to myself. You won't be safe otherwise."

"Slun Ceabb has been snooping around. He tried to get the details of my rescue from me. He knows Nox was involved on Pat'zan. He was also asking about the two Pazon battlecruisers you allegedly destroyed. Did you? How does he know? But I told him I don't know—I was unconscious."

"He knows because he was there. And didn't do a thing to help you."

"Can you prove it?"

"Yes. But to retain the advantage in a fight with him and people like him, it's better if he doesn't know what I know."

"So, a showdown is coming?"

"I'm not sure it'll be a showdown. I think it'll be more like a war, a long and bloody one. It's coming. I saw a Gaian battlecruiser not far from Coatera. My return is hardly a secret now."

∽

"Sit still!"

"It itches like crazy." Eli stopped giggling and gripped the armrests of the chair as Aura tried to remove the scar with a dermal regenerator.

"Almost done…"

"Already?" drawled Eli.

"Disappointed?"

"I missed this."

"Missed what?"

"Someone taking care of me. The last time it happened I was twelve… Or eleven?"

"Oh, poor baby… I'll take care of you!"

Eli smirked. "Don't tease the orphan." He slid off the chair and walked to a table covered with food.

"Come back, I haven't finished."

"The poor baby is hungry. Baby wants to eat." Eli surveyed the plates, grabbed a piece of cold meat, and immediately shoved it into his mouth. While chewing it, he snatched a baguette. Waving it like a sword, Eli proclaimed, "Ghohhh… hhuff."

"What's 'ghohhh… hhuff'? My translator doesn't get it."

Eli swallowed the meat. "It means 'good stuff.' Did you cook all that, or is it from a food synthesizer?"

"Synthesizer. I tuned it to learn a few Earth recipes I found on your internet." Aura hesitated before asking, "Do you always eat like this and speak with your mouth full?"

"Scared?" Eli burst into laughter. "I wanted you to know who you'll be living with. So that there'll be no regrets later."

"You cannot scare me with that. I'm looking at you—I'm coming back to life." Aura sobbed. "Do you know what that means? You know what it means to die? I still feel I cheated everybody. That I don't have the right to be alive, and maybe I don't."

"Stop that. Stop it now!" Eli rushed to her, and she buried her face in his chest. He cuddled her. "You're not the only one…"

"What do you mean?" Aura looked at Eli in horror.

"Nothing. Don't cry. I'll take care of you. Remember that. Promise?"

"I do. I'll look after you, too. I don't want you to feel like there's no one there for you."

"Hey, what about your parents? Are they still around?"

"Why?"

"On Earth, we care about families. I assumed that your parents love you. Don't they? Since I love you, I may want to share this feeling with them."

"I think it's wonderful. But on Gaia, we don't maintain close ties between generations. My parents are alive, we—"

The sound of long-range commsys chiming interrupted Aura. "What is it?" she asked irritably.

"Incoming call for Aurabella Thaleia from Mr. Rurik Cavell, ISS *Leobla*, Korango Independent Territory SA."

"Are you Aurabella Thaleia? I didn't know your full name—I love it."

"That's Ruke. He was so helpful and nice. The white dress, it was his advice…" Aura hurried. "Let's take the call."

"Sure!"

"Open channel."

Ruke's beaming face appeared on the screen. "My dear, why are you hiding my boy in your kitchen?"

Aura looked flirtingly at Eli and then at Ruke. "And why are you calling me if you want to talk to Eli?"

"Ha ha!" Ruke's broad smile became even wider. "Because I'm a man from the North, and nothing can escape the all-seeing eyes of the Northman's gods. My dear Eli is alive and well, and I want to hug him and drink a glass of Hopper or two if it's the gods' will—and the gods favor me lately."

"Your Holy Spirit, you're invited. Don't forget Shyster, your beloved wife."

Aura looked at open-mouthed Eli—a silent "Wife?" appeared on his face.

"Thank you, my dear, I accept the invitation. Forgive me—I know that I fished for it, but I couldn't help it!"

Eli stepped in. "Hi, buddy. Where are you? On Korango?"

"On my cruiser. I'm on my way to Cela. If you don't know, the Gaians selected Korango Enterprises as a general contractor for the final assembly on the restoration project, and it's completed. We'll be signing off on the project tomorrow."

"Wow! Congratulations!"

"All thanks to you, Eli. You know who paid for the labor? Pat'zan, your friend and His Lordship, Xiir Zanrod."

"Are you kidding? He's definitely not my friend."

"I'm serious. By the way, Yow is my project manager on Cela."

"How is he? I'd love to see him. Aura, is it okay?"

"Eli, it's your party, anything you want."

"Good. Hey, Ruke, I want to see Ash too. How is she?"

"They live together. Ash…" Ruke lowered his voice, "I have to say she's afraid of you. But she has a kind heart, and she's changed." Ruke went to whispering, "You know, she attempted another suicide. It was much worse than the first—"

Aura interrupted Ruke, "You kept it a secret from me? Why?"

Ruke sighed. "I don't know. I guess I wasn't sure if you could forgive her—"

"She had too much trust in people. Not a bad thing—Eli, what do you think?" Aura bestowed him with a smile.

"I'm thinking about the cave on Earth and the day that started our journey. And what a journey it was! If we all get together, that'd be something to celebrate."

"Eli!" exulted Ruke. "We'll get together like old times…"

At the bottom of the screen, below Ruke's face, appeared an announcement—"Incoming call for Elias Stroud from Ms. Nox Ell, ISS *Arisbe*, Gaian SA."

"Uh, Ruke…" said Eli after reading the note on the screen. "Something has come up. It may be urgent. I have to put you on hold." Signs of anxiety spread across his face. "Open channel to ISS *Arisbe*."

"Nice to see you both," said a stony-faced Nox. "Eli, the news of your arrival is out. We need to talk."

"Not from Aura's house. I'll go to *Night Stalker*. See you in five minutes."

She nodded. The screen went dark.

"Resume call to ISS *Leobla*," said Eli. "Ruke, sorry, I have to go. Let us know when you arrive. Our get-together is confirmed. Yow and Ash are invited. Please call Zarfo—I'd like to see him too, if you don't mind his absence on Korango. And he can bring Ash with him."

"Eli, don't worry, I understand. And Zarfo—yes. He always speaks well of you. See you soon. What a day! I love you both!"

The screen went dark.

"Where is your transporter?" asked Eli.

"I'll go with you."

"Aura, no. I told you."

Aura stubbornly shook her head. "I'm going with you. I will spend my life with you. If I don't start now, there will always be something between us. The Game, secrets, important things, Slun, Nox, the DRC, Ronda…"

"I don't know who Ronda is, but I don't want this life for you. If you set foot on this path, you can never go back."

"So what?"

"You'll have to do things that will disgust you. You'll have to deal with people who will disgust you. You'll have to smile while preparing to stab someone in the back. I know you—you aren't like that. You'll have to spend sleepless nights doubting your sanity and wondering whether you're doing the right thing."

"Are you that kind of person?"

"I wasn't, but I am *now*."

"If that's the way it works, fine. I'm ready. Thanks for the heads-up. I go with you, or you go nowhere." She stubbornly raised her head, but her eyes were pleading.

Eli stood up. "Give me a minute."

He went to the bedroom and returned with his guns tucked into their holsters. Then he held out his hand to Aura. "Give me your hand." Eli cast a long glance at her. Everything was in his eyes —love, angst, tenderness, and admiration for Aura. *Just don't die again...* "Please don't die next time! Swear!"

"I'll do my best."

Eli kissed her hand. "Then let's go."

Eli found Nox in a bad mood. She began with reproaches about his long absence and lack of communication, but it was Aura's presence that caused her greatest discontent. Eli stood firm. Looking straight into Nox's eyes, he presented her with an ultimatum— either she accepted Aura as his full-fledged partner, or Eli ceased to talk to Nox. After his sharp rebuff, the conversation continued in a businesslike manner. The apparent rift between Nox and Eli didn't go away, despite Aura's attempts to smooth over the breach.

Nox informed Eli that his return to the region of the Orion Spur, Coatera's location, hadn't passed unnoticed. According to her sources in the DRC, the Bureau had deployed battlecruisers with the order to monitor *Night Stalker*'s movements. She also told him that the rescue operation on Pat'zan had passed mostly unnoticed among Gaians due to the lack of any official news. D'Obba and Jour, true to their promise not to divulge anything they had collected on the DRC—from its operations on Korango, to its activity in space near Pat'zan—had also kept silent.

The real news was the Gaian government's growing concerns about Eli's possible possession of Game technology and the uncertainty regarding the nature of his connection to the Game. His homegrown rescue operation on Pat'zan irked the government most. According to Nox, the DRC and the Commission of the GAME saw Eli as a danger to Gaian society and had begun looking for ways to neutralize him.

One of their ideas consisted of building a criminal case against Eli for the alleged use of Game technology in the assault on Pat'zan. The second, viewed as more promising, targeted a special law to seize *Night Stalker* from Eli. Nox didn't know if the initial effort to prosecute him for his unproven triggering of the Game's quantum conversion was still on the table.

She said that a new element the Gaian authorities had to deal with was Eli's growing reputation on Gaia, threatening to transform into a grassroots movement in his favor. Nox couldn't explain the phenomenon or its origins, though noticed that, favorably to Eli, rumors had been spreading since his arrival on Coatera.

Eli, mostly silent, sat in his pilot seat, watching Nox with great interest. Most of the news, including the DRC plotting against him —which made Aura shiver—left him indifferent. He was waiting for the question related to the conversations they'd had on Kierus.

Nox, however, was beating around the bush, nervously looking at Aura and stepping back every time the conversation seemed to approach the real reason Nox wanted to talk to Eli.

The next time it happened, he interrupted her. "We've been circling around the same topic without addressing it, repeating things that, frankly, don't bother me. Anything else you want to talk about? Are you even glad to see me? You could mention it to be polite. Are we still friends?"

"We are." Nox blushed and nervously looked at Aura. "You're right. Have you decided what to do with The Great Satan's offer?"

Aura turned in her chair to Eli, her eyes wide with surprise. "Satan? Who is this? Is that a real person?"

"Yeah, that's the guy from Kierus," Eli smirked. "His name is Kond Phyns."

"What's Kierus?"

"Eli, no!" screamed terrified Nox.

"Oh, yes." Eli turned to Aura. "Aura, Kierus is the location of the Game. The Satan is the guy who developed it—well, most of it. He also happened to be my relative, great-great-great-grandfather, or something. That explains my odd DNA."

Eli turned back to the screen. "To answer your question, Nox—there was no offer. All he wanted to do was look at me. I didn't realize that at first. But soon after Kierus, I connected the things he said to what I knew because I had his gift—" Eli turned again to Aura. "*Night Stalker* was a gift—I didn't violate any laws. And the bastard killed my father on his way to deliver it to me."

"So," Eli was talking again to Nox, "evidently, my 'Fuck You' song impressed him—or I turned out better than his other offspring. The scales finally fell from my eyes—at that time, I was in the Andromeda galaxy, saving my ass from local savages. They detected the quantum core in my ship and wanted to pulverize me with their own version of the Game—I rushed back to Kierus—"

"You visited Kierus again?"

"No. Otherwise, I'd have known Aura was alive then. I received his entire hologram program while returning to the Milky Way, including the secret part he wanted to explain which I, like an idiot, didn't want to listen to on Kierus."

"Can you tell us what's in that secret part?" asked Nox.

"I'm going to. The Satan said it's at my discretion. But the three things he mentioned can have perilous implications." Eli was riding tall in the saddle in front of Aura and Nox—both of whom riveted their eyes on him. "So, buckle up, ladies." Eli donned a shit-eating grin—he had their undivided attention. "First, there's a new Game-like machine under construction. Kond sounded certain, though he gave no details. He discovered that before his death after analyzing some Game implementations. So the Games multiply like rabbits. If it's true, it'll be the third."

"Where's the second?" asked Aura.

"*Night Stalker*. She's not the real Game—there are no AI controls, but she has a fully implemented core, the quantum engine, and some additions to it. I'm the only person who can control it—it's hardwired in its design."

Nox gave a short laugh. "Okay, now I see why you don't care about the DRC plans to seize your fighter."

"The Bureau doesn't understand what they're dealing with. Their idiotic plans tell me they don't have the full picture. On Earth, a nuclear bomb was once a technology available to few nations. Right now, everybody builds them. Time marches on!"

"What else?" asked Aura. "You said three things."

"Right... Sorry, Nox, but it looks like I'm now the only one who can change the key algorithms controlling the Game—the one on Kierus, that is—if you haven't yet noticed. The switch in access rights to the Game took place when I got Kond's entire message. The irony is that I do not understand what those algorithms are."

"Son of a bitch!" Nox glanced at Eli. "Not you—Kond. I knew he could do something like that."

"Yeah, I think he never trusted you. But I do. If you figure it out, I'm willing to reverse the change and restore your access."

"Thanks, but let's wait with that. I kind of like it." Nox paused. "I admit it hurts my self-esteem, but with where things go, there's a chance they could coerce me to change the Game. I even regret you told me all this. I don't have the access now, but I know that you do. That becomes more dangerous for you."

"Could be," said Eli. "On the other hand, they probably won't harm the only person with the full knowledge of the machine and control over their beloved pet. But I still don't fully understand the implications of what Kond told me. I don't know how all this affects you. Eventually, the DRC and the Commission will learn the details of my visit to Kierus. Even if you were within your authority, I don't believe they'll be happy. That's why I share it with you and Aura.

"There's one more thing, probably the weirdest of all. It's not my DNA that gives me access to the Game—the one on Kierus. It's *Kond*'s DNA. He said that it may or may not be inherited. The thing is, the Satan was quite a loving fella, a prolific womanizer and father. Bottom line—there are others like me. I have the names of some of them who inherited the DNA, but the motherfucker didn't remember all of them and didn't even check the blood of many of his offspring."

"That's a mess. It's not only you—there could be an open season on people with such DNA—"

"Or on those who are suspected of having it," Eli interrupted Nox. "As they say, you can't make an omelet without breaking eggs."

Aura stiffened, and her voice gained an edge. "So, the dark times of the Game are back?"

Eli shrugged. "Honestly? I don't think they were ever gone for good. It seems you guys were burying your heads in the sand."

"Whatever it is, I'm scared. What are we going to do about all this?" asked Aura.

"That's an interesting question because it has a hidden assumption..." Eli smirked.

"Which is what?" Nox frowned.

"Which is whether we should do something at all. You, Nox, I'm sure, want to rush into the battle. But can you tell me why it's my war? Especially since I'm not the One anymore... Or not the only One. Besides, I don't want to endanger Aura."

"You hope the DRC will leave you and Aura alone?" asked Nox.

"I don't know. But I have my insurance policy, *Night Stalker*. If they don't touch Aura and me, I don't think I should interfere with anything. I've found good places where Aura and I can have a good, quiet life."

"So, after everything that happened, you're still that naive?" snorted Nox.

"Eli..." Aura looked into Eli's eyes. "Are you sure that's what you want? Or is it about me?"

Eli leaned forward to Aura. "And what do *you* want? You promised to stay out of danger." Frustration crinkled his eyes. "I'm tired. I want to die old. I want to die before you and in my bed. Is that so difficult to grasp?" Eli clenched fists and snarled, turning to Nox. "Can you even understand the abyss I was in all this time? I came to tell you what I learned from Kond. But no, that's not enough! Sorry, but for the moment, that's all I can offer."

"Eli, sweetheart…" Aura jumped up from her seat and dashed to Eli. She hugged him, pressing his face to her chest and caressing his shoulder. "I'll be with you no matter what. Anything you want." Then she looked at the screen. "Nox, I'm sorry, it's probably not a good time to continue this conversation." Aura returned to the co-pilot seat and looked askance at Nox.

A bitter smile showed on Nox's face. "Yes. Sorry, Eli, you're right, it was insensitive to start this talk. Thank you very much for getting back to me." Nox fidgeted, trying to rearrange something outside the hologram boundaries. "Another time, perhaps. Actually, I realized, based on what Eli said—"

"Nox!" Eli interrupted her. "You're my friend and will always be… Unless you don't want that. I'm not abandoning you. I'll do my best to support and defend you. And I'm *not* naive. I'm sure the DRC will be after me soon. But I want it to be like on Pat'zan."

"I don't understand what you mean," said Nox in a flat voice.

"When you didn't want me to shoot at the Pazons, and I said, 'If they don't shoot at us, I'll go away.' Remember?"

Nox nodded.

"Same now. I don't want to be an initiator. Besides, I think it would be a tactical mistake for us to make the first move. Aura, do you agree with this?"

"Absolutely!"

"Then let's keep in touch," said Eli with a smile. "So, friends?"

"Friends!" Nox brightened. "I never meant to push you into the fight. I only wanted to give you an update on what's happening on Gaia. We'll see. You guys enjoy your time together. Meanwhile, I'll keep myself busy with what you told me. Any suggestions on what I should focus on?"

"I think you should report to the authorities about losing full control over the Game. Other than that, I have no brilliant ideas," said Eli. "Maybe you can find out more about the new Game? What Kond told me is ten-year-old stuff. His DNA... If you can identify the way it controls the Game, that could be useful. Aura told me you're coming to Cela tomorrow? We can talk more then."

"Yes, I'm coming on official business. The restoration of the station is completed. I have to inspect some equipment delivered to the GAME Institute."

"We have a party tomorrow or the day after," said Eli, "All old friends. Will you come?"

"If I'm invited, I will. Though I'm not sure if it's a good idea to draw attention to our contacts."

"You're our friend, Nox. You're invited. Please come," said Aura.

"If I may... regarding contacts between us," piped up Eli. "The DRC knows about them anyway, and will be aware of what's happening on Coatera, at least in the near future."

"How?" Aura stared at Eli.

"Yow. He's Slun's asset."

"What's an asset?" Aura's forehead puckered.

"A snitch. A spy."

"What? How do you know?"

"I took my job as the head of Korango's security seriously." Eli screwed his lips into a grimace.

"So, the DRC—Slun?—recruited my contractor to spy on me? And you're only telling me this now?" Aura's eyes flashed with anger.

"I learned about Yow and Slun after the Pazons kidnapped you. Sorry. As far as recruiting him, it happened the other way around." A smile dangled on the corners of Eli's lips. "Slun recruited Yow before you hired him. He suggested Yow to you—you took him. Remember that?"

"You're full of surprises, my dear. I remember, and today is his last day on Coatera!"

Eli shrugged. "You can do that. But it would be a mistake."

"Why?"

"You don't expose your dirty laundry. Plus, there's no guarantee that your next contractor, Gaian, Pazon, or Korag, won't spy on you too. Finally, we can use Yow for relaying info to Slun that's beneficial to us. In other words, disinformation."

"That's disgusting!" Aura cried out.

"Well... it is. But you have to admit, I warned you about doing disgusting things. Didn't I? Recently—this morning!"

Nox, who so far was listening silently to the exchange between Eli and Aura, trying not to miss a single word, inhaled deeply and raised her hand, trying to get their attention. "Sorry to interrupt you both, but I have to sign off. I only wanted to say that everything we discussed should remain between us. Eli, I promise that I'll never tell anybody anything you share with me."

Aura smiled. "Nox, I agree with what you said. It's just that all this is new to me. See you tomorrow. Come to the control room when you arrive at Cela."

"Sure... Before I forget, your dress—you look lovely in it. White suits you. I don't remember the last time I saw someone in a dress. Does Eli like it?"

"Thank you! But don't make me blush." Aura beamed with pleasure and stole a glance at Eli. "Ask him yourself."

The hologram of Nox disappeared. Aura turned to Eli. "That was embarrassing. Nox is so blunt."

"Nothing embarrassing. On Earth, you'd be among the most beautiful and ravishing women I've ever seen. When I saw you the first time, I was afraid to even think about you—"

"Stop it! You're making it worse."

"The God, or nature, whoever gave you your body and eyes… And everything. You know, you're very, very sexy. The blue of your eyes is like a magnet. It pulls me into their chasm, deeper and deeper."

"Have faith in me—I'll rescue you." Aura smiled and then sighed. "We keep talking about me, but I wanted to say I understand better now what you meant this morning. Talking about disgusting things and facing them is not the same." Aura jutted her chin stubbornly. "But I won't go back. Never! I'll be with you—no matter what."

"People like you don't go back."

"I was watching Nox. I guess she doesn't have problems with the disgusting, but she seemed so miserable today—like she didn't expect the cold water you threw on her plans."

"She's a good person. Without Nox, you wouldn't be here. Most likely, I'd be dead. I'll be grateful to my dying day to Nox for what she did. But enough of her. I have a better idea."

Eli pressed something on the armrest of his seat and took out a ring from a small compartment that opened in the instrument panel. "This is the ring my dad gave my mother when he proposed." Leaping to his feet, Eli bent down on one knee in front of Aura, took her hand in his, and said, "I don't know how you do it here, so I'll go with what we do on Earth. Will you marry me?"

Aura, blushing red, squirmed in the co-pilot seat. "What am I supposed to say?"

"Say yes, if you want to marry me, or anyway, to stay with me forever. On Earth, a union between two people is called marriage when it's recognized socially or ritually."

"Yes! I want to marry you and stay with you forever!"

"Now I'll kiss you and put the ring on your finger. It's a symbol of my love." And that was what Eli did.

Aura stretched out her hand with the ring and held it to the light from the instrument panel. The five-carat diamond, in an old-fashioned cut, sparkled gray and white, throwing off flashes of fire.

"Spellbound stone!" she exclaimed. "It's carbon, I'm sure. But the purity is exceptional."

"It's a diamond, the hardest natural substance found on Earth, cut by hand. It's old. Passed from generation to generation in my family."

"What's the symbolism?"

"It doesn't tarnish—just like true love. The ring is a circle—no end, like our love for each other."

"Amazing! So simple and elegant. Can I wear it?"

"It's for you, Aura."

"I'll make a ring for you, too. I'll think about the style that fits you."

"You have diamonds on Gaia?"

"Probably, but I have the Game. I'll create the most natural and beautiful stone for you."

At Aura's remark, Eli stiffened. "What did you say?"

"The Game—I can reproduce the stone exactly as it is. For all intents and purposes, it'll be natural—all the impurities, isotope ratios—"

"Can I have the ring back for the moment?" asked Eli.

"Sure!"

Eli took it and examined it from all sides. Then he raised the ring. "*STALKER, MAGNIFY ONE HUNDRED TIMES.*"

A holographic magnification of the ring appeared in front of Eli. "*MAGNIFY THE LOWER THIRD OF THE STONE. ROTATE SLOWLY… STALKER, STOP!*"

Pointing at the small English inscription on the stone, Eli burst into laughter.

He tried to say something but couldn't. "I… I… Oh…" His stomach and chest were shaking with laughter. It was so contagious that Aura smiled and laughed too.

"My family ring… Oh…" Finally, he pried words out of his mouth. "It's Kond's ring!"

"Kond's?"

"Yes, my great-great-great-grandfather, the Grand Pilgrim Kond Phyns, a.k.a. The Great Satan, one of the original Game developers. You see here—'To my love, Isabel Gadol,' his name, 'Kond Phyns,' and the year '1872' engraved at the bottom of the stone. It's in English. He knew English."

Eli stopped laughing. "Shit! Was I wrong about Kond? Maybe he truly loved Isabel, my great-great-great-grandmother, and gave this ring to his wife? I never heard about her... I bet he could synthesize a much bigger one but was afraid that it could kill his love. In those times, to have an expensive diamond was dangerous."

"Are you upset that you gave me his ring?"

"No, but that's *Kond*'s ring. I don't know what to think."

"I believe that's even better. It stayed in your family, generation after generation of people in love. It's beautiful! I'm proud to wear it—it's mine, right?"

"It is. Here!"

Aura put the ring back on her finger and admired its splendor once again. "I love you, Eli!" She closed her eyes and buried her face in Eli's neck.

He raised his hand and ran his fingers into her hair. He kissed her forehead and whispered in her ear, "I love you so much, Aura. I love the way your name sounds. I love your smile. I love you more than anything." He cradled her head in his arms and looked into her eyes. "I can't lose you again, do you understand?"

"You won't. But enough of the darkness. I believe in the future. My heart is yours forever. Let's go home!"

THE END

AUTHOR NOTES: THE MIDAS TOUCH TRILOGY

The concept of The Midas Touch trilogy came to me long ago, perhaps in the late 1980s. The idea for the story combined several thoughts I had pondered for years. First, I believed the desire for power came from the survival instinct, where the more powerful were always better off.

But what about a society capable of providing its members with anything they wanted for free—sort of a communist utopia where their survival and much more were guaranteed? Would people still strive to gain power over others' lives?

So, I needed a thought experiment, and I decided that a sci-fi work of fiction would provide the best chance to observe such a utopia in action. To make my experiment as pure as it could have been, I also needed something capable of creating an unlimited wealth— a MacGuffin, a quasi-god entity. The King Midas and the legend about his touch seemed like a good metaphor, and that how the trilogy was born.

Introducing characters and building a world turned out to be Book I of the trilogy. It's a preview of what's coming in Book II, *Snares of Power*, where the exploration of the main theme takes center stage. I've already completed it, and the book is now under review and editing. I also started working on the final part of the trilogy, *The Crack of Doom*.

My journey to writing my first book was long and arduous. Long ago, I made several feeble attempts in writing of my own, but that didn't go anywhere. The energy of youth quickly dissipated in the daily routine of life in the former Soviet Union, where I was born. Was it all a waste of time? I don't know. Could be. But on the plus side, I learned a lot about human beings—everything good and bad in all of us.

In the early nineties, my wife and I moved to the United States. The need to settle in a new country also didn't leave much room for writing. Only after retirement, I seriously considered storytelling as something I would be doing to the end of my days. But even at that time, I decided to try something different, filmmaking.

Sergey Ilyn

That's because I loved everything visual, and I loved visual storytelling. The idea of making movies was always very appealing to me. Since the days when the trilogy plot stuck in my mind, I was dreaming of shooting the full namesake feature consisting of three episodes *a la* Star Wars trilogy, the original one. And that's where it got interesting.

I knew that serious filmmaking required great skills and experience. So I began practicing and experimenting. My wife and I made several short films, which turned rather successful; at least we received five awards. After our last movie, *Time Fuze*, I decided that it was time to tackle *The Midas Touch*.

I did so and wrote a script. I sent it to a former Hollywood executive and a well-known script consultant. Working with him turned out to be an eye-opening experience because I understood several things. They were all on the surface; still, I failed to see their importance. "Sergey, you've built a nice world, but where is the Death Star in your script?" I close my eyes right now, and I can see this line in one of his emails.

Alas, I didn't have a death star in my Episode I. I tried to convince the script consultant that it would appear in Episode II. "Sergey, why don't you write a book first?" was his response.

I talked to my wife, and she supported the idea. The next morning I started writing *Fun and Games*, Book I of The Midas Touch trilogy.

www.ingramcontent.com/pod-product-compliance
Lightning Source LLC
Chambersburg PA
CBHW071738110726

47908CB00006B/1623